tiaras
& teacups

Berry Lake
CUPCAKE
POSSE

friendship · romance · cupcakes

BOOK TWO

MELISSA McCLONE

Tiaras & Teacups
Berry Lake Cupcake Posse
Book Two

Copyright © 2021 by Melissa McClone

Cover and Photography by Cover Me Darling
Cupcake from SAS Cupcakes

ISBN 13: 978-1-944777-62-3 (paperback)
ISBN-13: 9781944777-61-6 (eBook)

Published by:

Cardinal Press, LLC
November 2020

get a free sampler

To receive a free copy of
Beginnings: A Sampler Collection,
join Melissa's newsletter.
Visit melissamcclone.com/join

🧁 dedication 🧁

For friends.
In good times and in bad, friendship sees you through.

A huge thank you to the iN Focused Flow DM group on Instagram and club on Clubhouse for their prayers and support. They lifted me up in so many ways while I wrote this book.

Special thanks to: my family, Elana Johnson, Julie Trettel, Melanie D. Snitker, Terri Reed, Elizabeth Bromke, Gigi Blume, Rachael Bloome, Danielle Norman, Jennifer Niles, Mary Moineau, Debbie Bishko, Kim Loraine, Sable Jordan, Shannon Humphrey, Shari Drehs Bartholomew, Kimberly Fields, Denise Stout Holcomb, Margie Lawson, and the Author Arena Writing club on Clubhouse.

A special shout-out and thanks to those involved with the first two books in the series: Cindy Jackson at When We Share, Trenda London at It's Your Story Content Editing, Rebecca Hodgkins, Kristine Moran at Author Bunnies, Rachel Christley at Beta Buddies, Sue Soares at SJS Editorial Services, Judy Zweifel at Judy's Proofreading, Julie Deaton at Deaton Author Services, Lia Fairchild with Your Best Book Editing, Hope Trettel, Aidan Niles, Lisa Lee Proofreading and Editing, Stephanie Anderson at ALT 19 Creative, Marisa-Rose Wesley at Cover Me Darling, SAS Cupcakes, Kate Farlow at Y'All That Graphic, Chas Patrick and Candace Fox at Essentially Chas, and Tressa at Prism Book Tours.

chapter one

AS JULIET MONROE added the last teapot to her box on Sunday afternoon, her heartbeat resembled a drumroll, the way it had since she arrived for the party. The Berry Lake High School drumline would be impressed. She was.

Today was the beginning of her new career, and she couldn't be more thrilled. The tea party had gone so well, her feet barely touched the floor. She even enjoyed cleaning someone else's house.

And it was a huge, HGTV-worthy house.

The stylishly decorated home had plenty of room for the Crawford family with six kids, two dogs, three cats, and a snake named Slick. Their menagerie might explain why the couple hadn't minded the laughing, screeching, and running all over the elegant downstairs during their daughter's eighth birthday party.

Juliet double-checked her supplies on the roller cart before making the last pass.

"Have everything?" Becca Crawford held a toddler on one hip and a sippy cup in her other hand.

Thankfully, Juliet had forgotten nothing. She secured the lid and set her purse on the top of the cart. "I do."

Becca adjusted the sleepy boy in her arms. "Charlene mentioned this was your first party. That's hard to believe. You handled the girls like a seasoned pro."

Pride filled Juliet, making her stand taller. That was so much better than hunching or cowering—two postures she wished she didn't know so well. But the Crawford family had been the perfect clients for her event-planning debut. "Thank you. That means so much."

"You deserve all the thanks." Becca's grin spread. "Everyone had a fantastic time, and I didn't have to do anything except take photos. The best win-win ever for a mom who was out of party ideas this year."

"Mama, Mama." Petra ran into the room, still wearing her fancy dress and the white gloves from the favor bags, but her feet were now bare. She glanced at Juliet, and a wide smile burst across her face. "Oh, good, you're still here. This picture is for you."

She handed Juliet the piece of paper with a crayon drawing of a woman pouring tea for a table full of girls.

Juliet's heart swelled with warmth. She couldn't wait to put it on the refrigerator where she would enjoy seeing it. She hadn't expected to run the party on her own, but her boss, Charlene Culpepper, stood on the sidelines, letting Juliet do everything. This artwork was the icing on top of an already fulfilling day.

"Oh, Petra." Juliet studied the drawing and noticed the little details like her earrings. "This picture is lovely. Thank you so much. I have the perfect spot for it at home."

Petra flung herself against Juliet. "This was the best birthday party ever. Do this again next year."

"She will," Becca agreed. "I'll reserve the date early because I have a feeling you'll book up fast."

At a loss for words, Juliet held on to the little girl. She was thankful for this family who'd taken a chance on a new event planner and grateful to her boss for the opportunity.

Petra let go. "I want to teach my brothers how to drink tea. The proper way."

With that, she ran away and stampeded up the staircase.

Juliet hadn't felt such contentment since being a theme-park princess in her early twenties. Then, young girls had stared up at her with adoration, but she hadn't loved the job because of that. She loved doing her part—however small—to light up their faces. Those kinds of smiles had been missing from her own life for far too long.

But she had them today.

It was an excellent start.

After loading the party supplies into the car, she drove out of the luxurious neighborhood, located an hour west of Berry Lake. Bria Landon had told her to record her mileage, since it was tax-deductible, so Juliet had bought a small notebook to keep in the console. An app probably existed, but she preferred using a pen and paper.

A few minutes later, she turned the car onto the main highway. The drive home would give her time to decompress. She'd enjoyed working the birthday party, but her feet hurt from standing—she would need more-comfortable shoes—but nothing would dim the smile that lit up her entire body.

Whatever it took, Juliet wanted this feeling to continue.

A pop station played on the radio, but she wanted something…quieter. She switched to an adult contemporary one. That was better.

Juliet yawned, keeping one hand on the steering wheel.

Between partying in Missy Hanford's hospital room with her friends last night and staying up late and getting up early to prepare for the party, Juliet was tired. But it was the most satisfying tired she'd felt since her theme-park days.

When Charlene mentioned Juliet's first event would be a birthday, she'd pictured a luncheon or brunch with adults, not a tea party for a cute eight-year-old girl. Thank goodness the party details had arrived in Juliet's inbox last night, or things might not have gone as well.

With the party behind her, she realized that was part of her sixty-day trial period—work under pressure because event planners had to think on their feet and come up with quick alternatives in certain situations. Putting on a tea party for ten little girls took energy and patience Juliet hadn't realized she possessed any longer, but Petra claimed it was the best birthday ever—her guests and mom agreed—and Juliet received a fifty-dollar cash tip. Charlene told her to keep the entire amount, even though Juliet tried to give her half before her boss took off.

She tapped her thumb against the steering wheel to the music.

Of course, tea was lacking from this tea party.

Juliet laughed, making a mental note to herself.

It turned out kids preferred pink lemonade to chamomile tea. Charlene was aware of this, thankfully, or the day might have turned into a disaster. Juliet missed serving Berry Lake Cupcake Shop cupcakes—since the bakery was…not open—but the girls didn't mind the ones from the market. The rainbow sprinkles had been a hit. They ate and drank everything, including the pink wafer cookies and triangular-cut sandwiches. She'd also given an etiquette lesson like her grandmother gave her and the Cupcake Shop Posse years ago with an added pinky position since the girls wanted special instructions on proper tea drinking.

They were so sweet, wanting to do everything correctly.

Juliet couldn't wait to tell her four friends about it on the Posse's group chat. Selena Tremblay and Bria were flying home to Seattle and San Diego, respectively, so Juliet could wait to message everyone.

Excitement buzzed through her. She'd found herself in a magical groove nothing except being a princess had ever brought her. Not even acting. She didn't know how often Charlene booked birthdays like these, but Juliet hoped another was on the calendar soon.

Before she knew it, the *Welcome to Berry Lake* sign appeared. Almost home.

"Yes!" Juliet relished the hum buzzing through her. She turned the car onto her street.

She'd discovered she was good at something. And she wanted to tell Ezra, no matter what he might say. Until their marriage counseling appointment, less than a week and a half away, she could handle anything.

As she parked in her driveway, her cell phone rang. She turned off the ignition and glanced at the screen. Charlene's name appeared.

She accepted the call. "Hi, Charlene."

"Three people have called about scheduling children's birthday parties. You're magic, Juliet. Pure magic."

That was how she felt. Juliet danced in the seat, her moves only impeded by the seat belt. "Thank you."

"One person asked if you did princess tea parties. Is that something you'd consider?"

"I…I could do that." At least Juliet thought so.

She'd been through the princess training and worked for a few years as one, so stepping into the role again shouldn't be that difficult. It used to be organic—a part of her—because in her old job, Juliet Jones wasn't allowed to exist during working hours. Children needed to believe she was a real princess. No hint of reality or her true identity could seep through, or management would have fired her.

"I have an old costume Ezra had custom-made for Halloween years ago. I'd have to see if it still fits." She'd lost weight since then. His weekly weigh-ins increased her paranoia each time she stepped on the scale. Now, she limited calorie splurges to special occasions.

She would bring that up in counseling, along with the list of other things she wanted them to discuss.

"Wonderful." Charlene sounded like she was smiling. "You'll have to role-play as a princess, so I'll pay you a higher hourly wage."

Juliet forced herself not to scream her excitement. Instead, she wiggled. "Thank you."

"Are you home yet?"

"I'm in the driveway."

"Wash your tea set and then rest," Charlene ordered in her no-nonsense tone that no doubt drove the Culpepper sisters crazy.

The three women had no idea how lucky they were to have a mom like Charlene who cared about them enough to meddle in their lives. The alternative—indifference—hurt.

"Don't cook dinner," Charlene added. "Order or go out."

"That sounds like a great idea. Ezra's in Seattle and won't be home until later."

"Well, you deserve an afternoon of self-care, so pamper yourself. See you on Monday."

Juliet's body thrummed with elation. She put her phone in her purse.

She wanted to call Ezra, but he might be busy, and she didn't want to disturb him. He would arrive home soon enough.

Juliet had been trying so hard to make him proud. This job might do it.

Things were better between them since she'd brought up counseling and made the appointment. That gave her hope their relationship would not only improve, but she'd also have the marriage she dreamed about.

She removed the rolling cart containing her tea service. That had been a last-minute addition, but she'd thought the floral teacups with gold rims were a better fit for a kids' party than Charlene's statement-making white with silver trim.

Inside the house, she rolled the cart through the foyer. Thai food sounded good. Or tacos. Those were tasty on Tuesdays—and every other night of the week.

Something moved in the living room. Not something—someone.

Ezra sat on the couch with a glass in his hand.

She let go of the cart's handle. "I thought you'd still be in Seattle."

He said nothing.

That was odd. Juliet had never seen him so quiet. "Ezra."

His face was pale, and the lines around his mouth appeared deeper. Strange, given how hard he worked so his wrinkles wouldn't show.

Juliet sat next to him and touched his hand.

He stiffened, his muscles tensing beneath her palm.

"Are you sick?" She felt his forehead with the back of her hand.

Ezra jerked away. "Don't touch me."

She flinched but remained seated. "What's wrong?"

He gulped his drink. "*You* are what's wrong. I give you everything, and you do nothing."

Juliet swallowed, sorry she'd asked. But she wasn't about to be the timid wife he expected. Not today.

What had Selena told her? Oh, right. Juliet deserved…better.

She lifted her chin. "I take care of the house and you. Whatever you tell me to do, I do it. Everything I do is for or about you. I even got a job for you."

Ezra sneered. "What you do isn't a job."

"Have you been drinking?"

"Yes, Juliet. I have." He picked up a bottle from the floor, twisted off the cap, and refilled his glass to the top. "When a man's wife can't do anything right, whiskey is a big help." He downed a quarter of his drink. "I should have realized you only married me for my money."

Her mouth gaped. "I didn't. I fell for you long before I knew you were wealthy."

His lips curled. "No wonder you never made it as an actress. You possess zero talent."

His barb hit hard, but she didn't flinch. He must be drunk because his words were harsher than usual.

"Ezra." She held her voice steady. "Whatever has happened, I love you."

"You love my money." He hung his head. Something she'd never seen him do in twelve years of marriage and one of dating. "This is all your fault."

It usually was. Juliet squared her shoulders, preparing herself to face the onslaught of incoming fire. "What did I do this time?"

"You weren't enough." He raised his glass. "I had to find another way to cope."

"I don't understand."

"Remy."

Ezra made no sense. "What about Remy?"

"I was with Remy today," he babbled, so it came out like one word.

"In Seattle?"

"There was no trip or any late-night hours or dinner meetings," he jeered. "You drove me to her. You. That's why it's your fault she's…"

"She's what?" Juliet's shrill voice was loud enough for the neighbors to hear. She didn't care.

Ezra downed another swig of whiskey. He slammed the glass on the living room coffee table. Droplets of amber liquid flew everywhere.

She cringed. Tension spread from her shoulders to her stomach. A braver woman would stand to give herself an advantage over him, even if it was only a couple of feet. Not her. She stayed seated next to her husband on the couch, waiting for him to answer.

His accusing gaze met Juliet's. "Remy's pregnant."

Ezra's words ran together again, so Juliet wasn't sure if she'd heard him correctly. She held her breath as if that would help her make sense of what she thought he'd just said.

It wasn't true.

It couldn't be true.

Not true.

She'd misunderstood because of how he'd spoken so fast—created the worst-case scenario in her imagination.

Yes, that was what happened. Juliet was tired, and seeing him in the living room caught her off guard. That explained why she wasn't sure what he'd said. Yes, that had to be it.

Thank goodness.

She wiped her palms over her skirt.

Her husband always said she never paid attention to him as she should. She disagreed, but this proved him right. When they attended their first marriage counseling session next Tuesday, she would admit to doing this. That might help improve their marriage faster.

Juliet exhaled, but the hardness in her stomach didn't lessen, nor did the ache in her chest.

Tiredness.

She needed him to clarify his words.

That would settle her mind. She worried too much. That was what Ezra always told her.

She focused on her husband, who looked nothing like the handsome VP of sales she'd last seen on Friday morning before he'd left for Seattle. His hair was a mess as if he'd not combed it after waking up. Spots of whiskey stained his untucked polo shirt.

Except, he said he hadn't gone golfing for the weekend. He'd also mentioned being with Remy Dwyer.

Juliet's ribs squeezed tighter.

No, it wasn't true.

Ezra stared at his drink like a lifeline.

He must be drunk. It wouldn't be the first time. Alcohol removed what few filters he had. Or he wanted to get back at her for putting the toilet paper on the roll wrong or not polishing his shoes correctly or one of the other stupid, meaningless things he demanded she do a certain way.

That was why he mentioned Remy.

To get a reaction from Juliet so he could yell at her more.

Not that he needed a reason.

All she had to do was ask him to repeat what he'd said.

If she listened more carefully, the gnawing at her gut would stop.

His mouth twitched.

Did he want to say more? She waited.

Coward.

But she knew that. Otherwise, her lips wouldn't remain glued together.

The ticking of his ridiculously expensive, ugly clock amplified the silence between them. The second hand moved, echoing the beat of her heart.

Come on. All she had to do was ask him. Not that hard to do, but her thick tongue wasn't cooperating.

Juliet inhaled and exhaled slowly. She clasped her hands on her lap. No sense in putting this off any longer. "What did you say?"

His Adam's apple bobbed. "Remy's pregnant."

Ezra's words slammed into Juliet with the force of a runaway train. Her breath caught. Her heart split in half. Her blood turned to ice.

"Remy?" Juliet's voice grew sharper. "The bimbo from the art gallery who's young enough to be your daughter?" The words came out fast, speeding up like her pulse. She balled her hands, digging her fingernails into her palms. "Remy? The one you said you weren't having an affair with?"

Juliet took a breath.

He didn't look at her.

Her entire body shook. Heat flooded her face. Sweat beaded at her hairline, and a lump, hot as glowing charcoal from the smoker, burned in her throat.

But the tears…

There were none.

Her ribs tightened, squeezing her aching chest. She wanted to scream and shout and dump the glass of whiskey on his head.

A litany of what would happen to her without Ezra pounded in her brain—divorced, penniless, homeless. Being traded in was her worst nightmare, and why she'd tried to be the perfect wife for so long.

Tried and failed.

Why wasn't she crying? Shouldn't she be crying? Wailing? Begging him not to leave her? Why, with her comfortable world falling apart, did the corners of Juliet's mouth want to curve upward and her stomach flutter as if on the precipice of something new? As if she stood at the edge of a cliff, ready to jump into the raging waters below, wearing her favorite Oscar de la Renta dress and shoes?

It made no sense.

Risk was a four-letter word. She rarely took a chance on anything. And Ezra was her husband.

Would a loving husband cheat and get another woman pregnant?

The little voice inside her head she'd grown to hate, especially these past months, mocked before snickering.

It was true.

Everything she'd suspected.

True.

A black hole swallowed Juliet's heart. She inhaled, but her lungs didn't fill with air. She tried again, her breath quickening with each attempt. Her eyes stung, and tears blurred her vision.

Crying must be a delayed reaction.

"I never meant for this to happen." Ezra's voice was raw. His shoulders slumped, and the lines on his face added ten years. He would hate that.

Not her problem.

Juliet blinked, trying not to lose it. He would enjoy watching her fall apart.

She took a breath and another, working to gain her composure so she could say more than one word.

Juliet raised her chin. "You didn't expect to get caught."

"I didn't," he snapped, a vein pulsing at his jaw. "But this is your fault. If you'd been a better wife, a younger one, I wouldn't have needed Remy."

She froze so she wouldn't nod. Not because she agreed but out of habit and self-preservation. That hadn't worked out so well.

Her throat tightened. "Thirty-five isn't old."

"Compared to twenty-four, it is."

A pressure built above the bridge of her nose. She'd been twenty-two when they met.

"Men age like fine wine, whereas women…don't." His gaze darkened, making his eyes beady—Ezra, the rat. "That's why I've been looking for a replacement since you turned thirty."

Her mouth gaped. She closed it.

Juliet's eyes burned. Heat pooled in her cheeks.

The two of them were nothing but a cliché. The affair and impending divorce would upset her grandmother—unless she and others already knew somehow.

Did Grandma know? What about the town's busybodies? What if she was the last person to know?

Juliet's insides twisted until she thought they—she—might snap.

Hand trembling, she reached for his glass and drank. Her eyes watered, and she nearly spit out the mouthful of whiskey, but she forced herself to swallow.

Juliet returned the glass to the table before wiping her face with her hand. Her mouth was hot and dry. She needed water.

"That's mine." Ezra grabbed the glass, sloshing more liquid onto the table. He cradled his drink, gazing at the whiskey with more affection than he'd looked at her in…months.

Possibly years.

A weight pressed against the center of her chest. Her body hurt as if she'd aged fifty years in the last sixty seconds.

Idiot.

Him, but her, too, for not being courageous enough to stand up for herself.

To leave her comfortable life.

To put her rotten excuse for a husband behind her.

Ezra glared. "Aren't you going to say anything?"

She looked past the fancy moisturizers, Botox injections, and hair-color job every four weeks. Underneath the designer clothes, expensive cars, and over-inflated job title was a horrible, petty man who would be a first-time father at fifty-five. Make that fifty-six when the baby was born. "This situation isn't in my etiquette book, but I pity you."

He sneered, his lip curling like a B-actor playing the role of a villain. "You're the one who'll have nothing. God gave you beauty but no brains. That was clear when you signed a prenup giving you only a small settlement when we divorce."

When, not if.

Her muscles knotted. Her teeth clenched.

Thirteen freaking years. How had she spent over a decade loving this man?

She loved him, or rather she'd loved the character she'd created in her imagination. Reality didn't come close to her fantasy husband.

"You're right. I'm not very smart because I thought you were my Prince Charming. I must be stupid not to have seen what you really are. A pathetic man having a midlife crisis." She stood, smoothing her skirt. "I'm too tired to find a place to stay tonight, so I'll sleep in the guest room. Tomorrow, I'll pack my things and be out of here before you get off work."

Ezra's face scrunched. "Why are you leaving?"

"You and Remy—"

"Remy's not capable of raising a child or keeping this house clean." His words grew louder, the stench of whiskey hitting Juliet's nose. Yet another verbal assault, even if he wasn't criticizing *her* for once.

"Have my dinner ready when I walk in the door tomorrow night." His demand smacked her like a left jab.

She doubled over before forcing herself to straighten. She wrapped her arms around her stomach as if that would give her more strength to remain standing. "You can't be serious."

He downed more whiskey. "Why not?"

Tell him. Juliet had to say something. She squared her shoulders. "Nothing you offer would make me stay."

"Are you sure about that?" Wicked laughter lit his eyes. "You wanted a child. Raise Remy's. You're a competent maid and cook. You should be a decent nanny."

Juliet's jaw dropped. "No."

"You'll need a place to live and a job after the divorce." Ezra swayed slightly before leaning against the couch. "Babies wake in the middle of the night. You can live in the room above the garage so you'll be close to the nursery."

Her heart exploded into a million jagged pieces.

He raised his glass as if what he'd said was normal. Perhaps in his mind, it was.

"There isn't a bathroom up there." Not that Juliet was considering it. Of course, she wasn't. But she was so used to doing what he wanted. She was having a hard time understanding how he'd fooled her for so long. And that prenup she signed would haunt her for years. But a part of her had known that once she'd read it six months ago.

"I'm sure Remy will allow you to use one in the house." Ezra slurred his words. "It's not as if you can rent a public toilet with a shower by the minute."

His voice grated like gel fingernail extensions on a chalkboard.

"Face it. Your days as a trophy wife are over, Juliet. You're too old and no longer beautiful enough to find another rich husband. Unless you want to be homeless, working for me is your only option." He removed the gold band on his left ring finger—the way it slipped off so easily suggested he'd done this before—and tossed it next to his glass on the table. "Remy can't cook or keep her apartment clean. She won't be able to handle this house and entertain guests. She's too immature to raise a child properly. This will solve your problems and mine."

Juliet's knees went weak, but she wouldn't buckle. That was what he wanted. To see her on the ground with tears streaming down her face.

"Say something," he snapped.

She had lots to tell him, but not when he'd been drinking. The safest thing was to get away from him.

Juliet pushed back her shoulders and stared down her nose, the same way she'd done with demanding guests at the theme park years ago. She hadn't needed to rely on her Princess 101 training in her current life, but the perfect princess posture came as naturally to her as breathing.

"Not tonight." She turned and walked away.

Her purse sat on the cart. Juliet didn't want to wash dishes, but leaving her tea set within Ezra's reach wasn't an option. She lifted the cart handle, marched upstairs and into the guest bedroom, and locked the door.

She plopped onto the queen-sized bed and buried her face against a down pillow.

What am I going to do?

chapter two

"I HATE BEING IN the hospital." Missy Hanford clutched the blanket, her fingers digging into the thin fabric. They'd elevated her burned foot, and her head hurt. It was Sunday night. That meant she'd only been there for two and a half days, but she wanted to throw a tantrum to show how much she hated it here.

Suck it up.

Rob would tell her that. And he would be correct, as usual.

She shouldn't complain to her friend Nell Culpepper, who worked in the emergency department. It wasn't her fault Missy wanted out of there.

Not tomorrow, but today.

Now.

She sat up.

Pain sliced through her head.

Ugh.

Horizontal might be the best position. The trip to the bathroom earlier had tired her. Walking—okay, limping—had hurt all over, but the nurse, who was the antithesis of Nell, made Missy put weight on her foot despite the burns, claiming it was necessary.

She rested against her pillow, wanting to ignore the IV in her hand and the circular pads on her chest connected to wires plugged into a machine. But after being unconscious for almost two days, her awareness seemed heightened, as if the coma sent her senses into overdrive, soaking up the sights, sounds, tastes, and smells whether or not she wanted it to.

The beeps and blips irritated her teeth and increased the throbbing at her temples. A nurse had removed the tube from Missy's throat, but it still hurt. Not even ice water helped. That turned out to be a good thing because getting up to go to the bathroom was a pain—literally.

"I don't understand why I have to stay another night." If Missy subtracted thirty years from her age, she would be two, and the tantrum itching to come out could. She loosened her grip on the blanket so she didn't poke a hole through the fabric. "That one doctor said they would release me today."

Nell, still in her nursing scrubs from her shift earlier, shook her head. "He said the hospital *might* release you. You're doing better from the smoke inhalation, but you have a concussion. And don't forget the burns on your foot. One more day won't kill you."

It wouldn't, but…

Missy's vision blurred.

Smoke. Heat. Flames.

Tension formed between her shoulder blades.

She hadn't been able to see.

Dark. It had been so dark.

Her pulse kicked up a notch.

And smoky. So much smoke.

No air to breathe.

She inhaled, filling her lungs without difficulty this time. The air was clear except for a scent that was more chemical than citrusy. Missy held her breath, trying to calm herself before she exhaled. Slowly.

Not real. None of it was real.

She flexed her fingers.

Safe. She was safe.

Only a memory.

It couldn't hurt her.

That didn't stop bits and pieces of Thursday night at the bakery from flashing in her mind like a movie trailer.

Missy blinked to reorient herself and motioned to the dinner tray on her bed table, hoping Nell, who was checking the water level in a flower arrangement, hadn't noticed the momentary freak-out.

"If I stay any longer, I'll starve to death." Missy tried to keep her voice steady when all she wanted to do was whisper and ask for a hug. If only Rob would visit her again. But it had been more than twenty-four hours and nothing. Not while sleeping overnight or when she napped today. She raised her chin. "I need to lose at least ten pounds, but I'd rather not do it this way. I'm not even sure what kind of meat this is."

"You ate the mashed potatoes."

"I was hungry, and carbs are my friends." Missy had tried being positive, but optimism wasn't working. She wanted to go home. Mario and Peach needed her, and she needed her cats.

Plus, her photos of Rob were there. She wanted to see him, to compare what he looked like versus what she remembered about the man in her dream. "Can't you pull some strings with your coworkers?"

"Sorry." Nell's tone was compassionate. "I'm just an RN."

"An RN who is one of my oldest and dearest friends and practically runs the emergency department." Missy would beg if necessary. "Please try. I'll repay you with cupcakes."

Nell perked up. "I like cupcakes."

"You love them." After each shift, Nell stopped by the Berry Lake Cupcake Shop on her way home. Missy looked forward to the visits, but now… No, she wouldn't think about the future of the bakery. Not yet anyway. "You choose what flavor, and they'll be the first batch I bake once I'm on my feet again."

Which would be soon. It had to be.

Nell didn't reply, but she bit her lip.

Hah! That meant she was considering it. Missy held her breath. *Please, oh please.*

"Are you baking them at the Huckleberry Inn?" Nell asked.

Penelope Jones, who was Juliet's grandmother, had offered the use of her commercial kitchen to help them fulfill the bakery's special orders. Missy didn't know how badly the fire had damaged the cupcake shop. No one would tell her. But that only led to more questions about the future and everyone's jobs, including hers as manager.

But overthinking hurt.

Both her heart and her head.

Most especially the latter.

This concussion might not be such a bad thing. She had an excuse for ignoring stuff.

"I don't know." Missy didn't. "If not at the inn, I'll bake them at home. Cupcakes aren't as complicated as, say, a wedding cake. All I need is a bowl, ingredients, a pan, cup liners, and an oven. Depending on the flavor, I might have the recipe memorized. Well, once my brain stops wanting to crack through my skull."

Nell's tired face brightened. "The pain should lessen each day. You look better than last night. I'll mention that when I talk to your doctor tomorrow."

That was better than nothing, even if Monday was too far away. Okay, not that far, but Missy had to ask. "Why not tonight?"

"It's Sunday. Most doctors have gone home."

Oh, right, but that reminded Missy of something. "That's where you should be. You worked all day before coming up here to be with me. You must be exhausted."

"I told Jenny I'd stay until you fell asleep."

Of course, Nell did. Missy swallowed a sigh. Everyone thought they had to take care of her. It wasn't as if she'd thrown a real tantrum. "My sister-in-law isn't my keeper. And you're not my caretaker. I can fall asleep on my own. Until the fire, I did it every night. I'm not a child."

Even if she kept acting like one.

"No, but you could have died."

"I didn't. I'm very much alive thanks to Welles Riggs, paramedic and hero around town."

Nell groaned. "Please don't say that to his face. The guy has a big enough ego. Not that I've seen him since Friday morning. The chief must have disciplined him for disobeying orders."

"I hope not, because if he hadn't…"

Missy gulped, unable to continue. If not for Welles, she might have more than second-degree burns on her foot…or she might be dead.

If that had happened, would she be with Rob now?

Probably best not to think about the answer after the strange dream she'd had about him yesterday.

It was a dream, right?

It had to have been a dream.

He was dead, and dead people didn't just show up in real life. At least that had never happened to her before.

"But Welles did," Nell finished for her, pulling Missy out of her thoughts. "And as I said, you've improved since last night. You're no longer as pale, and your bruises are slowly fading, but you need time to heal."

"Do comas make you have weird dreams?" She needed to know.

"It depends on the type. Some people have vivid dreams or nightmares." Nell came closer, standing at the side of the hospital bed. "Did you?"

"I…" Missy hesitated, torn whether to say more. She wanted to go home, not to have a psychiatrist examining her. Because saying her dead husband visited her yesterday might be a sign of something more than the injuries she'd sustained in the fire. She wasn't the same as she'd been before that IED killed Rob nine years ago. Everyone knew she wasn't, but this felt…different.

Nell touched her hand. "You can tell me anything."

Of course, Missy could. Nell wasn't some random stranger who worked at the hospital. They'd been friends for over fifteen years. She wouldn't judge.

Still, Missy inhaled deeply. "I dreamed about Rob yesterday. I was in the coma, I think. Because I hadn't opened my eyes."

"Did the dream scare you?"

"No. The opposite. I was so happy." Warmth balled at the center of her chest before spreading to her fingertips and toes. "It was so real, like he was right next to me. I didn't want it to end, but…"

Nell leaned closer. "What?"

"Rob told me I needed to wake up." Even though Missy asked to stay with him.

The corners of Nell's mouth lifted in a soft smile. "And you did."

"I didn't want to." Part of Missy wanted to return to that dreamlike state—okay, coma—to keep the feeling alive, not only as a memory but forever. "But I did for him."

She hesitated to say more, especially about agreeing to live again. Well, try to. Her friends had wanted that for a long time. If she told them Rob wanted her to make the dreams they'd had come true, they would push harder. She didn't want that. Besides…

Dream or not, Missy had no idea how to make her dreams come true when they'd died with him. Rob was her one true love, the love of her life, the only man she'd ever kissed. She wanted no one else.

Only him.

Nell's face lit up. "I'm happy you did. You're the cornerstone of the cupcake shop and the Posse. And what would I do if you weren't around?"

"Learn to bake cupcakes yourself," Missy joked.

Nell laughed. "I'd have to because I'm addicted."

That made Missy smile. "You are."

"It's not the same situation, but I struggled after Andrew. I truly believed after our month apart, we'd live happily ever after. I even tried on wedding dresses during our break."

Missy's heart ached for her friend. "Oh, sweetie…"

"I found the gown. The one that makes you feel like a princess. Gorgeous and special."

Her dress had been from a consignment shop in Portland, but that hadn't stopped Missy from feeling the same way. "Magical."

Nell nodded. "When he married a woman he'd only known a couple of weeks, after being with me for years, a part of me died. It took a long time before I wanted to date again. I can't imagine what losing your husband must be like, but Rob adored you. You were his entire world since you were kids. Your happiness was all that mattered to him. And subconsciously, you might realize that, and it's why you dreamed what you did."

"That makes sense." Missy clung to the memory of being in his arms, even if it was only a dream. But a part of her wished it had been real.

"If you decide to date or fall in love again, it won't take away from what you shared with Rob," Nell continued.

Weird. Her words echoed what he'd said.

"I'm not trying to push you after what you've been through." Compassion filled Nell's voice. "But when a trauma or life-altering event happens, a person reassesses their life."

Was that why Missy had dreamed about Rob that way? Part of her hoped not. She wasn't ready for anything more, except for getting out of the hospital.

You're never alone, Missy. I'm always with you.

She'd believed that in her heart. But hearing Rob say those words in the dream had given her such peace—contentment missing for the nine years he'd been gone. But thinking it was only her mind doing it…hurt.

She wanted it to be *him*.

Emotion clogged her throat. Missy couldn't reply, so she nodded.

"Selena did a podcast on love. I'll send the link," Nell said. "On it, she talks about the human heart's infinite capacity to love. The heart doesn't choose between one person or another. There's more than enough love for both. For all."

Missy's breath hitched. More similarities from her dream. It didn't surprise her Selena—also known as Selena T to her rabid fans who listened to the life coach's podcast, took her courses, and bought her books—would discuss this. But the timing for hearing about it was…odd.

Tingly, hair-stand-on-end strange.

"Thanks." Missy had a concussion, but she recognized the signs.

The dream. Nell. Selena T's podcast.

Missy didn't want a man who wasn't Rob, but was she making that decision for the right reason? Okay, no one knew that more days than not, a dark cloud pressed down on her. At times, more tears fell than she thought humanly possible. "I should probably talk to Selena."

Nell's eyes widened, matching the "o" her lips formed. "You should."

Her friend's surprise was understandable. Missy hadn't done well with grief counseling—private or group sessions. She'd turned down help from Jenny and her friends, including Elise, who begged Missy to see somebody—anybody. When that failed, her boss wanted her to speak with Selena and offered to drive Missy to Seattle to make a face-to-face meeting possible. The least she could do was honor Elise's friendship and memory by talking to Selena.

Even if Missy didn't think it would help much since nothing else had.

But it was a step.

One step.

When she'd been standing still for...

Nine years.

Missy raised her chin slightly. Any farther would hurt her head. "I will, once I recover."

Nell's relief was palpable. "I'll hold you to it. I'm texting Selena tonight, so she knows to reach out if you don't."

That brought a laugh. So typical of Nell, who took care of her patients and friends alike. Through and through, she was a caretaker, which explained why she was such a highly regarded nurse and excellent at her job. "I wouldn't assume otherwise."

"That's what friends do."

"Especially you."

Nell held out her hands. "Guilty."

"You're also guilty of not telling me about Gage." Missy appreciated her friend wanting to help, but it was time to change the subject to something not about her. "I was unconscious when it happened, but I'm wide awake and want to know all the details about the new guy."

Nell laughed. "You heard Gage when I met him."

"His friend was injured hiking, and you'd made plans to have coffee."

"On Friday morning, which was a day off for me. But I came to the hospital to check on you, so I texted him to reschedule."

Missy recalled what she'd heard when the Posse threw an impromptu party in this room last night. It had been fun to be together for one last time with Nell, Juliet, Bria, and Selena before the latter two left town. "Friday was two days ago, so I'm guessing you saw Gage somehow."

Nell blushed before nodding. "He showed up at the hospital with coffee and snacks from Brew and Steep and a bouquet."

"Impressive for a first date."

She nodded, pink rising on her cheeks. "My mother thought so."

Oh, no. "Charlene met him?"

Another nod. "She was in the waiting area when Gage arrived."

That had disaster—or a line of questioning à la the Spanish Inquisition—written all over it. Missy couldn't wait to find out which. "What happened?"

"She introduced herself, forcefully if I might add, and asked him what he did for a living."

Poor Gage. "Typical Charlene."

"Right? She's the one who suggested Gage and I find a quiet place to drink our coffees, which wasn't a bad idea. But she hasn't stopped talking about him. I'm guessing she's planning our wedding."

"I'm pretty sure your mom had that planned before your fifth birthday."

Nell laughed. "You're probably right. An occupational hazard when your mom is an event planner."

"I'm assuming Gage is handsome, the kind of guy you take home to meet Mom."

As Nell sighed, heart-eyes practically appeared. "Gorgeous, and I would have rather waited until we'd gone on a few dates to introduce him to my mom, but he's so nice and understanding. Not only about her, but I fell sound asleep when we were having coffee in the atrium."

"Oops."

"Pretty sure I was snoring, too." Nell groaned. "So embarrassing, but I enjoyed a glorious nap with my human pillow, who smelled amazing."

"I'm so excited for you." Everything about Nell seemed lighter, and her eyes twinkled. Her friend's happiness lessened Missy's feelings of being so stuck. "When do you see Gage again?"

"Saturday."

"I'll need a full report."

"You'll get one. I'm trying not to expect too much. I did with our coffee date on Friday, and then—"

"Me. Sorry."

"What happened at the cupcake shop isn't your fault. Blame the stupid arsonist."

Missy couldn't believe someone had set fire to the bakery on purpose. She hoped the person hadn't known she'd been upstairs asleep in the office.

How could they?

Only Jenny knew.

Still, arson… Missy had spoken to Sheriff Dooley and the fire inspector earlier today. She hoped they were close to catching whoever did it. "I keep trying to remember that."

"It's true. But—"

"I should have never gone back inside for Elise's recipe journal," Missy finished for her.

"You must hear it from everyone."

"You have no idea." Since she woke up yesterday, that was all she'd heard from friends, medical staff, and official visitors.

Nell patted her hand. "People care about you."

"I know, but I didn't run into a wall of flames and thick smoke. It wasn't bad at the time."

"A fire can change on a dime."

"I learned that the hard way. But the journal. There's so much in there. Each page screams Elise." Missy pointed at her head and her foot. "My injuries were worth it."

"I wouldn't go that far, but I can't wait to see what you do with her recipes."

Me, too.

Only that task appeared daunting with her in the hospital and no more cupcake shop. But she wouldn't lose hope. She couldn't. That was why she prayed the Berry Lake Cupcake Shop would rise like a phoenix from the ashes. Otherwise, getting injured for the journal would be for nothing.

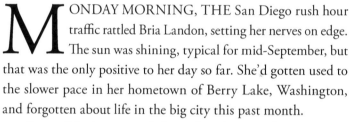

chapter three 🧁

MONDAY MORNING, THE San Diego rush hour traffic rattled Bria Landon, setting her nerves on edge. The sun was shining, typical for mid-September, but that was the only positive to her day so far. She'd gotten used to the slower pace in her hometown of Berry Lake, Washington, and forgotten about life in the big city this past month.

Be careful what you wish for, unless it's a cupcake.

That was one of Aunt Elise's many sayings.

Bria ignored the pang of grief and focused on the freeway. She turned on the radio to find out this wasn't only a traffic jam. There'd been an accident up ahead.

Her neck muscles tightened, but rolling her head from side to side did nothing.

A horn honked somewhere behind her. Others joined in. The line of red brake lights in front of her appeared longer.

She gripped the steering wheel. A good thing she'd left early so she would arrive at work with time to spare.

Traffic moved at a snail's pace until it picked up. After what felt like hours, Bria parked in the employees' lot behind the building that had become her home away from home. She grabbed her laptop case and purse.

The stately columns and brick façade screamed traditional, appropriate for an accounting firm, which defined old-school when most companies had gone high tech. Still, Bria found comfort in the traditions. That had been the case, even when she'd been an eager twenty-three-year-old CPA interviewing for a job. The pluses outweighed the cons.

She planned on being one of the first women to rise to the upper-management ranks. Someday, she would say goodbye to her cubicle and move into a private office with windows. That might take time because a firm like theirs didn't have many resignations, only retirements. That was fine with her.

After working there for a decade, a couple of more years didn't matter.

When she entered the lobby, the receptionist's desk was empty. Typical. She usually was the second employee to arrive, and after four weeks away, she wanted to get back on her regular schedule. Today, if possible.

As she climbed the stairs, Andy, a junior accountant, was on his way down.

"Hey," she said. "How's it going?"

Andy kept walking. *He must have AirPods in.*

She would rib him about that later. It would have been nice to say hello to someone. Her condo had been too quiet when she arrived home last night. The same this morning.

Her chest squeezed tightly. It was a familiar feeling since her aunt's death, the funeral, dealing with the estate, seeing her dad, finding out an arsonist set fire to the cupcake shop, Missy getting injured, and reconnecting with Dalton Dwyer.

Bria nearly laughed at everything that had happened over the past week and a half. She wasn't big on change. If she focused on what remained the same in her life—being at the job she loved—that might help.

As she continued up the stairs, she planned her day. The few calls she'd received from her boss, Mr. Howe, and her friend Susan, who'd handled Bria's accounts while she was away, had been easy to answer. She hoped that meant everything would be in order, so she could contact her clients to see how they were doing. Otherwise, she would spend her Monday getting things where they needed to be instead of doing actual work.

Her stomach churned.

That was what she got for not eating breakfast. Her kitchen was bare, and she didn't stop on the way this morning. But there was more to it than that.

Which surprised—no, shocked—her.

Last week, Bria had been counting the days until she returned to San Diego, wishing she were home, but now Bria missed her friends in Berry Lake. Aunt Elise would want the Cupcake Posse—what she'd named them when they worked at her bakery one summer fifteen years ago—to stay in touch this time. Bria wanted that to happen, too. That was why she would check in via their group chat at lunchtime. She would make an effort this time and not forget how much those four women meant to her.

Her cell phone buzzed.

She pulled it from her purse's outside pocket and glanced at the screen.

DALTON: *Have a great day at work. I miss you.*
BRIA: *Miss you, too! TTYL*

Her smile spread to her toes. She hadn't stopped thinking about Dalton since he'd dropped her off at the airport yesterday with a kiss and a "call me when you get home." She did, and they'd talked for two hours—the reason she'd never made it to the grocery store.

No worries. She would go out for lunch and swing by the market after work.

Bria entered her cubicle and…

"Huh?" The desk, chair, and file cabinet were there. A monitor, keyboard, and landline phone, too. But her personal items were missing.

She shuffled forward and opened a drawer.

Empty.

No pens, mechanical pencils, erasers, and paper clips. A tissue package, lip gloss tube, and coaster were gone.

She glanced in the other drawers. All cleaned out. The filing cabinet, too.

Nothing hung on the cubicle's walls. Someone even removed the wall calendar.

Bria pinched herself. Okay, she wasn't dreaming. "What's going on?"

No one answered her.

"Is anyone here?"

No reply.

A shiver inched along her spine.

Remember, you're usually the second person here each morning. The first was…

She placed her laptop bag and purse in the largest desk drawer, hoping they'd be there when she returned.

Stop.

This wasn't a Stephen King novel. There had to be a logical explanation. The job was the one constant in her life—never changing, and she relished in that. Besides, she was the most requested accountant with a waiting list to add new clients.

As if on autopilot, she headed to Mr. Howe's office. She could count on one hand how many times she'd arrived before him. Only…

The scent of freshly brewed coffee was missing. No matter when Bria got to work, the aroma filled the air because Mr. Howe needed a cup to start his day.

Maybe upper management had given people the morning off and left her off the email distribution list.

Except she'd seen Andy.

No worries. She would find out what was going on soon enough.

Bria knocked on Mr. Howe's door.

"Enter."

Relief surged through her. She opened the door. One step inside and Bria froze.

She expected to see Mr. Howe, not Fritz—her ex-boyfriend— sitting behind the massive mahogany desk. He wore a tie, which wasn't unusual. His suit jacket was.

His eyes narrowed. "Close the door."

She did before taking a seat in the leather chair opposite his desk. "My cubicle is empty. What's going on?"

"The firm is restructuring, Bria." He steepled his hands in a gesture out of a mafia movie. "Mr. Howe retired, and they promoted me to take his place."

That meant her ex-boyfriend was her new boss.

A slight chill shot through her. She flipped her hair behind her shoulder.

Okay, no big deal. They'd remained friends and teamed up at the company picnic to win the three-legged race for their department in July. "Congratulations."

Working with him wouldn't be an issue, but the news unsettled her. The firm provided a stable job with excellent pay and benefits. They promoted managers from within. But length of employment counted for advancement, and Fritz was hired after her.

Jealousy nagged at her.

Why hadn't they asked her to apply?

Sure, Aunt Elise had been in hospice, but Bria stayed in contact. She'd also mentioned her interest in management at her last review. Mr. Howe had said she was a strong candidate for a future position. It made no sense.

She had to ask. "This all happened in four weeks?"

"It's been in the works, but only the upper level of the firm knew." Fritz's voice suggested he'd known, which made even less sense. "There are other changes."

Changes as in more promotions?

Oh... The pieces of the puzzle clicked together.

Bria wiggled her toes. She must have received a promotion, too, and someone moved her things into her new office. That explained her cubicle and Fritz's promotion.

She leaned forward, eager to hear more. "What changes, Fritz?"

He stiffened. "It's Mr. Carson now."

Another shiver ran along her spine, but a foreboding of dread accompanied this one.

Mr. Carson?

They'd dated for years. At one point, she assumed they would marry. They had so much in common—it turned out they'd been too much alike. Fritz was a little stuffy, and she wasn't exactly Miss Lighthearted and Carefree, but his tone and posture set off warning bells. Especially if she'd been promoted, too.

"Mr. Howe was old school." She spoke in a cheery tone. "Most of the managers don't make us—"

"With Mr. Howe's retirement, we're reorganizing. That means a reduction in workforce."

Wait. What? She clutched the chair arms. The firm had never laid off employees in the past.

Fritz rubbed his hands together. Something he did only when he was nervous.

Bria's heart slammed against her chest. He wouldn't fire her, would he?

She squeezed her fists so tight the veins on the tops of her hands showed.

Enough. No torturing herself with what-ifs when Fritz sat across from her with all the information she needed to know.

"Say what you have to say." The impatience in her voice was unlike her, but she didn't care. This job defined her life—her future. "What is it?"

He opened a folder on his desk and pushed a piece of paper toward her. "The firm has eliminated your position."

As the air rushed from Bria's mouth, her stomach clenched. Bile rose in her throat. She thought she might be sick.

No, this couldn't be happening.

All her plans. Her safe, comfortable life. Gone.

Why?

She read the sheet with her name printed at the top. The terms of her severance package were listed below. She was being laid off.

Tears pricked her eyelids. Bria swallowed, trying to pull herself together. She hadn't cried when they mutually agreed they would be better off as friends. She wouldn't cry now, especially when Fritz appeared almost gleeful.

That made no sense. None of this did.

"I don't understand." Her voice cracked, so she cleared her throat. "I've worked here for over ten years. I have excellent reviews from management and clients. My roster is full, and I have a waiting list of people who want to work with me."

"The firm has eliminated your position," he said as if he'd told her there were no paper towels in the restroom.

"But why?" California was an at-will state, which meant the company didn't have to give her a reason for termination. "Was it because I took family leave?"

"It's illegal to punish an employee for that. And your aunt wasn't considered kin per state law. The firm gave you that time off for your service."

Time off using her vacation days and unpaid when she ran out of those. "You knew in August?"

His face reddened. "It doesn't matter when management decided."

The words tumbled out one on top of another.

"It does to me." Tears burned the corners of her eyes. She blinked to keep from crying. "I need to understand."

"This isn't personal." His voice was tight. "It's a business decision."

"One that drastically changes my life. I love my job and working for this firm."

He stared at the paper in front of her. "You're receiving a generous severance package that includes a week's salary for each year you've worked here. You have no time off remaining, so you won't receive a lump sum for that, but you can use COBRA to keep your health insurance until you find a new position. With your experience, it won't take long. We've provided a letter of recommendation, of course."

Of course.

His matter-of-fact voice grated on her nerves. Bria didn't want another job. She also disagreed with one week of pay per year employed being "generous."

But what could she say?

She'd been away for a month, and they hadn't missed her.

Not that she regretted spending those last three weeks with Aunt Elise. But why would Mr. Howe tell her about a potential client he wanted to introduce?

"Any questions?" Fritz asked.

Bria had no idea where to start, but one question rose above the others. "Who else?"

"Excuse me?"

"Who else's position was eliminated, Mr. Carson?"

"I'm not at liberty to divulge that." He wouldn't meet her gaze. "Your belongings are with HR, but double-check nothing was forgotten before heading downstairs. They are expecting you and will review your package. I wish you all the best."

Disbelief coursed through her veins. "Do you?"

He startled. "What do you mean by that?"

"You're not the same person you were a month ago. The man I dated for years." She studied him. Same haircut and clothes, but his eyes and facial features were different. "What happened to you?"

He shifted, averting his gaze once again. "Goodbye, Bria."

Knowing he'd dismissed her in more ways than one, she picked up the severance package letter and returned to her cubicle.

Warm tears wet her cheeks. She quickly wiped them away.

Bria wanted to get out of there, but she plopped into her chair instead. Or what had been hers until a few minutes ago.

Her rib cage felt like a vise, tightening with each passing second, making it impossible to fill her lungs with air.

A minute. She needed a minute or ten to hold herself together and breathe.

The feeling of loss added to the ones already weighing on her heart.

She pulled out her phone and pressed her favorites on her contact list. Aunt Elise's number was at the top.

Bria's finger hovered over the name. And then she remembered.

Her aunt was dead, but for a moment, Bria forgot.

Oh, Aunt Elise. I wish you were here.

Bria squeezed her eyes shut. Her hands shook.

Stop procrastinating and do what you have to do.

She opened the same drawers she'd checked a few minutes ago and looked underneath and behind the desk. Whoever cleaned her cubicle did a thorough job.

The hollowness inside her grew.

"Hey." Susan Dunlop, who'd started at the firm a month after Bria, stood at the cubicle's entrance. She wore khakis and an orange sweater set. Only her chunky necklace and earrings hinted at the woman's gregarious personality she hid at work. "I'm sorry about your aunt."

"Thanks." Bria wiped her clammy palms over her navy pants. "Did you know about me losing my job?"

"No, but Fritz cleaned out your cubicle on Friday. He wouldn't tell anyone why."

Ugh. It wasn't as if she had anything to hide, but knowing he'd gone through her things and packed them felt like a violation, an invasion of her privacy.

"I assumed you'd been promoted, too. I mean, why would he get Mr. Howe's job over you?"

"Not to sound entitled, but I thought the same thing."

"It's true." Susan glanced over her shoulder and lowered her voice. "He told everyone to come in later today. That raised a few eyebrows since you and Mr. Howe were the only ones who arrived early."

"That must be why Andy was heading down the stairs and ignored me."

"He's out front complaining because he'd promised to send something to a client this morning."

Bria rubbed her face. "Mr. Howe told me he planned on working until he turned seventy. I can't believe he retired."

"Retired isn't the word I'd use. Rumor has it, someone higher up on the food chain shoved a voluntary retirement package at Mr. Howe and told him to shut up and take it."

Bria's jaw dropped. "Fritz said…"

"Did Fritz mention he's engaged to Carlisle Mulligan?"

Engaged? Bria let the info sink in. "I didn't think they were that serious."

"You don't date a founding partner's only child lightly. Especially one who is as spoiled and bratty as her." Susan glanced around before leaning toward Bria. "Carlisle wanted Fritz promoted, even though he isn't as qualified as you or Allen."

Allen Alexander joined the firm a year before Bria and trained her when she started. He was a nice guy with a wife and two kids. "Was he laid off, too?"

"Only you."

"I'm the only one?"

Susan nodded.

"I don't understand. Fritz mentioned a reorganization."

"I guess you could call it that, only I think Carlisle orchestrated it. Not upper management."

"You lost me."

"Carlisle wanted Fritz promoted and you fired. Remember the company picnic?"

Carlisle hadn't been friendly to her, but it had been right before Aunt Elise went into hospice, so Bria had forgotten about it. "I haven't dated him in a couple of years. We're friends."

"Jealous harpies with narcissistic tendencies don't act logically."

"Unbelievable." She wasn't sure that reason made her feel any better. "That makes more sense than it being my performance."

"You were the firm's most recent Employee of the Year."

Bria had been awarded that three times. She pointed to the plaque she'd won in December—only it was no longer hanging on the cubicle wall. "I can't believe I lost my job because of my ex-boyfriend's fiancée when this place has been..."

My life.

Susan glanced to her left. "Fritz is hovering outside his office."

"Probably waiting for me to head to HR."

She leaned closer. "Sign nothing during your exit interview. Tell them your emotions are too raw after losing your aunt and your job."

"You're not wrong."

"Talk to Mr. Howe. I'll call you later, okay?"

Nodding, Bria rubbed her eyes, but her insides quivered. She never thought this would happen to her.

What do I do now?

chapter four

J ULIET OPENED HER eyes to daylight before squeezing
her eyelids shut.

Ouch. Ouch. Ouch.

Something pounded in her head. Forget a woodpecker tapping
its beak or even a jackhammer against her skull. This was a wreck-
ing ball, demolishing and leaving her brain in bits and pieces. The
sip of whiskey hadn't been the problem. She'd removed any trace of
that by brushing her teeth and gargling with mouthwash—twice.

No, the pain came from crying.

Once Ezra shut the master bedroom door last night, tears
fell for hours. She wished she meant that figuratively, but nope.
Hours it had been. Fat, wet tears had poured out and streamed
down her face, leaving her eyes swollen and the pillow damp
enough she'd flipped it over.

She'd cried for herself and not knowing what she would do
or what her future held, for the baby who deserved better parents

than Ezra and Remy, and for her grandmother, who would be so disappointed in Juliet being the first in the family to divorce.

Upset enough to disown her?

Possibly, and the uncertainty clawed at Juliet.

Grandma was the only relative she had left.

She clutched the comforter to her chest, looking up at the ceiling to keep more tears from falling.

What would Penelope Jones do when she found out her granddaughter's marriage was over?

As worst-case scenarios flashed in Juliet's mind, she shivered.

Don't do this to yourself.

Even if the worst happened, Juliet wouldn't be alone.

She opened her eyes, blinking until her vision adjusted to the sunlight streaming in the room through the open blinds.

Not alone.

Two critical words—ones she hadn't forgotten.

She grabbed her phone from the nightstand and typed a message for the Cupcake Posse group chat, set up a week ago to help them stay connected. They'd needed something with Bria and Selena living elsewhere. But who knew in less than twenty-four hours after saying goodbye, Juliet's life would implode? She wanted to believe their vow to be there for each other was true, but Ezra hadn't honored his vows. Why should her friends?

Here goes nothing.

She took a breath before hitting send.

> **JULIET:** *Last night, Ezra told me Remy is pregnant.*
> *He's the father. I needed time to process. Now,*
> *I need to figure out what to do. I have to visit*

my grandmother and ask if I can move into the
Huckleberry Inn. I want out of here ASAP.

Juliet exhaled. No matter how Grandma reacted, her friends would have her back. At least, she hoped so.

Doubts, however, surfaced, ready to take her out like a rogue wave on the coast. After nearly fifteen years apart, the five of them had reunited last week. Sure, they picked up right where they'd left off as if they still worked at the Berry Lake Cupcake Shop and Elise Landon was alive. But what did that mean today and tomorrow and every day after that?

A vow was only words. The intention behind it was what mattered.

She waited, staring at her cell phone as if she could wish a reply into existence. But people might be busy or not have their phones with them.

Dots formed on the screen.

Someone was replying.

Her hands trembled, so she tightened her grip on the phone.

NELL: *I'm so sorry. But I don't think you want to move out of the house voluntarily. Not sure why, but I remember hearing that. I can call the Carpenters. They handle all kinds of legal cases.*
JULIET: *Thanks, but you don't have to ask. I signed a prenup, and even if I hadn't, I couldn't afford to keep this house. Ezra wants me to move into the room above the garage and be his and Remy's maid and nanny. I need to get away from him. Today!*

NELL: *You're welcome to stay with me. I'm fostering a cat. Not sure if you're allergic.*
MISSY: *Hugs. My place is small, and Mario and Peach are there, but we can all fit.*
BRIA: *Those are great offers, but stay at Aunt Elise's house. The spare key is under the painted rock near the front porch. You'll need food. I got rid of everything in the kitchen before I left.*
SELENA: *Move into Elise's place. I'll call a divorce attorney I know. She'll get the prenup tossed out.*

Not alone.

Juliet's breath hitched, and tears—relieved ones this time—welled in her eyes.

Her hands shook, but she typed and sent another message.

JULIET: *I appreciate the offers, Missy and Nell, but Elise's house is within walking distance to work and my grandmother's. I'm not sure if the car is in my name or not, but knowing Ezra, it isn't.*
BRIA: *Elise signed over her car to me when she stopped driving. The insurance is up to date. Use it. The keys are in the top drawer in the kitchen.*
JULIET: *Thanks.*

And thank you, Elise.

Despite her former boss's lightning-fast temper, Elise Landon had loved her family, friends, and customers fiercely.

More dots appeared on Juliet's screen.

MISSY: *I'll be out of the hospital this afternoon, but I can't do much to help now.*
SELENA: *Your job is to recover, Missy. We'll pick up the slack until you're better.*
NELL: *Yes, we will, so put away the phone, Missy. You're not supposed to be staring at screens with a concussion.*
NELL: *I'm at work, but I'll grab groceries when I get off and bring them to Elise's.*
SELENA: *I'll come to Berry Lake this weekend. If Ezra cleaned out your bank account, text me, and I'll send money ASAP.*

Uh-oh. Juliet hadn't considered their money. She opened the banking app on her phone and did a double take at the balances in the two accounts.

Only $150 remained in their checking account and $25 in their savings.

Her shoulders drooped. "Why, Ezra?"

On Saturday, there'd been over ten thousand dollars in each account when she'd taken out her weekly allowance for groceries.

Her muscles bunched. All she wanted to do was scream. Instead, she dropped the phone onto the bed.

Okay, until this past week, he'd been the only one earning a paycheck. She kept him fed, clothed, and the house clean, which made her…his glorified maid and nanny.

Juliet buried her face against her hands before straightening.

She needed to stop pretending life was a fairy tale. That storybook had ended years ago.

Why wouldn't Ezra drain their accounts?

The man had cheated and gotten another woman pregnant. *A rat, remember?*

At least she had a withdrawal slip with the amounts that had been in both.

After three deep breaths, she picked up her phone and typed.

> **JULIET:** *I need a good divorce attorney, Selena, so please pass on my number to your friend or give me hers. Ezra cleaned out the bank accounts, but I have some cash to tide me over.*
> **JULIET:** *Feel better, Missy. You can help me later. And, Nell, milk, eggs, cheese, butter, and bread would be great. I want to lie low for a few days.*
> **BRIA:** *If you have questions about the house or car, text or call me.*
> **JULIET:** *You guys are the best friends ever.*
> **SELENA:** *You aren't in this alone.*
> **BRIA:** *We promised to be there for each other.*
> **NELL:** *We sure did.*
> **MISSY:** *Cupcake Posse forever!*
> **NELL:** *Off the phone, Missy, or I'll talk to your doctor again.*

Laughter bubbled over. Something Juliet never expected to experience this morning. But wasn't that why she texted her friends? So she wouldn't have to face this by herself?

Their offers, however, left her stunned but oh so grateful for their friendship and them.

No more dots appeared.

It didn't matter.

Juliet clutched her phone to her chest. Her friends had solved pressing questions, but one remained.

What next?

Staying under the covers appealed to her. But she'd been too comfortable in her marriage and look where that got her. She needed to get out of bed and take action.

It was Monday.

She listened.

Silence.

For the first time in years, Ezra hadn't asked Juliet to weigh in. Something he required her to do once a week. He might have forgotten, or her weight no longer mattered, or he might be hungover.

I hope not the latter.

Hungover meant he would be here. She wanted him gone so she could…

Pack.

The vise tightened around her heart—squeezed.

Don't think.

Do.

With her phone in hand, she tiptoed across the guest room floor and placed her ear against the door.

Quiet, if Ezra was home, he wasn't making a sound.

That wasn't like him.

Juliet opened the door.

The house remained silent.

She muttered a prayer.

A peek in the master bedroom showed an unmade bed, his clothes from yesterday on the floor, and an empty whiskey bottle on the nightstand.

He must have gone to work this morning.

Thank goodness.

She headed downstairs, each step more cautious than the last.

Splashes of whiskey remained on the living room table. The kitchen looked the same as she'd left it before going to the birthday party. The coffee pot was empty. Not a surprise, since she'd never seen Ezra use the coffeemaker. He might not know how to turn it on, let alone brew a pot. That was her job each morning, no matter the day of the week.

Not any longer.

If Juliet worked fast, she could be out of there before he returned home after work.

Where to start?

She glanced around at each piece of furniture or décor she'd selected for the new house less than a year ago. Most of it was more of Ezra's taste, but a few items she loved. Only a handful of things had belonged to her before they married. They hadn't been "upscale" enough for him.

The doorbell rang, slicing through the silence.

Juliet jumped. She didn't want company, but habit sent her to the entryway.

She opened the front door, surprised to see her boss standing on the porch. "Charlene?"

The woman was in her late fifties but looked fifteen years younger and dressed impeccably, no matter the time of day. She held a disposable drink tray containing two cups of coffee from Brew and Steep on Main Street.

A mix of curiosity and concern filled Charlene's gaze. "Is it true?"

Juliet clutched the doorknob. Okay, Nell—Charlene's oldest daughter—knew, but Juliet didn't think her friend would say anything to her mom. At least not *this* fast. Maybe Charlene meant something else had happened. Given all that occurred in Berry Lake last week, it was possible. "What do you mean?"

"It's all over town that Remy's pregnant, and Ezra plans to marry her."

All over town.

The words reverberated through Juliet. Her knuckles went white. News spread fast in Berry Lake, and Charlene was known as a busybody with gossip. Only this time, they were talking about Juliet and her hus—Ezra. And this was only the beginning.

Divorce. A wedding. The birth of a baby.

Her husband's.

Not hers.

She lowered her gaze with a combination of embarrassment and shame, even though she'd done nothing wrong. Except if she'd been a better wife—more loving, smarter, prettier—this wouldn't have happened. "It's true."

"Chin up." Charlene entered the house as if she owned it, pried Juliet's fingers from the knob with one hand, and used her hip to close the door. "None of this is your fault."

Juliet wanted to believe that, but Ezra had accused her of being the problem. Of course, he'd blamed her when his investment portfolio lost money. As if leaving a teacup in the sink for more than an hour affected the stock market. And she couldn't make herself younger. Still… "He said—"

"Come here." As Charlene one-arm hugged her, a flowery fragrance surrounded Juliet. "You'll get through this."

Juliet hugged her back, relishing in the woman's warmth. "Thank you."

Charlene let go. "Even after crying and not sleeping based on the dark circles under your eyes, you're beautiful and the kindest person in Berry Lake. Your husband made a terrible choice. That's on him, not you. Trust me, he'll regret his decision because Remy is a mini-Deena. What can I do to help?"

Juliet appreciated Charlene's offer. "I need to pack. Bria told me I could move into Elise's house."

"If you leave…"

"He's planning to stay. It's not as if I could afford the house on my own. I want to go."

"Elise's place will be perfect. But first, caffeine." Charlene handed Juliet a coffee. "Let's sit for a minute."

Juliet went to the kitchen. The breakfast nook and family room were more her style than the elegant formal dining and living rooms. She sat and sipped. The warm liquid tasted good, but the best part was she hadn't made it.

Charlene took a drink. "How much have you heard about Deena DeMarco?"

"Other than she's the wicked witch of Berry Lake and changes her last name like a seasonal wardrobe, not much."

"Thirty-four years ago, Deena told Paul Dwyer she was pregnant. He was in love with someone else, but they'd broken up, and Deena made her move. After he reunited with his original girlfriend and they planned to get married, Deena mentioned the baby."

"What did he do?"

"What Paul Dwyer always did. The right thing. He married Deena."

"Honorable."

Charlene rolled her eyes. "Stupid, because Deena wasn't pregnant."

"Seriously?"

"Deena claimed to miscarry, rather conveniently when Paul wasn't around. This all happened before medical record laws, but the receptionist spilled the tea about a negative pregnancy test."

Juliet fiddled with the cup sleeve. "Why didn't Mr. Dwyer divorce her and marry the woman he loved?"

"Because she'd married someone else. A total rebound, but it was too late because Paul's former girlfriend was pregnant with her husband's baby by the time the truth came out."

"So sad."

"Heartbreaking, and I wouldn't put it past Remy to pull the same con on Ezra."

Juliet's breath rushed out. Her stomach hardened into a heavy cement block. She opened her mouth, but then closed it.

Charlene leaned toward her. "If Remy is lying about being pregnant, would it change you wanting to move out?"

Juliet drank more—stalling. The answer should be immediate. N-O.

Ezra's taunts over her figure and fading looks screamed in her head. If what he said was true, this was her only chance at a relationship. Yet, he'd lied to her. He'd implied cheating with other women besides Remy, so Juliet had no reason to believe anything he said about her appearance. Even with her future so uncertain, the sense of freedom lingered on the edges. She wanted to escape the years of being told what to wear, do, and think. She wanted to be free.

"Whether or not Remy's pregnant doesn't matter." Juliet's voice remained steady while her insides trembled. "He's been looking to replace me for years. There's no reason for me to stay."

She wished saying the words didn't hurt so much. Or that she feared leaving was a huge mistake.

Charlene patted her hand. "I've got your back."

"Thanks." Juliet hated how she questioned everything. But she'd made no significant decisions beyond what groceries to buy and to apply to work for Charlene in years. "I hope it's the right one."

"It is." At least Charlene sounded certain. "Max and I remained amicable when we mutually decided to split, but that's not always the case. Take anything and everything you might want. You can return items later, but don't assume Ezra will let you into the house again. Be sure to grab any important paperwork and bank statements, too."

"Ezra handled the money, so I'm not even sure what statements he has, but I'll check his desk when I get my birth certificate and passport. I only have my clothes, jewelry, a few photos, and tea sets. I decorated for him to entertain. Not much holds any sentimental value other than a couple of pieces." The coffee cup warmed her hand. "Oh, wait. One of Hope Ryan Cooper's paintings arrived on Saturday. It was a gift from Ezra, and I love it. I'd like to take that with me, but it's too big to fit in my car."

"Max has a truck. If you don't mind, I'll send him a text and also call his wife, Sabine, who has boxes from when Sheridan got evicted so that Remy could move into the apartment."

"Remy is both an evil stepsister and home-wrecker." Saying the name made Juliet want to gargle with mouthwash.

"Like I said, she's a mini-Deena." Charlene pulled out her phone. "Max and Sabine have flexible schedules and will be happy to help."

"Thanks." Sabine ran the local animal rescue, where Juliet had worked for a high school volunteer project. "You weren't kidding when you said your divorce was amicable if you feel comfortable asking your ex-husband and his wife for help."

"I've never been happier, and Max is, too. Sabine has been a wonderful stepmother to my three girls. A divorce doesn't mean the marriage was a failure. Some people just need to move on. That was the case with us."

Juliet needed to move on, too, but her marriage had failed. Nothing would convince her otherwise. "I appreciate any help. I'd like to be out of here before Ezra gets home from work."

"We'll have you packed and moved into Elise's house in a few hours."

Juliet sipped the coffee. The hot liquid heated her insides. Now all she needed was for the caffeine to kick in. "Nell's at the hospital, but she's picking up groceries for me later."

"These next few days will be rough, but you deserve better than Ezra Monroe. That's what Elise would tell you."

"She said something similar to me. Elise never liked Ezra."

"I know. We were best friends and told each other everything." Charlene smiled. "I never liked him much myself."

Juliet laughed. "You're not alone. I should have listened to everyone."

"Love isn't logical. The heart wants what it wants. Nobody can make us see the truth until we're ready."

"Sometimes, not even then." She sighed.

Charlene patted her arm. "Show me where your bedroom is."

"It's upstairs." As Juliet climbed the stairs, she glanced over her shoulder at Charlene, who followed. "I don't know how I can thank you for your help."

"Pack your princess costume. That'll be thanks enough. I wasn't kidding yesterday when I told you three people want to book you for their daughters' birthday parties."

Juliet half laughed.

"What's so funny?"

"I was working as a princess when I met Ezra. Now, I'll be putting on a tiara and gown after he's gone."

"You kissed a frog for a while. It's time to find your Prince Charming."

Or was it time for Juliet to find herself?

chapter five

SELENA PACED THE length of her kitchen, rereading the texts from the Cupcake Posse's group chat. Her muscles twitched. The usual calmness she exuded to her listeners, clients, students, and herself had vanished with Juliet's first text.

Each time she reread the messages on the screen, Selena's frustration grew. With each lap, her feet moved faster as if that would transport her from Seattle to Berry Lake so she could hug Juliet. But Selena had to wait until this weekend to go there. Unless...

Patience.

She needed to be patient.

She rarely had an issue with that, but today was extraordinary. That was why she wanted a reply from Tamika Rayne, divorce attorney extraordinaire, now. Selena would pay the retainer and any fees so Juliet would have the best legal representation possible. Money should be spent, and Selena and Logan supported several charities, but she couldn't imagine a better way of spending more than on her dear friend.

Juliet needed support, both financial and emotional.

Selena had been trying to help her friend last week. She'd hated what Juliet implied about Ezra Monroe's demeaning and abusive-sounding treatment. But when he'd shown up at the hospital on Friday, she'd seen a self-centered bully hidden underneath his sharply tailored suit and plastic smile. Oh, she hoped she was mistaken about him—even if that was a rare occasion—for Juliet's sake. But now...

Selena tightened her grip on the phone.

Nope. She wouldn't take her emotions out on an electronic device. A better idea popped into her mind.

She placed her phone on the island, a safe distance from the sink. As she stomped to the fridge, each step reverberated through her and echoed in the kitchen. Getting out her emotions, not stuffing them inside her, pretending they didn't exist, was key. She wouldn't recite positive affirmations to hide the actual pain.

Nope.

Selena T wasn't that kind of coach.

Her personal-development clients either dug deep into themselves to discover what blocked them from receiving what they wanted or asked for a refund. Some people needed a gentler, passing-out-candy approach to manifesting, focusing on vision boards and positive thinking. For those, they were better off with a different coach because Selena was more the kind to trigger them, making them face what they'd been ignoring.

As she opened her fridge, Selena's gaze zeroed in on the stack of egg cartons. She removed one of the three.

Years ago, her third mentor taught her not to hold in or ignore her emotions. It had taken months, nearly an entire year, to get out all the junk she'd pressed down inside of her that affected her self-worth, everything from the teasing, taunts, criticisms, sexual innuendos, and self-hate. Before doing that, she'd tried to be positive and upbeat all the time, but it hadn't worked. Her brain wouldn't let her say the affirmations it didn't believe in without her bursting into laughter or shaking her head with a big N-O.

Not everyone was like her, though, which was why so many coaches, who did it differently from her, were thriving with their online businesses and hitting six-, seven-, and eight-figure incomes. She fell into that last group. Hard to believe when she'd grown up dirt-poor with limited options in her hometown, but she was oh-so grateful. As she told her clients, if she could do this, so could they.

She would keep saying that to her friend.

Juliet needed to see herself as strong, intelligent, and beautiful. Not only see it but believe it wholeheartedly so she loved herself. And that self-love was all that was required. Juliet didn't need to find her worth in a no-good husband—because *she* was enough.

More than enough.

Right now, however, Selena had to get her emotions out because she wanted to hit Ezra Monroe.

With her fist or her car.

One or the other would do.

Which told her she had work to do on herself before she could support Juliet properly.

Selena didn't condone violence. Humans were meant to be loved by themselves and each other. Logan had taught her that sometimes when emotions flared, punches flew during a hockey game. The instinctive reaction—often ill-timed in a game—resulted in being sent to the penalty box until a player served his time and returned to the ice.

It was too bad life didn't operate the same way as a hockey game because Ezra needed to pay for cheating on Juliet, demeaning her, and treating her more like a possession than his wife.

But Selena had her way of dealing with what the jerk did. One that wouldn't get her arrested for assault. She opened the carton and removed an egg. The shell was cold against her hand.

She pictured his slimy face and grimaced. "Ezra Monroe, you are a poor excuse for a husband and a weak, horrible man."

Selena threw the egg as hard as she could against the sink.

The shell shattered, but that didn't lessen her need to avenge or hit. She grabbed another egg and stared at it, imagining Ezra again with his fake smile, colored hair, and pampered skin. "You'll rue the day you hurt Juliet because the Cupcake Posse takes care of our own."

Selena threw overhanded, aiming for the bottom of the sink but hitting the side. Pieces of the shell, whites, and yolk dripped down, slow and gooey.

That was better than the first one.

She pulled out another egg and studied it from all angles, thinking about how carefully Ezra had dressed, not to look good for Juliet but to show off to others, including Remy Dwyer.

"Your baby mama will make your life so miserable. You'll think about Juliet every day and regret losing her. She, however, won't miss you because she'll be living her best life without you."

With a burst of love sent to her friend, Selena tossed this one harder than the other two. It hit the bottom of the sink and splattered.

Air rushed out of her lungs, and her shoulders relaxed. The tension evaporated as if it had never been there. That release was what she'd needed.

Selena breathed in through her nose slowly, holding her breath for an instant before exhaling. The corners of her mouth curved upward. No more ickiness remained. She'd cleared what had built up. Of course, she had. The method worked every time.

"Uh-oh." Logan stood in the doorway, his hands on either side of the doorjamb. Even in his sweatpants and a ratty T-shirt, he was the hottest man she'd ever seen. "Who upset you? And do I need to get involved?"

Her heart swelled with affection. Logan Tremblay didn't understand her coaching or woo, as he sometimes called what she did with clients, but he supported her one hundred percent. He was her safe place—her home.

"You don't, but Juliet's husband cheated on her and got the other woman pregnant."

As Logan shook his head, his eyes darkened. Before she'd married him seven years ago, he told her about teammates cheating. Some marriages survived; others didn't. She'd seen it play out several times since then. But she trusted him, or she wouldn't have stuck around.

He motioned to the fridge. "Use all the eggs if it makes you feel better."

She placed the carton back in the refrigerator. "It only took three."

"Last time, it was nine." He stood behind Selena and wrapped his arms around her. "You must be leveling up."

"Probably." She leaned against his chest, soaking up his warmth and strength. "And what happened to Juliet is for the best."

He stiffened. "How can you say that?"

She faced him, placing a hand on his whisker-covered face. The season didn't start until the first week of October, but the team had been on a scoring streak during exhibition games, which meant no shaving for Logan, even though the scores didn't count. Hockey players had so many superstitions, but she supported him wholeheartedly. Selena, however, didn't take part since she wasn't on the ice with him. She happily continued to shave, wax, and pluck.

"Ezra is a jerk who treated Juliet horribly." Selena scrunched her nose. "She deserves better."

"We have plenty of room if she needs a place to stay. I can send a car or a plane to Berry Lake, whatever works best for her."

Her heart melted—an everyday occurrence around him. "How did I get so lucky to marry a guy like you?"

"I'm the lucky one." He kissed her. "Have I told you how much I love you?"

"You might have mentioned it about a hundred times since you got home last night." Selena had arrived a few hours before he did. She never took sleeping with her husband for granted during the season. That was all she knew with him. He'd been playing hockey when they met. "I love you."

"When are you going to Berry Lake?"

The man understood her so well. "Not for a few days. I haven't seen you, and Nell can handle things until I get there."

"You sure?"

"Positive." Selena kissed him, but something niggled at her. "Except…"

He laughed. "What?"

She picked up her phone. "Bria texted the group chat."

"That's what people do, babe."

"Not her. Elise once mentioned Bria never uses her phone at work, so she would have to call the office's landline to reach her during the day." A compelling need to talk to her friend grew. "I need to call her."

"Go ahead." He let go of Selena. "I'll make breakfast since you left some eggs."

"What time is practice?"

"Not until one."

"That'll give us time to catch up."

"Or we skip breakfast and catch up now." His sultry tone and not-so-subtle head tilt toward the stairs—and their bedroom—sent ripples of awareness pulsating across her skin.

A yes sat on the tip of her tongue.

Until she remembered…

Selena held up her phone. "I have to make that call, and you need to eat, or you'll fade on the ice."

"True." He tucked her hair behind her ears. "But I also want to make the most of my time with you."

"Same." She kissed his cheek. "Be right back."

Logan wouldn't have minded her talking in the kitchen, but Bria might not appreciate someone else being in the room, so Selena went into her office.

She pressed the call button.

One ring. Two.

"Selena? Is everything okay?" Bria's words rushed out with no pauses between them.

"I'm fine, but…" Selena listened more closely. Waves crashed in the background. "I thought you weren't allowed to text at work."

A gull's cry filled her ear.

The practical CPA wasn't the type to have a sound machine on her desk. Especially when Elise had once described her niece's office as an uninspiring, gray cubicle city, but that had appealed to Bria.

"What's going on?" Selena pressed, trusting her gut something was wrong.

Bria sniffled. "As soon as I got to work, I found out someone forced my boss to retire, and the firm promoted my ex-boyfriend ahead of me to take his place. He told me I was laid off."

Oh boy, the Posse had taken some big hits in the last twenty-four hours.

Selena had coached her clients through job losses, illnesses, divorces, bankruptcies, and deaths. Bria was dealing with a double loss. No, a quadruple one, if she counted the fire at the cupcake shop and her father, who'd disappeared from Berry Lake after the fire without saying goodbye.

"Are you at the beach?" Selena asked.

"Yes. I didn't feel like going to my condo." Bria's voice trembled. "But I need to get food and finish unpacking."

"Don't unpack." The words flew from Selena, but her gut told her she'd said the right thing. "Go back to Berry Lake."

"I have to find a job."

Bria had needed stability and certainty in her life at eighteen. That hadn't changed in fifteen years. "You can do that in Washington. Elise's house has three bedrooms, and Juliet would enjoy the company. I'll send you a plane ticket."

"Thanks, but I can use the frequent-flier miles I earned from the trips I made when Aunt Elise was sick."

"Does that mean you'll go to Berry Lake?"

Silence filled the line.

Selena bit her tongue to keep from saying more. This had to be Bria's decision, not hers.

"I might," Bria said finally. "I have to do a few things first."

"Like send out a bunch of resumes." It wasn't a question.

"Guilty," she admitted. "I also want to talk with my old boss. I'm pretty sure we were both let go because of my ex-boyfriend's fiancée, who is the daughter of one of the founding partners."

"That would be stupid on the firm's part."

"Which tells me it will be impossible to prove. But a colleague said not to sign the paperwork from HR without going over it carefully."

"Sounds like a good idea. Especially since you just returned from family leave."

"I was told my aunt isn't considered 'kin,' so it wasn't official."

"Semantics. I'll see if I can find an employment attorney in California."

"Selena—"

"I have an extensive network. I won't do anything but text you the names and numbers."

Bria sighed. "Fine."

Good. Because Selena wanted to do this. "Talk to your boss and figure out when you'll be in Berry Lake."

"Will you be there?" The miles between them didn't hide the hope in Bria's voice.

"I plan to be there this weekend to support Juliet."

Pans clanged, and Logan sang to himself. The sound filled her with warmth. She sent another text to Tamika asking if she had a referral for someone in California.

"And to support you." That gave Selena an idea. Her husband would understand. "If you can't come to Berry Lake right away, I'll fly to San Diego."

"Thanks, but I'd rather go there. Maybe I could see Dalton."

Of course, Dalton Dwyer. Selena had forgotten about the

new man, who was Bria's ex-high school boyfriend and first love. "Have you told him?"

"No." Bria's voice was whisper-soft. "You're the only one who knows. Well, besides the firm. It's just…"

You never expected this to happen.

Selena didn't say it because this wasn't her story, but thanks to Elise, who'd worried about her niece, Selena knew Bria had majored in accounting so she'd have a stable, recession-proof job. She'd purchased a condo in her mid-twenties as if afraid someone would rip away her life if she didn't put down roots or take on a thirty-year mortgage.

"We only decided to date yesterday." Bria's voice rose an octave. "How do I tell him I lost my job? He'll think I'm a loser. Who am I kidding? I'm an unemployed loser."

"Elise told me about the award you won. That's not something they give out for just showing up. You earned that."

"Thanks."

"It's true." Selena could use this to work through Bria's emotional blocks, but not today. "All you have to say is, 'Dalton. I was laid off this morning. I have no idea why because I'm excellent at my job, but I intend to find out.'"

"That sounds too easy."

"It is. But the longer you wait, the harder it'll be."

"Like pulling off a bandage?"

"Exactly. It wasn't your fault. Remember that."

"I'm trying, but it's hard." Her voice went husky. "I thought my Employee of the Year plaque would be missing after my ex packed my stuff, but it was sitting on the top when HR gave me the box. I'm not sure whether to laugh or cry. I still don't."

"Do one or the other or both, whatever you feel like doing. Don't hold in the emotion. Get it out. Otherwise, you'll have problems later."

"You've mentioned that in podcasts."

"Because it's brilliant advice, and clients pay me to help them remove what they've stuffed down from ignoring their emotions or pretending nothing bothered them."

"This bothers me. I, uh…"

"What?"

"Kicked over a sandcastle." Guilt oozed from Bria's voice as if she'd stolen something. "It had been abandoned, but…"

"Good for you." Selena wouldn't allow her friend to beat herself up.

"Really?"

She swallowed a laugh at Bria's surprise. "Yes. Punching your pillow works well, too. A few minutes ago, I hurled eggs into the sink, imagining they were Ezra Monroe."

"I may have to buy an extra carton of eggs."

"You should, and let loose." If Juliet were as open to what Selena said, everything would turn around for her. "And do you know the good thing about sandcastles?"

"They're pretty."

"Yes, but you also can rebuild sandcastles, bigger and better than the last time."

Silence filled the line until Bria sniffled.

Selena wouldn't push. Not yet anyway.

"I'm not sure there's anything for me in San Diego."

The anguish in Bria's voice hurt Selena's heart. "Then go home."

"But if I do that, I'll have failed."

"Why do you think that?"

"Because I left Berry Lake for too long. When Aunt Elise got sick, I visited, but this last time was the longest I'd stayed. I feel like if I was going to move there, I should have done it three years ago when she was diagnosed with cancer."

"You weren't ready."

Bria said nothing.

Not unexpected.

"We can't change our pasts." Selena shifted into coach mode. "But when something negative occurs, we can do two things. Let it stop us, or we pick ourselves up and keep going, learning from the situation, so we don't repeat a pattern. It's not immediate and might take time, but that's the silver or tarnished lining to tragedy. But only if we pay attention."

"I'll start paying closer attention."

Juliet and Bria needed to rebuild their lives, and having each other close would help both women. Nell and Missy would be there to support them. Berry Lake was the right place for Bria.

Without a doubt.

And for Selena, too.

Seattle wasn't that far away. Selena would visit as often as she could.

She and Logan wanted to buy a vacation home. A lakefront property there would work well for multiple reasons. But first…

Selena repositioned the phone against her other ear. "What are you doing now?"

"I'm walking to my car. Then I'll go to the store. I plan to call a dozen eggs Fritz."

"Who's Fritz?"

"What I've temporarily named my pillow. It's also the name of my ex-boyfriend who fired me."

Selena laughed. "Love it."

"Me, too." Bria inhaled. "Do you mind not saying anything about my job or rather lack of one yet? I don't want Juliet to worry when she's got so much going on."

"The Posse would want to know."

"I'll tell everyone as soon as I figure out what I'm doing."

Selena understood. "I won't say a word."

"Thanks. And I'm so glad we found each other again."

"Me, too, and I believe it was Elise who did this. Your aunt knew we'd need each other."

"And the cupcake shop."

Selena's stomach tightened. The bakery where they'd worked together had been destroyed. Arson. And whoever set the fire was still out there.

"The Berry Lake Cupcake Shop won't be down for long." No other option was acceptable to Selena. No matter what it took—money or effort. She was all in. Elise Landon deserved her legacy to continue, and so did all of them. "And don't forget my idea of us buying your dad's share."

"I haven't. Especially now that I need a job." Bria laughed.

Selena smiled.

Laughter was a good start. But the best was yet to come for all of them.

🧁 chapter six 🧁

I N THE MASTER bedroom, Juliet sat on the unmade king-sized bed with an empty box on the floor. Her fingers itched to change the sheets. She usually—okay, always—did that first thing on Monday mornings.

Not today.

Still, the list of chores danced through her head like a conga line. Only doing what Ezra expected of her each day was never much fun, which was why she'd forced herself to leave the bed-sheet crumpled and ignore his pants, shirt, and damp towel on the bathroom floor.

Not her job any longer.

Packing, however, was.

Purses, shoes, hats, scarves, and clothes surrounded her. Pretty, expensive, colorful items—nothing she'd selected for herself—but they were all she had, so they would come with her.

Her practicality would impress Bria. Nell would praise Juliet's efforts before asking to try on stuff. Missy would fold everything. And Selena would tell Juliet to take only the pieces she loved.

But this wasn't the time to go all Marie Kondo. Nothing brought Juliet joy except her tea sets and the painting that arrived on Saturday. If worse came to worst, she would sell things online or visit a consignment shop in Portland.

Just keep going.

It wasn't easy.

The sound of the tape roller in the bathroom intensified the pain in her heart. Everything was changing in her life, and she was afraid.

Not that she wanted to be with him.

She didn't, but…

Was Remy pregnant?

The answer wouldn't change Juliet's plans. Okay, she didn't really have plans. She had friends, a place to stay, a part-time job, and some cash. On the flip side, she didn't know what would happen tonight, tomorrow, and every day after that.

The lack of security stole her breath.

Her muscles twitched.

Not wanting to be left out, her stomach roiled.

A good thing she hadn't eaten today, or she might be sick.

Anything is better than staying here.

She knew that logically. But knowing wasn't the same as believing it.

A swatch of pink fabric stuck out from the pile of clothes from her dresser. Juliet tugged on it.

The fifteen-year-old T-shirt showed its age. The Berry Lake Cupcake Posse logo—a takeoff on the shop's—had faded along with the color. It smelled like the detergent Ezra preferred. But that didn't keep her from clutching the well-worn shirt to her heart as if it were the hottest, must-have piece from this year's Fashion Week.

There are no guarantees in life, but a cupcake always helps.

Elise had said that many times. It was a favorite saying of Juliet's. Over the years, her former boss had sprinkled in tidbits of advice to her staff and customers. But this one had lodged in Juliet's heart and stayed there. After losing her parents at thirteen, she understood nothing was for certain. But for whatever reason, she'd believed her life would be different after that.

As if only that single bad thing would happen in her lifetime.

Yet here she was, packing her things with only the tip from the party, a few leftover dollar bills from this week's grocery allowance, and the cash in her savings jar. She used that to buy Christmas gifts so she could surprise Ezra without him knowing how much money she'd spent.

She folded the pink T-shirt and placed it next to her.

"I packed the items underneath your sink and drawers. I fit the extra toilet paper in there, too," Sabine Culpepper called from the master bathroom. "Your stuff is only on the right side of the counter, correct?"

"Yes. The fancy products in the white bottles belong to Ezra."

"Of course, they do."

"He spends more on his toiletries than I do on mine."

Sabine stood in the doorway with a sunscreen bottle in one hand and a tube of eye cream in the other. Her faded jeans, "All Animals Deserve a Forever Home" T-shirt, and tennis shoes were typical of what she'd worn for years, but she, in her early fifties, looked older than Charlene. Most likely because of Sabine's animal rescue and nasty divorce from Sal DeMarco. Those things would age any person fast.

"So, these belong to him, too?" Sabine asked.

"Yes."

Sabine studied the items before making a face. "Max wouldn't have a clue what to do with half the stuff Ezra has."

"That's not a bad thing."

"I'll never complain again." Sabine chuckled. "You know, if you'd moved to town a few months earlier, I bet Deena would have dumped my ex-husband and pursued Ezra herself instead of letting her daughter have him. She had to teach Sal how to groom. Ezra might have been able to show her a few things."

Laughter loosened the knot in Juliet's stomach as she imagined mother and daughter fighting over her husband. The only problem? Ezra appeared too gleeful. "Probably, except Deena appears to be around the same age as him. He wouldn't look twice at her since he thinks I'm too old for him."

"Cradle robber. That's the only male equivalent I know for a cougar."

"Daddy might work, though Remy took that literally."

Sabine nodded. "The Dwyer women seem to be Berry Lake's remedy for men having a midlife crisis. My ex is an idiot, and your soon-to-be ex-husband is following suit."

"He is now." But once upon a time, Ezra had treated Juliet like a princess. She wasn't sure how that had changed or why she'd allowed him to steal her light—her life.

"Are any of your friends divorced?"

"No." She was embarrassed to admit she didn't have many friends. Ezra hadn't wanted her to do things without him. She saw Nell and Missy occasionally, but until last week when the Posse reunited after Elise's funeral, Juliet had been on her own, adrift in Berry Lake like an abandoned rowboat.

"Every divorce is different. I'm sure Charlene and Max sang 'Get Together' on the way to and from the courthouse in the same car, but mine and Sal's was bitter, and Sheridan found herself caught between us."

"She seems happy and well-adjusted."

"Yes, but that's all her. Nothing to do with Sal and me. Falling in love and leaving town has helped her, too."

"For once, I'm glad we never had kids."

"It'll still be hard." Sabine sighed. "Divorce is a loss, and your emotions ping all over the place. No matter how low you feel today, you'll probably feel worse. But remember, it gets better. And when that happens, the ache consuming your heart and body right now will have been worth it. The thought of being on your own can be scary, but the freedom is a vast improvement over being married to the wrong man."

"I hope so."

"Max and I work together. Talk. Compromise. Laugh. It wasn't like that with Sal. Both of us were too stubborn, and we drew lines in the sand far too often."

Ezra didn't ask for Juliet's advice because compromise wasn't part of his vocabulary. He made demands. He picked out her clothes because, according to him, she had no style or taste. "I doubt I'll get married again, but I'm happy your second marriage has worked out better."

"You need time to heal before you decide about relationships. I waited years to date. Max was the third man I'd gone out with, but I knew during our first dinner, he was it for me."

Juliet rubbed her chest. "That's what I thought about Ezra, but I was twenty-two. I wanted to be swept away."

"You'll know how to do it differently next time."

She shivered. "Not interested in a next time."

"Which is what you *should* say right now. I'll finish up in the bathroom so we can get you out of here."

"Thanks." Her throat closed up. A part of her wanted to hold on to this life for a moment longer, even if her heart told her it wasn't hers anymore.

She pulled out her jewelry box's top drawer. A gold engagement ring and two wedding bands, all she had left of her parents, filled one velvet-lined square. They'd died together, doing what they loved—traveling, seeing the world instead of spending time with her.

As she closed the drawer, the overhead light reflected off the diamond on her finger, sending colorful prisms around the bedroom, mocking her.

She held on to both platinum rings and pulled on them before stopping at her first knuckle. She'd worn the band for over twelve years—the engagement ring six months longer than that. Ezra had removed his ring last night, but she wasn't ready.

Her marriage was over, but she needed…time.

Juliet packed the jewelry box and placed the pink T-shirt on top. She dumped the other clothes and accessories on the bed inside before taping it shut.

Sabine stood in the doorway to the bathroom once again. "Everything fits in two boxes. If you'd wanted the scale, it would have taken three."

"Thanks." Juliet would never weigh herself again unless she had a doctor's appointment. "I think we're finished upstairs."

Heavy footsteps sounded in the hallway. That must be Max, Michael, and Sheridan returning after dropping off the painting and tea sets.

Instead, Ezra stormed into their bedroom with Charlene at his heels. He wore a suit, but his face was red, and a vein pulsed on his forehead. He must have been combing his fingers through his hair because it was a mess, an adjective he hated.

"What do you think you're doing?" Spit flew with each word.

Insides quivering, Juliet stood even though she wanted to cower. That was a habit. Conditioning. Either way, it had to stop.

She gripped the tape roll and raised her chin a notch, hoping he didn't see through her. "I'm packing."

With a don't-mess-with-this-mama-bear expression, Sabine stood in the bathroom's doorway, ready to charge.

Juliet gave a subtle shake of her head.

Sabine stopped, pulled out her phone, and typed.

Juliet tossed the tape on the bed with false bravado, picked up the box, and walked with careful, measured steps toward Ezra. Well, toward the doorway. Except he blocked it. "We're almost finished. Please get out of the way."

Behind him, Charlene typed on her phone before mouthing *911*.

Juliet hoped the police weren't necessary, but she hadn't expected Ezra to come home in the middle of the day.

His nostrils flared. "Where do you think you're going?"

Anywhere but here.

She wouldn't tell him. "I found a place to stay while I figure things out."

He widened his stance. "Stop acting like a child, Juliet. I told you last night there's a place for you here."

"And I told you no."

"I spoke to your grandmother this morning."

Anger flared. Juliet tightened her grip on the box. "You had no right to do that."

He smirked with glee in his eyes. "Guess you're not staying with Penelope."

Such a liar.

She wouldn't give him the satisfaction of riling her. "I'm sure Remy wants a ring on her finger ASAP. Text me the name of your attorney. I'll have mine contact yours."

His face blanched. "Why do you need an attorney? If we share one, it'll save money."

"No." Lesson learned after signing the prenup.

He rocked back on his heels. "It doesn't matter what you do. You signed the prenup."

Yes, but Selena's text had led to a quick internet search while she and Charlene waited for Sabine, Max, Sheridan, and Michael to arrive. "Did you know a judge in Washington can throw out a prenup if the terms are unfair to one party? And this is a community property state?"

Ezra's face turned even redder.

Juliet didn't know if it would make a difference in the divorce, but seeing him squirm was worth repeating her newfound knowledge. "It'll be interesting to see what a judge has to say when I show the bank accounts' balances from Saturday and today. Over twenty thousand dollars. Poof. Gone."

He tried to speak—unless he was mimicking a fish, the way his mouth opened and closed.

"Charlene, would you mind getting the other box from the bathroom?" Juliet asked in her politest tone.

"Gladly." Charlene side-eyed Ezra as she passed.

He glared at Juliet. "You're nothing without me."

"I'm okay with that." Juliet's voice remained firm, but she wasn't lying.

"You'll regret leaving me."

"No, I won't." She was sure she would feel like celebrating. Not this week, or month, or year, but…someday. "You, however, may find a younger, new wife…lacking."

The words sounded nothing like Juliet. The years of not speaking her mind, not showing her emotions, not standing up to him ballooned inside her. She needed to get it out.

"Just remember, when you realize what you lost, this was all your fault." Not holding back, even though she was politer than she probably should be under the circumstance, boosted her confidence. She glanced at the bathroom where Sabine and Charlene stood with the boxes. "Ladies, it's time to go."

Carrying a box, Charlene strutted past as if she were the Queen Bee. As the center of the Berry Lake grapevine, that wasn't too far from the truth. Nell complained about her mom's meddling, but Juliet was grateful to have a boss like her.

Sabine followed with her head held high and a snotty air to her, which was hilarious given the woman worked herself to the bone at the animal rescue she founded. Usually, hair and fur covered her. But she might as well be wearing a fancy gown and tiara.

Both women were her new heroes. She hoped Nell and Sheridan realized how lucky they were to have moms like them.

"Don't do this." Funny, but Ezra almost sounded sad. "I agreed to marriage counseling."

"While having an affair."

"We can work through this."

Juliet didn't think so, but she wasn't the only one involved in this situation. "Is that what you want?"

"I don't want you to leave."

She had no reason to believe him, but she had to ask, if only for her grandmother's sake. "Why should I stay?"

"You're my wife."

More like his maid and cook. Sure, he bought her things. Fancy things. Expensive things. But all she'd wanted was to be loved for who she was without conditions or requirements.

"We'll make this work," he pleaded, reeking of desperation.

Not that she felt sorry for him. "What about Remy and the baby?"

His jaw tensed, and his silence spoke volumes.

If Remy lied about being pregnant, the joke would be on Ezra.

Not Juliet's problem. "I'll cancel our counseling appointment on Tuesday unless you want to go with Remy."

Juliet marched out of their bedroom without a word or a glance over her shoulder.

chapter seven

FROM THE PASSENGER seat of her sister-in-law's SUV, Missy stared out the window at the kids walking and skipping on their way home from school. Pop music played on the radio, but the volume was low, most likely because Jenny worried about Missy's head. It didn't hurt as much as before, or she might have gotten used to the dull throbbing. She hoped it wasn't the latter.

Lukewarm air blew out the vent, and she inhaled the fresh scent of autumn—falling leaves and blue sky, even though the official season didn't start until next Tuesday. Fall brought to mind pumpkin spice cupcakes with cinnamon-flavored cream cheese icing. She'd been making those since Labor Day weekend, but as September gave way to October, the flavor picked up in popularity. Cinnamon evoked memories for most people. Hers were of high school football games, homecoming, and trips to corn mazes. Such good times.

Tension seeped from her muscles, but not all of it disappeared.

She wouldn't be baking those cupcakes or any others until she recovered.

But thinking about the cupcakes reminded her of something no one except the sheriff and fire investigator wanted to discuss with Missy. And even though she missed her two cats, she didn't want to go home yet.

Not until she saw the damage for herself.

That might help her make peace with what had happened the other night and the uncertainty her future now held. The only question was, would Jenny—who'd taken overprotective to a new level the past few days—agree?

Honestly, it could go either way.

Missy wanted to ask a different question first. One that would likely get a no, but that might make Jenny say yes to her second one.

Missy drummed her right-hand fingers on the armrest. "Can we stop by Elise's house to see how Juliet is doing?"

"You heard the doctor." Jenny kept her eyes on the road. "Making social calls isn't listed on your discharge papers, either."

Jenny Hanford O'Roarke wrote bestselling, action-packed thrillers under the pseudonym Jenna Ford. Unlike her put-his-life-on-the-line, risk-taking character named Ashton Thorpe, she was shy and quiet, the definition of introverted and cautious. She didn't speed, made a complete stop on a yellow light, and did whatever she could to help a friend or stranger so long as she didn't have to leave her comfort zone. However, she was stepping outside of that box more often now thanks to her husband, Dare, a former Army Ranger.

She glanced at Missy, but only for a moment. "In case you forgot, you need to rest."

"Juliet needs—"

"*You* to be one hundred percent to help her. Her entire life imploded. You know what that's like. It can't be fixed in a day. She'll need time to work through this."

Missy sank lower in the seat. "Okay, you're right."

Perhaps she should go home and do nothing until they— whoever that was—deemed she could have her life back. Until that happened, she would be a burden to the people she loved.

Family and friends had put their lives on hold to be with her at the hospital. No doubt that would continue once she was home. The same way it had when...

Rob.

When he'd been killed, her world fell apart. She'd been frozen, breathing but just barely, unable to cope with being alone, totally on her own. The thought of moving on without the man she'd loved for most of her life had crushed her. Missy had wanted to give up, but Elise and Jenny wouldn't let her. Thanks to them, Missy had kept working at the cupcake shop and as an author assistant to keep the grief at bay and...survived.

"Heal." Jenny's voice was soft. "That's all you need to do."

Missy never wanted to be a burden again. "I plan on it."

This time wasn't the same as nine years ago. Her injuries would eventually disappear. A scar or two might remain, but there wouldn't be something inside her that never seemed to heal. However, she was better now than she'd been before. The darkness no longer engulfed her every day as it had. She might only get by on some days, but it wasn't all day, every day as it had once been.

"You have a deadline." Missy didn't handle Jenny's calendar any longer, but the production schedule was etched in her brain. The next thriller manuscript was due in a few short weeks. At this point in her writing process, Jenny always hated the story and freaked out, saying no one would buy it or another one of her books again. She didn't need her sister-in-law relying on her. "And Dare is busy with Briley and being your assistant."

He'd taken over when Missy had been promoted to manager at the cupcake shop. "The two of you have done enough for me."

"That's what family does for each other. Without you, I wouldn't have met Dare."

Missy had convinced Jenny to go on a Caribbean vacation with her online book club where she'd tossed a message in a bottle into the sea, and Dare had found it. Missy also told her to visit him after he'd been injured in a military training exercise. "Not the same thing."

And it wasn't.

Jenny had grieved losing her parents and brother. She was naturally a homebody, so she needed a little push. Okay, shove.

Missy, however, got out of the house. She had a job and volunteered with Sabine Culpepper's rescue. She didn't need someone to take care of her. Not the same as when she'd been widowed at twenty-three and her friends no longer lived in town. Even though two were in Berry Lake now, she didn't want to be in the way.

And Juliet needed her help.

Missy wouldn't be sad to see Ezra go. She'd never liked him, and his cheating didn't surprise her. The guy was not nice. He demanded a discount on his orders because Juliet had worked at the cupcake shop over fifteen years ago. As if she were the only one, not half the teens and adults in town, who'd worked part-time job for Elise Landon, the best boss in Berry Lake. Given Remy Dwyer's reputation, Ezra deserved her. No doubt that relationship would be like watching a train wreck about to occur. The only things needed would be popcorn, soda, and a direct line to the town's rumor mill.

Jenny glanced her way. "You're quiet."

"Happy to be out of the hospital."

"I heard you didn't want to be there any longer." Jenny laughed. "Another night, and you might have earned the worst-patient award."

That wasn't a lie. Still, Missy shrugged. "Guess I'm old and stuck in my ways."

"You're only thirty-two."

"True." But some days, Missy felt much older as if she'd lived a hundred lifetimes. She didn't think that would change. But it made the uncertainty facing her scarier.

Jenny and Dare considered her part of the family, but that was only because of Rob. He'd been Jenny's younger brother. The truth was, it was only Missy, Mario, and Peach now. Yes, she'd reconnected with her friends from the cupcake shop, but they had their own lives. Selena and Logan defined #relationshipgoals. Bria seemed enchanted by Dalton. Nell and Juliet would fall in love with the right guys one of these days. And Missy would still be alone.

No matter what Rob said in her dream, that was the truth. T-R-U-T-H.

As Main Street came into view, she straightened. Curiosity poked at Missy like her cats when their food bowl was only half-full. She had thought about letting this drop, but now... "Do you think we could..."

"See the cupcake shop?"

"What's left of it anyway." She bit her lip. "Is that weird?"

"No, healthy. Better than you avoiding what happened."

"I can't forget, given my bruises, cuts, and burns." She tried to sound lighthearted but wasn't sure if she succeeded.

"You left out the concussion." Not sounding amused, Jenny gripped the steering wheel.

"I was hoping you forgot that one."

"Nope. And you're not getting your phone until the doctor says it's okay."

Nell had caught Missy texting on the Posse's group chat this morning. "I wasn't on it much."

"Enough that Nell called me on her lunch break."

Of course, she did. "Nell needs a family of her own, so she doesn't keep mothering all of us."

"That guy who showed up at the hospital might be the one."

"I hope so. Nell seems to like Gage. And Charlene isn't trying to meddle or play matchmaker for once."

That might explain why Nell was so interested in the new guy. However, Missy would take a meddling parent over not having one. Her mom and dad left town while Rob was deployed and never told her where they moved. They'd never forgiven her for skipping college and marrying her childhood sweetheart instead. "Nell says Gage is hot, so there's that, too."

"I'll admit, he's easy on the eyes."

Jenny drove onto Main Street, slowing as she came to the Huckleberry Inn on one side and Events by Charlene on the other, which started the stretch of blocks with businesses.

Missy stared out the window, recognizing people on the sidewalk. Most tourists had stopped visiting town, so anyone out was local and recognizable. "Everything looks normal."

Jenny nodded. "They closed the street until noon on Friday to clean up. It was a mess before that."

Brew and Steep came next on the right and then the art gallery. The cupcake shop was across the…

Missy's hand flew to her heart.

A gut-wrenching groan sounded.

Her.

She hadn't expected…

This.

The fire had gutted the ground level. Soot stained the front. The fixtures inside and the photos of employees on the wall were destroyed as if they and Elise had never existed.

Her breath hitched.

The second floor, where she'd been when the fire broke out, appeared to be there still, but the damage to the structure was significant. If not for Welles…

She struggled to fill her lungs. Tears stung her eyes.

Jenny pulled to the curb across the street from…it. She touched Missy's arm. "You okay?"

Missy opened her mouth and then closed it. She stared in disbelief. Gone. It was all gone. "I had no idea it was this bad. There's not much left."

"Now you understand why everyone has been on you about returning inside to get Elise's journal."

Missy nodded before wiping her eyes. She cleared her tight throat. "Seeing the shop like this would have killed Elise if cancer hadn't. It'll take a lot of work and money to repair."

"People say insurance won't cover the damage because it was arson. A few think Bria should fundraise on the internet."

Not a bad idea because Bria would need to find a way to pay for the repairs. Elise had set aside some money for an interior remodel, but that had never happened after her diagnosis. But those changes had been cosmetic. This… This would require a complete rebuild.

Uncertainty over what Missy should do during the reconstruction quadrupled. She needed to work, or that would give her too much time to think at home. Dare enjoyed being Jenny's assistant. Missy wouldn't take that away from him. And there were only so many special orders the cupcake shop might receive once she was on her feet again.

"Are they going to tear it down and start over?" The words sliced Missy's aching heart wide open.

"I don't know. Bria tried to reach the insurance agency all weekend. I'm not sure if she succeeded."

"Why did someone do this?"

"The entire town wants to know that."

It made no sense. "The sheriff and fire investigator talked to me at the hospital."

Jenny stiffened. As her hands tightened around the steering wheel, her knuckles turned white. "Do they consider you a suspect?"

Missy shrugged. That was something she'd never thought to ask. "They asked a lot of questions but never mentioned if I was a suspect or person of interest. But I'd be the world's stupidest arsonist to set a fire in my bare feet, call for help, and return inside while on the phone with them."

"If they want to talk to you again, have an attorney present."

She rolled her eyes. "Jenny—"

"What?"

"You don't need to use your worst-case-scenario writer's imagination with this. They just wanted to make sure they hadn't missed anything or see if I remembered anything else now that my head doesn't hurt as much as it did."

"I'm not being a writer. I'm being cautious because I love you." The words were full of sincerity. "I want you to be safe and not find yourself arrested for something you didn't do. Tensions are high. People are out for blood."

"I love you, and I am safe. I doubt anyone thinks I set the fire. What would be my motive? A long vacation if the cupcake shop had to close? That makes no sense. I'm… I'll be fine." Missy took a breath before glancing at the bakery once more. "We can go now."

There wasn't anything left to see across the street. Missy's heart was heavy.

Ten minutes later, Jenny pulled into the driveway and parked. The large house sat on a piece of property on the outskirts of town. The home and the lot were bigger than either of them had needed, but it was what Jenny wanted. A house she could grow into someday. The charming guest cottage in the backyard where Missy lived had been a bonus.

She squirmed in her seat, eager to be there. "I can't wait to see Mario and Peach."

"They missed you." Jenny pulled the keys out of the ignition. "We played with them. Briley and Yeti, too. But they want their mommy. Stay there until I come around."

Great. Jenny was going to hover. Missy wouldn't fuss, though. Not after all Jenny had done for her and gone through the past few days. Missy would put up with the caretaking until she got to the cottage and was alone again.

"The cats are in the guest room. Where you'll be staying."

"No." The word came out sharp and fast. She didn't care. "The cottage is fine."

"It's too far if you need us. And the guest bedroom is on the first floor with a bathroom attached."

"You have a manuscript to finish."

"I'll make it, no problem. I always do."

"I don't want to intrude."

"You're family. I'll say that as many times as it takes to sink into your concussed brain." Jenny grabbed her purse. "My getting married and having a baby changes nothing. You being here is what I want, and it's what Rob would have wanted."

True, but in Missy's dream, he wanted something else. It had been so different from any dream she'd had of him before. So real. But she had a concussion and been through a fire. Perhaps the trauma set off her subconscious.

Who knew what her brainwaves were doing?

But for a moment, one spectacular moment, her heart and mind believed he'd returned to her. And she would cherish that moment for as long as she lived.

Jenny opened the passenger door. "Are you okay?"

Missy jumped, not much with her seat belt tightening across her chest, but she hadn't realized her sister-in-law had gotten out of the SUV. "I'm...tired."

"Let's get you inside." Jenny helped her out, so Missy's feet didn't hit the cement too hard. "I didn't want you to trip when you went into the bathroom, so I put the litter box in the closet. Leave the door cracked so the cats can get in and out."

"Thanks. You've thought of everything."

"I'm trying." Jenny's eyes darkened. "But please, never scare me like that again. I don't know what I would do without you."

Missy tried not to let Jenny's emotional tone affect her. "You have Dare and Briley."

"Yes, and I have you, too, and want to keep it that way." Jenny's voice sharpened. "I would have never made it this far on my own. And if it takes every single day for the rest of our lives proving what you mean to me…"

Guilt coated Missy's mouth. She swallowed. "You don't have to do that."

"Okay, but I'm dedicating another book to you."

Missy laughed. "Sure, but please make sure Ash is hot in it. You know how much I love my book boyfriend."

It was Jenny's turn to laugh. "I do because I love Ash, too."

"I heard that." Dare walked out, carrying Briley, who tugged at her daddy's ears. "If you grow up to be a writer like your mommy, don't fall in love with your hero. Your future spouse might end up with a complex, thinking they don't add up to all the brave things her fictional character does."

That was funny, given Dare had been an Army Ranger sergeant before his medical discharge.

Jenny kissed him. "You're my hero. You know that."

"I might need some more convincing." Dare winked.

They helped Missy into the guest bedroom. The saying "no pain, no gain" was overrated. It was a good thing she didn't have to walk to the cottage, or she wouldn't have made it.

Mario and Peach popped up from their naps on the bed where someone laid out her pajamas and meowed. Yeti, Jenny and Dare's cat, remained sleeping.

"Hey, babies." Missy went to them and sat on the mattress. The relief to her foot was immediate, but she held in a sigh to keep Jenny from worrying more. "Did you miss me?"

Mario and Peach rubbed their heads against her. Their purrs soothed her soul.

She kissed each one. "I missed you, too."

Dare laughed. "They act as if we ignored them. We didn't. They got extra treats, which Yeti enjoyed, too. It took me a half hour to find the toys they scattered in here so you wouldn't fall."

She loved on her cats, and they soaked up the attention. "Thanks."

Briley squirmed as if she wanted down, but Dare didn't place her on the floor.

Missy yawned.

"Time for bed," Jenny announced.

Missy hated to admit a nap sounded good. "I could use a rest."

Jenny turned to Dare. "Take Briley out so Aunt Missy can get some rest."

"See you later." Dare had Briley wave before they left.

"Please don't hover," Missy said.

"I'm not." Jenny plumped a pillow. "Just making sure you do what you're told."

"That's hovering."

"I'm practicing for when Briley's older. Now sleep. You'll make the cats happy."

"The cats, huh?" Missy laughed. "Thanks, Jen. For everything."

"Don't have to thank me. This is what family does."

Jenny wouldn't let Missy forget that. "You don't have to keep reminding me."

"I'll be the judge of that. Need help changing?"

"No, thanks." That would be too much. She wasn't infirm, only injured.

Jenny picked up Yeti from the bed. "If you need anything else—"

"I'm good." Missy had no choice to be anything else because the one thing she needed for things to be perfect—the only thing she wanted—was Rob. And unfortunately, no one could give her that.

chapter eight

AT THE NURSES' station on Monday afternoon, Nell waved goodbye to a patient and his wife, walking hand in hand on their way out. She turned toward the wall before stopping herself. No more clock watching. Even if the one hanging behind her drew her attention like a tractor beam.

Nope.

Not doing it.

The seconds wouldn't speed up, no matter how much she wanted time to go by faster. Besides, her patients deserved her complete focus, and the shift ended soon enough. Then, she would make the call she'd been dying to make all day.

Her gaze traveled to the phone on the desk. The landline was for business only, usually for calls made within the hospital or for discharged patients if they had questions, but that hadn't stopped her mom from using it to reach Nell.

Often daily.

Sometimes more than once a shift.

Except for today.

Ring.

Oh, it had rung several times, but her mom hadn't called. Today of all days.

Figured.

Nell half laughed.

The one time she wanted her mom to tell her about moving Juliet into Elise's house, no call.

Typical.

But it sucked.

Sure, Nell would find out soon enough, but she'd wanted to know if extra wine or chocolate—perhaps both—should be added to the grocery list. Or if Juliet might need something else to make her feel better.

Not that stuff like that would help.

Despite the Posse's efforts, Juliet wouldn't be okay. Not for a long time.

That made Nell's heart hurt.

Even though she hadn't even been married, only dreamed about it, that kind of betrayal cut deep, making a person question themselves, their self-worth, and the decisions that led them to where they now found themselves—heartbroken and alone. Wine, chocolate, *and* cupcakes needed to go on the list.

Her coworker Cami approached. Her loose ponytail appeared to be ready to fall apart. The circles under her eyes had darkened since she arrived for their shift. One of her twins had been having nightmares lately, which meant restless, often sleepless nights for the single mom.

"Are you doing okay?" Nell asked.

Cami stifled a yawn. "I'm hanging in there."

Barely, but Cami didn't need Nell to say that. The two had worked together since she returned to Berry Lake after living in Boston. They'd been on the third shift until moving to days when a couple of senior RNs left for jobs at more prominent hospitals in Vancouver and Portland.

"Sit for a minute," Nell suggested.

Cami plopped into the chair at the computer monitor. She didn't sigh after her bottom hit the seat, but her shoulders relaxed. "I'm ready for quitting time."

"Same."

Cami glanced at the board. "Did you discharge the fractured ulna in four?"

"Yes. The couple in three also left." Nell erased the info for those exam rooms. Things were finally slowing down, which would make for a quiet shift change for once. Tourists and weekend— sometimes weekday—warriors kept the small, regional hospital busy. "How is the woman in two doing?"

"She's getting kicked upstairs." Cami glanced toward that exam room. "A good thing her husband told her it might not be indigestion from something she ate, or she would be dead."

Nell rubbed her neck. "Yeah, he mentioned that when I took him a cup of coffee. Scary."

And it was. She hadn't been able to stop thinking about it.

The man's wife, in her fifties, had come in after experiencing a heart attack. Though she kept denying that was the problem. They were from out of town and staying at the Huckleberry Inn for a few days of hiking the many trails around Berry Lake. The woman, fit and active, reminded Nell of her mom, who had two speeds: full power and off.

Her mom seemed invincible, but now Nell was as concerned about her health as she was about Juliet's situation and emotional state. "I'm going to remind my mom to make an appointment for a checkup. She gets so busy with her event planning she forgets or pushes it off."

Cami raised a brow. "Who's meddling now?"

"Truth." But Nell wasn't about to apologize. "My mom butts into my life all the time. Yes, it annoys me, but that's how she's always been, and I'd like to keep her around. Plus, now she can get a taste of her own medicine."

"I hope the twins feel that way about me when they're older. Not the annoying part, but the keeping me around." Cami appeared to deflate, her shoulders hunching forward. "They tell me they like their dad better."

"That's because he's the fun dad who only sees them on weekends." The couple had divorced but tried to stay on good terms because of their children. "The kids love you."

"Only when they get their way," Cami countered. "Otherwise, the twins prefer 'fun dad' to 'strict mom.' If he had them all the time, I doubt he'd seem so cool to them."

Cami rolled her shoulders with a dejected expression on her face.

"One day, they'll see how lucky they are to have you as a mom." Nell meant it. Cami did everything for those two kids. She even sent meals with them to eat when they spent nights or weekends with their dad and included enough for him.

"Thanks. That, however, might take years. Though I'm not going anywhere." Cami rubbed her eyes. "But honestly, I'm the lucky one. The twins can push my buttons even more than my ex, but they're great kids. I say that knowing I'll be shuttling them between their soccer practices at two different fields later this afternoon."

"You've got this." And Cami did. No matter how exhausted she was, she did all the things for her children and then some. She never held back from Nell, either, sharing the highs and the lows of life—sometimes a lack of one—as a single mom.

"Thanks." The corners of Cami's mouth curved as if a smile would take too much effort. "I needed to hear that. It's been one of those days."

"It's almost over."

Cami often said she felt this way, and Nell did what she could to get through the hours or minutes until their shifts ended. She envied Cami because Nell wanted a family. She had since she was little and dreamed of being a wife and mother. Becoming an RN was something she would do until she had children, and then she'd take a break to stay home and raise them. After her kids were grown, she would return to work.

A solid plan.

Until Andrew married someone else.

And she hadn't fallen in love again.

Have you really tried?

That voice in her head sounded a lot like Selena T on the podcast, so Nell ignored it.

For the umpteenth time.

She'd toyed with the idea of having a baby on her own, but hearing about Cami's life had changed Nell's mind. She wasn't ready for single motherhood.

Instead, Nell clung to her dream of a family and a happily ever after. There was still time for it to come true. But the older she got—she was three years away from turning forty—the more her anxiety ramped up.

Selena kept telling her to believe it would happen. And Nell was trying.

Try harder.

That was what Selena T would say in that compassionate yet tough-love voice of hers.

Thirty-seven.

That wasn't old. Not really, given the life expectancy these days, but her fertility decreased with each passing year. Sure, getting pregnant was still possible and technology helped in some cases, which was why she'd considered investigating options for doing this on her own. Sure, it was doable.

Doable but challenging.

After seeing what Cami went through, even with an ex-husband to share some responsibilities, Nell reconsidered.

"Uh-oh," Cami muttered. "Incoming at eleven o'clock."

That could only mean one thing—well, person.

Welles Riggs.

Nell stiffened, preparing herself.

Three…two…one…

"Well, if it isn't my two favorite RNs." The hottie firefighter strutted toward the nurses' station as if he was not only the defini-tion of swagger but also God's gift to womankind. Okay, he sort of was if a woman liked the clean-cut, handsome, and drool-worthy types. He was fit, and charm oozed from every pore, which only made her want to keep more distance from him. That probably amused him and was why he kept bothering her.

Each time he saw her, which was often several times a day when they both worked the same days, Welles asked her on a date. He'd been doing that since he was a kid—he was four years younger than her—and it had become a big joke to him.

Though seated, Cami stared down her nose at him. "And here I thought Bigfoot had abducted you during one of your dad's Sasquatch tours."

The navy pants and T-shirt brought out Welles's blue eyes. A woman could drown in those pools and not mind as she went under, forgetting to breathe. "That must mean you missed me."

As Cami focused on her computer monitor, she nailed a cold, disinterested expression.

Come to think of it, Nell hadn't seen Welles around since Friday morning for an exam from his injuries sustained in the fire. "Have you been gone?"

"Sort of." He shifted his weight between his feet. "Chief put me on probation for disobeying orders during the cupcake shop fire. That means while the others go on fun runs, I'm stuck at the station cleaning or doing maintenance."

His definition of fun must differ from hers. "Fun runs?"

Welles shrugged. "Beats cleaning."

The guy never slowed down. When he wasn't at the fire station, he worked at his dad's Sasquatch Adventure Tours, either being a tour guide or selling Bigfoot and Berry Lake memorabilia at their shop. He also mowed lawns for senior citizens like Mrs. Vernon.

"But I have no regrets going into the bakery, and the station's all shiny, and nothing's broken." Pride sounded in his voice. "A win-win."

Nell agreed. "Great attitude."

"It is." He sidled up to her, a little too close for comfort when his spicy, woodsy scent tickled her nose and made her want to take another sniff.

Welles studied her. "You appear a tad anxious. Does that mean it's true?"

Alarms blared in her head. An image of Juliet popped into Nell's mind. She took a step away from him. "I need more context before I answer that."

"Missy," he clarified. "Someone said she might get out today."

Okay, he wasn't talking about Juliet. *Good.* Nell released the breath she'd been holding. So far, no rumors about Ezra and Remy had circulated through the hospital, so she hoped that meant no one knew.

Yet.

Once they did, the news would travel lightning quick.

Nell crossed her fingers. "They discharged Missy an hour ago."

He pumped his fist. "Yes. I figured she wouldn't be in here that long. Now, it's time for you to show your eternal gratitude."

The guy had saved her best friend, and Nell had thanked him on Friday. That was enough, except… "I'll leave that to Jenny. I bet she puts you in a book for saving Missy."

Welles's chest puffed, and he stood taller. "Guess I better read them."

Nell laughed. The guy was too much, but he'd been the same way as a kid.

Cami was more skilled at hiding her grin. "Wait. You read?"

He wiggled his fingers. "I'm the total package. Brains and brawn. One day soon, Nurse Nell will see that."

He'd been saying that for nearly twenty-five years if her math was correct, but she gave him props for persevering. "Whatever you say, Paramedic Welles."

He leaned casually against the counter. "So, who was the guy with all the presents on Friday morning?"

"I should have gotten popcorn during my break," Cami mumbled.

Nell ignored her. "His name is Gage."

"Have you gone out with him yet?" Welles asked.

Cami snorted.

Nell side-eyed her coworker. "We had coffee in the atrium."

"She fell asleep. Even snored in front of the guy," Cami chimed in unexpectedly, sounding gleeful. "Classic Nell."

"I was tired and worried about Missy." Not that Nell needed to defend herself. And what Cami said wasn't untrue. It *was* classic Nell. She nearly laughed.

"At least the guy didn't appear to mind. A video of you sawing logs didn't end up on the internet, so my guess is he likes you," Cami continued.

"I hope so." Nell crossed her fingers.

A puzzled expression formed on Welles's face, not what she expected to see from him. He was infamous for joking and teasing the nurses on duty. It was his way of flirting. "Aw, sweet Nurse Nell, if you need a pillow, use me. Anytime."

That was more like him, but his tone was too serious for, well, Welles. "Thanks."

"Are you going out with him again?" Welles picked something off his T-shirt.

"Saturday." Gage mentioned a hike and a picnic lunch. A walk was more Nell's style, but she enjoyed picnics, so she would survive the hiking part.

"Lucky for you, I'm off that day." Welles narrowed his gaze as if to see her reaction clearer. "I'm happy to chaperone…"

That was more like him. "Thanks, but we should be good."

He appeared to want to say more, but his mouth slanted, and his lips pressed together.

Strange. He enjoyed getting in the last word. Perhaps being on probation was mellowing him. That wouldn't be a bad thing. "I need to check on some things. Bye."

She headed toward the exam room, unsure why Welles was here if he hadn't come in on his rig, as he usually did.

"Nurse Nell," he called after her.

She faced him. "Yes, Paramedic Welles?"

He flashed her a charming smile that hinted at slow, passionate kisses that made her wish he'd just say goodbye. "One of these days, you'll wake up and realize what's been right under your nose this entire time."

Nope. Probation hadn't mellowed him at all. She knew the answer, but this was part of the game. It was her turn to play. "And what would that be?"

"Me." He raised his chin. "Which is why I keep asking you out, even though you continue saying no. Admit it. You love me."

The guy was too much. She laughed. "Be careful, people will think you're delusional, my friend."

"We are friends. Good friends."

"We're friends." She would leave it at that.

His grin widened. "It's meant to be."

"You lost me." Again.

"Friends to lovers?"

She hadn't a clue what he meant. "Huh?"

Cami rose slightly from her chair. "Friends to lovers is my favorite romance novel trope. Slightly ahead of enemies to lovers and grumpy and sunshine."

Welles beamed as if she'd given him an A+ on a final exam.

Uh-oh. The last thing Nell needed was for the guy to think he had a chance with her. Flirting was one thing. His job brought him into the hospital, but they also lived next door to each other. "Go get your popcorn, Cami."

Cami groaned. "You're no fun."

"I can teach Nell how to have fun," Welles said without missing a beat. "You should borrow some of Cami's books. Educate yourself on the genre."

"I left my romances in Boston." Nell hoped her tone was nonchalant instead of bitter. She was over Andrew now, and it wasn't too late for her dreams to come true. "I prefer thrillers these days."

Welles shook his head. "Romance can get your adrenaline flowing much better."

She shrugged, not wanting to play along.

"Forget this Gabe guy."

"Gage," she corrected.

"Whatever." Welles stepped toward her. "Let me show you what a real HEA looks like."

"A what?" Nell asked.

"Happily ever after," Welles explained. "That's romance novel jargon, which you would know if you kept reading them."

He probably read manuals for work. A magazine or two for fun, but he didn't appear to be the novel-reading type, especially romance books. "And you do?"

"I've read a couple for research."

Nell shouldn't, but she had to ask. "What kind of research?"

"This."

"You lost me." That seemed to be commonplace around him.

Welles pointed at her and himself. "Woman and man."

"He means flirting." Cami sounded aggravated.

The guy was incorrigible. Few men would research women by reading romance novels. That straddled the line of impressive and frightening. "I'm sure that comes in handy with others."

Welles wagged his eyebrows. "I'd rather it work on you."

"Not today."

"Tomorrow?" The hope in his voice matched the gleam in his eyes.

She didn't know whether his tenacity annoyed or flattered her. "What am I going to do with you?"

He winked. "Wrap me up and take me home."

Nell shouldn't laugh, but she couldn't help it. "And with that, I'm out of here."

The guy was too much, but she had a feeling when he finally fell in love with some woman, she would miss the attention. But that day wasn't today.

And she was happy about that.

Later that afternoon, Nell juggled the grocery bags in her hands. She stood on the front porch of Elise's house.

Elise.

A pang hit Nell's heart.

Her former boss no longer lived there.

Nell inhaled the fresh air on this warm September afternoon. The breath filled her lungs, and the smell of cupcakes baking was missing.

Elise would never again make delicious cupcakes for customers to savor, add a wise adage about life at precisely the right time someone needed to hear it, nor tell everyone "I told you so" about Ezra Monroe, who she feared would hurt Juliet.

"You were correct."

Once again.

But being right about this would have devastated Elise. She along with everyone else in town adored Juliet. Well, except for her horrible husband. Elise, Missy, and Nell had tolerated Ezra Monroe for one reason only—Juliet.

Nell had wanted her friend to find happiness, even if no one thought her husband was good enough for her. Now he would be *persona non grata*. Remy Dwyer, too.

Nell fumbled until she could poke the doorbell with her index finger.

A *ding-dong* sounded.

The front door opened.

Juliet wore a ruffled apron and her blonde hair in a messy bun, yet those only brought out her beauty. Still, she was so much more than her looks. Juliet Jones Monroe was as sweet as a slice of huckleberry pie. Ezra would regret choosing Remy Dwyer over his lovely and kindhearted wife.

"Sorry to keep you waiting." Juliet's face flushed. "I was cleaning."

"I didn't wait long. Besides, this is the only place I have to be tonight." Mr. Teddy, her foster cat, had an automatic feeder, so he would receive his dinner on time whether or not Nell was there.

Juliet motioned her inside. "Come in."

Nell stepped inside. A few boxes sat on the living room floor, and a large flat container leaned against the wall. "Settling in?"

"Not yet. It's been a rough day." Juliet wiped her forehead with the back of her hand. "Cleaning is something I can do where thinking isn't required, so I thought I'd do that before I unpack."

"And now you have food." Nell headed into the kitchen.

"That's way more than I asked for."

"You mentioned not going out. You need more than that short list to survive."

"I suppose it's true."

"Trust me as a food expert, it is."

Nell unpacked the items she'd purchased: chicken breasts, a bag of salad, broccoli, tomatoes, peanut butter, Italian sausages, mozzarella, pasta sauce, ziti, chicken noodle soup, bread, bagels, butter, eggs, yogurt, cheddar cheese, cream cheese, coffee, tea, sugar, salt and pepper, chocolate, cookies, ice cream, chocolate sauce, lemons, limes, apples, oranges, bananas, sparkling water, wine, and cupcakes.

That should give Juliet enough to make meals for a few days. "I bought cupcakes, but if you tell Missy I got them from the market, I'll deny it."

"Your secret is safe with me." Juliet came closer. As soon as she saw all the food, she covered her mouth with her hand. She blinked rapidly. "All my favorites."

"It's been a while, but I remembered some of them."

"Of course, you did. Because that's who you are." Juliet shook her head. "You shouldn't have gone to so much trouble."

"That's what friends do. And it was no trouble. Even if it had been, which it wasn't, you're worth it."

Gratitude shone in Juliet's eyes. "Thank you."

"I ordered a pizza to be delivered. I figured you might want some company for dinner, and I'd enjoy a cupcake for dessert."

"It'll be like those slumber parties we had that summer."

Nell nodded. Except Elise and the others were missing. "Yep."

Tears gleamed in Juliet's eyes. "Thank you."

Nell hugged her. She wanted to take away the hurt and pain. "You're not alone."

"I know." Juliet clung to her. "And that makes all the difference in the world."

Nell held on to her tightly. "I'm so sorry this happened."

"Thanks." Juliet backed away, wiping her eyes. "But if it hadn't been with Remy, it would have been another woman. I'm too old for Ezra."

"You're not. He just has some ridiculous notions about what it takes for him to feel young." Nell had never wanted to hurt another person as much as she wanted to hurt Ezra. And to be honest, other than Andrew, she hadn't wanted to hurt anyone before. "He doesn't deserve you."

"He doesn't." Juliet's voice was soft but didn't waver. "After everyone left earlier, I found Selena T's podcast. I started with the first one and am listening to them in order. I probably should have done this a long time ago."

"Better late than never."

Juliet nodded. "I can't change the past, but I took a baby step forward today."

"Not a baby step." Nell wanted to burst with pride. "A gigantic leap. And that was so brave of you."

"Maybe."

"Definitely."

"Fine, but not so brave. I didn't have a choice."

"Still brave, and I won't hear otherwise."

Juliet laughed—the best possible music to Nell's ears. "I'm so glad you're here."

"Me, too." Her friend had a long road ahead of her, but she wouldn't travel this path alone. The Posse would be by her side to support and help Juliet figure out what she wanted to do and be next.

Juliet had been the princess among them, even before her job at the theme park years ago. And no matter how much Ezra might have wanted to take away her tiara and give it to Remy, Juliet would be the princess of Berry Lake, and the rest of the Posse was happy to be her court.

Well, as long as Selena got to be queen.

chapter nine

O N WEDNESDAY, JULIET approached the Huckleberry Inn with hesitant steps. The three-story Victorian stood proudly on the corner of Main Street and A Avenue. Even before her parents' death, she called the place home because she'd spent most of her time there, but all she wanted to do right now was turn around and run to Elise's place, crawl under the covers, and hide.

Be brave.

Juliet imagined Selena T urging her on.

Too bad Juliet's courage had deserted her two blocks ago.

You can do this.

She needed to see her grandmother.

The well-tended lawn and flowers in pots on the porch provided postcard-picturesque curb appeal to the Berry Lake landmark. Unfortunately, her grandmother expected her family to be as perfect as her inn—at least appearance-wise. Juliet, however, was committing the ultimate sin.

Divorce.

Juliet climbed the steps until she reached the welcome mat, but she didn't open the door. She...couldn't. Not yet anyway.

She took a breath. And another.

Her hands smoothed her skirt. She'd chosen the outfit, a black ensemble, in the hopes it would appeal—perhaps, appease—her grandmother's sensibilities. Juliet wasn't mourning the loss of her marriage. But showing up in cheery colors to discuss her impending divorce from Ezra would make a tough conversation harder.

Open the door.

The staff left it unlocked during business hours.

Yet, her arm remained glued to her side.

Coward.

She was.

Her grandmother was a loving woman who'd supported Juliet as a child, teenager, and adult—but Penelope Jones was intimidating, too, which was why Juliet had always done what was asked of her.

Until now.

Worry clawed its talons into her heart like a vulture, ready to swoop down on an injured animal lying in the road. If this didn't go well...

Chin up, princess.

The odds weren't in Juliet's favor. She'd known that the first time her grandmother ignored her call. Each message she left reaffirmed it. The question was...

How badly would her grandmother react?

A lecture? A cooling-off period? Or a get out of my life?

It could be one of the above or something else.

Penelope Jones followed her own set of etiquette rules, like Emily Post's book but on steroids. People, including her granddaughter, weren't allowed to drop by unannounced. Only guests could do that.

But she couldn't wait any longer, even if this visit changed her life.

You are strong. You are brave. You are enough.

Juliet repeated the mantra. For whatever reason, the words didn't help. Probably because she didn't believe them yet.

This is another baby step. And if it turns out to be a life-changing one, so be it.

She grabbed the handle, opened the door, and stepped inside, inhaling the vanilla, rose petal, and sandalwood potpourri. The scent of home surrounded her, slowing her pounding heart and reminding her of better days.

Breathe.

She flexed her fingers. "Grandma?"

Footsteps sounded on the hardwood floor. Heavy ones, as if someone stomped their way from the kitchen.

Her grandmother, wearing a lace-trimmed apron, rounded the corner. Her gray bun added two inches to her five-seven height. "What are you doing here?"

"You didn't return my calls."

Grandma wiped her hands on her apron. "Most people would take that as a hint not to bother me."

Juliet's heart stumbled. "Is that what I am to you? A bother?"

Her grandmother's breath heaved, and her gaze narrowed. "We might as well get this over with."

That didn't sound promising. Still, she pretended a shiver wasn't inching its way along her spine and stepped toward the parlor.

"Not in there. That's for family."

The air rushed from Juliet's lungs. At least she understood how this would likely go.

Her grandmother motioned to where the inn served breakfast, lunch, and afternoon tea.

With feet that felt as if she were wearing cement-filled boots, Juliet trudged her way into the dining room. Unsure if they were sitting at one of the tables or standing, she waited to follow her grandmother's lead.

Her grandmother stood with her hands on her hips. "Please tell me what's so important you had to burst in here without calling first."

"I called. Several times since Monday." Juliet kept her head high even when she wanted to cower. "I want to tell you about Ezra and me."

"That's unnecessary." The lines around her grandmother's mouth deepened. "The entire town knows, and it's an embarrassment—a mark against the Jones name. Your grandfather must be rolling in his grave. How could you let this happen?"

Wait. What? Juliet stared in disbelief. "Ezra's the one who cheated."

"That happens sometimes, but a loving wife won't allow an indiscretion to derail a good marriage."

Juliet's jaw dropped. She closed it. "It hasn't been a decent marriage for years."

"Counseling will—"

"He's having a baby with another woman. He no longer wants to be married to me."

"Convince him—"

"No," she blurted, unable to understand her grandmother's thinking. She and Ezra had no children, so doing what was best for the family didn't factor into their decision. Though Juliet had helped him advance in his career and thrown parties and dinners for his colleagues and clients, he earned all the money. But she'd stayed long enough—too long really—for the financial security and to not upset her grandmother. It had stopped being a marriage and turned into a transactional relationship. "Just no."

Her grandmother gasped. "I beg your pardon?"

Juliet startled. She'd never said no to her before. But this time, Ezra had left Juliet with no choice.

She lifted her chin. "I said no."

Her grandmother's face pinched as if someone had used the wrong fork with their salad.

"I love you, Grandma." Juliet's voice was steady. Her hands didn't tremble. Her shoulders remained straight. "You're my only family. But Ezra has controlled me and been verbally abusive for years. He gave me a weekly allowance, picked out my clothes, and limited my interactions with people."

Her grandmother crossed her arms over her chest. "Not me."

"No, but you're the reason we moved to Berry Lake."

"That shows your husband is a good man who cares about you and me."

"A good man wouldn't do what he did."

"One time—"

"It was more than once." Juliet couldn't believe the direction of this conversation.

"You need to keep him from straying."

"I did everything for him for years. There was no pleasing him. I'm done. I found a divorce attorney." Well, Selena had, and Juliet liked what Tamika Rayne had to say. "I won't go back to him."

Her grandmother shook her head. "Marriage is sacred."

Juliet's aching heart hurt more. "I honored my vows. Ezra didn't."

"I cannot condone you divorcing your husband. That's the easy way out."

She had a feeling this would happen. That was why she'd tried so hard to make things work with Ezra. "Staying with him would be easier."

"Then stay," Grandma urged. "Your grandfather had a few dalliances in his younger days, but they meant nothing, so I forgave him. He eventually settled down, and we had a happy life together."

Ugh. Juliet didn't need to hear that. "You chose that path. I'm choosing another."

"Leaving your husband is a huge mistake." Her grandmother's lips thinned. "I won't watch you ruin your life."

And there it was.

Pain slashed through Juliet.

Memories flashed through her brain of holidays and birthdays, of tea in the parlor and bedtime stories, of burying her parents and crying in her grandma's arms after the wake, of introducing her grandmother to Ezra for the first time and knowing she'd made the woman proud.

For years, Juliet had tried to earn love, thinking she didn't deserve it on her own.

No longer.

She wanted to be loved with no conditions. She deserved that.

Still, the pain kept building. She was losing the two people who should have stood by her no matter what.

Juliet took a deep breath. She blinked, trying not to cry. "I'm sorry you feel that way. I've tried not to disappoint you, and that's why I stayed with him for so long. But I must do what's best for me. That's getting away from a husband who admitted he's been wanting to replace me since I turned thirty. The man you think is so good asked me to be his and his new wife's maid and nanny. I can't stay with someone like that."

Juliet waited for a reply.

None came. Not even a blink.

It shouldn't surprise her, but she'd hoped…

She'd hoped for a miracle.

"I doubt we can avoid each other completely in such a small town, but I won't come to the Huckleberry Inn," she said finally. "If you ever need me, you have my number."

Her grandmother's expression remained the same. She stood still as if carved out of marble.

Juliet struggled not to lose it. She kept waiting for a reply, anything, but none came. A lump burned in her throat. She swallowed around it. "Goodbye, Grandma."

As numbness spread through Juliet, she moved toward the front door. She didn't glance over her shoulder. Grandma wouldn't call for her or change her mind unless Juliet returned to Ezra. That was so not happening.

A part of her wanted to rush to her grandmother and beg for her forgiveness. But this wasn't Juliet's fault. She'd done nothing wrong. The only way to move forward was to stop begging for crumbs of affection, doing what someone thought she should do to be loved, and trying to be what they wanted her to be.

Her hand hovered over the doorknob for a moment, and she opened it.

Goodbye, Huckleberry Inn.

Juliet stepped out, wiping tears away, and closed the door behind her.

Cupcake Posse Group Chat...

> **JULIET:** *I spoke with my grandmother. She wants me to stay married to Ezra. I said no. And she said she wouldn't watch me ruin my life.*
>
> **NELL:** *Do you want me to come over?*
>
> **JULIET:** *No, I'm tired. Going to bed early.*
>
> **BRIA:** *I'll be there on Friday!*
>
> **SELENA:** *I'm sorry, Juliet. I'll be there Friday night.*
>
> **NELL:** *Jenny took Missy's phone away. She's on the road to recovery.*
>
> **SELENA:** *Brunch at Jenny's on Sunday so Missy can be there!*
>
> **NELL:** *Great idea. If you need company, text me. I have a date with Gage on Saturday, but that's it.*
>
> **JULIET:** *Thanks. It hurts, but I'm better off on my own than with people who'll only love me if I do what they want.*
>
> **SELENA:** *You are. Great attitude. And you're not on your own.*
>
> **BRIA:** *You have all of us.*
>
> **NELL:** *Cupcake Posse Forever.*
>
> **NELL:** *That's usually Missy's line, so I'm posting it on her behalf.*

On Friday morning, Juliet woke to the sound of bells and bolted upright in bed. Daylight streamed through the windows. She rubbed her scratchy eyes.

At least she hadn't cried herself to sleep last night.

Ding-dong.

Not bells.

The doorbell.

She scrambled from under the covers.

Charlene had given her the day off, so Juliet hadn't set her alarm.

It must be a delivery. Bria doesn't arrive until later today.

Juliet padded her way to the entryway and opened the door. Her boss was the last person she expected to see. Well, third on the list. Her grandmother and Ezra took the top two spots.

Charlene grinned. "Good morning, Juliet. Did I wake you?"

Juliet combed her fingers through her hair. "It was time for me to wake up."

Past time, but she hadn't been able to sleep, so she had watched shows on HGTV until exhaustion forced her to bed.

"Well, I have a surprise for you." Charlene's eyes twinkled with mischief. "Butterscotch is moving in."

The name sounded familiar, but… "Butterscotch?"

Charlene entered the house. "Elise's cat. He's spoiled but a real love. He's been fine with me, but I believe he'll be happier here with you."

Juliet's heart leaped. She'd always wanted a pet, but her parents enjoyed traveling too much, and her grandparents hadn't allowed them at the inn. "I know nothing about cats."

"A good thing I brought a cat expert with me." Charlene winked.

Juliet had no idea who her boss meant unless she was talking about herself. "Will Bria be okay with this?"

"I'm sure she will be. Bria loves the cat, but she and Elise thought Butterscotch would be happier with me since she lives in a smaller condo."

"Okay." Despite Nell dropping by and messages on the Posse's group chat, Juliet had been lonely. She rubbed her palms together. "Looks like I have a housemate. It'll be nice to have company."

"It will." Charlene's gaze softened. "I heard what happened with your grandmother, and I'm so sorry, but you're better off not trying to please someone who doesn't want the best for you. I still can't believe Penelope dared to ask me to organize a baby shower at the inn for the pregnant home-wrecker."

Juliet's knees nearly buckled. Only the door kept her from hitting the ground. "She didn't!"

Charlene nodded. "No worries. I said no. We don't want or need the business. But the nerve of her."

Juliet's shoulders sagged until she stood straighter. "My grandmother's trying to send a message by choosing Ezra's side."

"Which shows you how little you're losing."

Unfortunately. "I feel like an even bigger fool."

"Not a fool. You love wholeheartedly. That's nothing to be ashamed about." Charlene pushed her way inside. "Now step aside."

Juliet did.

As if on cue, a handsome man entered, carrying a hard-sided pet carrier in one hand and a fluffy cat bed in the other. He was tall, fit, and around Juliet's age or a few years older, given the slight creases at the corner of his eyes. His dark hair was thick and wavy. The kind meant for running fingers through while kissing.

She wet her lips.

Butterscotch meowed.

"This is Dr. Roman Byrne," Charlene announced.

"Next-door neighbor." He motioned to the boxes in the living room. "Looks like you're new to the neighborhood, too."

His hands were full, so she didn't extend her arm. "Juliet Monroe."

"Soon to be Juliet Jones," Charlene added without missing a beat.

Juliet had no idea how to respond. "I moved in on Monday."

"Sunday for us." He placed the cat carrier on the floor and the bed on the couch. "I'll get the other things from your car, Charlene."

"Juliet and I can take care of those later. You were on your way to work when I ambushed you." Still, Charlene closed the door. "But thanks for your help with Butterscotch. I never expected to see Berry Lake's newest veterinarian in the driveway next door. Juliet's never had a cat. I'm telling you, it's fate."

Was fate another name for Charlene? She was laying it on a little thick.

Juliet ran her tongue over her teeth. She should have brushed them before answering the door. Not that a man as attractive as Roman would notice her. "Nice to meet you."

"The pleasure is mine."

Charlene beamed as if she'd invented calorie-free cupcakes. "I'm sure you'll be seeing lots of each other, being next-door neighbors and whatnot. It's a match made in heaven."

Heat rushed up Juliet's neck and pooled in her cheeks. No wonder Nell complained about her mom's meddling.

Butterscotch meowed louder.

"Do you have any advice for someone who knows nothing about cats, Dr. Byrne?" Juliet asked.

"It's Roman. Cats enjoy eating and sleeping." He opened the gate on the carrier. The movement made his muscles flex. The guy was in great shape.

An orange furry head stuck out. A pink nose sniffed the air before an enormous cat who looked as if he hadn't ever missed a meal and ate a second breakfast daily lumbered out. Butterscotch headed straight to the couch, jumped up, sat, and purred.

"See." Charlene clapped her hands together. "Butterscotch is happy to be home. I thought he would be."

The cat appeared content. "Is there anything else I should know about taking care of Butterscotch?"

Roman closed the gate on the carrier. "Cats enjoy playing each day. A laser light or a feather toy works well for that. Most cats will tell you when they want attention and when they'd rather be left alone. Think of him as a tiny despot in a fur coat, and you're here to do his bidding. As long as he's happy, you won't have to worry about anything."

"Sounds like my soon-to-be ex-husband." *Oh, no.* Juliet cringed. Had she said that aloud?

Charlene laughed. "It does."

Roman gave a closed-mouth smile. He most likely had no idea who Juliet meant.

"Anything else?" Juliet wanted to change the subject.

He nodded. "Keep his water bowl filled and feed him per his usual schedule."

"Twice a day," Charlene chimed in. "And he's particular about having a clean litter box."

"I don't blame him for that." Juliet wondered where his litter box would go. She hoped Charlene knew. "Thank you."

His grin spread. "You're welcome. If you have questions, I'm right next door. I need to get to the clinic."

"I appreciate the cat tips." Juliet opened the door for him. "Have a nice day at work."

"Enjoy yours with Butterscotch." With that, Roman walked outside, and she closed the front door.

Butterscotch remained on the couch. His purrs were loud enough to be heard across the room. *He must be happy to be home, but does he understand what happened?* Juliet would open Elise's bedroom door so he could see she no longer lived there.

"Isn't he attractive?" Charlene whispered.

"Roman?"

She nodded.

"Why are you whispering?" Juliet asked in an equally quiet voice. "I doubt he's standing on the other side of the door listening in."

"You never know."

"That would be creepy."

Charlene's eyes twinkled. "So, what do you think?"

"About?"

"Dr. Roman Byrne."

"He's nice and knows more about cats than I do. But I suppose it's his job to know about all animals."

Charlene sighed. "I don't mean his skills or brain. The man is gorgeous. He didn't mention it, but he's his niece's guardian. I'm sure he'll be looking for a wife as soon as he gets settled. If

Nell hadn't met Gage, I'd steer her toward him. She would be a wonderful mother figure, but she's adamant about never dating another doctor after what that loser Andrew did to her. I don't think either Evie or Jojo is ready to be a mom, so that leaves…"

Juliet stepped away from her boss. "Not me."

Charlene frowned. "Why not?"

Juliet held out her left hand with her wedding rings on it. "I'm still married."

"You'll be single soon enough. And being married didn't stop Ezra."

"I'm not him."

"Of course not, but you and Roman would make a lovely couple."

"Um, have you looked at me?" Juliet motioned to herself. "I'm wearing sleep-rumpled pajamas. I'm barefoot, have no makeup on, and my hair is a mess. I'm sure he's horrified by my appearance. Ezra would be."

Charlene rolled her eyes. "We've already established that Ezra is an idiot. You look as beautiful as ever. Less put together than usual, but natural. Many men like that, and I believe Roman is one of them. He couldn't take his eyes off you."

Ezra's taunts about Juliet's looks and age replayed in her brain and battered her self-confidence once again. "Not true. Roman's a vet. He wanted to make sure Butterscotch would be okay. That's all."

Charlene laughed. "He glanced at the cat, but you had his full attention."

Her boss was only being polite, but Selena asked Juliet to accept compliments better, so she would try. "I appreciate that, but even if Roman were…interested, I'm not ready. He'll have his pick from any of the single women in Berry Lake, and he'll want a single one."

"Semantics," Charlene countered. "Any man with half a brain would choose you."

"Not Ezra."

"No brain. Come on, a brief flirtation and romance might do you good."

"No." The word shot out. The thought of any of that terrified Juliet. "I'd prefer to enjoy the pleasant view next door."

"Eye candy like Dr. Byrne is to be savored, no matter how old a woman is. Women will throw themselves at him as soon as they see him. I'm guessing the hubbub about the arson overshadowed his arrival because I didn't know he'd moved in."

Perhaps, or the guy was smart and kept it quiet on purpose. Not that it mattered.

"But that gives you time to get chummy with him," Charlene added.

Juliet now fully understood what Nell meant about her mom's matchmaking. It wasn't only annoying but a little frightening. "I'm sure you'll find the perfect person for the nice veterinarian. Someone not married."

She hoped that was enough to let Charlene know to back off. Enough was going on in Juliet's life without her boss playing matchmaker.

Despite what Sabine had said on Monday, Juliet didn't think she wanted to fall in love again.

She'd had her chance at happily ever after. And failed.

chapter ten

ON FRIDAY MORNING, Bria hurried out of the restroom at the Portland International Airport. She'd texted Dalton that her flight had arrived and she would meet him outside the baggage claim area on the lower level. Not that Bria had to pick up a suitcase. She rolled her carry-on luggage behind her. Selena had told her to pack more, but Bria couldn't stay for long in the middle of a job search.

No, this trip was all for Juliet.

That was why Bria also hadn't told the Posse the bad news she'd received from the insurance agent.

I'm sorry, Bria. I wanted to discuss this with the corporate office before talking with you. Bottom line, the cupcake shop's fire insurance policy doesn't cover arson.

Aunt Elise's insurance agent hadn't been avoiding Bria's calls. He'd been trying to see if there was more he could do. There hadn't been. And now…

Forget about it.

125

Juliet needed Bria to focus on her, nothing else. Paying for the fire damage would be complicated—perhaps, impossible—to figure out on her own. She'd left a message for Marc Carpenter, her aunt's attorney, since the building was part of Elise's estate. As for Bria's job, she would submit resumes in the early morning or late at night while in Berry Lake. A few days away wouldn't set her behind too much when she flew back to San Diego on Tuesday.

Don't think about leaving when you only just arrived.

Enjoy the moment was what Aunt Elise would tell her.

Bria's throat constricted. A heaviness weighed against her.

She missed Aunt Elise so much.

But at the moment, all she could do was keep moving—literally. She headed toward the main terminal.

The last time she flew into this airport, her aunt had still been alive. When she'd left Berry Lake, the house had been nothing but filled boxes in the living room and garage and empty bedrooms except for the furniture. At least the place wouldn't be empty now. Juliet was there, and she needed Bria and all the Posse. No matter the uncertainty in Bria's life, she would help her friend.

Knowing she was coming to support Juliet had given Bria purpose and direction after her disappointing discussion with Mr. Howe yesterday. Before accepting his retirement package, he'd spoken to an employment attorney, which required him to sign an agreement not to discuss the terms or sue the company in the future. Bria understood why he'd done that. His package was much better than hers. Now, she had to decide whether to accept what they offered—something else she didn't want to think about right now.

The buzz of conversation mixed with the PA announcements. She passed a couple holding hands and staring lovingly into each other's eyes. In a few minutes, that would be her and Dalton.

Flutters filled Bria's stomach.

She couldn't wait to see him. They'd said goodbye on Sunday, but she missed him more with each passing day. The texts, calls, and video chats helped, but none of those things were like being together, especially since they only decided to "date" five days ago.

As she continued with purposeful steps—okay, impatient ones—toward the exit, a man hurried past her, nearly hitting her with his duffel bag. He mumbled *Sorry, I'm late* before continuing forward.

The fact his bag missed Bria suggested her luck had changed for the better.

Good, because it couldn't get much worse.

She crossed her fingers for extra luck.

"Bria!"

She turned toward the sound of her name.

Dalton stood outside the security area with a big smile on his face and a bouquet in his hand. He wore jeans. His forest green Henley complemented his hazel eyes perfectly.

Her heart slammed against her ribcage before exploding and covering her insides with sparkly pixie dust.

Dalton was waiting inside the terminal, not sitting in his car at the curb. And he'd brought her a gift.

Bria savored the tingles. She quickened her steps to reach him sooner.

People walked between them, getting in her way, but she didn't take her gaze off Dalton. She couldn't.

So handsome and sweet and…

She swallowed, hoping to find her voice. "Hey."

Her tongue appeared to have grown three times its normal size.

Dalton wove around those in his path.

Bria met him halfway. All she wanted to do was hug him, but she kept her arms pressed at her sides. He might be her boyfriend, but this was a brand-new relationship. She didn't want to mess it up, acting too needy, even if she was.

He kissed her lightly on the lips. "I can't believe you're here."

"Sorry, not sorry."

He laughed, and the sound surrounded her, making her wonder why she hadn't packed more clothes so she could stay longer. Though Aunt Elise did have a washer and dryer...

"Welcome home," Dalton added. "I feel as if I should buy a lottery ticket."

"Me, too." She cleared her dry throat. "I thought you were picking me up downstairs at arrivals."

He kissed her forehead. "What kind of boyfriend would I be if I didn't come inside to meet you?"

More tingles shot through her. Being with Dalton brought up those first-love feelings from high school, but this second time with him was so much better already.

Oh, wait, she hadn't answered him.

One word popped into her mind. "Practical."

"Yes, but with you, I'll choose romantic."

Her heart sighed. Honest-to-goodness sighed.

He handed her the flowers. "For you."

The sweet fragrance tickled her nose. She sniffed again. "They're gorgeous. Thanks."

"Let's get your suitcase."

"I have everything."

His forehead creased. "That's all you brought with you?"

The disappointment in his voice stabbed at her heart. "I have plenty to last me."

"I thought…"

"What?"

He shook his head. "It's nothing."

His reaction and tone suggested it was something. "Tell me. Please."

Dalton led her out of the way. "I thought you were staying at your aunt's."

"I'm staying there for a week."

"I meant forever."

Bria's lips parted. She wasn't sure what to say to that. "I haven't decided what I'm doing, but I can't walk away from my life in San Diego and abandon the condo."

"Of course, you can't." Dalton brushed his hand through his hair before chuckling. "I'm excited you're here but impatient. California might as well be Mars. I've missed you that much."

"I'm here now, so let's make the most of it."

"I plan to, but I have another goal during your visit."

That sounded intriguing. "What?"

He gazed into her eyes. "I plan to convince you the Northwest is where you belong."

That could be a possibility. The Posse would be happy about that, but… "Define the Northwest?"

"Portland, Berry Lake, or anywhere in between."

"If convincing me means I get more flowers and kisses, I'm game."

"I can get behind those things, especially more kisses."

Bria pressed her mouth against his. "Same."

"I'll take this." He took the handle from her. "You're here for Juliet, but I've got you. Whatever you need."

"Thank you." Bria's nerve endings tingled. Who was she kidding? Her entire body danced and wiggled inside. "All I need is you."

She might hate having so many balls up in the air and juggling to keep one from hitting the ground, but everything except Dalton could wait.

For now.

"This place looks amazing." Bria stood in Aunt Elise's living room. The boxes she'd left were nowhere in sight. Juliet had turned the place into a mini showcase. The painting on the wall behind the couch, the throw on the chair, pillows, and half a dozen other little touches that Juliet had added to make it feel warm and welcoming. "Thank you for making this place a home again."

Juliet beamed. "I didn't want to do too much, but…"

"Do whatever you want." The house had felt so empty after Aunt Elise's death, but Juliet had filled it with life again. "Make this place your own. Really."

Dalton carried Bria's suitcase into the house. "Huge improvement given everything was in boxes the last time I was here."

Butterscotch stalked from the kitchen to the living room. He stopped, stared at Bria, and meowed.

She inhaled sharply. "Butterscotch."

"Surprise." Juliet sounded nervous. "Charlene dropped him off this morning. She said he would be happier here."

Bria scooped up her aunt's beloved cat. "Hello, handsome."

"Should I be jealous?" Dalton asked.

Juliet laughed.

"There's room for both of you in my life." She kissed the cat's head. He purred like a race car engine. "It feels like Auntie Charlene gave you extra treats."

"A second breakfast, too," Juliet chimed in.

"I'm glad he's here. The house wasn't the same without him." *Or Aunt Elise.*

Bria hugged the cat tighter.

Dalton came closer. He held out his hand to let the cat smell him. "Who is this?"

"Butterscotch. He was my aunt's pride and joy."

"Her second one." Juliet adjusted a pillow. "You were Elise's first."

Before Bria could say anything, Dalton kissed her. "For sure. That's why I wasn't allowed inside the cupcake shop."

"You're allowed in now." And then she remembered. "Or when it's open again. If—"

"When." Confidence filled Juliet's voice.

Bria should take a lead from her friend. She nodded. "It's good to be in Berry Lake."

"I'm so happy to see you. Thank you for letting me stay here."

"I love knowing the house isn't empty, so stay as long as you want."

"I don't know where I'd go, so I'll stay. But what would be even better is if you'd move home, and we could be roommates. Wouldn't that be fun?"

Juliet didn't know about Bria losing her job, but Dalton did. She glanced at him.

He winked at her. "I could get behind that idea."

The thought of permanently returning to Berry Lake appealed to Bria. The two hours she'd spent with Dalton where they'd grabbed a bite to eat and drove there had given her a taste of what it would be like if she lived closer to him. No job tied her to San Diego. She could work as a CPA anywhere. Her condo was a lonely place that no longer felt like home. Not the way this house did, thanks to Juliet. Plus, Butterscotch was here, too. "I haven't had a roommate since college, but it *would* be fun."

"It would be," Dalton encouraged. "And closer to Portland than San Diego."

Bria had to laugh. He'd been pointing out all the pluses about living there. "One-track mind."

"Over what?" Juliet asked.

"I want Bria to move here, too," Dalton admitted.

Juliet rubbed her palms together. "Two against one."

"You guys are tag-teaming me." Not that Bria minded. She enjoyed people wanting to be with her.

Unlike her father.

Wherever he might be.

Nope.

Not going there.

Butterscotch squirmed in her arms, so she placed him on the floor.

"It's a discussion for later." Bria focused on Juliet. "Right now, I want to know how you're doing."

As Juliet's smile disappeared, she sat on the couch. Butterscotch hopped onto her lap. "I have good days and bad days. I'm working part-time at Charlene's and have a party to do tomorrow afternoon. My grandmother wants nothing to do with me and appears to have sided with Ezra and Remy. Selena found me an attorney, and ever since the lawyer contacted him, he keeps blowing up my phone."

"I'm sorry." Dalton sounded sincere. "But on the bright side, it can only get better."

Juliet half laughed. "That's true. Oh, the new vet and his niece moved in next door."

That got Bria's attention. "You mean the hottie Sabine and Charlene kept talking about?"

"The same. His name is Roman Byrne."

Dalton scoffed. "So what if the guy takes care of animals? You've got a hottie right here."

"Yes, I do." Bria kissed him on the cheek.

Juliet grinned at them. "A good thing because competition will be intense."

The guy must be handsome. "That'll be fun to watch from the sidelines."

Juliet nodded, but she seemed...down.

Bria had to ask. "You okay?"

"It's hard when everyone knows what happened in my personal life, is talking about it, and is taking sides."

Bria sat next to her friend and touched her arm. "I'm sorry."

Juliet shrugged, but she didn't appear to be indifferent. Far from it. "Life in a small town, right?"

"Still sucks," Dalton said. "I remember what it was like after my dad died and when my mom remarried for the first time. I was glad to be away from here when that divorce happened."

"It's so hard." Juliet rubbed Butterscotch, and the cat soaked up the attention. "I've only been to work and the inn until today.

I ran to the market to get more things for Butterscotch, and I ran into Remy. She gave me this *hate-me* look, and I expected to see her blow smoke at me. I don't know why she acted like that when she won. Not that Ezra is the best prize."

Despite Juliet's words, the hurt was unmistakable.

"My sister and I don't talk anymore, but she and my mom sometimes seem to be two halves of a whole," Dalton admitted. "They've perfected hate-me eyes, scornful sneers, and evil eyebrow raises. Owen isn't much better, but he's Remy's twin, so that might be why."

Bria rarely heard Dalton mention his family, except for his youngest brother. "What about Ian?"

"I call him a few times each week, but I don't know what my mom says to him. He's a senior, and I hope once he heads off to college, her influence on him will lessen as it did with me. I told him he always has a place with me if he needs one."

Bria's heart warmed at what a good brother Dalton was. He would be a wonderful father.

Uh-oh. It was way too soon to be thinking about him like that, wasn't it?

Slow down. Slow it way down before you ruin things with him.

"I hope your brother takes you up on it," Juliet said. "Your mom scares me."

Dalton laughed. "Welcome to the club. I love my mother, but I keep my distance. I'm grateful for her doing what she had to do for us after my dad died, but she's out of control now."

Bria remembered what her aunt had said about his mom being a social climber and wealthy-husband collector. The two women had hated each other. "Don't let Deena DeMarco get to you. She's all talk."

"That's right," Dalton agreed. "Anything more would require work, and my mom doesn't do that."

"Your sister, too," Juliet joked.

That was more like her friend. Well, the one Bria remembered from fifteen years ago. However heartbreaking the divorce from Ezra would be, Juliet would be better off without him.

He stared at Juliet with compassion. "And your husband—"

"Soon to be ex-husband," Juliet and Bria said at the same time.

"Jinx," they also said in unison before bursting out in laughter.

Bria grinned. "This is like when we were younger."

"Except instead of owing a Coke, let's do champagne or wine."

Yep. The old Juliet still lived inside her. However, Selena would call this glimpse the new and improved Juliet. Speaking of which… "When does Selena arrive?"

"Later tonight."

"Have you spoken with her?"

Juliet nodded. "Lots of calls and texts. Selena also connected me with a divorce attorney, who I like. We had a video call yesterday. I-I'm in expert hands."

Bria didn't know how Selena ran an eight-figure business, supported her husband, and counseled her friends. Bria had spoken to Selena every day this week. She'd also given Bria the name of an employment attorney. "Sounds like it."

"How did you take today off?" Juliet asked. "I thought you used up your vacation time?"

Dalton glanced at Bria, who shook her head slightly. Thankfully, Juliet didn't appear to notice.

"It turned out not to be an issue with work, so I flew up earlier." Bria wasn't ready to tell her friend what happened. Maybe before she left.

"That's sweet of you. It'll be great to have the Posse together. I must admit I worried we'd go our own ways again."

"Same," Bria admitted. "But we're committed, and the chat group helps."

Juliet nodded. "It was hard typing that text on Monday morning, but I'm glad I did."

"Me, too." Even though guilt coated Bria's mouth for not doing what Juliet had done. "So, which room should I take?" Bria asked.

"Your old one. I'm in the guest room."

"Not Elise's?"

Juliet shook her head. "Selena said she'd stay there."

"Does anything ever bother the mighty Selena T?" Bria asked.

"I don't think so, but she might find Butterscotch sleeping with her. I've found him in there twice already."

"I'm not surprised." The cat loved sharing her aunt's pillow. "Elise spent her last days in a hospital bed she'd rented, but Butterscotch still slept next to her each night. He always did, even as a kitten."

"I never noticed him when I visited her."

"He usually hides when company comes over."

"He's out now," Dalton said.

Juliet grinned. "Butterscotch must like you."

Dalton's chest puffed. "Though your aunt wouldn't like that much. She hated me."

"She didn't appreciate you breaking my heart," Bria clarified, not wanting him to feel bad.

He stared at the floor. "I'm sorry I was such an idiot in high school."

"We both grew up, and I forgave you. No looking back."

"Don't you dare even consider breaking her heart again, or you'll have to deal with the Posse," Juliet teased, but there was a steely glint in her eyes.

"No breaking hearts ever again." He crossed his heart. "Promise."

"We'll hold you to that," Juliet warned.

His words filled Bria with light. She stood taller as if her feet only skimmed the floor. "Me, too."

But she was only teasing. Dalton was the one thing going right for her, and she had nothing to worry about with him. It was the best feeling in the world.

chapter eleven

SELENA WOKE UP early on Saturday. As she lay in Elise's bed with her eyes closed, she imagined Logan in their bed at home. Pink, purple, and white energy swirled in her mind, and she sent a burst of love to him. Selena did the same thing with her parents in Palm Springs, her friends, and her clients. It was something she did each morning and night—a way to reach out to those in her life.

A purr vibrated against her right side. She'd read that the frequency was in the range that helped heal everything from infection to broken bones.

With her eyes still closed, she touched Butterscotch. "I miss your mommy, too."

The cat rolled closer.

His fur was soft against her fingers. "She loved you so much."

The purring increased, soothing Selena's soul. Elise was in a better place. Selena only wished her friend and mentor had been more open to alternative cancer treatments. Elise had claimed it wouldn't make a difference, and no matter how hard Selena tried, she couldn't convince her to give it a chance.

But she'd done her best.

That was all anyone could do.

Still, grief remained. Even if life and death were more entwined than most humans realized. She opened her eyes.

Butterscotch kneaded his front paws.

"Okay, I see what you want now." The same as last night.

The cat had scratched at the bedroom door until Selena let him in and left the door ajar in case he needed out. He'd fallen asleep before her, and as far as she knew, not moved from his spot.

"I'm happy you have Juliet. Nothing against Charlene, but this is your home. And soon, Bria will be here once she gets over herself and realizes Berry Lake is where she belongs." Selena continued rubbing the cat. She closed her eyes again, visualizing her friends living in this house and overflowing with abundance, both financially and in love. Warmth flowed through her. "It'll all work out."

That would make Elise happy.

I miss you.

Selena cuddled with Butterscotch. Elise had believed in Selena from the beginning, telling her she could do and be anything she wanted. She'd taken that to heart, and Elise supported each step on her journey to become Selena T, Queen of the Internet and a multi-millionaire. They'd commiserated each setback at the start and celebrated each milestone after things took off.

But no more.

Selena sighed. "I've made over a million dollars each of the last three months."

She knew Elise wasn't there, but she said it aloud anyway. Selena had planned to tell her in person and celebrate with champagne and cupcakes, but she thought she had more time. Only things happened so fast—too fast—at the end.

"It'll be a million dollars a week soon."

She didn't have a time frame for the goal. It would happen when it happened. No trying to force it because she'd selected an arbitrary date to reach the milestone. Some needed a set date, but this worked for her.

"Logan and I will make sure Butterscotch and all the Posse members never have to worry about anything. I have big plans for your cupcake shop, too. Ones I want to discuss with your attorney. Today, if Marc has time to talk to me."

Selena opened her eyes once again.

The cat stretched, taking up a considerable portion of the mattress.

"You remind me of Logan." Selena continued petting the orange fur. "He hogs the bed, too."

The cat didn't appear to care. Neither did Logan.

She grinned.

"I enjoy waking up with a cat. Maybe what's missing in my life is a pet."

Because what else could it be? She had the career and husband of her dreams—more money than she could spend in a lifetime. She lived in a gorgeous house in Seattle with a view of the Puget Sound, but when Logan was on the road, the place seemed too big for only her. She supported him wholeheartedly, but a part of her looked forward to his retirement so that they could spend more time together.

Oh, she'd known what married life to a professional athlete would be like, but she thought he would have retired by now. Each time it was supposed to be Logan's last season, he'd received accolades, awards, and contract extensions and kept playing. She was happy for him and shouldn't complain, but this had been going on for years.

"I'd take you to Seattle with me, except you need to be in this house where you lived with your special human. But this must be a sign I need a cat. I could give two cats a forever home. A pair is better than one, right?"

Butterscotch continued to purr.

"I'll take that as a yes. And you know what? It's time Logan and I stopped talking about buying a vacation home and actually purchased one." When Bria returned to town, a nice place on the lake would come in handy. "Yes, this feels right."

The feeling and emotion behind something—whether it be an idea, a decision, or a physical item—was what drove her to take action.

She pictured the perfect second home. The images were fuzzy in her mind until they sharpened, her desire coming into focus—on the water with a deck, hot tub, outdoor fireplace. There would be lots of trees, wood, and glass.

As long as the bones are solid, a contractor and designer can fix interior issues. A familiar voice said that inside her head. That meant one thing.

"Looks like I'm buying a vacation home today."

They had plenty of cash, which would appeal to a seller. Yes, this was doable, but first...

She reached for her phone. They needed to have a conversation about adopting cats, but that had to happen in person because Logan had always said no children, no pets, and no plants. He'd relented a year ago and let her have a succulent. She now had twelve. But she understood why he remained firm on the other two things.

He didn't want to worry about taking care of anyone else. He'd been responsible for keeping his younger sister safe from their dad, a drunk who liked to beat up his kids. Logan had taken the brunt of the hits, and he wanted the abuse to stop, not keep the pattern going. His grandfather had been as brutal.

Not that it would continue with Logan.

He wasn't like that. Okay, sure, he was a defenseman for his hockey team, and things got rough on the ice, but he was a big softie outside of the rink. He rarely drank. She'd only seen him buzzed twice in their entire time together.

But she respected him enough not to show up with a pet. That wouldn't be fair or right. But she wanted to have the discussion. She'd been feeling as if something were missing, and a little furry being or two to love appeared to be it.

But she would mention the vacation home. They'd discussed it before. Time together to view properties for sale was the only thing standing in their way. Call the voice in her head a download or a ping, a sign or intuition, but this was what they were supposed to do, and the timing was now. She typed a message.

> **QUEEN:** *It's time to buy a vacation home.*
> **HOTTIE32:** *Today?*
> **QUEEN:** *Yes. I'm sure I'll find what we want.*
> **HOTTIE32:** *Go for it.*
> **QUEEN:** *Want to see it first?*
> **HOTTIE32:** *You know what I like. But send me a video.*
> **QUEEN:** *I love you.*
> **HOTTIE32:** *Love you.*

"That was easy," Selena said to Butterscotch. "But most things are."

It hadn't always been that way in her life, but as she grew, doing inner child and shadow work to overcome the wounds holding her back from getting what she wanted, things fell into place. She saw no reason to make life more difficult than it had to be, and her method had worked.

A knock sounded.

Selena rose on her elbows. "I'm awake."

Juliet pushed open the door farther. Her eyes were puffy and red.

Oh, no. She must have cried herself to sleep after telling Selena and Bria what happened with Ezra and her grandmother. But letting out the emotion was better than holding it in.

Selena sat up. "How are you doing?"

"I look like a mess, but I feel better."

"I'm glad to hear it."

"You'd heard the story with Ezra before, but I think I needed to tell it again for Bria's sake and mine. Thanks."

Her features appeared more relaxed than yesterday—a good sign. Juliet had a long journey ahead of her. Selena would do what she could to help, but she could only do so much, or her friend would find herself in the same place. If not with Ezra or her grandmother, then with another person. "Sometimes, you need to tell a story a few times before you're ready to let go."

"I want to let this go, so I hope I'm getting there." A hint of uncertainty remained in Juliet's voice, but she sounded stronger than she had all week during their calls and chat last night.

That was a positive sign. Progress. But healing would take time. Divorce often played out like a grief cycle. But once Juliet passed the various stages, she would thrive. "You are."

"Are you hungry?" Juliet asked. "Bria made cinnamon toast."

Memories of a similar breakfast made Selena's mouth water. "That's what Elise served when we had sleepovers that summer."

Juliet nodded. "There's also bacon and eggs. Everything should be ready shortly."

Selena's stomach growled. "As much as I enjoy a lazy morning in bed, that sounds too delicious to miss."

The breakfast would be as good or better than what she would have eaten at the Huckleberry Inn. Selena wouldn't stay or eat there again. Penelope Jones was a gracious innkeeper, but she was also a shrewd businesswoman. Selena saw right through her games. The woman would do whatever it took, including embracing Remy and Ezra, to convince her granddaughter not to divorce her husband.

But Penelope's plan wouldn't work. Her actions weren't out of love. They were to manipulate and hurt Juliet to get her way. And because of that selfishness, putting more importance on appearances than what was best for her granddaughter, the woman would lose the best thing in her life—Juliet.

Mindful of Butterscotch next to her, Selena carefully slid from between the covers. "I'll brush my teeth and be right out."

As if understanding that meant breakfast time, the cat stood and arched his spine.

Juliet's mouth formed a perfect O. Despite her swollen eyes, she was beautiful. "You had company last night."

"He wanted in around midnight, so I opened the door."

The house had been so still and quiet. The only sign of life had been the cat and the hum from the refrigerator. Juliet must have fallen asleep before that.

"Come on, handsome." Selena kissed the top of the cat's head. "It's time for breakfast."

A few minutes later, she sat around the kitchen table with Juliet and Bria. Butterscotch watched them from his cat tree.

Juliet sipped orange juice before setting her glass on the table. "I've been listening to your podcasts, and I enjoy them. But I'm such a hot mess. How do I get to a place where I'll have what I want?"

If Selena had a dollar for every person who asked that question. Wait. She sort of did. "Keep doing the work."

Juliet straightened. "Oh, that reminds me, I have a party to host this afternoon. I'll be busy from one to five."

"Not a problem." Selena hadn't meant her actual job, but she would use this opening. "I'm guessing Bria wants some alone time with Dalton."

Bria stared into her coffee cup before looking up. "I don't have to see Dalton today."

"Yes, you do," Selena answered quickly before her friend came up with excuses. "I have a few things to take care of here."

Like buy a property and talk to Elise's attorney about the cupcake shop.

"Okay, it would be nice to spend more time with him," Bria admitted.

Selena winked. "You mean awesome."

Bria blushed before sipping her coffee.

Selena focused on Juliet. "I'm happy to hear you have another party to do, but event planning isn't the type of work I meant. I'm talking personal-development work."

"Oh." Juliet tilted her head. "I'm guessing putting on parties is easier than the stuff you discuss on your podcast and in your books."

"It depends. There isn't one path, even though many wish there were." Selena tried to figure out what would work the best for each client. Human Design often helped, but sometimes it only took hearing something a fresh way from what they'd heard before. "But if you're committed to growing, to leaving your past behind, that requires digging deep, and you won't always like what you find. Some people decide it's easier to stay where they are."

Juliet tentatively raised her hand. "That's what I've done for years. I knew things weren't right with Ezra, but I was so afraid of what that might mean for me and my relationship with my grandmother, I rationalized and pretended my way through a bad marriage. I don't want to keep doing that."

"Then don't." Selena didn't miss that Bria, who'd been quiet last night, was listening intently. "I'm not trying to be flippant, but setting an intention is a great step."

"More baby steps," Juliet said, and Bria nodded.

"Baby and big ones." Selena said that for both women, but until Bria trusted all her friends with the truth about her job situation, Selena couldn't say anything more specific to her. "But you've got this."

Juliet sighed. "I sure hope so. A part of me wants to change the past, so I no longer feel like a failure."

"You haven't failed," Selena affirmed. "You're who you are because of all you've been through. But sometimes bad things happen for no rhyme or reason."

"Like my parents dying?"

Selena nodded. "People often come into our lives to show us something about ourselves. Some are there for a brief time, others longer. But when we don't pay attention, or we ignore what we see, we keep repeating the pattern by having the same situation show up."

"I don't want another Ezra."

"I know you don't."

"But I see what you mean. It was easier to ignore stuff until things escalated to the point where I had to take action."

"And now that you have, and you're ready to look at your marriage more openly and honestly with yourself, you will grow. The end of a relationship doesn't mean you failed. It means you learned what you needed to, and it's time to move on."

Juliet nodded, but her lips pressed tightly together.

"What?" Bria asked.

"I miss my grandmother. These past few days are the longest we've gone without talking."

"That's all on Penelope," Selena replied fast. "You've been a wonderful granddaughter. All you can do is work on yourself and hope she does the same regarding this situation."

And likely others, but Selena didn't want to go there.

Juliet shrugged. "I can't imagine her listening to any meditations or journaling."

That made Selena laugh because she couldn't see it either. "No, but there's another kind of work besides that. And sometimes, as we change, it affects the people around us when they see us shift."

"Even if she doesn't want to see me?"

Selena's heart hurt for her friend. "Yes."

"The town's not that big," Bria said finally. "She'll see you, eventually. Unlike my father, who's vanished. I've texted him every day, but no reply."

"I'm sure he'll turn up. He's done this before, right?" Selena asked.

"Lots of times, but Aunt Elise was always the voice of reason when it happened."

"Then we'll have to be that for you." Juliet smiled at Bria. "Well, Selena. Though I hope to be more on track soon, so I can help everyone, too."

"You will be." Selena glanced between the other two. "How about we go on a walk after we eat?"

Juliet nodded. "And you guys can help me get ready for my party. It could use a queen's touch."

"Always happy to help." And Selena was. She would do anything for her friends.

After the walk, Selena and Bria helped Juliet prepare for her party. Items covered the kitchen table.

The muted sound of a lawnmower provided the soundtrack to their work. A musical or film score would have been much better.

Selena glanced out the window to the backyard. "It was nice of Dalton to mow the lawn."

"He'd offered to check the house each week when I left."

"And I moved in the next day," Juliet chimed in.

"It's great to have you here, but he wants to watch his brother's football games, so he'll keep up the yard and maintenance."

"A very boyfriend-ish thing to do."

Bria flushed. "That's what he is."

"And you're cute together." Selena had known of Dalton Dwyer in high school, but he'd been four years younger and one of the rich, popular kids in town—the opposite of her. She hadn't liked him because of how he'd broken up with Bria. But she'd forgiven him, and Selena wasn't one to hold a grudge.

"Very cute." Juliet glanced at the microwave clock. "I need to put on my princess costume. Do you mind loading the rest of the tea set into the container?"

"I've got this." Selena motioned to Bria and the yard. "Go flirt with your boyfriend."

"You just want to fight me to try on Juliet's tiara," Bria joked.

"Guilty." Selena laughed. "I'll see you later."

Bria nodded. "If no one's home, the house key is under the painted rock in the flower bed."

That was the same place it had been fifteen years ago. "Still?"

"That's how I got in on Monday." Juliet smiled. "Bria had extras in the kitchen drawer, so I put that one where it belongs."

Bria headed toward the kitchen door, obviously eager to see Dalton. "Marc Carpenter had me change the locks since we didn't know who had a key."

After taking selfies wearing a tiara, Selena carried a tote out to Juliet's car. The scent of freshly mowed grass hung in the air. "From everything I've seen, you go all out on these events."

"Charlene has high standards, but I'm glad she's over-the-top. It's more fun for the girls and me. Plus, the moms love it. They aren't the kind looking to save money on the party."

Selena loved the way Juliet's eyes lit up. "You enjoy putting on tea parties."

"I love it." Juliet popped the trunk with her key fob. She wore an elaborate costume that was nice enough for a theme park and piled her blonde hair artfully around a tiara. She was the quintessential princess. "I'd never considered what my dream job would be, but this is it. Thanks for talking to Charlene for me. I wouldn't have ever thought of it."

"You would have eventually. I just gave you a little push."

Juliet lifted her roller cart into the trunk. "I may need to find something else part-time, but this is perfect for now."

"Have you spoken to Tamika?"

"Yes, and I like her. She's hopeful about getting the prenup tossed out, but I want to be more conservative in what I'll get. Ezra will play hardball with money involved."

"If you need anything…"

"I'll ask. But so far, I've been fine. I plan to pay rent to Bria. I told her I'd cover the utility bills, too."

Pride swelled. "You're doing great."

"I'm doing my best. Having all of you on my side helps."

"Juliet," a man called from next door.

Selena turned to see a tall, handsome man walking toward them. He appeared to be in his mid-thirties or early forties. No ring on his left hand, but not all men wore wedding bands.

"Oh, hi." Juliet shut the trunk. "This is my friend Selena. Selena, this is Roman Byrne. He's the new vet in town."

Selena tried not to laugh. She might as well be invisible the way the guy looked past her to stare at Juliet. "Nice to meet you, Roman."

"Oh." He startled. "Same."

The man was smitten, and Juliet seemed oblivious. That was probably a good thing since she needed to learn to love herself, not rely on someone else to love her.

"You look like a fairy-tale princess." He sounded a little breathless.

Juliet curtsied. "I work for Charlene's event-planning company. I have a birthday party to do this afternoon."

What appeared to be relief flashed across his face. He took a step forward. "You do birthday parties?"

"She does," Selena answered for her friend. Not the best move, but she wanted Juliet to bring in events, not rely only on Charlene. "Adults and kids."

Roman blew out a breath. "I can't believe my luck."

Not luck. More likely fate or destiny. But Selena would keep that to herself.

"What do you need?" Juliet asked.

"I'm the guardian for my niece. She's eleven going on thirty. But she turns twelve in a couple of weeks, and I'm assuming she'll want a party."

"Has she mentioned what she wants?" Juliet asked.

He brushed his fingers through his hair. "No, but I haven't asked. I'm new to this parenting thing. Her parents, my twin and her husband, were killed in a car accident. This will be Katie's first birthday without them. She hasn't been interested in much since we moved to Berry Lake, but staying in Montana, where we lived, was too hard, so I...we...decided to try something different."

"Ask Katie what she wants." Selena knew nothing about raising kids. All her clients were eighteen or older, but her gut told her that. But her friend would know better than most. "Don't you think so?"

Juliet nodded. Her hand was on her heart, probably empathizing with the girl. "I'm so sorry to hear about your sister and your brother-in-law. I lost my parents when I was thirteen, and I lived with my grandparents after that. You should talk to her unless you want it to be a surprise, but that might not go over well, depending on how she's feeling."

"I'll ask her."

"If she wants a party, I'm happy to help. I just need to make sure the date is open with Charlene."

"I can check with her, too," he offered.

Juliet nodded. "Whatever works best for you."

Selena liked the way Juliet didn't hesitate. The uncertainty in her voice at breakfast was gone.

"Any advice in the meantime?" Roman asked.

"Be patient," Juliet said.

He half laughed. "I've been working on that. Sometimes I'm not very successful. Her dad homeschooled her. I gave that a try. Failed. And a few weeks into the school year, she's enrolled in a new school in a new town in a new state."

"You're grieving, too."

He nodded. "My sister was my twin."

"That's so hard."

"We were both vets and shared a practice. We worked long hours, so we didn't see each other out of the office except on major holidays. But she was there for me until she wasn't. Everywhere, from work to their house, the memories were too much for us. Not that Missoula is huge, but I thought a smaller town might be better for Katie."

"I grew up in Berry Lake with Juliet." The guy seemed to be trying his best with a rough situation, but Selena didn't want him to have on blinders. "Kids can get into the same trouble here as anywhere."

He held up his hands as if stopping her. "Please don't destroy my illusion of a Hallmark movie life."

Juliet laughed. "If that's what you want, you'll love Berry Lake during the holidays. Lights, snow, and holiday cheer wherever you look. Very Christmas-movie-worthy."

"That's a relief." He moved onto Elise's driveway. "What do I do until December arrives?"

Juliet rubbed her chin. "You make this place home and be there to listen and give as many hugs as it takes. My grandparents did that with me."

Selena waited for what she knew would come next.

Three...two...one...

"And I'm happy to help however I can," Juliet added. "You know where to find me."

"I do." He glanced over his shoulder at his house before focusing on Juliet again. "Could I get your number? That might make it easier if we don't bump into each other."

Not exactly smooth, but the guy had some game. Selena watched as her friend handed him her phone.

A cell phone beeped.

"I texted myself." Roman gave the phone to Juliet. "I'll be in touch."

Selena knew he would text or call soon and not only about the party.

"And if you have questions about Butterscotch, now you have an easy way to reach me," he added.

Juliet's smile brightened her face. "Thanks."

"Nice meeting you," he said to Selena, but his attention was still on Juliet.

"You, too." Selena wondered if she should let things play out or if she needed to say something to Juliet about her neighbor's interest. "I hope you and your niece enjoy Berry Lake."

"Me, too." With a slight wave, he returned to his yard.

Juliet checked her phone. "I should get going."

Curiosity got the best of Selena. "So your neighbor is the new vet people talked about last week?"

"Yes. Charlene is trying to play matchmaker. And not subtly."

"He's interested in you."

"He's being neighborly." Juliet's keys jingled. "Even if he was, I'm in no position for more than being neighbors. But I want to help Katie. If you think I could and not make things worse."

Selena touched Juliet's arm. The satin and velvet fabrics were soft against her palm. "You can help her because you know what she's feeling. It might be cathartic for both of you. But be careful around Roman because he does like you."

Juliet laughed. "Didn't we go through this in middle school once or twice?"

"High school," Selena corrected. "You're two years younger than Nell and me."

"That's right." Juliet opened the car door. "Are you sure you'll be okay alone?"

"Positive." Selena had texted a local real estate agent and was meeting her in thirty minutes. If all went well—and why wouldn't it—she would leave town with an offer pending on a dream vacation home.

chapter twelve

I'M. GOING. TO. Die.

Muscles Nell didn't know existed ached.

Put one foot in front of the other.

Not so easy to do when her feet kept slipping thanks to the small pebbles and dirt on the narrow edge along the mountainside—this was so not a trail unless it was aka The Path of Death.

She sucked in a breath. Barely any air filled her burning lungs. They weren't high enough where altitude would be an issue, but she huffed and puffed.

I'm not going to make it.

Nell stopped, placed her hands on her knees, and bent over. That would help her breathe. She also needed to stop the lactic acid from continuing to build up.

Gage glanced over his shoulder and smiled at her—a smile that sent the choirs of angels in heaven singing and the sun turning up its brightness. Why did he have to be so attractive?

"We're almost at the top, Nell." Gage had to yell because he was that far ahead of her. He'd also been saying that for two freaking hours.

This is a light hike, he said.

Not much more than a walk, he said.

Minimal vertical climb, he said.

Wrong, wrong, and *dead* wrong.

She might as well be on a trek up to Everest or another peak in the Himalayas. It was going to kill her. Lunch better include cold lemonade, French fries, donuts, and chocolate-covered strawberries when they reached the top.

The farthest she'd walked recently was in December at a mall in Portland—only because she'd had to park at the most distant spot in the lot.

Out of Shape R Us.

Nell took another breath.

"Come on," Gage encouraged from what appeared to be a mile away, but she doubted his voice would carry that far. "You're doing great."

No, she wasn't.

And the worst part?

She'd resigned herself to death on this mountain, but midway up, she realized she didn't have a last will and testament. Only thirty-seven, she hadn't thought she needed one, which was stupid considering what she saw each day at the hospital. At least her sisters were named as the beneficiaries on her life insurance from work, but was there anything embarrassing—her stash of See's Victoria Toffee aside—that people would find when they came to pack up her apartment? Mr. Teddy was a foster cat, so he'd return to Sabine's rescue.

Don't think about it.
You'll be dead.
It won't matter.

"Let's get going, or we won't have time to eat before we have to turn around."

One glance at him reminded her why she was putting herself through this torture. But that only brought more questions to mind. He was hot. Hotter than hot. So hot someone like him shouldn't look twice at her.

"I packed a yummy lunch," he called down to Nell.

With her luck, she'd eat and puke. That would be a nice bookend date, given she'd fallen asleep on their first one. She would end up a meme and go viral.

"It's only seven miles," he added.

As if that would tempt her.

Ha.

When he'd said seven miles at the trailhead, she'd assumed a round trip and a flat trail.

"Life's meant to be an adventure." He wouldn't stop trying to get her moving again. "Isn't it fun not to know what's coming up?"

Only if he meant being surprised by what commercials came on during the breaks of her favorite shows.

He hiked to her. "Rested enough?"

No, that would take a week of lying in bed with an IV of sugar water and hourly doses of cupcakes.

The image of his hurt friend popped into her mind. Funny, but she hadn't thought of that guy until now.

She took a breath and another. She might be able to talk without sounding like she was wheezing. "How's your friend who broke his arm doing?"

"He's okay. He'll need physical therapy at some point. But his wife has grounded him."

"Grounded him?"

"He can't go anywhere with me unless she's with us. She blames me for his injury."

Smart woman.

Unlike Nell.

"Caught your breath?" he asked in a hopeful tone.

While her breath had left her two miles ago, her lungs were hanging on by a thread. Her heart was ready to throw a fit. Gage, however, wasn't winded, and he'd eagerly added more distance to his hike by coming to her.

So not fair.

Still, she nodded.

Lunch.

The one word swirled in her head. Her reward for surviving the rest of the way would be food.

He clapped his hands together as if that would make her move faster. "Let's go."

As he had all day, Gage took off first at a fast clip, much quicker than she could walk. She didn't mind because that gave her a delightful view of his backside.

If she had to die, which appeared likely based on the steep slope ahead of her, at least she'd have that as the last thing she saw.

Five minutes later, she reconsidered Gage's appeal. Everything hurt again. Tiredness turned into exhaustion.

Forget the food. Not even that was motivation enough.

She wanted to turn around and head to the car. That was the smartest action to take before she injured herself.

"Gage," she called to him, but her voice sounded as weak as her legs. "I'm tired."

"Keep going. We're almost there. And I have lunch."

He treated her like a three-year-old by dangling a piece of candy in front of her. It had worked so far, but now...

"I can't make it." Nell cringed, hating to admit defeat. But she was a couch potato, and he wasn't.

Looks and killer body aside, why did I want to go out with him?

Because your mom's thrilled, and she's stopped meddling in your life.

That would only continue if Nell kept going out with him. And if she did, his love of adventure would lead her on more outings like this. Was that what she wanted?

"Come on, beautiful." He cranked up his charm with a model-worthy pose. "Trust me. All this will be worth it when you see the view."

Nell doubted that, but she wasn't a quitter. At least, she tried not to be, so she forced her right foot forward, followed by her left. She hoped he gave her a kiss and some chocolate when they reached the top, or this would have all been for nothing.

On Sunday at eleven, Nell stood on the front porch of Jenny and Dare's house. She held a box of donuts. Okay, propped against her hip was a better description since her arms hurt too much to bear weight. No one had asked her to bring anything, but she needed a donut. Okay, three. But she hoped the others would eat some so she wouldn't scarf down the entire dozen.

As she raised her arm to press the doorbell, a pain sliced through her shoulder. Still, she touched the round button.

It had taken every ounce of energy to get out of bed so she could stop by the market's bakery and arrive on time. More than once, she'd thought about turning the car around, but she didn't want to miss this brunch while Bria and Selena were in town. Both Juliet and Missy needed all of them, even if Nell hurt worse today.

Dare opened the door. He held Briley, who sucked on a pacifier. "Good morning."

Not for her, but she wouldn't take out her frustrations on a man who'd routinely risked his life to protect their country and made Jenny so happy. "Is everyone here?"

"Yes, but three of them arrived together."

Oh, right. Selena had stayed with Bria and Juliet. Nearly dying of exertion must kill brain cells because Nell had forgotten.

"The Posse is in the dining room." He kissed the top of his daughter's head. "I'm on Briley duty. But I'll take the donuts into the kitchen where Jenny is setting up a buffet."

He took the box, and Nell dropped her arms to her sides.

Pathetic.

She stepped into the house. Pain shot through her right knee. She grimaced and shortened her stride.

As he closed the door, he studied her. "You okay?"

No, but Dare didn't need to know that she was an out-of-shape couch potato, and the extra weight she carried made going uphill more difficult. But then again, Gage's idea of "easy" and hers differed significantly. She needed to recover fast, or tomorrow would be a miserable day at work. A good thing she'd taken today off to spend with the Posse, or she'd be an even bigger mess.

"Sore from hiking." The only way to save face was to leave off how her muscles felt as if they'd been hammered with a mallet and run through a grinder.

Dare grinned. "Nothing like getting fresh air and sunshine."

She would rather breathe circulated indoor air and never see blue sky again. A shower hadn't helped last night. Neither had this morning's. Nell would have taken a bath, but she feared in her current state not being able to get out by herself. She would rather die a slow, agonizing death alone in dirty bathwater than call 911 and need to be rescued from her tub. Hot firefighters saying hello and flirting at the nurses' station in the emergency department was one thing. Requiring them to rescue her naked, stuck self was so not happening. The embarrassment from that would kill her.

With careful steps to make sure she didn't aggravate her achy muscles, she followed Dare. He headed into the kitchen, and she veered into the dining room.

Somehow, she made it without groaning. Of course, the empty chair at the table was on the far side of the room.

Please shoot me now.

"Good morning." Her body might be ready to shut down, but her heart danced at the sight of her four friends. "It's so great to be together again."

"We were just talking about that." Selena stood and hugged her.

Nell stiffened, gritting her teeth to keep from crying out.

Selena jerked away. "What's wrong?"

"The hike with Gage turned out to be a seven-mile climb." As Nell tried to walk as normally as possible, she moved toward her spot.

"Wait." Missy's nose scrunched. "Round trip?"

Nell lowered herself into the chair. She forced herself not to sigh when her legs no longer had to support her weight. "No."

Everyone gasped.

She didn't blame them. Even a seven-mile round-trip would have been pushing it. "In my defense, Gage is the definition of gorgeous, and ever since my mother met him, she's stopped meddling in my life."

"But you don't like to hike." Selena's voice sounded as shocked as her expression. "You never wanted to go hiking when we were in high school."

"Why would I?" Nell shuddered. "My favorite distance to walk is from my couch to the fridge."

Her friends laughed, as she expected.

"I'm paying the price, though. My entire body, including my toenails, is voicing displeasure over yesterday." Nell stared at the table. "I brought a dozen donuts. Please eat several so I don't. Because I think that's the only thing that will help until Missy is baking again."

Her friends laughed.

"Donuts are wonderful substitutes in situations like this." Missy was halfway on her feet when Bria stood.

"I'll get one for you now," Bria said.

"I can wait." Nell didn't want to be rude and eat in front of her friends. "Dare said Jenny was putting together a buffet."

Missy slumped in her chair. "I'm healing, but she treats me like an invalid. I still don't have my phone, and I'm staying in the guest bedroom when I want to move back into the cottage."

Missy's bruises had faded more. Her color looked better, too—all good signs.

"You're recovering because of the care you're getting," Nell said.

Missy shrugged. "I hate to be a burden."

"You're not!" Jenny yelled from the kitchen.

"I am," Missy mouthed to them.

The four shook their heads. Nell knew Dare's proposal to Jenny thrilled Missy, but she'd worried where she would fit in the newlyweds' lives. Nothing had changed, however.

"After such a horrible hike, I hope Gage rewarded you with a kiss when you reached your destination," Bria joked.

"No," Nell admitted. "I was nearly hyperventilating from lack of oxygen."

"Classic Nell," Missy joked, and everyone agreed.

"It's true." If everything didn't hurt, Nell would laugh. "When he drove me home, I was in so much pain. I told him not to walk me to the door, said good night, and slid out of his truck. I'm sure he'll never call me again."

And to be honest, that might not be such a bad thing. Gage was so into the outdoors, and Nell...wasn't.

"At least you got a picnic out of it." Despite what had happened to Juliet with her husband, she was still an optimist. "That had to be nice."

"Not really." Nell fought a groan. "Gage wore a backpack, so I assumed it was full of food. It turned out he carried weights because it was a 'training day' for him. He had tucked healthy granola bars, fruit leather packages, and trail mix, only not the kind with chocolate, into the front pocket. Not only was I dying from the exercise but starving."

Her friends either pressed their lips together or bit them.

"Go ahead and laugh," Nell said. One day she would look back and do the same.

Full belly laughter filled the dining room.

At this rate, her mother would play matchmaker for the rest of Nell's life.

"I'm sorry for laughing so hard." Bria raised her coffee. "But that doesn't sound like a fun date."

"It wasn't." Nell took a cup from Juliet. Steam rose, and she blew on it. "The only plus was seeing Gage's backside all day. The view when we reached the top was lovely, which he said it would be, but I needed to rest so I could make it down without falling, so I forgot to take a photo."

"Think of the calories you burned off." Juliet was such an optimist.

"I assumed I would have lost weight from the exercise and lack of food, but this morning I stepped on the scale, and I'd gained two pounds. Life is so unfair."

No one said anything. But what could they say?

"So my big date was a huge fizzle." Nell sipped the coffee that had precisely the right amount of sugar. She had no idea how Juliet remembered that. "What's going on with everyone else?"

"Nothing with me." Missy sounded resigned. "Mario and Peach enjoy having me with them all day, so there's that. But I miss baking. I can't wait to try the new recipes and make the special orders."

"Penelope Jones left me a message." Bria's voice was husky. She cleared her throat. "She's decided not to let us use the inn's kitchen."

Juliet hung her head. "Oh, no. This is my fault."

"No. You aren't involved with the cupcake shop." Selena didn't miss a beat. "This is your grandmother's choice, and it's hers to make."

"Okay." Except Juliet didn't appear convinced.

"Selena's right," Bria said. "Tell Missy and Nell about your party."

Juliet's frown disappeared, and her face brightened. "It was so much fun. I loved dressing up as a princess again. The girls enjoyed themselves. I got a big tip. And two moms asked for cards."

The table cheered.

"Now, tell them about your next-door neighbor," Selena said.

Juliet blushed. "The new vet Charlene and Sabine mentioned lives next to Elise's house. He has guardianship of his niece and texted me this morning about having a birthday party for her."

Selena's eyes twinkled. "I knew he'd get in touch."

"Is he as good-looking as my mom said?" Nell asked.

"Yes," Juliet and Selena said at the same time.

"Roman is attractive," Juliet added.

Selena rolled her eyes. "The new barista guy at Brew and Steep is attractive. The vet is a total looker. Gorgeous."

Uh-oh. Nell hoped her mom wouldn't go into matchmaker mode when she found out about the horrible date with Gage. "He probably won't be single for long, given the lack of dateable guys in Berry Lake."

"That's what your mom said." Juliet grinned. "But don't worry. Charlene told me you won't go out with another doctor, so you have nothing to worry about."

Relief flooded Nell. Perhaps she could wait to tell her mom that she and Gage were over before it began.

"Roman appears interested in Juliet," Selena teased.

Juliet's face turned redder. "Do you want to date a vet, Missy?"

"Nope," Missy answered quickly. "He's all yours."

"Still married," Juliet reminded. "And he'll be a client."

"He can be a friend like Welles, who is my neighbor." Only Nell hadn't seen him around this weekend. She usually caught him going in or out of his place. "He flirts, but it's all in fun."

Juliet shrugged. "My focus is his niece. She lost her parents recently. I want to help her, and putting on her birthday party will be a good start."

"It's perfect," Selena agreed. "For a friendship with both of them. The last thing you need is a relationship. This is the time to work on yourself."

Juliet nodded. "Be sure to tell Charlene."

"You can tell her until you're blue in the face, but she might not hear you." Nell had a lifetime of experience with her mother. "I'll mention it, too, though she doesn't listen much to my sisters and me."

"If we all say something, it has to help," Selena said. "But, Nell, your mom interferes because she loves you."

Nell shrugged. "Sometimes I wish she loved me less."

"Be careful what you wish for." Missy drank her coffee.

Oh, no. Nell cringed. Missy's parents had never forgiven her for marrying Rob. Nell shouldn't have said that. "I'm so sorry."

"Don't worry about it." Missy took another sip. "How are you doing, Selena?"

"Great." Selena's face glowed. "Logan's excited for the season to start. I've taped a few podcasts, and I'm preparing to launch a new program next month. And yesterday afternoon, I bought a place on Berry Lake."

Bria leaned toward Selena. "Wait. What?"

Missy squealed. "You bought a place here!"

"Oh, my!" Juliet covered her mouth with her hands.

Thank goodness. Now the focus would be off Nell's lousy date. She owed Selena a cupcake.

"This is awesome." And it was. "So we want details."

"It's the old McMurray place." Selena lit up. "Good bones, but we'll have to do a complete remodel. The house has to-die-for views. And the property is amazing. It has a private beach, a new dock, and a boathouse."

"I'm so happy you did this." Nell's vision blurred with tears of joy. She and Selena had been inseparable in high school. "You can spend the off-season here."

"That's the plan, and fortunately, if he wants a rink to practice on, there's one not too far away, or we build our own."

Bria stared at her. "I can't believe you just bought it."

"Logan and I have been discussing a vacation home. And now that the Posse is together again, Berry Lake makes the most sense of where we should buy. Yesterday morning, I had a gut feeling I'd find what we were looking for, and I did that afternoon. The property wasn't on the market yet, but the real estate agent was planning to list it soon, so she took me over there, and I knew the second I stepped through the door."

"This is perfect because now everyone has a place to stay here." Missy's excitement was palpable, and Nell agreed.

Bria shifted in her chair before glancing at Selena. A look passed between them.

Uh-oh. Nell had known both women long enough to know when something was up.

"About that…" Bria cradled her cup in her hands. "I may be spending more time up here. A lot more."

Selena patted Bria's hand. Lines creased Bria's forehead.

Nell ignored her soreness and leaned forward. "What's going on?"

"Are you okay?" Juliet asked.

Missy bit her lip. "Tell us, please."

Bria took a breath. "I lost my job."

A pin-drop silence enveloped the room.

"I don't understand." Missy broke the quiet. "You're like a super-CPA. The only things missing are a cape and a calculator attached to your arm."

Juliet nodded. "What happened?"

"Management forced my boss to accept a retirement package, and the firm promoted my ex-boyfriend to take his place. He laid me off when I returned to work on Monday."

"But why?" The question burst from Missy's lips.

Bria shrugged. "A colleague thinks his jealous fiancée wanted me gone. Whatever the circumstances, they're sketchy, so I'm talking to an employment attorney this coming week."

One thing was clear to Nell. This hadn't just happened on Friday. "Why didn't you tell us?"

Bria glanced at Selena before staring into her coffee cup. "None of you could do anything, and we needed to focus on Juliet."

Missy shook her head. "It doesn't work that way."

"No, it doesn't," Juliet agreed.

An I-told-you-so expression crossed Selena's face, but she said nothing.

Selena knowing didn't surprise Nell. That was how it had always been. People came to her for advice as much as they had gone to Elise, but for different issues. Even as a teenager, Selena was destined to be a life coach.

"So what are you going to do?" Nell asked Bria.

"Talk to the attorney." Bria rubbed her hands together. "Find another job."

Missy sat taller. "Move here. You can work anywhere and have Elise's house. You'll also be closer to Dalton."

Bria blushed. "He wants that, too. I'm considering it."

"Don't consider it," Missy urged her. "Do it."

"I might."

"So things are going well with him?" Nell asked.

"It's been a week since we decided to date, but yes, it's wonderful, and seeing him this weekend has shown me how good we are together. I hope... I want this to work. Long-term. He feels the same way."

Missy raised her orange juice. "When it's right, you know. Though with Rob, we were so young. We didn't understand what was happening. We clicked, and that was it."

Selena nodded. "That's how it was for Logan and me."

"I can't remember what it was like with Ezra." Juliet sounded sad. "It was sudden and exciting, and I couldn't believe a handsome, older man would be interested in me. I guess I should have realized it was too good to be true."

"He was the lucky one." Selena was quick to answer. "What feels right can be different depending on the person and their situation."

Given what Juliet said, Nell wanted to add her two cents. "I thought Andrew was it for me. I was sure he was, but what I felt might not be the same right you all mean."

"That means someone else, someone better, is waiting for you." Missy shimmied her shoulders. "With the Posse together more, I bet things fall into place for all of us. Well, except Selena, who already has everything."

Selena said nothing but gave a closed-mouth smile.

That wasn't like her. Nell would have to find out what was up.

"And it's only a matter of time before these get-togethers become regular during the hockey off-season," Missy added.

Selena nodded. "But I'll visit when Logan travels."

"And if I move up here," Bria clarified.

"When," the others said in unison.

They all erupted into laughter, even if it hurt Nell.

Jenny stood in the doorway to the dining room. "You all haven't changed in fifteen years."

"Not really," Bria admitted.

Juliet nodded. "Other than some wrinkles and pounds."

"Lessons learned," Selena added.

It was Jenny's turn to laugh. "I'm sure you're ready to eat. I remember how you used to scarf down all those cupcakes at

Elise's bakery. There's a buffet for you on the breakfast bar, so help yourself. I'm going upstairs to take Dare a donut."

With that, she walked away.

Nell glanced at her friends. She would fix Missy a plate, but first, Nell wanted to say something. "This feels like old times, only better."

"It does," Juliet agreed.

Selena and Bria nodded.

"Cupcake Posse forever." Missy rose. "Now, let's eat—Jenny's right. I'm starving. And before Nell says a word, I'll get my food myself. Thank you very much."

Nell held up her hands, palms facing out. "Did I say anything?"

Missy's gaze narrowed. "No, but you thought it."

Guilty, and based on the look on Missy's face, she knew it.

"What can I say?" Except there was one thing that came to Nell's mind. "Cupcake Posse forever."

🧁 chapter thirteen 🧁

NOT AS MANY customers filled Brew and Steep on Sunday afternoon as there'd been the day before. That made Bria happy as she sat at a round table for two—fewer people to ask her about the cupcake shop. They'd been asking wherever she went in town except at Jenny and Dare's house earlier. Sure, Bria understood the interest, but the fire had only been ten days ago, and she lived in San Diego. It would take time to figure things out.

But something else weighed on her. The instrumental music playing didn't lessen the thoughts swirling in her mind. She'd enjoyed brunch with her friends, but Selena's announcement this morning about purchasing a vacation home made Bria the odd person out.

Move to Berry Lake, and you won't be.

It was possible.

She had the house. A business, well, a fire-damaged one. And a boyfriend who lived not that far away.

Yes, a move made sense except—Berry Lake had no accounting firm.

Bria didn't have to work for someone else. Some accountants struck out on their own, but the stability of a regular paycheck and benefits appealed to her in a way few understood. Life with her dad had been so uncertain growing up, never knowing if there'd be enough money or not. She'd learned the meaning of bankruptcy at far too young an age. And during those times, she didn't blame her mom for taking off when she was two. Bria only wished her mother hadn't left her behind.

Portland had accounting firms, so that was something to look at. The city wasn't that far from Berry Lake, and Dalton lived there.

Dalton.

Chills—the good kind—ran through her.

As if on cue, he waved from where he placed their order. At least two people worked behind the counter, but all Bria saw was Dalton. Even from across the shop, she noticed how his brown T-shirt deepened his hazel eyes. The color changed based on what he wore. Too bad that didn't happen with his emotions. She remembered Aunt Elise's old mood ring. Yes, eyes that acted the same way would be helpful.

He spoke to the barista, an attractive man who had to be the one Selena meant earlier, but the guy wasn't nearly as good-looking as Dalton. The barista must have said something funny because Dalton laughed. The deep, warm tone smacked into her.

As he stepped from the counter, Dalton flicked hair off his forehead with a gesture that would make a fashion photographer rapidly click the shutter button.

Gorgeous.

Butterflies performed an aerial show in her stomach. Not the first time that had happened since they reunited. She associated the flutters with him now. The tingles, too. And the chills. She loved all the reactions.

Funny how she'd hated him for over fifteen years, yet once they'd finally spoken, she could understand why Dalton did what he did. No, that hadn't taken away her heartbreak or hurt, but he'd had his reasons and done what was easiest for him. Even though it had made her life…

No dragging up the past again. Not when the two of them had moved beyond that.

Bria sent a grin his way, and he rewarded her with one in return.

He'd gotten more attractive over the years. She didn't want to stop staring. Not that she could, when her gaze kept traveling to him no matter what she did. A giddiness flowed through her. She didn't remember the last time she'd crushed like a teenager.

Yes, she did—with him when she'd been in high school.

Bria nearly laughed. But she couldn't shake the feeling something would go wrong. So far, nothing had. Their impromptu wine tasting and appetizers at a nearby winery yesterday afternoon had been the best date she'd had in…well, ever.

Today was more chill, and that was fine. All Bria wanted was to spend time with him while her friends had other stuff going on. Selena was on her way to Seattle. Juliet had received an emergency call to help Charlene at an event when someone else failed to show up. Missy needed a nap. And Nell wanted to take another shower to soothe her sore muscles.

Dalton approached the table. He no longer played sports as he had in school, but he still moved with strength and grace. "They'll bring our order to us. You okay?"

"Yes." She glanced around, happy no one appeared to notice her. "A part of me can't believe I'm here with you. This is our third day in a row."

"And we have two more days after this."

"Wait. What?"

"I'll be here until I drive you to the airport."

Excitement surged, but… "That isn't until Tuesday. What about work?"

"I'm working from here. Tanner is still intent on making his plans for Berry Lake happen."

The firm Dalton worked for wanted to buy up property in Berry Lake. Bria recalled the proposal she'd seen when they'd made an offer for the cupcake shop. Tanner's amount was now significantly less after the fire. "Berry Lake two point oh."

Dalton laughed. "Yes. But this is an improved version."

"I kind of like how it is now."

He shrugged and then laced his fingers with hers. "Some is okay. Other parts need upgrading, but as long as he wants me to do some legwork here, I'm good."

"Me, too."

They sat staring into each other's eyes and holding hands. Gold flecks shone in his irises.

Selena and Logan had defined #relationshipgoals for Bria, but she thought she and Dalton appeared to be headed that way, and it was the best feeling in the world. She wanted it to continue—to grow into…more.

"How did brunch go?" he asked.

"Good. Selena surprised us all by saying she bought the McMurray place yesterday."

Dalton straightened. He let go of Bria's hand. "When did the property go on the market?"

"It wasn't yet, but the real estate agent knew it would be soon, so she contacted the owners. It was a lucky break, though I'm guessing Selena would call it something other than luck." The way his eyes grew darker reminded her of when her dad would tell her it was time to move to a new city or state just as soon as she settled into a new school. "What's wrong?"

"Tanner wanted that property." Dalton shifted in his chair as if he were suddenly uncomfortable. "I spoke to the owners last week and asked them to contact me if they wanted to sell."

The plans she'd seen were mainly of Main Street. The concept mentioned a lakeside resort but with no details. "How would that property fit into Berry Lake two point oh?"

Dalton stared at the table. "Tanner is interested in the property."

Not surprising, when his boss only cared about the building that housed the cupcake shop and not the business itself. "The McMurray house isn't an official landmark, but it's well known. The family might not have wanted it torn down."

His intense gaze met Bria's. "Selena won't?"

"She mentioned a remodel." Bria hated that he appeared hurt by not getting to buy the place first. She covered his hand with hers. "You and Tanner are excited about your company's plans for remaking Berry Lake, but not everyone will be on board with your vision. There's history here that shouldn't be erased and replaced with something new to fit an architectural concept better. You don't need to rebuild the entire town."

"True." He rubbed his chin with his free hand. "My boss's enthusiasm is contagious, and most of his plans will be good for the town. But I don't want to disappoint him. He's given me so many opportunities."

"I get that. I'm the same way with my work." Or she had been until Monday. Her stomach clenched. "But you only have so much sway. You're not a magician who can make people do what your boss wants. If Tanner wanted the McMurray property, he should have had you make an offer they couldn't refuse. He didn't, so that's on him for losing it to a cash buyer."

Dalton's face brightened. "You're right."

She squeezed his hand. "Of course, I am."

He laughed.

"Order for Dalton." Bentley Strauss carried a tray with two coffee cups on it. He'd worked at the cupcake shop until the fire. "Cappuccino?"

Bria raised her hand from Dalton's. "That's mine."

"You must be the Americano." Bentley placed both drinks on the table before looking at Bria. "I didn't think you'd return to town so soon. Does that mean something's happening with the cupcake shop?"

"No, I'm here to visit friends." She winked at Dalton. "And my boyfriend."

Dalton grinned wryly, making her heart beat faster. "I was hoping you wouldn't lump me in with the first group."

"So, you found a new job?" she asked Bentley.

"Yes." He lowered the tray. "But I told the manager I'll quit when the cupcake shop reopens."

The teen sounded so confident. Bria wanted to feel that way, too. "I hope it's soon."

"Me, too." He leaned closer. "I prefer working for Missy."

"Good to know." Bria would have to tell Missy. "Have you met Dalton Dwyer?"

Bentley nodded. "You came into the cupcake shop a few times before the fire."

Would her life in Berry Lake be defined by "before the fire" and "after the fire"? She'd assumed "with her aunt" and "without her aunt" would divide it.

She held on to her cup. The warmth seeped into her hand.

"I did." Dalton sipped his coffee.

"Your brother Ian is in the same grade as me. He played well on Friday night. Some of us drove to the game." Bentley glanced at the counter. "I should get back to work. I'm learning how to use the espresso machine. Enjoy your coffees."

He hurried away, conscientious as ever.

She wondered if Missy knew Bentley was working here. "I'm glad he found a new job."

"Seems like a nice kid."

"The best. He closes on the weekends and fills in whenever we need extra help if it's not during school."

"I wonder if he's friends with Ian."

"Did someone say my name?" A young man with similar features, brown hair, and athletic build to Dalton strutted to the table as if he owned the place. His tight T-shirt showed off muscles he must use as the quarterback. Two bigger guys stood behind him like bodyguards. Maybe they were offensive linemen.

"Speak of the devil," Dalton teased. "Bria, meet my youngest brother Ian."

Ian flashed a charming grin, similar to one Dalton used. "Youngest and most handsome brother."

"Nice to meet you," Bria said. "I see you're as modest as Dalton."

Ian winked. "More so."

She bit back a laugh. The teen acted larger than life, the same way Dalton had been fifteen years ago. *It must run in the family.*

He motioned to his friends to go to the counter. "Be there in a minute."

The two giants lumbered past the table.

Ian focused on Dalton. "I didn't know you were in town this weekend."

"You said you were busy, so I didn't want to bother you."

"We had an away game on Friday night."

"Bentley mentioned that to us," Dalton said.

Ian did a double take. "How do you know him?"

"He brought us our coffees," Bria explained. "He also worked at the cupcake shop until the fire."

"The fire. Right." Ian rubbed his nose. "Last night, a friend had a party. It was fire, though not the kind with flames if you know what I mean. Today, I'm staying out of the house. I'm tired of listening to Mom and Remy make wedding plans. Mom asks Sal to pay for everything, and the guy says yes to whatever she wants. It's so pathetic."

Bria sipped her coffee to keep from saying anything. The words wouldn't be nice after what Deena and Sal had done to Sheridan DeMarco and Remy had done to Juliet.

"Wedding plans, huh?" Dalton raised his coffee mug.

Ian rolled his eyes. "She's having some old guy's baby. He must be rich. Otherwise, my sister wouldn't give him the time of day. Remy's just like Mom."

"Is Mom excited about being a grandmother?"

Ian snickered. "She's freaking out and wants to be called Mimi because it sounds younger than Grammy or Nana."

Dalton took a sip of his coffee. "Is she leaving you alone?"

Ian shrugged. "Pretty much. Remy is her focus."

"How's school going?" Dalton asked.

"The same as it was last week. My GPA is good enough to get accepted into most D-One schools except the top tier." He glanced at the counter. "But I can't let it drop, so Sal's paying for a tutor. Mom told him it's cheaper than paying college tuition."

It didn't surprise Bria that Deena would want Sal to pay for Ian's college. According to Aunt Elise, the woman used her husband as her personal bank or charge card. "Do you have a number one school you want to play for?"

"Whatever place is the farthest from her," Ian joked, but the glint in his eyes suggested he was serious. "I took my recruiting trips last fall. I have one offer, but the first signing day isn't until December, so I have time."

"Good luck."

He nodded. "Well, I'm going to hang out with my friends."

"I'll call you before I leave town," Dalton said.

Another nod. "Nice meeting you, Bria. Don't let my family dissuade you about my big brother. Dalton and I are the normal ones."

With that, Ian hurried to the counter.

She watched the teenager give a half nod in acknowledgment of Bentley before jabbing one of his friends. "Ian seems like a good kid."

"He is, and I want him to stay that way. Sports keep him out of the house and give him direction, so Mom hasn't had as much time to ruin him like Owen and Remy."

"Their choice."

"It is." Dalton took a sip. "Enough about my family. Let's not discuss them. I want to enjoy this time with you."

Bria liked the sound of that. She stared over the lip of her mug at him. "What do you have in mind?"

As Dalton walked next to Bria on Main Street, his fingers entwined with hers. The sun peeked from behind a cloud. But that wouldn't change this September afternoon from feeling like a bluebird day. He fought the urge to wrap his arms around her and not let go. But so much had changed in her life recently. Should he tell her how he felt or wait?

It wasn't as if they didn't have time.

They did.

And he would keep telling himself that, even if he wanted to ask her to leave San Diego, forget about Berry Lake, and move to Portland.

With him.

Today.

As they passed the gallery, Bria stopped and peered closer. "That's odd."

"What?"

"There's no artwork on display in the window."

"Whatever was there must have sold."

"I suppose so, but I noticed it last weekend, and nothing's changed. When Sheridan ran things…"

"You don't have to stop."

"It's your family."

He shrugged. "Remy's like my mom. She'll do the bare minimum to get what she wants. Owen works more, but he's still looking for an easy meal ticket."

"I'm so glad Ian has you. And vice versa."

"Me, too." Dalton raised her hand to his mouth and kissed it. "And I'm happy to have you."

"Same."

Penelope Jones walked toward them in a dress with sensible pumps and a cardigan sweater. She carried a reusable grocery bag. The brown purse hanging from her shoulder bounced against her hip.

Her face pinched. "Bria Landon? You're back already. Does this mean an arrest for the arson will happen soon?"

Dalton squeezed Bria's hand.

She appreciated the sign of support. "I don't know what's happening with the investigation. I'm only in town to visit my friends."

The woman's finely arched eyebrows shot up. "Friends, you say?"

"Yes, including Juliet." Bria couldn't stop herself from saying the name.

Penelope harrumphed. "Well, I hope the sheriff does something quickly. I, for one, don't feel safe knowing an arsonist is running around Berry Lake."

"We don't know the arsonist lives in town."

"True, but few come here this time of year, and it might scare tourists away if the person isn't caught."

She was correct about that.

"Good luck with the cupcake shop." Penelope peered closer at Dalton. "You look so much like your father. God rest his soul."

Without waiting for a response, she stepped around them and continued on her way.

Bria glanced over her shoulder. "I'm surprised Penelope didn't bring up my dad."

"You think he's a suspect?"

"A person of interest, at least. I'm assuming I'm one. As is Missy."

"The sheriff asked me where I was. The place I stayed had cameras all over the property for the owners to monitor renters. It's not walking distance, and my car never moved, so that must have taken me off the list since they've never reached out again."

"I hope you don't hear from them."

"They'll find whoever did it."

She nodded. "I keep telling myself it was random. Bad luck. My dad knows stuff about business, so surely, he had to know arson means no insurance coverage and that the building would lose value."

"You think he did it?"

"I don't want to believe it, but he was here the day of the fire and then he took off. Other than his phone call to you, he hasn't reached out to anyone. That seems suspicious."

"You mentioned your dad disappeared in the past."

"Yes, but there wasn't a fire investigation going on those times. I don't want to jump to conclusions because innocent until proven guilty, but it's…hard."

"Don't think about him now." Dalton hated the uneven tone of her voice. He glanced up ahead at the florist shop. That gave him an idea. "Stay right there."

Bria stopped. "Why?"

"No questions." Dalton hurried into the flower shop and paid for a single red rose. He came out and handed it to her. "This is for you."

"So sweet." She sniffed the flower. "Thank you."

"I want to spoil you."

Bria smiled at him. "I'm happy to let you do that."

"I don't want to pressure you, but have you ever considered that you got laid off from your job because you're not supposed to stay in San Diego?"

"You think the universe gave me a push?"

"Selena T might say it was a shove."

Bria laughed. "You *do* listen to her podcasts."

"Every week. And some things sink in."

"Only some." Her lips parted.

That was the only invitation Dalton needed. He brushed his lips over Bria's. "But I've learned enough to know that now that I've found you again, I have everything I need."

"If you keep talking like that, you won't have to spoil me. I'll swoon at your feet."

"If that happens, I'll catch you." He touched his forehead against hers. "I'll do whatever I must until your heart believes what I say."

He placed his mouth against hers. The kiss was slow and tender. He savored the taste of her. His arms wrapped around her, and she came closer to him, never missing a beat with their kiss.

Dalton wanted this.

chapter fourteen

O N WEDNESDAY, JULIET sat in the front room at Events by Charlene with a stack of boxes at her feet. She sliced the tape on the first one and opened the flap to see boxed miniature tea sets.

Charlene walked out wearing the vinyl apron she put on when working with flowers. There was a florist in town for more significant events like weddings, but her boss created arrangements for dinners and showers.

"What do you think of the favors?" Charlene asked.

Juliet removed a tea set from the box. All the pieces were visible through a plastic front: a small teapot, sugar bowl, creamer, cups, and saucers. She didn't know where Charlene found stuff like this, but Juliet knew one thing. "The kids will love them."

"I bought top hats for any boys who might attend as well." Charlene beamed. "Wait until you see the princess items."

"I'm sure they're wonderful."

She came closer and her gaze sharpened with interest, looking more like a mom than a boss. "Nell was over for dinner last night. She said the brunch on Sunday was fun."

"It was." The time with the Posse not only filled Juliet's stomach but also satisfied her soul. Selena was rubbing off on her. Before leaving for Seattle, she'd given Juliet a morning routine to do each day: walk outdoors, do a short gratitude practice, and journal. For the past three days, she found herself more focused and in a better frame of mind. She wasn't sure what Nell had told Charlene, so Juliet didn't want to say too much. "But I miss having Bria and Selena here."

Bria had flown back to San Diego yesterday. Juliet and Butterscotch were adjusting to only the two of them in the house. It wasn't bad, per se, but she enjoyed having her friends there.

"Sounds like Selena will be in town more often. Possibly Bria, too."

"I hope so."

Juliet wouldn't get too excited yet. Bria was waffling over what to do. She'd confided she didn't want Dalton to feel rushed with their relationship if she left San Diego for the Pacific Northwest. Juliet thought he wanted to hurry and dive into the deep end ASAP, given how the guy looked at Bria. Even though Juliet hoped her friend moved to Berry Lake—okay, into this house with her—she'd told Bria to forget about everyone else and decide based on what she wanted. Selena would be proud.

Juliet stacked the tea sets on the coffee table. Usually, she wouldn't work where clients could see, but items for a wedding reception on Saturday night filled every horizontal space. "I'll wrap the boxes in tissue paper. All we have to do is tie them with ribbon when we find out the guest of honor's favorite color and add a personalized tag."

"Perfect."

She opened the next box and peeked inside. "Tea party lollipops."

"Aren't they adorable?"

There were two different styles of cups and teapots. "So cute."

Charlene grabbed a rectangular basket. "Store them in this until we make room for the kid supplies."

Juliet straightened. "We need a space for them?"

Charlene nodded. "The calendar is booking up with tea parties. Our most recent addition is your neighbor."

Heat rose up Juliet's neck, but a party in Berry Lake might help her book more events closer to home. "He texted me about his niece's birthday. It's in October."

"Which is coming up fast. So I saved Roman the second Saturday. You'll have to discuss the details for a theme and location. If he doesn't want to host it at his house, we can use the dining room here."

"You'd do that?"

"I have in the past for baby or wedding showers when other places weren't...available."

Her boss meant times when clients couldn't afford to pay for a rental or might not have enough space in their homes. Despite her meddling and matchmaking, Charlene Culpepper had one of the biggest hearts in Berry Lake. Perhaps the biggest, now that Elise was no longer there.

"Thanks. I'll tell Roman." Even though they lived next door, she hadn't seen him, but she'd texted him to set up a time to talk.

"I have no idea what kind of party his niece wants. I haven't met her yet."

"Some middle schoolers will still be into princesses."

"A few of us thirty-somethings are," Juliet joked.

"There's no age limit on wearing a tiara."

"I hope not." Juliet often wore one while doing housework. She only wished small animals would help her with the chores. So far, Butterscotch remained uninterested in doing his part. Thinking of the cat reminded her of a call she'd received from Sabine's daughter. "I spoke to Sheridan this morning about wedding favors. They decided on a Christmas stocking for each guest. They texted a list of ideas and wanted us to see if we have any suggestions. The price range is two fifty to five hundred dollars each."

"Their wedding will make our year."

It was high-end with no set budget. "Yes, but knowing Sheridan found a great guy like Michael is everything."

Sheridan had been through so much with her dad, Sal DeMarco, and his second wife, Deena—Remy's mom—and deserved things to go right in her life.

"You mean a great *wealthy* man," Charlene joked.

"That, too." Michael Patterson had made his money through some sort of investment. Not bad for a guy in his late twenties. Sheridan had mentioned her father and his new family weren't invited to the wedding in December. That was a relief. "Such a cute couple."

"They are." Charlene glanced out the front window. An odd expression formed on her face. "Have you seen your grandmother?"

"For a moment on Monday, at Brew and Steep." Juliet forced herself not to shiver. "We didn't speak, but the chilly glare she shot my way gave me goose bumps. Why?"

Charlene clasped her hands together before tipping her head to stare at the ceiling.

Her boss was procrastinating. That meant she'd seen something out the window. She'd done the same thing during a meeting with a client who'd wanted to serve hot dogs and potato chips at her wedding. Charlene had convinced her to go with a sausage food truck.

Juliet placed the rest of the lollipops in the basket and stood.

Ezra's car was parked in front of Charlene's building, but he and Remy were crossing Main Street toward the Huckleberry Inn.

Juliet squinted to get a better view. Remy carried lilies. One of Grandma's favorites, which Ezra knew.

But he'd never brought her grandmother flowers before. That was Juliet's responsibility. So maybe this was Remy's idea? Only, why buy lilies? Coincidence?

Before Ezra and Remy reached the porch steps, the inn's door opened. Penelope Jones stepped out. She wore the lace apron Juliet's grandfather had purchased in Germany. Her grandmother's happiness was clear from across the street, even with the others in front of her. The woman glowed like a spotlight and looked a decade younger.

Juliet's chest tightened. Seeing her grandmother with the two people who had betrayed her hurt. She rubbed the spot over her heart.

Her grandmother hugged both of them. She stepped away and appeared to touch Remy's flat stomach.

Juliet's mouth dropped open.

Grandma rarely minced words, but Juliet hadn't realized when her grandmother asked about her having children last week, there'd been more to it than a general question—she wanted to be a great-grandmother. The baby's parents, or who'd been hurt by the conception, didn't matter to her.

Charlene touched Juliet's shoulders. "Are you okay?"

Juliet should've looked away, but her gaze remained glued to the porch. She didn't think the pain in her heart could get any worse, yet it did. She had wanted kids, but Ezra had said no. Now… "I'm not sure whether to laugh or cry. It hurts, yet a part of me is numb."

"Numb is good." Charlene angled Juliet so she couldn't look out the window. "Any fool can see Ezra's trying to suck up to your grandmother. He'll do whatever it takes to make sure she remains on his side."

Juliet forced herself not to glance toward the inn. They would be inside by now. "I don't know about that. He's been nice to my grandmother, but they aren't close."

Not like she and Grandma had been.

"They might not have been close before, but he spends lots of time with her now."

"I wonder why."

"He wants the Huckleberry Inn."

That made no sense. "My grandmother would never sell it to him. Developers have tried to buy it several times over the years."

"Oh, sweet child. You see only the best in people. That's what I love about you." Charlene hugged her. "Why did Ezra want to move to Berry Lake?"

"After my grandmother fell and was hurt a year and a half ago, he thought I should live closer to her."

"Very altruistic." Charlene rolled her eyes. "Did he give you any other reason?"

"No, he knew I missed her. Why?"

"Rumor has it, Ezra only moved here to make sure Penelope left you and him the Huckleberry Inn."

"Left?"

"When she died."

Juliet's mouth dropped open. "I've never seen her will or even asked about it. That's…"

"Ezra. The man is devious."

That was a valid point. "He must want my grandmother to cut me out if I'm named and leave it all to him."

Or the baby.

"Yes, but he hasn't managed it yet. Penelope hasn't contacted the Carpenters, and that's who handles the inn's legal affairs."

Juliet didn't know that, but she had no reason to doubt her boss's knowledge. Somehow, Charlene Culpepper kept tabs on everything that happened in Berry Lake, whether it occurred in public or behind closed doors.

"I have a feeling it's only a matter of time," she added. "Perhaps, you should—"

"My grandmother is free to do what she wants with the inn." Juliet didn't hesitate to interrupt, even if it was impolite. But she was firm about this. "She can leave it to Ezra. I won't try to change her mind. Not that I could if I tried. She doesn't want to hear anything I have to say."

Her grandmother hadn't drawn a line in the sand. She'd erected a stone wall—one that Juliet wouldn't attempt to scale. She no longer wanted to peer over the top either, something she felt she'd been doing for days.

No more.

Her grandmother had recently called Juliet "the light of her life." Well, she'd flicked off that switch fast. Whether it was the divorce or a baby not even related to her or a combination of the two, Grandma's feelings for Juliet had changed.

So be it.

"I'm finished with her." She no longer had a grandmother, but it would be okay because she had her family of the heart—the Posse, Charlene, and Sabine. Juliet lifted her chin. "It hurts and probably will for a while, but I won't let Penelope Jones get to me again."

On Thursday afternoon, Juliet walked home from work. It was only four o'clock, but nothing more needed to be done today, so Charlene had called it a day. The weather varied in the fall, but Juliet only wore a sweater today. The temperature would drop when October hit, but she would enjoy the sunshine as long as it stuck around.

Two kids riding bikes waved.

As she waved to them, a warmth flowed through her.

The children, the tall trees providing a canopy of branches over the sidewalks on either side of the street, the neighbors watering their yards and plants, the welcome autumn flags, and the leaves changing colors were signs of life. At her old house with Ezra, no one played outside or even rode bikes. The only people she regularly saw out were lawn maintenance crews.

She preferred this neighborhood with the older, smaller houses. The location, so close to Main Street, reminded her of growing up at the Huckleberry Inn. That was no longer part of her life, but the memories had been good ones, so she would hold on to those and let go of the rest.

"Juliet!"

She glanced at the house next to Elise's. Sunrays surrounded Roman, making him appear otherworldly as if he were a demigod from a movie.

Stunning.

Her mouth went dry.

It might be hanging open, too, so she pressed her lips together.

He wasn't alone. A girl with glasses, straight hair, and clothes two sizes too big stood beside him. She clutched a book tightly against her chest and hunched her shoulders as if that would make her invisible.

That must be Katie. Juliet's heart ached.

She walked over to them. "Hello."

"I got your text, but I've been so busy I didn't have time to reply." His words came out fast and flustered.

"There's no rush." Juliet focused her attention on the girl. "How are you doing?"

"This is my niece." Roman placed his hand on her shoulder. "Katie, this is…"

"Juliet." She extended her arm. "It's so nice to meet you."

Katie hesitated until she reluctantly held out her hand to shake, but she said nothing.

Juliet wanted to hug the girl. Instead, she shook hands and let go quickly. "I hope you're enjoying Berry Lake."

Katie shrugged. She held the book in front of her like a shield.

"I hear you have a birthday coming up. Are you excited?" Juliet asked.

Another shrug.

Roman dragged his hand through his hair. Lines around his mouth tightened. "I mentioned you do parties, and we would talk to you about doing hers."

There was no time like the present. Butterscotch didn't eat until later, and late afternoon was all about his naps. "Do you have any ideas about what kind of party you want?"

Katie shook her head. Her knuckles were white around her book.

Juliet decided to try a different tactic. "Do you enjoy reading?"

"Books are everything." Katie's face lit up. "I'd rather read than do anything, especially talk to other people. Books are the best friends ever."

Roman's please-help-me expression told Juliet he felt over his head with his niece. "Have you been to the library yet?"

Katie perked up. "There's one here?"

Roman mouthed a *thank you*.

"Yes," Juliet said. "It's a decent-size for a small town, but if they don't have a book you want, you can request it from another library, and they'll send it."

Katie's eyes widened. "That is so cool. Can we go, Uncle Roman?"

"Sure." He sounded as relieved as he looked.

"Now?" The hope in the single word was palpable.

Roman hesitated.

"If your uncle is busy, I'll take you." All Juliet had to do tonight was feed Butterscotch dinner. She would love to do something with Katie. "If he doesn't mind."

He rubbed his chin. "Why don't the three of us go?"

Katie nodded enthusiastically. "Please come with us."

"Of course." The girl had been disappointed enough. "Let me run inside and check on my cat, Butterscotch, and then we can go. Will that work?"

Katie lowered her book. "Yes!"

One side of Roman's mouth curved in a lopsided grin. "You're calling him 'my cat' already?"

Oops. Juliet hadn't realized she'd said that. "Well, I take care of him, so that makes him mine. At least for now."

But she hoped longer. She was attached to the orange furball.

"Cats choose you," Katie said, surprising them. "My mom told me that's how we ended up with Smalls. That Smalls picked us."

"That's true," Roman agreed. "Some breeds, like Siamese, pick one person within a family to attach themselves to."

"Smalls is a domestic tabby, right, Uncle Roman?"

"Yes, she is. And those are some of the best cats in the world," he answered.

Juliet nodded. "Your uncle would know since he's a veterinarian."

"My mom was a vet, too." Katie sounded proud, but her gaze dropped to the ground, and the book came up to her chin again.

Roman sighed, but Juliet didn't miss the way his eyes gleamed or his rapid blinking. Both of them were grieving.

"Give me a minute." She wasn't the light of Penelope's world any longer, but that didn't mean Juliet couldn't shine her light on these two. "I'll be right back."

At the library, Roman stood to the side. Katie and Juliet sat on the floor in front of a bookshelf. He doubted they knew he was there because he was supposed to be finding a book in the adult section. But he hadn't wanted to leave his niece. It wasn't that he didn't trust Juliet or being in a public building. Katie herself made him want to stay.

And so did Juliet.

He told himself that it was because she had a way with Katie. His niece's sad face and the weight of whatever she carried on her shoulders appeared to be gone. She finally looked like a happy eleven-year-old, and parts of Marlena shone through her daughter.

Roman missed his sister. He might work medical miracles with animals, but he was clueless about his niece. That explained why her cat Smalls was the most well-adjusted in the family.

Yet, for the first time in months, the knot in his stomach loosened.

Katie removed a book from the bottom shelf, looked at the cover, and read the blurb. "What do you think?"

"Sounds interesting." Juliet gave Katie her full attention. "I love anything with princesses."

"The story sounds good." Katie studied the book as if it contained the secret to potty training puppies. "I'll add this one to the maybe pile."

That was when he noticed two stacks. One was taller than the other.

"I brought a tote bag, so we'll use that to carry whatever ones you borrow."

"Thank you." Katie stared at the stacks. "I read fast. Do you think we can come back when I need more books?"

"Of course." Juliet didn't miss a beat. "Your uncle has my number, or I'm right next door."

"Convenient."

"Yes, it is." Juliet pulled out a book. Whatever she saw made her return it to the shelf. "That one doesn't sound good."

Katie nodded, even if she had been busy checking out other books.

His niece had finally made a connection.

Meeting Juliet Soon-to-be-Jones gave him hope. A few minutes in her presence had transformed Katie from a sulky, silent, sending-judgy-glares girl to an excited-bouncing-on-her-toes, carefree kid. Juliet made him feel good, too.

But, despite being in the middle of a divorce, she wore her wedding rings.

Talk about a huge red flag.

He'd learned his lesson about dating a soon-to-be divorcee the hard way and had an engagement ring to show for it. Speaking of that, Roman didn't know why he still had it.

A symbol of his stupidity, perhaps?

He should sell it and take Katie on a vacation somewhere—Anaheim or Orlando. She might prefer that to Hawaii or Mexico. And he could splurge without guilt. Her college savings account had enough to pay for an Ivy League education if she got accepted. After selling the practice, half of the proceeds had gone into a trust fund for Katie, too. He'd taken his share and the money from selling his townhome and would use that to pay off his loans from vet school and as a down payment on a house in Berry Lake. He hadn't rented in years, but that made sense until they decided where they wanted to live—in town, on the lake, or on the outskirts. The place they rented was fine for now, especially with Juliet next door.

She held a book of fables. "So, your birthday?"

Katie's posture suggested an exaggerated eye roll. "I don't need a party."

"Your uncle thought you might want one."

She stared at the books on the shelf. "This is important to him, isn't it?"

"He wants to make your day special."

Roman hadn't meant to eavesdrop, but he enjoyed watching Juliet. Still, he took a step away from them.

Katie's shoulders hunched in a posture that was becoming way too familiar. "My mom said birthdays should be the best days ever, but she's dead."

"I'm sorry. I know those are words people say when they don't know what else to tell you. But I am sorry. My mom and dad died when I was thirteen, and I wouldn't wish that on anyone."

Katie's gaze jerked to Juliet's. "Me either. It sucks."

"It does."

Roman released the breath he'd been holding. He didn't want to stay here without them knowing he was near enough to hear them.

He came closer to them. "How's it going?"

Katie pointed to the stacks. "Juliet's helping me pick out books."

Of course, she was.

Juliet was a natural with Katie. Not only because she'd been orphaned at a young age. The woman didn't talk down to Katie but listened. He'd known about his niece's fascination with stories, yet he'd never once thought to take her to the library—in Berry Lake or Missoula. Yet, Juliet had the first time she'd met Katie.

Juliet moving next door the day after they'd moved in might be nothing more than coincidence. Or could it be something more?

He stared at Katie, seeing her mother in her green eyes, in the smile that should come out more often, and in her love of reading. Marlena had been four minutes and twenty-eight seconds older. From the time they were little, she promised to watch out for him.

Did that include beyond the grave?

An odd thought, given he and woo-woo weren't well-acquainted.

Yet Katie needed a mother figure, and he needed someone, too.

Juliet was beautiful, kind, caring—the total package.

Except she was still married. But once her divorce...

You just met her.

That wasn't all Marlena would say.

You promised not to jump headfirst into another relationship and propose before you got to know someone.

All true. Roman's sister had known him better than anyone.

"I'm having a book birthday." Katie tilted her head. "Even though I'm not sure what that is."

"I usually do tea parties. Some are themed, so we can do that but with a book. An example would be to use a classic novel like *Alice's Adventures in Wonderland.*"

Kate stared at her. "That might be fun, except don't you do princess tea parties?"

"I told Katie I saw you in your princess costume," he said.

"I do those, too. Would you like a princess one?"

Katie shrugged, but even Roman could tell the idea piqued her interest.

"A princess tea party works for me." Based on what Charlene said, he wouldn't have to do much but put together a guest list and pay. She'd even offered to host it at her building so no cleaning on his part.

"Yes, but..." Juliet stared at the two stacks of books. "What if we have a literary princess tea party?"

Katie rose on her knees, visibly excited. "What's that?"

"Guests come dressed as their favorite princess from a book," Juliet explained. "It can be a fairy tale, a classic novel, or something more contemporary. That would give people a wide range to choose from."

Katie's narrow shoulders sank. "I don't have any friends here."

Roman had only seen messages from her friends in Missoula on the tablet she used. He hadn't thought about guests, only the party.

His chest tightened.

This might not have been a good idea.

"Not a problem." Juliet's calm demeanor would soothe even a frightened puppy. "Invite your class."

Katie wrinkled her nose. "Not the boys."

"Okay, just the girls," Juliet suggested.

Roman tried not to laugh. "Does that mean I don't get to come?"

Her look was so much like her dad it was eerie. "You're a man, not a boy."

"Oh, right." Roman grinned.

He hoped Juliet saw him as a man, too. Possibly the man for her.

chapter fifteen

SITTING ON JENNY and Dare's living room couch instead of lying in their guest bedroom thrilled Missy. Unfortunately, that only showed how low she'd set the bar for her life. Nell and Jenny, however, were going overboard at the moment. Sure, they were only looking out for her, but her sister-in-law and her best friend both needed to dial down their concern.

"It'll be okay." Worry appeared in the lines on their faces and their tense postures. Missy wanted them to relax. "They just want to talk to me again. No big deal."

"Not talk." Jenny paced across the floor. She wrung her hands. "The sheriff and fire investigator have more questions for you, which is a big deal. Or it could turn into one, depending on your answers. You need a lawyer present. The Sixth Amendment—"

"Please don't feel the need to pull out the Constitution." Missy wasn't trying to be a pain, but seriously, she rescued animals and put any bug she found in the cottage outside. She was the least likely person to set a fire.

"Let's turn on one of those crime dramas you watch because Jenny's right." Nell sat in a chair with a drooling Briley on her lap. "We know you didn't do it, but having a lawyer there during the questioning can't hurt."

Missy shook her head. A TV show wasn't real life. She didn't know the fire investigator well, but she trusted the sheriff. Royal Dooley had come into the cupcake shop every day. He would watch out for Missy the same way her boss had. "I have nothing to hide."

"It doesn't matter whether or not you did it." Jenny's voice rose an octave. "Emotions are high. People in town, including Mayor Prescott, want the arsonist brought to justice. Penelope Jones has been making a fuss over no one being arrested yet. If there's a rush to justice—"

"Do I look like an arsonist?" Missy wasn't stubborn, or maybe she was. The idea anyone would think she did it was ridiculous. "I'm a thirty-two-year-old widow. People in town placed bets on whether or not I'd kill myself nine years ago. Most still pity me, not see me as a criminal with a flame fetish."

Jenny rubbed her neck. "You're the only person they can place at the cupcake shop."

"Because I was asleep in the office upstairs. Yes, I'm the one who cleaned out the storage room earlier and put the stuff in the table area, and that likely fueled the fire, but it was bad timing. Nothing nefarious. I called nine-one-one and returned inside, but not to destroy proof of what I'd done. I wanted Elise's journal, which Welles found under my shirt. I was also injured." She raised her foot to emphasize her last point. "Those things prove I didn't do it."

"Common sense doesn't always matter." Nell tapped the tip of Briley's nose. "If there's enough circumstantial evidence, a person can be arrested."

"No one will arrest me."

"Fine. I'm overprotective. I plead guilty to that charge." Jenny's words rushed out. "But please, for my sake, let me call the Carpenters and see if one of them is free to be here with you."

Missy had nothing against the three generations of attorneys, who always left generous tips in the jar at the cupcake shop, but… "They aren't criminal lawyers."

Nell raised Briley in the air, and the little girl squealed. "They're still attorneys."

Missy glared at her friend, but she didn't like how the worry in Jenny's voice kept ramping up. "I guess it can't hurt."

"I'll call them." Jenny hurried out of the living room as if she feared Missy would change her mind.

Missy blew out a breath. If only she could get rid of her problems, the frustrations, and other people's worry with an exhale. "This is silly. Now I'm going to have to pay for an attorney I don't need."

"Not silly, and you won't see a bill."

Her muscles bunched. "I don't want Jenny to pay."

"She can afford it."

Yes, but that wasn't the point. Family or not, Jenny had done enough for Missy. She needed to stand on her own two feet. Well, her one healthy one.

Briley cooed, and Nell made a funny face at the baby. "Everyone knows you didn't do it, but you need to be smart about this. It's your future at stake."

"A jobless future."

Nell shook her head. "The cupcake shop will reopen, but I understand why you feel that way. Did you speak to Selena when she was in town?"

"No, I told Selena we'd talk after I recovered. She needed to support Juliet and Bria while she was here. I'm fine. Nothing is happening with the bakery or with me for a while."

Nell studied Missy. "You don't have to wait."

"There's no rush. Really." Missy stared at her foot. "But I will speak with her."

"Good, because you promised."

"And you won't let me forget that."

"Nope."

Nell was such a caring friend. Missy needed to remember she and her sister-in-law were only trying to help. "I did something productive after everyone left the brunch the other day."

Nell had Briley stand. "What?"

"Jenny helped me research options for baking without having a commercial space. She did the computer work and printed out stuff for me. Turns out, you can get a cottage food permit. I emailed Bria all the info, but we should be able to use my kitchen in the guest cottage, not only for special orders but items to sell directly to customers through the website or by a form."

"That's great."

"It is." Missy hoped Bria agreed. "You pay a fee and fill out a huge multi-page form that may require your firstborn child. I gave up reading after page four. If the application passes, then an inspector needs to visit and sign off on everything, so it can take six weeks or so. But at least the Berry Lake Cupcake Shop could be back in business sooner rather than later."

"That sounds great."

Missy nodded. "You can't have pets in the house when preparing or packaging the food, so I'd have to bring Peach and

Mario over here while I bake. But Jenny and Dare won't mind, and the cats can play with Yeti and Briley."

Nell's gaze narrowed. "You did this all on Sunday?"

"Once I had the info, a plan clicked into place. My concussion is much better. I only get occasional headaches now. Do you know how boring it is not to do anything?"

"No, and I would enjoy lying around and doing nothing for a couple of weeks."

"Be careful what you wish for."

"I suppose you're right, especially if it meant staying with my mom," Nell said.

"Wait. I thought Charlene was leaving you alone."

"Oh, she is, but when my mom finds out Gage hasn't called…"

Missy's lips parted. "He's ghosting you?"

"Well, I haven't contacted him." Nell stared at Briley. "My muscles needed a cooling-off period."

Missy laughed. "I'm sorry."

"Don't be. If it's meant to happen, it will."

Jenny returned. "Any lawyer may be present. It doesn't have to be a criminal attorney. Elias is happy to come over and be here as a friend."

"I don't have to pay him?" Missy asked.

"He's not officially representing you, just looking out for your best interests for me."

She could handle that. "Thanks."

"But I doubt he'd mind if you baked him some cupcakes." Jenny didn't miss a beat. "He's missing them as much as Nell."

"As soon as I'm back on my feet."

"I get the first dozen," Nell reminded. "You promised them to me at the hospital."

Oh, right. The conversation came back to Missy. "Fine, Elias can get the second dozen."

"I'm off today." Nell danced with Briley on her lap. "I can stick around and play with this pretty girl during the meeting."

"Thank you." Jenny sounded relieved, which was better than her previous worry.

This was a lot of trouble to go through for a few questions, but Missy's friends all seemed happier, so she would go along with them. For now.

Two hours later, Missy still sat in Jenny and Dare's living room. The only difference? It was more crowded now. Jenny was next to her, but Nell had retreated upstairs with Briley. A tray of cookies sat with cups and a pitcher of iced tea on the table.

Elias Carpenter was in the chair where Nell had been earlier. He wasn't that old—late twenties if Missy remembered correctly—and he looked more like someone's younger brother or friend in his khakis and navy polo shirt. No one would think Elias was here as an official lawyer, especially without a briefcase or even a pen and legal pad. Instead, he held a glass of water in one hand and a cookie in the other.

That put Missy at ease. She didn't want anyone to believe she was lawyering up. Despite what Jenny and Nell thought, Missy thought that would make her look guilty.

Sheriff Dooley sat on the loveseat with a small, spiral notebook next to him. His bald head gleamed, and he patted his forehead with a handkerchief. "We appreciate you taking the time to answer a few more questions."

"Not a problem." It wasn't for Missy. "What more did you want to know?"

Reggie Lemond, the forty-something fire investigator, sat in a chair. His military haircut reminded her of the time Rob had shaved off his curly locks when he became a Marine. He readied his pen and pad of paper. "Can you go over what happened the night of the fire once more?"

She'd told them at the hospital, but maybe they thought now that her concussion was better, she would remember something different. "A delivery of supplies arrived on Thursday afternoon. I realized the storage room had gotten to be a mess, so after we closed, I took everything out so I could reorganize it."

"Did you lock the front door when you closed the bakery that night?" Reggie asked.

"Yes, I was the only one there. Sometimes another employee will close, but that night I used my key."

He scribbled something. "Go on."

"When I realized I wanted to clean the storage room, I moved the supplies into the seating area. I sorted and organized every-thing there."

Reggie tapped his pen on his pad. "Everything means what?"

"Baking ingredients, liners, boxes, inserts for boxes, bags," she rattled.

He wrote more. "The ingredients include flour?"

She nodded. "Flour, sugar, salt, baking powder, vanilla, and lots more. Do you need to know the rest?"

Sheriff Dooley shifted positions. His notepad fell off his leg, but he caught it. "I don't think that's necessary. Do you agree, Reggie?"

The man nodded. "So what happened after you moved everything?"

"I wiped down the shelves, swept, and mopped. It was time to feed my cats, so I ran home to do that, eat, and change clothes. I returned to the cupcake shop. I thought about moving the stuff into the storage closet, but I was worn out, so I worked on recipes instead."

"Where did you work on them?" Reggie asked.

As if there were a desk in the kitchen or even a chair, but she refrained from saying that. "In the office. I lost track of time. Jenny texted me after midnight. I told her I was staying the night there so I could get an earlier start in the morning on the supply closet."

Reggie's mouth slanted. "Do you normally sleep at the cupcake shop?"

"No, but I've done it a few times, There's a daybed."

"Did you hear anything?"

"I had music playing, so no."

He studied his notes. "When did you notice the fire?"

Missy shivered. "I noticed the smoke first. The scent hung in the air. I thought I'd left the oven on."

The sheriff leaned forward. "Have you ever done that before?"

"No." Missy half laughed. "Elise would have killed me if I did that."

"Sounds like Elise." His expression and tone were bittersweet.

"So you smelled smoke?" Reggie pressed.

He'd heard this already, and Missy didn't enjoy thinking about that night. But she hoped this would be the last time she had to go over it. "I did, so I headed to the kitchen, but nothing was on. I returned upstairs and fell asleep. Something loud woke me up. It was the smoke detector. I grabbed my phone and ran downstairs barefoot. There was smoke, but no flames. I turned on the light to see smoke coming from the front of the shop. I looked out there. The smoke was heavier. Flames lit up the eating area, where I'd put stuff. I thought about grabbing the fire extinguisher, but I called nine-one-one instead."

Her throat was dry. She reached for her iced tea and sipped. Jenny picked up the pitcher and refilled Missy's glass.

Elias ate a cookie.

"Take your time," the sheriff said kindly.

Missy took another sip. That helped.

Reggie tapped his foot. "Do you remember what color the flames were?"

"Orange and yellow? I don't remember."

"What about the smoke?"

"It was dark, but it looked white or gray."

"Did the fire smell?" he continued.

"Like smoke." She didn't know what these questions would tell him. "I headed out the door to the alley. I must have pushed the door all the way open so it caught because it didn't close. That's how I got inside the bakery to get Elise's journal."

Reggie kept writing until he flipped the page. "Was anyone else in the alley?"

Missy shook her head.

"Did anything seem abnormal or out of place?" he asked.

"I didn't notice. My mind was on what was happening inside the bakery, not outside it."

Reggie gazed intently at her. "What happened?"

She closed her eyes as memories assaulted her senses. "I remembered Elise's journal and headed inside. The dispatcher told me to stop, but I continued up the stairs. I grabbed the journal and tucked my phone in my pocket. On my way down, the smoke was worse. The floor seemed hotter. I couldn't see. It got bad fast. I shoved the journal under my shirt to protect it. I must have fallen because I ended up on my stomach in the kitchen. It was hard to breathe. I tried to get up, but my head hurt too much. I don't remember anything else until I woke up in the hospital on Saturday."

"What about your keys?" Reggie asked.

Missy blinked. "Keys?"

Sheriff Dooley grunted. "Give her a minute to regroup, Reggie. This isn't easy to go over."

The fire investigator nodded. "Your keys to the bakery."

Elias grabbed another cookie. "Missy told you she left with only her phone and the journal. Can you tell me the significance of her keys?"

Reggie stared at his spiral notebook. "Bria Landon said she, Missy, Heidi Parker, Bentley Strauss, and Charlene Culpepper had keys to the bakery."

"That's right," Missy agreed. "There's also a spare in the office in case someone works a different shift and needs a key to close."

Reggie leaned forward. "Was the spare there the night of the fire?"

"I don't know because I had mine." Missy tried to picture it on the hook by the desk, but she came up blank. "As for my keys, they are in the office. Probably on the desk since I used them to get into the bakery after dinner."

"Can I see them?" Reggie asked.

Hadn't he heard what she said? "I don't have them."

Reggie's gaze darkened. "Where are they?"

She started to speak, but Jenny touched her hand, so Missy pressed her lips together.

"Missy has established she left her keys in the office, and that's where the spare is kept, too." Elias stretched his legs out in front of him. "If you want them, I suggest the investigation team search for them at the site. Do you have another topic you'd like to ask about?"

Reggie glanced at the sheriff.

Sheriff Dooley snorted before grabbing a cookie. "Don't look at me. You're the one who wanted to talk to her."

Reggie was only trying to do his job, but this round of questioning felt different compared to the last one. He seemed to be implying she was guilty of something. She was grateful Jenny had asked Elias to be there and for Nell watching Briley. Missy would make cupcakes for Sheriff Dooley, too. But none for the fire investigator.

"There's a reason for my questions. Only Missy's key and the spare are unaccounted for," Reggie said finally. "But whoever set the fire had access to the bakery and/or possessed a key. You were inside the bakery with both keys."

He thinks I did it.

As Missy straightened, every muscle tensed. "I—"

"The questioning is over with, gentlemen." Elias stood. "If you need to speak with Missy again, please go through my office."

Reggie made a beeline to the front door and outside.

Sheriff Dooley took his time. He tipped his head toward her. "Reggie's under a lot of pressure to solve this. I'm sorry, Missy."

With that, he left and closed the door behind him.

"I don't believe this. Reggie thinks I did it." Missy looked from a teary-eyed Jenny to Elias, whose jaw jutted forward. "What am I going to do?"

chapter sixteen

TUESDAY AFTERNOON, JULIET'S phone rang. She glanced at the name on the screen—Grandma—and the phone slipped from her fingers.

It clattered onto the kitchen floor.

The teakettle whistled from the stove.

She jumped.

Her hand trembled, but she turned off the stove, picked up the phone, and accepted the call.

"Hello?" Her voice sounded weak, but the call caught her off guard. It shouldn't. For all she knew, her number had been pressed by mistake.

"I need a favor."

Penelope Jones rarely wasted words, but Juliet would have preferred a greeting of some sort given how their last conversation went. But she wouldn't automatically say yes as she had in the past. No way would she agree to anything involving the upcoming baby shower. "What?"

Silence filled the line.

Surprisingly, Juliet didn't care. Not much anyway. She reminded herself she wasn't the one who called and waited for a response.

"Mrs. Vernon needs your help."

A heaviness pressed against Juliet's shoulders. She'd hoped... *Stop.*

She took a deep breath. Mrs. Vernon had been in the hospital recently. None of her kids lived in Berry Lake, so in the past, Juliet had brought her items from the market when it was too icy for her to go out. "Should I go to her house?"

"No. Are you home now?"

"Yes. I'll be here all evening." *In case you want to come over, too.*

Juliet gripped her phone. She fought the urge to plead her case once again, but she didn't want to get her hopes up, only to have them dashed one more time.

"I'll pass it on." The line disconnected.

No thank you.

No how are you?

No goodbye.

She shouldn't have expected anything different, but perhaps whatever this favor Mrs. Vernon needed would soften her grandmother's heart toward Juliet. *And the tooth fairy will leave a million dollars under my pillow.* Those odds might be better than the ones involving Penelope Jones.

But on the off chance she accompanied her long-time friend, Juliet tidied the living room. Not that it was messy. The only things out of place were two of Butterscotch's toys. She put those into the basket under the end table the way she did each night before bed so he could take them out and play with them. Yes, they already had routines.

Juliet ran her finger over the edge of the TV.

No dust.

She refolded a throw blanket and arranged it differently on the back of the chair.

"That should do it," she said to the cat stretched out on the top of the couch.

Ding-dong.

Juliet walked to the door with measured steps, trying to calm her nerves. She'd known Mrs. Vernon her entire life. No big deal.

Except it felt like an enormous deal.

The "favor" might be a test. It wouldn't be the first time that happened. But now Juliet was worried. If she did the right thing, would everything be forgiven? Or would she be given points to redeem herself?

Not that she'd done anything wrong.

Her fingers tightened around the knob, and she opened the door. Only Mrs. Vernon wasn't standing there. It was her youngest daughter. "Sheila?"

"Hey." Sheila was in her mid-forties if Juliet remembered correctly. A box sat next to her on the porch along with a small dog crate. "I can't thank you enough. My mom has been beside herself about what would happen to her beloved Lulu. The two of them are in the car saying goodbye. It's been a hard day."

"Where's your mom going?"

"To an assisted-living center." Sheila picked up the crate by the handle and gave it to Juliet. "Mom needs more care than I can provide. The assisted-living center is only a few minutes from my house in Vancouver. My husband is allergic to dogs, so we can't take Lulu. None of my brothers or sisters want the dog. I was about to call Sabine and surrender her to the rescue when your grandmother said you'd be happy to take Lulu."

Juliet's stomach dropped. "When did my grandmother say that?"

"At lunchtime." Sheila carried in the box. "She came to tell my mom goodbye. They've been friends for over sixty years."

That was typical of Penelope Jones, who would do anything for other people but not… Juliet's fingers gripped the handle.

Her grandmother hadn't asked for a favor. She'd volunteered Juliet to make a lifelong commitment—at least for the rest of Lulu's life. Sheila appeared so relieved. And Mrs. Vernon had always been so sweet to her.

How could Juliet say no?

She couldn't.

Which Penelope knew.

"Where do you want this?" Sheila asked.

"On the floor." Swallowing a sigh, Juliet set the crate next to the door. She glanced at Butterscotch and hoped the cat forgave her.

"I have a doggy bed and a few other things in the car." Sheila headed onto the porch. "I'll get those while my mom tells you about Lulu."

Juliet closed the front door behind her so Butterscotch wouldn't get out. She walked to the silver minivan parked in the driveway. The hatch was open, and Sheila removed items from the back.

Mrs. Vernon, with a headful of loose gray curls and sad blue eyes, sat in the passenger seat. She clutched a little white dog to her chest.

Juliet forced a smile. "Hi, Mrs. V."

"Hello, Juliet." With a tear-filled gaze, Mrs. Vernon kissed the top of the dog's head. "I told Lulu to be a good girl for you."

"I'm sure she will be." Juliet couldn't believe she'd been put into this position. Charlene might have brought over Butterscotch, but the cat had lived there. Cats were also self-sufficient. Juliet knew nothing about dogs. "I can send photos of her, and if you're in town, please visit anytime."

Sheila mouthed a thank-you before slamming the hatch close. She had a dog bed tucked under her arm and a tote bag overflowing with what appeared to be stuffed animals and toys.

Juliet hoped Bria didn't mind.

"Thank you, dear." Mrs. Vernon opened the passenger door, kissed Lulu once more, and handed over the dog wearing a pink collar with a matching leash attached. "I usually cook her dinner. I put the recipe and other instructions in the bag. Lulu eats a half cup of kibble for breakfast and gets a dental bone in the morning and a treat before bedtime. She'll beg for human food, but it's not good for her tummy. She loves children and has bitten nothing but her chew toys. If she is scared, she'll tinkle, but otherwise, she does her business outside. Though, she needs a little coaxing in the rain and snow. But I wrote all the info for you."

"Thanks." Because Juliet would never remember.

"Lulu's fourteen, so old like me, but we both have a few more years left."

"I'll make sure Lulu's are good ones." And Juliet would, even if she didn't have a clue how to take care of a dog. But she'd said the same about a cat, and so far, Butterscotch was doing well.

"I know you will." Mrs. Vernon sighed. "I'm sorry for what you're going through with Ezra and Penelope. I tried to talk some sense into the woman and told her a man like him doesn't deserve you and should be kicked to the curb ASAP, but she's stubborn, as usual. When she finally opens her eyes to see her mistake, I fear it will be too late, and I wouldn't blame you for cutting all ties. Do what you need to do and don't worry what anyone else thinks."

"Thank you." Juliet hugged Lulu. "I appreciate you saying that."

"It's the truth." A thin, veined hand reached out to touch Lulu. Mrs. Vernon sniffled. "Take care of each other."

Despite her grandmother's shady way of getting Juliet to take the dog, perhaps this was meant to be. "We will."

Sheila came to the passenger side of the car. "I'll carry these in, Mom, and then we'll head home."

"Your home. Mine will be put on the market and sold to a stranger." Mrs. Vernon didn't sound happy. "I suppose a place with bingo, a hair salon, and other activities might be fun. But no man better hit on me, or I'll knee him where the sun doesn't shine. My heart belongs to Walter."

Sheila rolled her eyes. "Don't get yourself kicked out, please. We were lucky to find you a spot so close to our house."

Mrs. Vernon shrugged.

"Tell them you're spoken for," Juliet offered. "If they keep bothering you, you can take more action."

"Excellent advice." Mrs. Vernon's eyes no longer appeared to be sad but resigned. "Thank you, dear."

Juliet held Lulu's paw to wave goodbye.

Mrs. Vernon blew a kiss before staring at her lap.

Sheila headed to the house. "I left my number with the instructions. The dog is up to date on her shots and appointments, but if you need a vet, phone the clinic. 'That's where Mom took her, and she called them with your info this afternoon."

The clinic.

Where Roman worked.

He would know about dogs.

Juliet followed Sheila, who opened the door and placed everything in the entryway.

"Thanks again." Sheila petted Lulu. "You're a lifesaver. And I don't care what Penelope Jones thinks. My mom's right. You deserve better than Ezra Monroe."

"Thanks."

"Let us know if you have questions about Lulu." Sheila looked at the dog before shaking her head once. "Bye."

The door slammed shut.

Butterscotch hissed.

Lulu barked.

Butterscotch's tail tripled in diameter, and he arched like a cat from a Halloween decoration.

Some wetness ran down Juliet's arm. "Oh, no, Lulu. Did you just tinkle on me?"

"What do you want for dinner?" Roman asked his niece, who sat at the kitchen table doing her homework.

"Anything except chicken. We've had way too much of that lately."

People—okay, women—had been dropping off meals for them this week. But Katie was correct. Most of the dishes had chicken. "How does pizza sound?"

"Pepperoni?"

That was her favorite. "Is there any other kind?"

"Well—"

"That was a rhetorical question." He should have known better than to ask that.

"Oh, so you didn't want me to list all the types of pizza?"

A knock sounded.

Katie's eyes widened. "If that's the pizza, teach me how to do that."

"I don't have that kind of magic." However, that would be a fun trick. He went to the entryway and opened the door.

Juliet stood with a trembling white dog in her arms. She appeared to be near tears. "Help."

"Whose dog?"

She gulped. "Mine?"

He opened the door. "Come in."

"Lulu tinkles when she's scared." Juliet looked at her arm. "I had to wash before I came over."

"I've dealt with worse than tinkle from dogs."

She stepped inside hesitantly. "Thanks. You said if I had questions to let you know. I have about a million."

"Puppy!" Katie ran toward them.

"Stop," he said in a firm tone.

She did.

"How did your mom teach you to approach a dog you aren't familiar with?"

A guilty expression flashed on her face. "Slowly and quietly. Ask the owner for permission first and let them sniff me."

"Do you want to try again?" he asked.

Katie nodded.

"Go ahead," he encouraged.

She took a step toward Juliet and the dog. "Can I pet your dog?"

"This is Lulu, and I'm sure she'd love a rub. I'm told she loves kids, but please go slow because she's had a rough afternoon."

It sounded as if Juliet had, too. That gave Roman an idea. "Would you like to have dinner with us tonight?"

"We're having pizza," Katie chimed in before placing her hand under the dog's muzzle so Lulu could sniff it.

"I…" Juliet stared at Lulu.

She was worried about the dog. For someone who'd never had a pet, Juliet's heart cared about animals. He would make this easier on her. "Lulu can stay. Katie's cat, Smalls, won't care."

"She eats a home-cooked dinner. I haven't looked at Mrs. Vernon's instructions."

Juliet sounded overwhelmed. Roman didn't blame her. "Dogs are an enormous responsibility. What if you leave Lulu with us, get the instructions, and we can review them?"

"Really?"

Roman wanted to kiss the worry off her face, but Katie and Lulu were in the way. Plus, he didn't know if that would go over well with Juliet. His gaze zeroed in on her wedding rings. "Yes."

"Do you like pepperoni pizza?" Katie asked Juliet.

"It's my favorite."

Katie bounced on her toes. "Mine, too."

"Give me Lulu." Roman held out his hands. "I'll order the pizza while Katie takes Lulu out to the backyard in case she needs to tinkle more."

Juliet's cheeks turned a charming shade of pink, but she didn't give him the dog.

"It's okay, Juliet," Katie said with the voice of a thirty-year-old in an eleven-year-old body. "Uncle Roman might not be sure what to do with me, but he's good with dogs. You can trust him with Lulu."

With a slight laugh, Juliet gave him the dog. "I'm trusting you."

"Won't let you down." He tried not to laugh. "Promise."

A few minutes later, he'd ordered the pizza, Smalls watched everyone cautiously from the couch, Katie had forgotten about her homework to play with Lulu, and Juliet returned with her list.

Nerves radiated off Juliet. She crinkled the edge of the paper before handing it over. "A cat seems like less work."

"They can be, but a senior dog won't be as much work as a puppy. From what I've seen, Lulu is well-behaved and soaks up attention like a sponge."

Juliet blew out a breath. "That's a relief."

"First, a cat. Now a dog." Roman studied her. Something in her eyes bothered him. "Was this planned?"

She bit her lip. "Not exactly. My... Someone volunteered me, and I was stuck since Mrs. Vernon is going into an assisted-living center and can't take Lulu with her. I didn't feel right saying no."

"A dog is a commitment."

"That part scares me when I'm still learning how to be on my own. Now I have the responsibility of a cat and a dog. At least I have more to think about than my failed marriage." She blushed. "Sorry if that's too much information."

"It's not." Roman found her openness refreshing. Everything about Juliet intrigued him. "How are you doing with Butterscotch?"

Her mouth curved upward. "Great. That cat has me trained already."

He laughed. "That's what cats do. Dogs aren't that way."

Juliet's slight smile disappeared.

Roman hadn't meant for that to happen. Maybe this would make her feel better. "But dogs will bring you joy each day. They could teach humans a thing or two about unconditional love."

A grin spread until her face glowed.

His breath caught in his throat. *So beautiful.* He swallowed.

"In that case…" She glanced at Katie and Lulu on the floor. "This was meant to be."

Roman had the same feeling.

Juliet had a dog and a cat. He had a kid and a cat. Together that made…

A family.

chapter seventeen

"**Y**ES, I WAS over at Jenny's again. I just got home." Well, sort of. Nell sat in her car outside her apartment building. She'd answered Bria's call after she pulled into her spot. The worry in her friend's voice echoed each concerned beat of Nell's heart.

"Is Missy any better?" Bria asked.

Nell rested her forehead against the steering wheel. She didn't want to upset Bria, but the truth would come out soon enough. "No. Missy's still as stunned as she was the day Reggie was over there. Jenny's beside herself. Me, too. Elias Carpenter has been a godsend. But I can't believe Missy's just a suspect because her keys are missing. Especially when they're in the rubble somewhere."

The words spilled from Nell's lips. The group chat kept the Posse informed, but only she had been with Missy to see how this affected their sweet friend.

It wasn't good.

"I'm flying up there this weekend." There was no hint of uncertainty in Bria's voice, suggesting she'd already decided this. Bria wasn't spontaneous. "I'll search for a job up there."

Nell straightened. "That'll be great. Thank you."

"I'm in the process of applying for a permit to do the baking at Missy's place, so I need to make sure she has what she needs. If we can get her making cupcakes again, that'll help keep her mind off everything else. At least, it worked when Rob died."

Elise had known what Missy needed—work. Nell hadn't been in Berry Lake, but she was there now and would do what she could to help.

"Sounds like a great plan. And that's not me being purely selfish because I miss her cupcakes." Nell tugged on the loose waistband of her jeans. "Though I've lost a couple of pounds not having them daily, so I might have to watch what I eat."

"Whatever makes you happy."

"I am. Happy, that is."

She would be the best surrogate aunt to Briley. Nell had loved holding and playing with the little girl. And though her heart longed for a child of her own the entire time, life didn't always work out as planned. And when Evie, Jojo, or Sheridan had kids, Nell would smother them in love and advice the way Elise did with Bria and each of the Posse.

"Still, it would be nice if a guy noticed me," Nell said.

"One will."

Nell nodded. She would never say never, but she wasn't feeling it right now.

"Did you hear from Gage?"

"Nope, and it's okay. Yes, he's hot, but we'd only gone out twice." As long as her mother laid off the matchmaking, she would be fine. "Do you need someone to pick you up at the airport?"

"Thanks, but Dalton has me covered."

"Of course, he does." Nell hoped things worked out between the couple, and so far, so good. Each successful relationship gave her hope one was possible for her. "The two of you are so sweet together."

"We are." Bria's laugh sounded like heart-eyes, and Nell could picture an I'm-so-in-love grin accompanying it.

"Text me when you want to work on Missy's kitchen. I'm happy to help."

"Thanks. Selena doesn't know if she'll make it this weekend."

"Probably not because Logan's team is in Seattle, but she'll be with us in spirit."

"For sure." Silence. "Thanks for the update on Missy."

"Anytime." Bria's tone implied she wasn't saying something. She'd mentioned Dalton, so it wasn't him. "Any word from your dad?"

"Nope. I keep trying, but he hasn't returned any of my texts or voice messages."

Where could Brian Landon be? But Bria didn't sound that concerned. Something else must be on her mind. That left only one thing for Nell to bring up. "How's the job situation?"

"The employment lawyer is smart and savvy. I'm so impressed by her, but she thinks proving my ex-boyfriend's fiancée got me fired would be difficult and expensive. That's not where I want to spend my money, so I understand why my former boss accepted his retirement package."

"Have you taken their severance package?"

"Not yet. The lawyer's contacting the company on my behalf, first. It may be for naught, but she said it couldn't hurt to see if they'd renegotiate mine. I'll need money for the cupcake shop repairs."

"You're going to reopen?" Nell hated asking, but fixing the fire damage would be expensive—even more expensive to do without insurance.

"I want to try." Bria's tone, however, wavered. "Dalton's boss lowered his offer after the fire. It would be an insult to Aunt Elise's legacy if I sold for that price."

"He wants a bargain."

"Yes, but that won't work with me."

Nell's heart panged. "You sound like Elise. She would be proud."

"Thank you." Bria's gratitude reflected in her voice. "Hearing you say that makes me happy."

"It's true." Nell slid out of her sedan and tucked her keys into her front pocket. She grabbed the two grocery bags and her purse and closed the door with her hip. "Now text the group chat, so we can plan accordingly."

"You mean I can plan, and you all will fall in line."

"That's what I said."

"See you soon."

Nell looked forward to it. "Bye."

As she climbed the steps to her unit, the line disconnected. Male voices grew louder.

Five years ago, she'd rented the apartment at the then-new complex based on photos on the internet. The place was great, but now she wondered if she should buy a home. Having a kid on her own might not be in her future, but a house could be. She didn't have to wait for a partner or husband to become a homeowner.

She reached the landing and spotted two men. She recognized Welles right away. He was speaking to another guy, who wore a hat and faced away from her.

Welles's gaze met hers with the relief she felt at the end of a shift, but the grin on his face was too sincere to be fake. "Here she is."

The other man turned and flashed a brilliant smile straight off a whitening toothpaste ad. It was also so familiar. Her muscles tightened in protest.

Nell blinked. When she opened her eyes, he was still there. "Gage?"

"Hey." He wore shorts, a long-sleeved shirt, and hiking boots. Smudges of dirt suggested he'd been in the woods; though, based on what she knew about him, he might have been doing a training run from one end of the lake to the other while blindfolded with his hands tied behind his back. "I was in town, so I thought I'd stop by."

A little out of his way since he lived across the Columbia River in Hood River, Oregon, but she had no reason not to believe him. "Out for a hike?"

"Training."

"For what?" Welles asked so she didn't have to.

Gage beamed as if he were about to make the first ascent on a mountain in Alaska. Something he'd mentioned on their date—four times. "My next adventure."

Welles rolled his eyes. He stepped forward and took the bags from her left hand. "I'll help you with these."

He'd offered in the past, but today she wouldn't say no. It wasn't Gage, per se. But her worry over Missy and Juliet and Bria might make Nell agree to do something like agree to go mountain biking or spelunking so she wouldn't be alone. She was still recovering from their last outing. But he was as attractive as she remembered.

"Thanks," she said.

Welles did a double take. "Are your keys in your purse?"

"Nope." She pulled them out of her pocket, unlocked the door, and stepped out of the way so Welles could go first. Gage followed. She went in last and shut the door so Mr. Teddy wouldn't escape.

The cat rubbed against Nell's leg. He gave the same greeting each time she arrived home, whether from one of her twelve-plus-hour shifts or getting the mail from her box at the apartment complex's office.

She rubbed behind Mr. Teddy's ear. "How's my handsome guy?"

Gage preened as if he were staring into a mirror and not at her. "He's great."

Welles shook his head. "She's talking to Mr. Teddy."

Gage glanced around. "Who?"

"The cat," she and Welles said at the same time.

"Jinx." Welles winked before putting away her groceries. Surprisingly, he knew where everything went. He'd been over here a few times—they'd been neighbors the entire time she lived there—but she hadn't realized he paid that much attention.

"Oh, right." Gage didn't appear impressed, but Mr. Teddy had been the same with him the first time they met. "So I was thinking…"

"Be careful you don't hurt yourself." Welles spoke loud enough so Gage would hear it.

Nell almost laughed, but she didn't want to encourage Welles or be rude to Gage.

"What?" she asked Gage.

"I have tickets to a movie tonight in Hood River. Want to go?"

"Rom-coms are Nell's favorites." Welles put the milk carton into the refrigerator. "But as long as the film has a love story, she'll enjoy it."

True, but how did Welles know that? Only a wall separated their apartments. Could he hear her television in his?

Oh, man, she hoped not. She nearly shuddered. She'd ugly-cried through several films.

Gage's nose crinkled as if he smelled Mr. Teddy's litter box. "It's not that kind of movie. This is an extreme-skiing movie to get people fired up for winter."

Of course, he skied. Nell assumed the answer, but on the off chance she was wrong, she had to ask. "You must love the black diamond runs."

Gage's eyes brightened. "I do. But backcountry skiing is my favorite."

"That can be dangerous." Welles put the rocky road ice cream in the freezer. "Every season, avalanches kill skiers who go outside resort boundaries."

"There's a risk with most things that get the adrenaline pumping." Gage's chest puffed. "But I've had training, so it's not an issue. Do you ski, Nell?"

Both men stared at her as if world peace depended on her answer. "I haven't skied in years, but I only did green and blue runs."

"Nothing wrong with that," Welles spoke in a matter-of-fact tone, which she appreciated.

"You're missing out on so much fun and excitement by sticking to beginner and intermediate slopes," Gage said a beat later.

"That's okay. I enjoy having two functional legs." Nell didn't hesitate to answer. But she understood why his friend's wife had grounded him from taking part in any more of Gage's so-called adventures. "To be honest, après-ski with a hot cocoa with whipped cream and chocolate shavings on top is more my style than heart-racing activities."

An appreciative smile spread across Welles's face. "That's my Nell."

Not his, but she kind of liked Gage's territorial expression and stance.

"So the movie?" Gage asked.

"I have a ticket for it, too," Welles chimed in. "Let's ride together, Nell. That way, Gage doesn't have to drive you home since he lives in Hood River."

Nell had no idea how Welles knew that much about Gage unless the two men had discussed it before she arrived. She didn't need a chaperone—especially her next-door neighbor—for a movie, but this was one more data point showing how little she and Gage had in common. Call her shallow, but that didn't stop her from enjoying the package.

"It would save me a drive." Gage stared at Nell. "Are you game?"

"Sure." A movie with two handsome men would be better than an evening with her TV and Mr. Teddy. Nothing against her foster cat, but she could mention seeing Gage and put off her mother's questions about her dating life and relationship status for another week. "It sounds like fun."

"Let's grab dinner in Hood River," Welles suggested. "I forget the name of the brewpub near where it's playing."

Gage nodded. "I've been there. Great stout."

"One of my favorites on their menu," Welles agreed. "You'll love the French fries, Nell."

"French fries are my second favorite food group after cup-cakes, so I'm in." And she was, but she had an ulterior motive for going. Welles enjoyed the outdoors. Not in a crazy let's-climb-all-the-peaks-in-the-Cascades-in-a-weekend way, but he would be a better fit for Gage's so-called adventures. That would leave Gage to do the boring stuff like meals and movies and binge-watching TV shows with her.

It could work. "Let me grab a jacket, and we can go."

The brewpub was loud and full of people dressed in jeans and T-shirts. Nell had never been there before, but she enjoyed the casual atmosphere, delicious food, and tasty beer. But most of all, she loved being the center of attention of two attractive men trying to one-up themselves in front of her.

If that made her vapid.

Or pathetic.

So be it.

She didn't want to be anywhere else. Seriously, the only thing that could make tonight better was if the place served cupcakes.

Still, no complaints.

The envious glances from other women hinted at what walking a red carpet must feel like during the award season. Talk about a confidence boost. So what if questions about her relationship to the men filled those same stares? She was the one sitting with them.

That was more than enough.

She'd also been correct about the two guys having things in common. She was sure they were on the way to becoming friends—a bromance in the making.

Cue the violins. Or maybe an air horn would be a more apt noise in this case.

The idea of skydiving or bungee jumping off a bridge—two activities Gage mentioned over appetizers—didn't appeal to her in the slightest. Sorry, she was addicted to walking and breathing. Welles didn't appear keen on the skydiving, but he'd thought the bridge sounded fun, and the men exchanged numbers.

Success.

Her heart, lungs, legs, and muscles wanted to scream for joy. Instead, she took a sip from the pilsner she'd ordered.

So good.

Gage checked his phone. "We should head over to the theater."

They each tossed money on the table to pay the bill, which reminded Nell. This didn't feel like a date—more like three friends hanging out—so… "How much do I owe for the movie ticket?"

"Twenty-five should cover it," Gage said.

A twinge of disappointment shot down her spine, but it was similar to a hair blown across her face with a breeze—quickly brushed aside.

Welles, however, rolled his eyes as if he couldn't understand what she saw in Gage.

A part of her understood the reaction, but this wasn't a date. Nell was happy to pay, so she handed over twenty-five dollars.

As they walked to where the movie was being shown, Gage took off at a fast pace.

Welles slowed his steps to walk next to her. "The guy might look good on the outside, but you deserve better on the inside. You've never been into his kind of adventure."

Once again, he wasn't wrong, but this wasn't the time for that discussion. "We're just getting acquainted."

He started to speak before pressing his lips into a narrow line.

Whatever he had to say mustn't have been important.

During the movie, she sat between Gage and Welles. That part didn't suck. The rest, however...

No popcorn.

Who watched a movie without buttered popcorn?

There should be a law against it, but this auditorium only allowed water.

Ugh.

There was also no plot, only skiing that had her holding her breath or covering her eyes.

She didn't mind documentaries or avant-garde films, but action-adventure flicks?

So not her thing.

As a skier jumped off a sketchy cornice, Gage whooped and hollered. Welles cheered.

Nell forced herself not to check the time on her phone. The light would be a dead giveaway. She wanted to know when it would be over. With no clock, she resorted to counting from one-Mississippi to sixty and keeping track of the minutes on her fingers.

People clapped and stood.

She startled, halfway through the seventeenth minute.

Nell stood and applauded.

Gage whistled. Welles had a big grin on his face.

Yep, a bromance was born tonight. That thrilled her. Only, she was once again the odd person out.

Stop it.

Gage wasn't Mr. Right. He wasn't even Mr. Right Now. He appeared to agree based on how he'd preferred talking to Welles about rock climbing than chatting with her.

Nell wouldn't deny the obvious, either. Chances were he'd bought her ticket for someone else. No one spent twenty-five dollars and waited until the day of the event to invite a person to attend. At least none of her friends did.

Man or woman, it didn't matter. She'd been his second choice. Maybe a third or fourth even. Whoever was supposed to go must have canceled. That was why Gage hadn't called. He'd probably stopped by knowing she would be free.

Gage's eyes lit up. "Enjoy the movie?"

"I've seen nothing like it." That was totally true. "I had no idea people could ski on the edge and live to talk about it."

He nudged her arm with his. "Good one."

Except Nell wasn't kidding. She would rather visit the dentist, see the gynecologist, and have a mammogram all on the same day than ski as they did in the movie.

"Tonight was fun. I'll give you both a call," Gage said. "I need a new partner in crime to help me get in better shape, Welles. And, Nell, we should hang out again."

If Welles became Gage's adventure buddy, she would never have to do another hike again. Yet, she could keep her mom off from meddling a little longer. "Sure."

Welles's hand settled at the small of her back, and Nell stiffened. She hadn't expected him to touch her.

"It's getting late," he said. "And we have a drive ahead of us."

Gage surveyed the crowd. "Take off. I'm sure I'll find someone I know."

She didn't doubt that. "Have fun. Thanks for inviting me tonight."

"And letting me tag along," Welles said.

"Always good to make new friends. And now I have two in Berry Lake."

*Friend*s.

"You can't have too many friends," Welles agreed with an enthusiasm she saved for her favorite desserts. "Isn't that right, Nell?"

Nell nodded, trying hard not to let her grin be fleeting.

So much for her plan. Friends were good. But a boyfriend would be better.

When would hers show up? She'd been patient, but she was getting tired of waiting for her chance at love.

chapter eighteen

O N THURSDAY NIGHT, Juliet sat in her living room chair with Lulu at her feet. She kept getting I-will-murder-you-in-your-sleep glares from Butterscotch, who no longer hissed at the dog but still wasn't happy. As if in protest of the canine interloper, the cat sat between Roman and Katie on the couch.

"I think we've covered everything for the party." Juliet reviewed her notes. "You have the invitations ready?"

Katie bit her lip as if they hadn't had spaghetti and garlic bread for dinner thirty minutes ago. "Yes, but what if no one wants to come?"

Juliet didn't want the girl to worry. She would talk to Charlene about what to do if no RSVPs came. "Your classmates might be busy, but you won't know until you ask them."

Katie rubbed the cat. "I guess."

"You have the best event planners in Berry Lake working on your party." Roman messed up Katie's hair.

Katie's drawn-out sigh would power the windmills dotting the hillsides along the Columbia River Gorge. "They're the *only* event planners in town."

"We're still the best." Juliet flashed her princess-with-the-mostest smile, but Katie focused on Butterscotch. She knew something that might get her attention. "Would you like dessert?"

Katie's head popped up. "Please."

"Give me a minute." Juliet stood and headed into the kitchen. Bria wouldn't be there until tomorrow, but Jenny had convinced Missy to bake cupcakes today. Dare had delivered a dozen this afternoon, and they'd been tempting Juliet since then. But she'd wanted to save them for tonight.

Juliet had set out a platter after dinner. Now it was time to fill it.

Roman entered the kitchen. "Need help?"

"No, but I don't mind the company if Katie's okay by herself."

"She'll be fine." He leaned against the counter. "She's trying to negotiate a peace treaty between Butterscotch and Lulu."

"I hope she succeeds. Each day gets better, with less tinkling from Lulu, but I want them getting along by the time Bria arrives."

"When's that?"

"Tomorrow." Laughing at her optimism, Juliet placed two chocolate cupcakes on the platter. "Miracles happen."

"They do."

He came closer so that the scent of his aftershave or soap tickled her nose. It wasn't strong like the expensive brand Ezra wore that sometimes made her eyes water when he'd use a heavy hand to put it on. Roman's wasn't fancy like that, but the just-right mixture of citrus and cedar appealed to her senses.

Roman peered into the box. "Those cupcakes look amazing."

"Did you visit the Berry Lake Cupcake Shop when you interviewed at the clinic?" She removed a vanilla one with buttercream icing. Missy had outdone herself with the variety of flavors.

"I drove by it, but I was only here for a brief time. Katie stayed with her best friend's family, but I didn't want to leave her alone for too long."

"Good call." Next came two pumpkin spice cupcakes. "I remember wanting to know where my grandparents were or have them around me when I went to live with them permanently."

"Sometimes, I think we should have stayed in Missoula."

"You can always move back."

He nodded. "But other times, I feel like we're meant to be in Berry Lake."

Juliet glanced up at him. He stood close, an *in her space* close, as in *she could kiss him* close.

Wait. She shouldn't think about kissing him. Yes, she and Ezra were getting a divorce, but they were married for now, and…

She still wanted to kiss Roman.

Heat pooled in her cheeks. She stared at the cupcakes with an intensity she'd only used during her algebra final in college. That didn't stop the rat-a-tat-tat of her heartbeat.

His breath caressed her neck.

Had he moved even closer to her? Juliet didn't look at him. She couldn't.

Not when she was so afraid. Afraid of what she might see in his eyes. Afraid of what he might see in hers. Afraid of what she might do with her pulse pounding and heated blood rushing through her veins.

"Juliet?" His voice was a whisper and a plea that tugged at her heart and pulled at her dreams.

Temptation flared, only she didn't think he would be as easy to ignore as the cupcakes had been. She'd become skilled at pretending not to notice things with her husband, but she didn't want to do that with Roman.

Juliet wanted to give in. She wanted to—

"Guess what?" Katie raced into the kitchen as if a zombie were chasing her.

Roman stepped away from her as if she were a volcano about to spew molten lava.

Juliet didn't know how to feel by the interruption.

Probably for the best.

Not probably.

For the best.

At least, that was what Selena would tell her.

And what she should tell herself.

Juliet picked up a red velvet cupcake with a steady hand, even though her insides quivered like a plucked harp string. She took a breath to calm herself. It didn't help. "What?"

Katie's satisfied expression suggested she'd learned the secrets to the universe. "Lulu and Butterscotch are friends now."

"How did you manage that?" Roman asked.

Juliet turned away from the cupcakes. "I was about to ask the same question."

"Come see." Katie motioned them to follow her, and they did.

On the couch, Lulu sat on a cushion and Butterscotch on the one next to the dog. The two didn't touch or glance at each other, but this was the closest they'd been.

Juliet kept waiting for the cat to hiss or bop the dog's head with his paw. "How did you manage that?"

Katie stood tall with her chin raised. "We had a heart-to-heart talk. Uncle Roman isn't the only one with a magic touch with animals."

Standing behind his niece, he wrapped his arms around her. "Nope. You've got it, too. Like your mom, who had way more magic than me."

Katie leaned against him and sighed. "Do you think she'd be proud of me?"

The hope and wistfulness in those familiar words brought tears to Juliet's eyes. She'd said them a hundred—maybe a thousand times—to her grandparents.

Roman kissed Katie's head. "Both of your parents were always proud of you."

"And they still are," Juliet whispered as Roman said the words.

No one moved. The dog and cat appeared content with where they were, too.

Finally, Katie tilted her head up. "I think Mom and Dad would like Juliet a lot. Don't you?"

"They would. Your parents would like her a lot." He shot Juliet a smile that went from shy to scorching hot in a nanosecond. "Like we do."

Juliet's heart thudded. She swallowed around the cupcake-sized lump in her throat. Who needed dessert with such sweet talk?

Unexpected, but not unwelcome.

And that should worry her.

Way more than it did.

By the time Juliet had arrived at the cottage behind Jenny and Dare's house, the Posse—minus Selena—had Missy's kitchen cleaned and organized into something the health inspector would approve.

"I'm sorry I couldn't be here sooner." Juliet passed out coffees she'd picked up. "Charlene had a few extra things for me to do, and I needed to take Lulu for a walk."

Nell took a sip and then sighed. "Pumpkin spice latte. Perfect for this time of year. Thanks."

"Mine's a spiced cider with caramel." Missy held up her cup. "My favorite. You're the best."

"I got a cinnamon chai latte." Bria took another drink from hers.

"It's the least I can do." Juliet drank her maple cinnamon coffee.

"Rumor has it a certain new dog owner has been seen walking said dog with the new hottie vet in town." Nell eyed Juliet suspiciously. "By rumor, I mean my mom."

Juliet shook her head. That explained a few of her boss's innuendos this morning. "Charlene keeps her pulse on the gossip."

Missy raised her cup. "You didn't answer the question."

"Come on," Bria urged. "Spill."

"I'm drinking coffee, not tea." Juliet took a sip. "There's not much to tell other than Roman and his niece Katie have become friends."

"Friend-friends?" Nell asked.

"Or *friend-friends*?" Missy emphasized the last words and wagged her eyebrows.

Juliet shook her head. "You guys—"

"He stopped by the house this morning, but I thought he was being neighborly." Bria leaned forward. "Do you like him?"

"He *was* being neighborly," Juliet explained. "And I do like him and Katie, but this isn't middle school. I'm still a married woman."

"Who's filing for divorce," Bria reminded.

Missy nodded. "She's got you there."

"It's too soon." Juliet said that as much for her friends' sake as her own. "I'm not ready for romance. Forget a relationship."

Nell studied her as if she were checking a patient's vital signs. "I agree. So would Selena."

Juliet sent Missy and Bria a smug I-told-you-so look. "Another time or place…"

"Give it a few months." Missy stared over her drink. "Remember when we talked about things being right. If it's meant to be, it'll happen."

The two nodded.

Juliet hoped everyone stopped talking about her and Roman. She was bad enough on her own.

She kept thinking about being in the kitchen with him and what might have happened if Katie hadn't interrupted them. Not that he'd mentioned it when they said good night or when he'd shown up this morning with a bagel for her. But she'd kept quiet, too. Life was more like middle school than any of them realized.

"For now, I'm grateful to have them next door," Juliet admitted. "Roman and Katie have been an enormous help with Lulu."

"Friendship is the best foundation for a serious relationship." Missy limped to the counter where the cupcake box sat.

Nell nodded. "Unless you're Bria and Dalton. But they've known each other forever. And now they're in *lurve.*"

Bria rolled her eyes, but that didn't stop a blush from spreading across her face. Instead of replying, she drank her coffee.

Nice save.

Missy brought the cupcakes over to the small kitchen table. "Help yourself. I tried a few new things. Introducing Berry Lake, Huckleberry Dream, and Squatchy cupcakes."

"Oh, they look delicious."

"I want to try all three."

"I'm so impressed."

The accolades kept coming, and Missy deserved each one.

Juliet finished eating a Squatchy with mini-malted milk balls, coconut, and shaved chocolate on top of the chocolate frosting. "These are to die for. They'll be perfect for the Big Foot Seekers Gathering."

Bria nodded. "The Huckleberry Dream will be perfect for the summer festival."

"I'm in love with the Berry Lake ones," Nell admitted. "I usually prefer chocolate, but I like the gingerbread cake. And the gummy fish are too cute."

Missy sat with a satisfied expression. "Thanks. These recipes are Elise's. I've added a few twists, but it's why I wanted to save the journal."

No one said anything, but the atmosphere changed. Juliet and the others had told Missy she shouldn't have gone back into the bakery. No one needed to repeat it. But these recipes were Elise's. A way for her to still be with them, whether that was in this small kitchen or a rebuilt cupcake shop.

Juliet's eyelids heated. "Thanks for making these. They are the perfect combination of you and her."

"Yes." Bria wiped her eyes. "You've made my aunt proud in so many ways, Missy."

Nell nodded. "The weight I lost is going to return with a vengeance with these new flavors, and I won't mind a bit."

Missy grinned. "As long as we get the cottage food permit and I stay out of jail, the Berry Lake Cupcake Shop will keep going."

Jail. Juliet's heart dropped. She'd forgotten Missy was a suspect.

Bria's face pinched. She glanced at Nell and Juliet. "It'll be fine."

Juliet nodded, hoping it was true.

"Trust in the justice system." Nell picked up another cupcake. "Jenny and Elias will make sure you're okay."

Bria's phone rang. She glanced at the screen. Her mouth dropped open. "It's my dad."

"Take it," the rest of them said in unison.

She accepted the call and placed the phone to her ear. "Dad, where have… Wait. For what?… When?" Bria's face paled. Her hand shook. "Why?" She took a breath and another. "I understand. Dad… I'll head over there now."

All of them waited for her to disconnect from the call.

Bria scrubbed her face. "The good news is Missy is most likely no longer a suspect."

The pain in Bria's eyes kept any of them from cheering or even smiling, including Missy.

Juliet touched Bria's shoulder in hopes of comforting her. "What's the bad news?"

"My dad's being arrested." Tears streamed down Bria's cheeks. "They think he set the cupcake shop on fire."

chapter nineteen

B RIA SAT AT the Berry Lake Sheriff's Office with her friends and Dalton. She rubbed her arms. Her conversation with her father swirled in her brain with whirlpool intensity.

"He told me he didn't do it," she said to no one in particular. "He asked me to call Marc Carpenter."

Which she had.

I swear to you, baby doll. I promise with everything I have, which isn't much at the moment, I didn't do it. I wanted to sell the cupcake shop, not burn it to the ground. The bakery isn't worth anything to me now.

But he was a likelier suspect than Missy.

What if he did it?

Bria's throat burned as if she'd stuck a flaming stick into her mouth.

She rubbed her forehead to stave off a headache from erupting. But she might've been too late.

Dalton leaned against a wall with his arms folded over his chest. "Did he say why they arrested him?"

"He mentioned a tip from the anonymous hotline, and they took his keys."

Missy threw up her arms. "So much fuss about the keys."

"It must be their only evidence," Dalton said.

Bria nodded, but she hoped they had more than just keys to pin this on her father. She wanted the arsonist arrested, but she didn't want her dad to be the one who did it.

Sheriff Dooley stepped into the lobby. "Bria, your dad wants to see you."

She wasn't sure how the rules worked. "Can I?"

"For a few minutes." He motioned to her purse. "You need to leave your belongings here."

She handed her purse to Missy, who clung to it, and followed the sheriff, who led her to a room with a table and two chairs. Her father sat in one.

It was clean. Not like a hospital, but the air still had a funny scent. One she hoped never to smell again.

"I'm leaving the door open and stationing someone outside if you need help," the sheriff said.

"I won't." Bria wouldn't let him imply her father would harm her. He might not have given her the attention she wanted, but he'd never spanked her. She entered the room and sat in the empty chair. "Hey, Dad."

He'd aged ten years in a couple of weeks. "Did you call Marc?"

"I did. He was at the courthouse and will be here as soon as he can."

"Good. Good."

"Was one of your keys for the cupcake shop?" she asked.

Her father shrugged. "Your aunt gave me a few keys the last time I saw her. I don't know what they were for."

That sounded fishy. But Bria hadn't trusted her dad in over two decades. "Try to remember in case they ask."

"They're making me the scapegoat. I told Elise she could do better than Royal Dooley, and he never liked me after that. Reggie Lemond couldn't find a burnt log in a fireplace, let alone any evidence from a burned building."

"This isn't a vendetta."

"I didn't do it." Her dad glanced around as if searching for an escape route.

Not surprising. He'd been a flight risk for Bria's entire life. Would the court consider him one?

Her throat clogged with emotion, making it difficult to breathe, but she sucked in a breath if only to do something other than scream or cry. She exhaled for the same reason.

Her dad had let her down—disappointed her—so many times in the past. How was this any different? Other than the police being involved.

"Believe me, Bri." His voice faltered and cracked as if someone hadn't properly tuned the car radio to a station. "I'm innocent. I have an alibi."

She barely recognized him. Being in jail stripped away his confidence and bravado. No more boasting or acting as if he were making millions, if not billions. "Did you tell them that?"

He shook his head. "I can't."

Huh? It made no sense. "Dad, you must."

"Trust me. Please. You're all I have." He choked on the words and erupted into a coughing attack.

She nearly laughed. Not because she found him funny. Not at all.

But his words…

He'd been all she'd had since her mom took off. But her dad hadn't cared. Oh, he'd tried to keep her with him until it got inconvenient. Then, he'd dumped Bria at his sister's house, claiming Bria was too much to handle.

Bria tried to speak, but no words came. Probably a good thing because she didn't know where to start.

Last month, when she'd asked him to come to the hospital, he'd sent Dalton in his place. That had worked out well in the end, but she'd wanted—needed—her dad there, too.

But he couldn't be bothered.

Again.

Again. Again. Again.

The story of her life.

What little they'd shared together.

Aunt Elise had wanted them to be father and daughter—a family. That was why she'd left him half of the cupcake shop and Bria the other half. She didn't see that happening with her dad, but Bria wouldn't let him sit in jail. Innocent until proven guilty. The phrase, however, tasted like sour milk in her mouth. Still, she would try. "If Marc Carpenter doesn't feel capable of representing you, ask him to recommend someone who can."

"I will. Thanks."

"Your attorney is here, Landon," Sheriff Dooley announced. "Bria, it's time for you to leave."

"I'm so sorry." Her father spoke so whisper soft she had to lean over the table to make sure she didn't miss anything. "I love you, baby doll."

Her mouth gaped.

Bria was too stunned to close it.

Now, only when her dad needed her, did he say the three words she'd longed to hear for...years. Except this was only one more crumb he was tossing out. A crumb for her to hold on to, hoping to get more. The way it had been for as long as she remembered.

Her head hammered.

So did her heart.

Her vision swam.

Or it might be the room.

She walked out without saying a word and returned to the lobby.

Dalton rushed to her side and touched her face as if she were a treasured work of art. "You're so pale."

Am I? That would explain her lightheadedness.

He wrapped his arms around her.

Bria leaned into him. She needed his warmth and his comfort. And his strength.

"He claims he didn't do it, but I don't know what to think." Did that make her a horrible daughter or a smart one? She wasn't sure she wanted to know the answer.

Dalton rubbed her back. "You have every right to question him, given the past."

She appreciated him saying that. "I'm relieved Missy's not in there, but..."

"It's your dad," Dalton spoke with a tender tone. "Your relationship with him has been strained for years. Feeling uncertain and scared and angry and whatever else you're experiencing is okay. Trust me. I've run the gamut with my mom."

"Thanks." Bria looked at her friends, who appeared not to be watching her, but they kept glancing her way. "But go home. There's no reason for you to stay."

"Yes, there is." Nell stood and placed her hands on her hips. "Someone's going to need to get dinner."

"Bottles of water," Juliet added.

Missy nodded. "And dessert."

"Where else would we be but with you?" Juliet asked.

"Thank you." Bria remained pressed against Dalton, grateful for his arms supporting her. If he let go, she might fall to the floor. However, the Posse would catch her if he weren't there. "This is so unbelievable."

Missy blew out a breath. "I wish they'd arrested me."

"No!" everyone yelled in unison.

"But I'm innocent." Missy's tone was adamant. "They'd realize that, eventually. And Bria wouldn't need to worry about her dad."

Sincerity and sweetness coated Missy's words like frosting. In some ways, she was an old soul who'd suffered a horrible loss that changed her life forever. Yet, the young, carefree girl with her head in the clouds and her heart on her sleeve sometimes appeared.

"Thanks." Bria stared at Missy with appreciation and love. "My dad says he's innocent, so all we can do is wait to see what happens with him. The same as you said it would with you."

Everyone nodded, except there was a big difference. They all knew Missy wasn't capable of arson. The only fires she'd started had been in her cottage's fireplace.

Unfortunately, none of them could say the same thing about Bria's dad.

Innocent until proven guilty.

The phrase reverberated through her.

Dalton brushed his lips across her forehead. "What do you need from me?"

"This." She glanced up at him to see the concern in his gaze. Concern for her and something else she wasn't ready to name. "Stay with me, and don't let go."

He tightened his arms around her. "I won't."

"Until it's time to eat," Nell joked. "We love you, Bria, but none of us are hand-feeding you and your boyfriend. There aren't many limitations to what the Posse will do for each other, but that's a hard limit."

Laughter burst out, loosening Bria's knotted muscles. She didn't know what she would do without these people in her life. And she hoped she never had to find out.

The following week, Bria struggled for a sense of normalcy. Dalton had earned the Best Boyfriend in the World title, but everything else seemed…strange while she stayed in her aunt's house—okay, *her* house—with Juliet, a dog, and a cat. Bria missed her aunt so much. At times, grief swamped her. Her dad was still in jail—the judge denied bail.

The only bright spot?

It couldn't get any worse.

Late-night calls from Dalton, who was in Portland working, kept Bria from crying herself to sleep. Okay, it wasn't that bad except for the gossip mill. It had reached the wildfire stage, with one over-the-top rumor spreading across Berry Lake before another took flight. None, however, were correct.

As she placed the pan of lasagna on the table, she ran over her mental checklist. Garlic bread, salad, Parmesan cheese, and… The wineglasses caught her attention.

Chianti.

How had she forgotten that?

She opened a bottle. That had to be everything, right?

Juliet poked her head into the kitchen. "Everyone's here."

"Perfect timing." Bria placed the wine next to a pitcher of water. "Dinner's ready."

"Looks as delicious as it smells." Juliet disappeared. "Come and eat, everybody. Bria's spoiling us tonight."

Her voice carried into the kitchen.

Bria's face heated. "Not really. But thanks."

Selena, who'd driven over even though Bria had told her not to, sat down followed by Nell and Missy. All three oohed and aahed over the meal.

Halfway to the table, Juliet returned to the kitchen. She opened the silverware drawer.

Bria rubbed her face. "I forgot the forks and knives."

"You have a lot on your mind." As Juliet grabbed what she needed, metal clinked. "Sit."

Bria did, and everyone served themselves.

"So good." Nell slowly reached for the pepper and winced.

"You're moving a little slow again, Nell." Bria had been in the kitchen when her friend arrived. "Is everything okay?"

"I went rock climbing with Gage and Welles." As Nell stretched her neck, she winced. "I don't know why they wanted me there. I only slowed them down."

"Wait." Selena's gaze narrowed. "You're afraid of heights."

Nell shrugged. "I didn't look down."

Missy shot her a *you're-going-to-kill-yourself* look. "Seriously?"

Another shrug. "I was sure I was going to die twice, but I survived and earned a nice dinner with two handsome men afterward."

Selena continued studying her. "I didn't think you liked Welles."

"We're friends and neighbors," Nell explained. "But he and Gage enjoy being outdoors. I hoped that would leave Gage to do the more boring, unadventurous things with me, but that didn't work out today. That way, I can tell my mom I'm still seeing him."

Bria didn't like the sound of this. "Risking your life and limbs to stop your mom seems a tad…excessive."

"Not a tad. Extremely excessive." Selena took a sip of her chianti.

"Perhaps, but Gage promised to do something I love soon." Nell grabbed another slice of garlic bread. "So I see watching a rom-com flick and eating buttered popcorn in my future."

Ever cautious, Juliet shook her head. "This could backfire."

"Possibly. This will go one of two ways," Nell explained. "We become friends, or we might fall in love."

Selena rubbed her chin as if weighing the possibilities and calculating the odds. "If the latter happens, you can go mountain climbing on your honeymoon."

"That's too mainstream," Missy joked. "I bet Gage would be more into base jumping."

Nell shuddered. "No!"

"Never say never." Selena ate a bite of lasagna. "Who imagined me married to a professional hockey player? A new season means more road trips and nights apart."

A warning bell sounded. Bria was getting reacquainted with Selena, but this didn't sound like her. "I thought you didn't mind being away from Logan."

"Oh, don't mind me. I'm just getting used to another season with so much time apart. No big deal. My team runs my business. I have weekly client calls, podcasts, and courses, but the hard work's done. So now, the house feels…lonely."

"Get a dog or a cat," Juliet said.

"Or both," Missy suggested. "Sabine could find an excellent match for your and Logan's lifestyle."

"Or foster," Nell piped in. "That's what I'm doing with Mr. Teddy. Beyond him not liking Gage and loving Welles, the cat's been great."

Missy shook her head. "Animals have powerful instincts when it comes to humans. Dump the guy."

"We're hanging out, not dating." Nell wiped her mouth with a napkin. "And Mr. Teddy doesn't like Gage because he always sits in his spot. Well, when the guy sits. It's never for long."

"That's Nell's way of saying adopt an animal," Missy said.

"I've considered it." Selena rubbed her chin. "But I don't know if a pet is the right answer. Maybe I need more to do so I'm not bored."

Nell shook her head. "You run an eight-figure business. You do enough."

Selena shrugged, not appearing convinced. Strange, but her alter-ego persona, Selena T, seemed to have left the building or, in her case, the body.

Missy's gaze locked on Bria. "How are you?"

She didn't have to glance around the table to know all eyes were on her. She'd considered texting everyone, but it hadn't happened. Each time she tried, her thumbs froze, unable to type a single word. "Marc recommended a criminal defense attorney for my dad. The guy has a great reputation."

"Do you need money for the retainer?" Selena asked.

"I had enough to cover it." Bria had used her savings. Well, what was left of it after using up her vacation days when her aunt was dying. Once she signed the severance letter—her attorney was still talking to the firm—she would replenish the account, and everything would be fine.

Juliet sipped her wine, her fingers rubbing the stem.

Nell took another bite.

A pensive expression formed on Selena's face. It was the same look Aunt Elise had whenever Bria's dad came up in conversation.

And as with her aunt, Bria didn't know if her friends' silence was a blessing or a curse, but more wine would be good.

"Have you spoken to your dad again?" Missy asked, surprising Bria and, based on the way everyone stilled, the entire table.

"On the phone." She kept hearing his voice. He'd never sounded so...so vulnerable. "He swears he didn't do it."

Missy refilled her glass. "Maybe he didn't."

Juliet said nothing.

A glance passed between Nell and Selena. Their expressions said one thing—*guilty.*

They might be right. "My dad has lied in the past. He wanted to sell the cupcake shop."

"Sold is different from burned." Missy swirled her wine. "I'm not defending him. Whoever set fire to the shop could have killed me. But the fire investigator is under pressure to find the perp."

"Perp?" Bria asked.

Missy flushed. "I've been watching too many crime shows. But Sheriff Dooley has taken the case personally because of Elise. Public pressure has been high, which has to be why I was a suspect. So that's a situation where circumstantial evidence might lead to a rush to judgment."

"This isn't a TV show," Nell said in a matter-of-fact voice.

Missy's reasoning was both admirable and challenging for Bria to accept. "It isn't, and my dad appears to be the obvious person. He had a motive, and he left town. He claims he has an alibi, but he won't provide a name. I don't understand him."

A pained expression flashed on Missy's face. "He's still your father. Don't give up on him."

"I agree with Missy," Selena said. "Your past with him is complicated, but wait to see the evidence before deciding. Still, it's your decision, Bria. No matter what we say, you need to do what's best for you."

The others nodded.

"Thanks. Despite my dad being in jail for arson, things aren't all bad." Bria half laughed. Still, it was true. "I was so upset when I got laid off. But being in Berry Lake with all of you and seeing more of Dalton beats any job. I submitted the permit to sell cupcakes. I only wish Aunt Elise lived here with Juliet, Butterscotch, Lulu, and me."

A silence fell over the table.

A thoughtful expression formed on Nell's face. "She sort of is. She's in the cupcakes Missy bakes."

"Elise is in *you*, Bria," Selena added.

Missy nodded. "So much of her is still in this house."

A wistful gleam flickered in Juliet's eyes. "Elise taught us so much. I still hear her and her cupcake wisdom all the time. That tells me she's in our hearts and will always be there. No matter what happens with the bakery."

Bria blew out a breath. She'd cried so much, but the tears that welled now were happy ones. "Thank you."

"It's time for our usual toast." Selena raised her glass. "To Elise, who taught us a cupcake always makes things better."

The others raised their glasses before drinking.

Juliet took an extra sip. "So, I have a problem with Katie's birthday party next Saturday and could use the Posse's advice."

"What's going on?" Missy asked.

Juliet stared at her plate. "Only two girls have RSVP'd. Another girl is having her half-birthday party the same day, so Katie is considering canceling it. But I want her to have it."

"What is a half birthday?" Bria asked.

"A birthday party six months before your actual birthday," Juliet explained.

Bria's brows knotted. "That's a thing?"

Juliet shrugged.

"How old will Katie be?" Selena asked.

"Twelve."

"Ugh." Nell shivered. "I hated middle school."

Bria nodded. "It sucked."

Selena tapped her chin. "I have an idea."

Juliet leaned forward. "What?"

"What if I invite two young women I met the day of Elise's birthday sale? They're in high school, but they seem like sweet girls, and there will be a coolness factor of having them there. If not enough guests show up, they can take those spots. If more come, they'll help."

Selena always impressed Bria, who took more time planning things out. "That might work."

Juliet bit her lip. "Would they do it?"

Selena nodded. "I'll find them at the high school. Offer to take them for coffee or lunch and do a coaching session with each of them."

Bria had seen Selena T's website. She charged thousands for an hour of one-on-one coaching. "I'm sure they won't say no to that. Thanks."

"Yes, thank you." Juliet raised her glass to Selena. "I appreciate it."

"It's nothing." Selena shrugged it off. "What's the party theme?"

"It's a tea party, and guests are coming dressed as their favorite literary princess. Katie loves books. We're having it at Events by Charlene."

Missy wiggled in her chair. "That sounds fun."

"It does." Nell beamed at Juliet. "And we can be there to help."

"Oh, for sure. I'll make special princess cupcakes. As long as we don't sell them, we don't need a permit. Let me know what the color scheme is so they match the décor. I'll order tiara toppers from a supplier who reached out when they heard Bria submitted the permit application."

Juliet's eyes gleamed. She opened her mouth and then shut it before trying again. "Thank you, guys. Not just for the party… For everything."

Selena one-arm hugged her at the table. "That's what friends are for."

"That's right." Missy stuck out her hand over the table, and the others put their hands on top of hers. "Cupcake Posse forever."

If Bria hadn't known she'd made the right decision to make an impromptu visit to Berry Lake to help Missy, she did now. This small town where everyone knew each other's business was where Bria belonged.

Not San Diego.

Her life was no longer there.

Her heart had been telling her that for weeks, even before she'd lost her job.

After that, she'd known but fought it because of her condo, no accounting firms in the small town, and not wanting to rush her relationship with Dalton.

Tonight, however, her brain finally agreed.

Bria was...home.

chapter twenty

ON THE SECOND Saturday in October, at precisely nine o'clock in the morning, a knock sounded. Juliet padded her way across the rug. The visitor, coming over for a specific reason, was two hours early.

Not unexpected.

Which was why Juliet prepared last night, and Bria had gone to Events by Charlene to help decorate. She opened the door. "Happy birthday."

Katie beamed. She wore track pants, a button-up shirt—what she'd been told to wear—and fuzzy slippers. "Thank you."

Roman appeared with a colorful floral arrangement. "This is a girls-only morning, but I wanted to give you these. Flowers fit for a princess."

Juliet's heart thudded. She took the vase and sniffed. The light fragrance reminded her of a spring day—a new beginning. She hoped today would be that for Katie. And perhaps Juliet and Roman would have that someday. "Beautiful."

"Like you." He grinned at her, and her pulse shot into the ozone layer.

Katie bounced on her tiptoes. "I got pretty flowers, too."

"Your uncle knows how to do birthdays." As Juliet glanced at her floral arrangement, warmth flowed through her. Not delicate as the petals, but strong like the stems and the man standing in front of her. "How does being twelve feel?"

Katie shrugged. "No different from eleven, though I might have grown a little overnight."

Juliet guessed that Katie measured and weighed herself the night before. "You could be taller."

Katie glanced around. "I'm early. Uncle Roman told me to wait, but it's not his birthday."

Roman nodded. "It happened exactly as she says."

"Come in. Birthday girls aren't required to be patient here." Juliet opened the door wider. She wanted to make this birthday—Katie's first without her parents—as memorable as she could. She winked at Roman. "We'll see you later."

Katie nodded. "Go, Uncle Roman."

He held up his hands. Amusement flickered in his eyes. He appeared to be as excited as his niece. "I'm going."

Katie ran into the house, and Juliet closed the door.

"I got no more RSVPs." Katie petted Lulu. "I wasn't invited, but I heard everyone else will be at Fleur's half-birthday party."

Juliet's throat tightened, but she wouldn't allow her smile to falter. Kids could be mean, but their parents were cruel. "I'm sure they'll have fun, but they don't know what they're missing with yours."

Hope battled with worry in Katie's young eyes. "It's their loss, right? That's what you said."

261

The tremble in her youthful voice struck at Juliet's heart. Katie was trying so hard to be strong, but she needed reassurance.

"It is." Juliet's confidence often wavered by the hour, but she would be a rock—no, a steel beam—for Katie's sake. "My friends will be there, and you never know who else might show up."

"Do you think you can turn me into a princess?" Katie stared at her slippers. "I came early because I'm me, and you've got your work cut out for you."

Juliet hugged her.

"First, here's your birthday hug. Those were a thing in my family." She only winced a little, using the past tense. "And second, I want to let you in on a little secret."

Katie leaned closer. "What?"

"You're already a princess."

Her nose scrunched. "I am?"

Juliet nodded. "Not by title or bloodline. We all have a princess inside of us. Some are more blatant about it."

"Fleur Kirkpatrick."

And her mom, Heather Kirkpatrick, who'd been a mean girl in high school, but Juliet wouldn't say that aloud. "Our princess qualities come out on their own. There's no right or wrong way."

Katie shifted her weight from foot to foot. The motion sent Lulu toward her dog bed.

"What if I'm not like that?" Katie asked.

"Before we answer that, let's try to coax your princess out first, okay?"

Another shrug. "Guess we have nothing to lose."

Her use of "we" warmed Juliet's heart. "We don't. Follow me."

They went into the kitchen where the table had been set up to do hair, nails, and makeup. This was one area where Juliet excelled, and, as she'd arranged each item, she sang songs from Rodgers and Hammerstein's *Cinderella*. No princess classes required, though those had given her more skills to add to her arsenal.

Katie's mouth slanted. "Um, I'm not a girly girl. I'm a book girl."

"I know." Juliet set the vase on the counter. "But someone else is both."

Katie scratched her cheek. "That inner princess."

Juliet placed her hands on two thin shoulders and led Katie to a chair. "Yes, but also Princess Pea. Isn't that who you're dressing up as?"

"I love the *Tale of Despereaux*."

"I know you do." Juliet read the book after hearing Katie talk about it. She shouldn't have been surprised to discover the princess had lost a parent. "Why do you like that one so much?"

"Because it shows how even the most impossible things are possible."

Juliet tilted her head and touched her chin. "So that must mean making you into a princess *is* possible?"

"Oh." Katie straightened. "I guess so."

Juliet would show her how easy it was. "Let's get started."

Katie sat taller. "So what are you going to do?"

"We'll start with your hair." Juliet flicked a switch. "The curling iron needs to heat. After that, we'll get dressed and do your nails."

"Are you dressing up like a princess?" Katie asked.

"Not today because my costume is from a movie, not a book, though it comes from a fairy tale from long ago. But there will be plenty of princesses at the tea party."

Katie pointed to the makeup. "What about that stuff?"

Her sour tone on that last word suggested she wasn't a fan. That was okay.

"You'll get a touch of makeup for effect," Juliet said.

"I don't want to look like a clown or a try-hard."

She forced herself not to laugh. "You won't. Promise."

Juliet turned on the music she'd purchased earlier in the week, hit play, and picked up a hairbrush.

Katie's eyes doubled in size, but her expression screamed one thing—shock.

"What?" Juliet asked.

"That's the *Despereaux* movie soundtrack." The sentence rushed out as if it were one word.

Juliet feigned surprise. She touched her chest. "Imagine that?"

"You knew."

"I did. I want this to be a special birthday for you."

"Thanks." Katie got a faraway look in her eyes. "I wish you had known my mom. You would have been good friends."

"That would have been nice, but I'm happy we've become friends."

"Me, too."

And Juliet hoped her friendship with Katie only grew, as did the one with Roman.

Juliet ran the brush through Katie's hair. "Get ready. It's time to let our princesses shine."

Outside the entrance to Events by Charlene, Juliet stood with Katie. Anticipation danced through her, and a scepter-sized lump lodged in her throat. Charlene and Juliet had discussed and drawn up plans for the décor. Her boss had more experience than Juliet, and her four friends were here lending a hand. But she wanted everything to be perfect for Katie.

Juliet didn't glance across the street at the inn. Yes, it was a conscious effort not to do so, but eventually, she wouldn't feel the urge to look.

Katie wore a long green gown. Her hair fell in soft waves. She wasn't only a beautiful Princess Pea. She was also a stunning Katie.

"Are we waiting for something?" Katie asked.

The question jolted Juliet out of her head. She opened the door. "Welcome to your castle."

Katie bounced across the threshold as if her feet couldn't decide to stay on the ground or try to fly.

Two steps inside and Katie froze. "Whoa."

That was the perfect way to describe the tulle and fairy lights. Fresh flowers sat everywhere. Someone constructed an arched doorway out of cardboard that resembled a stone wall. A sign hung on it saying "Princesses" with an arrow pointing to the dining room.

Katie's face lit up brighter than a Christmas tree. "This is way better than I thought it would be. Thank you."

It was incredible. Charlene had taken their plans and quadrupled them. All for a girl she'd never met. "Let's see what else there is."

Juliet had no idea what they'd find, so she motioned for Katie to go first and then followed. When she entered the room, Juliet held in a delighted gasp. Katie released a loud enough one for the both of them.

The same faux-stone cardboard covered the dining room walls. Only, these were draped with more tulle, lights, and floral gardens. The table setting included books, flowers, and tiaras.

Two girls and two teenagers stood next to Charlene. The Posse crowded near the kitchen doorway. Roman was on the other side of the room. He filmed the scene using his phone.

"Happy birthday, Katie!" everyone shouted.

Katie's shoulders rose to her ears, and she clasped her hands under her chin. "Thank you so much."

"Before this royal tea party can begin, we must have introductions." Charlene bowed. "Princess Pea of Dor, I'd like to introduce you to your guests."

A girl in an old-fashioned dress stepped forward and curtsied. "Sara Crewe of London."

Katie whispered, "That's Alexis. She likes birds and eats lunch with me."

Next was a girl in a red gown tied with a gold sash. She curtsied. "Princess Buttercup of Florin."

"That's Chloe. She's super smart, especially at math."

Juliet glanced at Bria. "I have a friend like that."

"Our next two guests are surprises." Charlene stood with a regal air and dressed to the nines as if this were a black-tie event. Her grin was the biggest of them all. "They heard about the tea party and wanted to come."

The shorter of the teenagers stepped forward. She wore a long blue skirt, a white blouse, and a brown belt. As she curtsied, her long brown hair swayed. "Ella of Frei. My real name is Gigi, and this is the coolest birthday ever. I am so happy to be celebrating with you, Katie. I mean, Princess Pea."

"Same." A taller teen, also with brown hair, curtsied. She wore a plaid skirt, a light blue shirt, a navy cardigan, and a tie. "I'm Princess Mia of Genovia, but my real name is Belle. Like my namesake, I love to read, and I adore princesses. I'm so happy to be here."

Selena had come through in a big way, but she always had.

"I'm glad you're here." The excitement in Katie's voice was contagious. "All of you."

Juliet didn't know if her feet were touching the floor. She would soar by the end of the tea party. Speaking of which… "Why don't you princesses find your seats so we can get started?"

All of them, including the two teenagers, nodded.

Roman flashed her a thumbs-up before mouthing *Thank you*.

Juliet would talk to him later. She focused on the five girls seated at the dining room table with eager faces. All had put on the tiaras that had been on their place settings. "I'm Juliet for those who don't know me, and I'm so excited to be celebrating Katie's, aka Princess Pea's, twelfth birthday today. We're going to start with an etiquette lesson. Everyone ready?"

Five heads nodded.

Juliet took a breath. She pushed her shoulders back, raised her chin, and let her princess take over. "Let's begin."

And that was a wrap. Another successful tea party in the books, but Juliet had a feeling this would be her favorite one. As she stood in the doorway, Katie spoke to her four guests in the front room. The girls were so animated, talking and giggling and gesturing with their hands. None of them wanted to leave.

Juliet didn't blame them. She used to feel the same way about her theme-park job. Even after a tiring shift during the summer heat, she'd relished being a princess. The tea parties she did for Charlene allowed her to capture some of that feeling. But today, she was in full-on princess mode, even without her costume.

Someone came up behind her. The scent tickling her nose told her it was Roman.

"Thank you for today." His gratitude was clear in his voice. "It was more than Katie ever imagined. I would have made a mess on my own."

She faced him. "Not a mess. It would have been different from this, and that's okay."

He motioned to the dining room. "Katie needed this."

Juliet glanced at his laughing niece. "Katie did."

"I gave a tip to Charlene, but I want to do something special for you."

His words touched Juliet's heart, but… "That's unnecessary."

"I don't care. Have dinner with me."

She wanted to understand what he meant. "As a thank-you?"

"Yes, but…"

"What?"

"Not only a thank-you." A closed-mouth smile appeared, fleeting yet flirty. "I want to get to know you better without the party, Katie, Butterscotch, or Lulu around."

Heaven help her, but Juliet wanted that, too. "I'm not divorced yet."

"It's just dinner."

Roman made it sound so easy. Maybe it was. "What about Katie?"

"She says she's okay staying alone, but I can ask Chloe's parents if they mind watching her."

Juliet's friends wouldn't have a problem staying with Katie, either, but Juliet wasn't ready to ask them. Not yet anyway.

He took a step forward, closing the distance between them. "So is that a yes?"

Not trusting her voice, she nodded once.

"I like you, Juliet."

"I like you." Her voice sounded funny. Not at all like herself. She cleared her throat.

Roman came even closer. She moved toward him as if pushed by some unseen force.

His lips touched hers. Or maybe it was hers on his first. All she knew was they were kissing. The kiss full of tingles and tenderness made her want to melt into a pile of goo.

Someone squealed.

He stepped away from her. "I'm not sorry we did that, but I should have asked permission."

"I'm not sorry, either." However, a part of her wondered if she should be. "And I should have asked, too, because I might have kissed you first."

As he ran his finger along her jawline, shivers of delight shot through her. "Belated permission granted."

She swallowed. "Same."

"I should get Katie home. I'll be in touch."

In a dreamlike state and not wanting to wake up, Juliet nodded.

It's just dinner.

And it was just a kiss.

Except it wasn't.

Because Juliet wanted more kisses, and she would count down the time until she saw him again.

chapter twenty-one

AS MISSY SQUIRMED on her living room couch, her nerve endings performed the dance routine to Michael Jackson's *Thriller*. Only, no fun was involved. Not when worry gnawed at her insides. Keeping the promise she'd made to Elise was at the whim of the county inspector, aka the Food Safety Compliance Specialist, now in her kitchen.

I'll keep the cupcake shop going. I promise.

Eight simple words.

Missy had succeeded for the first three months. She'd thrived even. But one week after Elise's death, everything had gone up in flames.

Literally.

She rubbed her palms over the goose bumps on her skin. It wasn't even cold in here. But the thought of failing her boss and friend might make her break out in hives next.

"It's going to be okay." Dalton sat next to Bria on the couch. "It's hard to relax, but you look a little green."

Bria nodded. "You've done all you could."

"Not just me." Missy couldn't take all the credit. Her friends had helped to get her kitchen ready for today's visit from the county inspector, who'd shown up with equipment and other items that sent her nerves into overdrive. "I only hope it's enough."

"This place sparkles," Bria reassured her. "I'd feel safe eating off the floor."

Dalton chuckled. "I wouldn't go that far, but she's not wrong."

To be honest, the guesthouse had never been this clean. Not even on the day Missy had moved into this place. That didn't stop the doubts from growing.

"You put so much work into the permit application," she said.

Bria had filled out multiple pages with labels, ingredients, and a sales plan. A new business license with Missy's address had to be obtained. Lists of the recipes and processes were now in a shiny, white binder on the table. A new metal pantry with doors kept the bakery's supplies separate from her personal ones. *Still…*

Without the cottage food permit, the Berry Lake Cupcake Shop would remain shut down, and Missy couldn't keep her promise to Elise.

The oven door slammed closed.

Missy shuddered.

"Hang in there," Bria whispered.

Missy nodded when she wanted to walk outside and scream. That might release the tension between her shoulders. Throwing up might work, too.

"The inspector has a checklist to run through," Dalton explained. "It's the same as when they checked the cupcake shop."

It was Bria's turn to shiver. "Aunt Elise hated those visits."

"Me, too." At least Missy had known when this inspection of her kitchen would happen. She still wanted it to be over. "But Elise had been in business so long and knew what she was doing."

"So do you." Bria stood and came over to the chair where Missy sat. "You've worked at the cupcake shop for over fifteen years. There were a few breaks in there because of Rob, but not many. You know as much as my aunt did. The only difference is you won't be baking in the same commercial kitchen."

"Elise had a way of turning the stress into fun. But right now, I'm scared of failing her."

"You aren't. You won't." Bria's tone was adamant. "She trusted you with her legacy. You're the one who found a way for the shop to keep selling cupcakes. You're doing everything she'd want you to do."

"Thanks. I needed that." Missy pictured Elise in her bakery whites, hairnet, and cap. "Though she wouldn't be pleased with the twenty-five-thousand-a-year income limit."

"No, but we'll be back in full operation before then."

Missy nodded because she needed to believe that, even if common sense shouted how expensive the building repairs would be. "Elise told me there was always work to do and another cupcake to bake. I feel like that saying keeps hitting me in the face."

Bria smiled at her. "I hope in a good way."

"I'll let you know," Missy half joked.

"Elise had some great sayings." Dalton leaned forward, his hands on his knees. "You should write them down. Use them when you redo the bakery. They could go on the wall or in frames."

An idea popped into Missy's head. She straightened. "We could sell the sayings. Make artwork with the sayings. A book, even."

Dalton nodded. "Merchandising is a great way to bring in more income."

Bria laughed. "This is why I'm an accountant and not an entrepreneur."

Dalton patted the cushion next to him. "You're both now, sweetheart."

Bria sat next to him and kissed his cheek. "Thanks."

The couple was so cute together.

Missy fought a twinge of envy, missing having that kind of companionship and love. She glanced at Rob's photo on the mantel. They'd been like that, too. Elise had supported them getting married when the entire town, other than Charlene, had wanted them to wait. Without those two women, the wedding might have ended up turning into an elopement.

Grab love when you can. Just like a cupcake, it might not last as long as you think.

Her boss had been right. Then again, Elise Landon was correct about most things.

Maybe Missy had what it took to keep the cupcake shop going, here in her kitchen and whatever the burned-out building became someday. Supposedly, a few things in the office survived, and she had a feeling she knew one thing that had. She half laughed.

"Think of something funny?" Bria asked her.

Missy nodded. "That old filing cabinet Elise bought at a garage sale for five dollars. We used to joke it would withstand an apocalypse, so I bet it survived the fire and smoke."

Bria grinned. "She was so proud of her bargain. Sheriff Dooley nearly threw out his back, trying to move it upstairs. My aunt was swearing louder than him."

"Elise always let loose." She'd dated Royal on and off for years, never for long, sometimes only a few days, but it gave the town something to talk about every five or ten years. "But she was surprisingly quiet when she turned down his proposal."

Bria startled. "What proposal?"

Oops. Well, Elise wasn't here, so it didn't matter. "The sheriff proposed after her cancer diagnosis—the first one. I was at the cupcake shop when it happened. He wanted to make sure she had good medical insurance."

Dalton scoffed. "I hope the sheriff said more than that to her."

Elise had only mentioned it that one night, but she kept her life private. "There was always something between them, but they were so different and never stayed together more than a couple of weeks."

"My aunt was too independent," Bria said.

"That, too. I still remember Elise thanking the sheriff, saying no, kissing his cheek, and sending him off with a dozen of his favorite cupcakes. Of course, he returned the next day as if nothing had changed."

"It probably hadn't." Bria's forehead creased. "But I wonder how things might have turned out if she'd said yes."

"What-ifs only hold you back." Missy felt like a hypocrite saying that, but it was true. "If Elise loved Royal, loved him with her whole heart, she would have said yes to his proposal. On the flip side, if he'd loved her, he wouldn't have given up so easily. Love conquers all."

"You're right." Bria glanced at Dalton and rubbed her palms on her jeans. "Aunt Elise and I were close, but we lived so far apart. I feel like there's so much I don't know about her."

Dalton placed his arm around Bria and kissed her head. "Your aunt loved you. That's all you need to know."

Missy nodded. "Dalton's right. Your aunt loved you so much, Bria, and Elise would have done anything for you. She wanted only the best for you."

Someone cleared their throat.

Missy glanced over to the dining room and gulped a breath of fear.

The inspector stood, holding his gear. "I'm finished."

She jumped to her feet. Offering him a box of cupcakes might be against the rules, but she could say one thing. "Thanks."

Dalton also stood. "What happens next?"

"If you passed, we'll send you the cottage food permit. Otherwise, you'll hear from us with any corrections that need to be made."

"Thanks," Bria said.

"I'll walk you out." Dalton opened the front door for the inspector and followed him out.

Bria peered outside. "I think we passed."

Missy sucked in a breath. It didn't quite squish her fears but it buoyed her hope. "Why do you say that?"

"Because they didn't say we failed."

"After all the work to submit the application and prepare for the inspection, I hope you're right."

Bria crossed her fingers. "It was worth all the time and effort."

Missy glanced at Rob's photo again. Maybe her angel could pull some strings for them to make sure they were approved. But even if another inspection were necessary, Missy wouldn't give up.

She couldn't.

Because Elise's legacy wouldn't die with her.

Dalton kept thinking about what Missy had said about love conquering all. He'd been waffling over something for two days, but she'd made him realize the issue. This was a decision he wanted to make with Bria's input, not on his own.

He glanced at Bria sitting in the passenger seat. So beautiful. Things were going well. He'd promised he wouldn't rush her, but he had to give the owners an answer. That meant telling Bria sooner rather than later.

Now.

Nerves hit harder than the linebacker who'd sacked Ian during the last football game.

Dalton tapped the steering wheel with his thumb. "Do you mind making a detour by the lake?"

"Juliet's at Charlene's, and Lulu should be fine for another hour or so."

"It won't take that long."

He turned onto a narrow road with tall pines flanking both sides. If Narnia had a main entrance, this would be it.

Bria pressed her face closer to the side window. "Hey, this is Pinewood Lane. We used to come here."

Her remembering sent confidence flowing through him. "We did."

"I haven't been out here in years. Not since high school."

With him was implied.

"Me, either. Until recently." He kept his gaze on the road. For once, timing appeared to be in his favor. "It's changed a little."

"There are more houses. Is the pond still at the end of the lane?"

277

"Just beyond the trees." The tension eased in Dalton's shoulders. "We ice-skated there."

"*You* skated. I kept slipping and falling." She laughed before eying him sideways. "We did more than that there."

"We made snow angels."

"And?"

The road ended with a row of trees, so he turned the car to the right onto a narrower private driveway. The evergreens wouldn't lose their needles, but the maple leaves were turning yellow. A few had fallen onto the ground. He drove farther. A quaint cottage came into view, but she hadn't noticed it yet.

"Built a snowman," he replied, trying to keep this back-and-forth going until they arrived.

"There was something else." Her gaze sharpened. "Unless you forgot."

He parked the car. "I haven't."

Bria inhaled sharply. "This is the last cottage on Pinewood Lane."

She jumped out of the car.

Dalton removed the keys and joined her. She stared at the quaint cottage with shutters and a stone walkway leading to a Dutch front door.

He held her hand. "I kissed you here for the first time."

"I was afraid you'd forgotten."

"Never."

Her face lit up. "It was my first kiss ever."

"I remember that, too." Dalton squeezed her hand. They'd been so young and naïve. "I couldn't tell."

"Yes, you could."

They both laughed.

"You caught on fast."

She kissed him on the lips. "You were a good teacher."

"I gave you an A-plus."

The sounds of the forest filled the air: water from the creek feeding into the pond, the chirp of insects, the song of a bird who hadn't migrated yet.

Bria tilted her face toward the sun. "I love it out here."

"Remember when I mentioned talking to homeowners about selling their properties?"

Her color drained. "Tanner is interested in developing Pinewood Lane?"

The disappointment in her voice caused a physical ache in Dalton's body. "No, this isn't about my boss."

"Then what?"

"The owners of this place intend to sell. They've given me the first right of refusal, but I wanted to talk to you first. We keep saying there's no rush, and the cottage would be a good investment. But it'll tie up money, and it's in Berry Lake. Not San Diego. The owners have it booked as a rental until after New Year's Day and ask that I honor those, which gives us time, so…"

"Buy it."

He shook his head. "What?"

"All your rambling right now was your way of asking my opinion, right?"

Okay, he had been rambling. "Yes."

"That means so much…everything. You should buy it."

"Don't you want to see the rental records or statements?"

"Nope."

"And you don't care that it's in Berry Lake?"

She giggled, which wasn't the reaction he expected from his practical Bria. "I love that it's here. There's something I've been sitting on, waiting for the right time to bring up because I didn't want to push or pressure you."

"What?"

"I want to move to Berry Lake, but I need to know it's okay."

"It's not okay. It's perfect. I want you here."

She stared at the cottage with a wistful expression. "And I want you to buy this place."

"Then it's settled."

Bria nodded. "It's almost too easy."

"No one said it had to be hard." He hugged her. "But we should be better about bringing up what's on our minds."

"No more putting things off out of worry or fear."

"Sounds good to me." Dalton never planned on returning to Berry Lake, but plans might be overrated. With this woman in his arms and his life, there was no place else he wanted to be. Whether it was easy or hard, he would make sure they stayed together.

This time, it was his turn to kiss her.

And he did.

chapter twenty-two

J ULIET STOOD IN the living room of a large estate near Vancouver, Washington. It was Wednesday, a half day for the school district, and the perfect time for a birthday party. Seven six-year-olds, wearing crowns and dressed as their favorite princesses, gazed up at her with stars in their eyes. With mannerisms befitting royalty—well, the make-believe kind from storybooks—she swooshed the skirt of her Sleeping Beauty costume. The outfit went perfectly with the guest of honor's name.

"Thanks for celebrating Princess Briar's birthday with us." Juliet glanced at her first before looking at the others. "I hope you had fun."

The girls jumped up and down, cheering in a very non-princess-like manner. At this age, Juliet didn't rely on the princess handbook she'd had to follow at the theme park. It was all about having fun in sparkly dresses and tiaras while sipping pink lemonade with sugar cubes from dainty teacups.

Best birthday ever?

For princess-loving kids like these, yes.

Fresh-from-the-dryer-towel warmth balled in her chest before spreading through her entire body. Juliet picked up the pink tote containing the favor bags and held it behind her. "I'm going to assist Briar as she passes out your goodie bags."

Briar gave them out and hugged Juliet. "Thank you."

More cheers and clapping filled the air.

"You're welcome." Each party was a special gift that made Juliet's heart sing. "Now, let's say goodbye to your princess friends."

She still needed to clean and drive an hour and a half back to Berry Lake. The princess tea parties hadn't caught on in her hometown yet, so she traveled to put them on in different towns.

No complaints.

Juliet didn't make a full-time salary with event planning, but she had enough to live. Alimony from Ezra would help, but she preferred to think of that as bonus money. She didn't want to count on him for anything. Tamika believed a larger settlement was a sure thing, so Juliet tried not to worry about money.

Easier said than done.

She finally drove into town. The traffic light at the corner of Main Street and Third turned red. Juliet pressed the brakes. As a catchy tune played on the radio, she tapped her fingers against the steering wheel.

Crunch!

She jolted forward until the seat belt stopped her motion.

The radio played, but it sounded almost surreal.

Juliet clutched the steering wheel, her body stiff and unsure how to react. Someone had rear-ended her, but she didn't know what to do.

She had no idea how long she sat there.

A minute or an hour?

It might have been forever.

A person ran up to her car.

Bentley, the teenager who worked at the cupcake shop.

He knocked on her window.

Oh, right. Juliet released the steering wheel with her left hand. Her fingers shook, yet she pressed the window button. The glass lowered.

"Hey, you got hit hard." Bentley's gaze bore into her. "Are you okay?"

Was she? Her right hand still clutched the steering wheel so tightly her knuckles were white. She shivered.

Cold.

She was so cold.

Her body was numb.

The tightness across her chest must be from the seat belt.

"Mrs. Monroe?" Bentley pressed.

"I'm... I'm fine." A glance out the rearview mirror showed a black car with a folded hood. "We should check on the other driver."

She fumbled for the button to release the seat belt. On the third try, she pressed it.

Bentley opened her car door. "You're shaking."

Juliet was. "I'm fine."

"Adrenaline. You may be injured or in shock."

She stood, taking a moment to make sure she had her balance. Everything was off. As if her focus had become sharper, but the rest of her senses hadn't caught up. The teenager might be onto something. "You're a smart kid, right?"

He blushed. "I'm hoping to be valedictorian. We'll see how I do in physics."

She'd barely survived trigonometry. "Good for you."

Juliet took two steps and stopped.

Ezra's car.

That was what hit her.

She hurried to the window to see if he was okay.

Only Ezra didn't sit behind the wheel.

Juliet's mouth dropped open. She moved forward as if carried by a moving walkway. "Remy?"

The young woman rolled her eyes before getting out of the car. She wore a miniskirt that left nothing to the imagination and a camisole with straps thinner than her bra. An iceberg-sized, garish diamond engagement ring flashed.

"A princess costume." Remy snorted. "I thought Ezra was kidding when he told me you had one. Old ladies shouldn't play dress-up. Unless it's cosplay, but you're too uncool and boring to do that. And you're still wearing your wedding rings. Why? I've replaced you."

Juliet's muscles tightened.

Don't react.

Though she wanted to. Oh, she really, *really* wanted to.

Selena had told Juliet she didn't have to defend her choices, but this time she had one thing to say to the future Mrs. Ezra Monroe. "I'm on my way home from work."

"Tell it to someone who cares." Remy's bored expression matched her tone. "Why did you stop?"

Juliet trembled. She wrapped her arms around herself to try to stop the shaking. "Red light."

"You were looking at your phone, Remy." Bentley stepped forward. "I saw the entire thing."

She didn't like Remy, but the young woman was still a person and pregnant. "Are you okay?"

"A little sore." Remy rubbed her left shoulder and stared at the two cars. "Ezra's gonna lose it."

Juliet glanced at her car's crumpled trunk. Her tea set had been in there.

Her heart sank, falling faster than Rapunzel's hair from the tower window.

Juliet had wrapped each porcelain piece, but would that and the plastic cart be enough protection?

It was only one of her tea sets, but still…

Red and blue lights flashed from a sheriff's car. It parked behind Remy's—make that Ezra's—sedan. A man in a uniform exited. Tall and handsome, he reminded her of Josh Cooper, a high school classmate, only younger.

"Is everyone okay?" The man came closer. His nametag read Cooper. "I'm Sam Cooper."

No wonder he looked familiar. "Are you Josh's brother?"

"Yes, ma'am." Deputy Cooper glanced over at Remy, who was texting on her cell phone. "Who are you?"

"I'm Juliet Jones Monroe." Legally that was still her name, but she couldn't wait to drop the last part. "I was stopped for a red light when she rear-ended me."

"I saw everything, Deputy Cooper." Bentley pointed to Ezra's sedan. "Remy plowed into Mrs. Monroe's car without glancing up from her cell phone."

"Not my fault." Remy glanced up from her phone. "I didn't see the red light."

Deputy Cooper wrote notes. "You wouldn't have if you were on your phone. Not using a hands-free device is illegal."

Remy pouted, making her look to be the same age as Bentley instead of in her early twenties. "It was important."

Deputy Cooper studied the car's interior. "The airbag didn't deploy, so you mustn't have been going too fast."

The pout vanished, replaced by a flirty smile instead. "I never speed. I was on my way home."

Remy's apartment above the art gallery was at the corner of First and Main, the opposite direction, which meant she was probably headed to the subdivision where Juliet used to live. Of course, she was.

The worst part about this was Remy didn't care that she'd ruined Juliet's car, one she couldn't afford to replace, or that she'd damaged Ezra's. This appeared to be no big deal to her. Simply an inconvenience.

When it was a huge deal to Juliet.

For all she knew, Bentley was correct, and adrenaline masked any injuries. Speaking of which… "Does anything else hurt besides your shoulder?"

Remy's eyes lit up as if she'd stepped onto center stage. "I'm sore. All over. My neck hurts, too."

That would be enough. "Adrenaline masks injuries."

Bentley's chest puffed. "It does."

"If Remy feels any pain, she should be examined. She's pregnant."

Deputy Cooper studied the young woman with a professional expression. "How are you, ma'am?"

Remy's eyes widened to the size of quarters. Her mouth opened and closed like a fish's. Funny how Ezra did the same thing.

"She should be transported to the hospital to make sure she and the baby are okay," Bentley said.

When the cupcake shop opened again, Juliet would leave him a huge tip. "Yes, she should."

Deputy Cooper turned toward her. "What about you?"

"I'll make an appointment." The other problem was transportation. Elise's house was within walking distance from here. The hospital and medical center weren't.

"I can do the same," Remy blurted.

"Word of advice," Juliet cautioned, not knowing if the baby were real or a ruse. "See what Ezra says."

Stiletto heels flew from Remy's glare. "I texted him about the accident."

"I need to see your licenses, registrations, and insurance cards," Deputy Cooper said. Once they handed them to him, he glanced at Remy and then Juliet. "I'll be just a moment."

As the deputy walked toward his car, Ezra ran down the sidewalk. "What happened?"

As if on cue, crocodile tears flowed from Remy's eyes. "I didn't see the red light and hit Juliet. Both of your cars are damaged."

He hugged Remy. His hand cradled her head as if she were fragile and precious to him. "Are you okay?"

No punch in the gut. No slice to Juliet's heart.

Maybe she was over him. Or…in shock.

Remy nodded before sniffling. "I'm sore. My shoulder hurts, but—"

"The baby." He touched her stomach. "We need to go to the ER to make sure everything is okay with you and the baby."

Guess the fake pregnancy gig would be up soon, or the two would become parents next year. Juliet didn't care which, but she hoped for her future ex-husband's sake, it was the latter. Surprisingly, he appeared to care about the baby and Remy.

He turned toward Juliet, his eyes raking over her costume, but he said nothing. That was unlike him. "Are you okay?"

"The car is a mess, but I'm fine."

He started to speak, but Remy threw herself against his chest. "Hold me. I don't feel well."

Ezra did, but his gaze kept darting to Juliet.

The deputy returned. He handed her a piece of paper with her other documents. "I've called tow trucks. I suggest you trade insurance information, but both cars belong to Ezra Monroe and are insured by him."

"That's me." He continued holding on to Remy. "I'll take her to the hospital."

"I can call an ambulance."

"I'll drive her. We switched cars because mine had higher safety ratings." Ezra stared at Juliet. "Are you sure you're okay?"

She wasn't used to him caring about her. Not trusting her voice, she nodded.

Bentley stood taller. "I'll make sure Mrs. Monroe gets home. She's one of the cupcake shop's best customers. It's what Elise and Missy would want."

The kid's tip just got bigger. "Thanks."

Ezra grabbed Remy's purse from the car before leading her down the sidewalk. More than once, he glanced over his shoulder at Juliet.

She had no idea why, nor did she care. "I'm guessing the impact ruined everything in the trunk."

"I can go through the back seat and see," Bentley offered.

"Please." She wanted to know.

As the teenager opened the rear door, Juliet looked at Deputy Cooper. He'd been a few classes behind her in high school, but in a small town, everyone knew about him, especially when he was the Golden Boy's brother. "I thought you left Berry Lake."

"I used to live in Seattle." He placed cones on the street side of the cars. "I moved here last week. Today's my first day on the job."

"Welcome to Berry Lake."

"Not much traffic."

"There isn't except during the Huckleberry Festival and the Bigfoot Seekers Gathering. Then it's bumper to bumper." The way his mouth slanted made her want to laugh. "The rest of the year, not much happens in Berry Lake."

"That's what I'm counting on."

It sounded like Deputy Cooper had a story to tell. Two tow trucks pulled up.

"I'd get your purse and anything else you want," he said.

As she did, Bentley pulled her mangled cart out. "Not sure how anything fared."

"I'll look when I get home."

"The wheels are damaged. I'll carry it for you," he offered.

Her gut reaction was to say no because she wanted to do things on her own. But she'd been rear-ended. She was also shaky and on edge. Chances were her car was totaled. And her tea set might be in pieces.

A little help wouldn't hurt.

"I'd appreciate that." She glanced at the deputy, who spoke with the tow truck drivers. "Am I free to go?"

"Yes."

She smiled at Bentley. "Let's go."

The teenager adjusted the cart in his hands. "It's none of my business, but Mr. Monroe is stupid. You're like a real-life princess. And Remy is a caricature of the evil stepmother's daughter."

The kid was sharp. "Thank you, Bentley. I sense you have a bright future ahead of you."

"Same for you."

Funny, but for once, Juliet agreed.

Later that night, Juliet checked her phone. Bria wouldn't be home until later, but Roman hadn't messaged her. Not unusual if he worked late or Katie had a school event. Juliet wouldn't mention the accident to him or the Posse because a text wasn't the best way to tell them without more context. A photo of her car's smashed rear end—Bentley had taken it—would only cause worry.

She would survive on her own until Bria arrived home.

With Bentley's help, they'd gone through the plastic bin, salvaging the small gold sugar spoons, one teacup, and a saucer.

The rest was replaceable. The car, too.

She wasn't.

Ibuprofen and a hot shower eased the tightness in her muscles. She put on her pajamas and wiggled her toes in her fuzzy slipper socks. Now she would relax.

A knock sounded.

It must be Roman.

Juliet padded her way across the floor, excited to see him. She opened the door.

Ezra stood on the porch. His hair hung over his forehead. "May I come in?"

She clung to the door handle.

"Please," he added.

With a nod, she motioned him inside, and he entered. She closed the door.

Lulu and Butterscotch didn't get up from the couch. That was odd, or they were tired.

His gaze narrowed. "You're walking slower than usual. You're not okay after the accident."

Juliet tugged on her pajama shirt, wishing she'd put on a robe. "I'm sore, but I'm fine. How's Remy?"

"She's not pregnant."

He hadn't said miscarried. That was interesting.

This might not be a brief chat. Juliet walked to the couch and sat next to Lulu.

Ezra made a face at the dog and cat. Lulu growled. Butterscotch hissed. Both fur babies would get an extra treat for that.

He sat on the chair. "Remy said she miscarried last week but was afraid to tell me."

He sounded sad. Still, the two of them deserved each other for using people to get what they wanted.

Ezra blew out a breath. "I'm sorry."

Funny, but he almost sounded sincere. "For cheating on me?"

Ezra nodded. "I don't know if it was a midlife crisis—"

"You implied this wasn't the first time."

"It'll be the last. I swear. Please, forget the divorce. Come home where you belong. I was wrong about so many things. And the house isn't the same without you."

"It must be messier."

"Yes." He caught himself. "But I miss you. We were good together. Not lately, but before…"

For a moment, Juliet was twenty-two again, eager and full of dreams, and Ezra was the handsome, older man who'd swept her off her feet. For a few years, everything had been good—magical. Until it wasn't.

He hadn't come bearing gifts. Only himself. She nearly laughed at his confidence. "You always say the right things to me."

He glowed, beaming brightly like the North Star. "That's because I know you."

"Once upon a time, but no longer. You won't take advantage of me again."

"I never did that."

She straightened, pushing her shoulders back. "You took advantage of my youth and naïveté. I'm not that same young woman who put you on a pedestal and stared at you with starry eyes. I loved you, Ezra. I would have done anything for you. I did everything you asked and put my dreams of having kids aside because you didn't want them. And what do you do to repay me? You sleep around and treat me as if I'm nothing more than domestic help. So no, I don't want what we had. I won't take your lies and abuse any longer. You may not have hit me, but the way you spoke to me, especially these past few years, was abusive. I deserve better."

"You're still wearing your rings."

"Thanks for the reminder." Juliet grabbed the two rings and pulled them off her finger. It was easier than she thought it would be. "I never took you for granted, but you did me. Every day. And, Ezra, there likely wasn't ever a baby."

His face paled. "What do you mean?"

"I doubt Remy was pregnant. Deena told a similar lie when she was younger. That's how she married her first husband."

Ezra's nostrils flared. "Why didn't you tell me?"

Juliet shrugged. "I didn't know if Remy was faking it or not."

"You thought she was."

"Yes."

"You should have told me."

"You shouldn't have cheated."

"Juliet—"

"Remy's pregnancy makes no difference to me. The baby isn't why I left. Your cheating made me do what I've been considering for a while."

"You've thought of divorcing me?" His forehead wrinkled. "Why?"

"You stopped thinking of me as a wife when I turned thirty, but I'd hoped it would change. That's why I wanted to attend marriage counseling. I hadn't stopped loving you even though you only wanted me for my cooking and cleaning abilities."

"You need me." His voice was firm, his eyes cold.

She raised her chin. "I don't."

"If you think any other man will love you—"

"I don't need a man to love me." Juliet held her head high. "I love myself. And that's the only love I need."

chapter twenty-three

ROMAN STOOD AT the front window. He peered between the crack in the curtains at the sedan parked in Juliet's driveway. She wasn't home from her party in Vancouver, which was strange given the time, and he hadn't noticed the car when it pulled up.

Whose car was it?

"Whatcha looking at, Uncle Roman?" Katie asked from the couch where she and Smalls watched a movie—her treat for finishing her homework early.

"I don't recognize a car outside." He peeked out again. Nothing had changed. Weird.

"I didn't know you were on the neighborhood watch team."

Roman glanced at his niece. "I'm not."

"Mom and Dad were at our house."

Our house. Not her old house.

He didn't want to fail Marlena and Luke, but he was failing with parenting. Juliet had become his saving grace. She was everything he'd hoped to find in a girlfriend for himself and mother figure for Katie. He wanted to move forward as quickly as possible. All three of them needed each other. "I'll ask if this neighborhood has one."

Probably did. It wasn't as if people minded their business there, which he still wasn't used to.

Katie held a bowl of popcorn on her lap. "Can I help?"

Berry Lake didn't have a high crime rate. That had been a big appeal. "Sure."

"Cool." She refocused on the movie Juliet had recommended.

He would ask the neighbors on the other side. They'd lived there longer than Juliet. Not until tomorrow. Now, he needed to figure out who owned the sedan.

A door slammed.

Juliet's?

As if on cue, a man in a suit rounded the front of the car. The lights on each side of the garage door weren't bright, but they illuminated the area enough he could see who it was.

Ezra Monroe.

Roman's fingers tightened, balling into fists.

A moment later, the car backed out of the driveway.

What had Juliet's ex-husband been doing at her house?

Wait, they weren't divorced yet. Juliet still wore her wedding rings.

He remembered what had happened the last time he'd fallen for a woman who wasn't completely single.

His stomach plummeted.

Had Juliet been using him to make her husband jealous? That had happened the last time. It would explain why she asked him and Katie to take walks with her and Lulu. For all he knew, Juliet's divorce was...off.

Roman's blood ran cold. His muscles tensed.

The same scenario from Missoula was playing out. Only he didn't have Marlena to provide common sense and guidance. He had…

Uh-oh. Katie.

She assumed Juliet would be a part of their lives. Roman had, too. If that changed, he would have to do damage control.

"Hey." He tried to keep his voice calm when his stress level wanted to spiral. "Do you mind if I run next door? It won't take long."

She didn't glance away from the screen. "I'm good here. Say hi to Juliet for me."

"Be right back." That was something he'd made a habit of saying after she'd lost her parents when they'd taken a short drive to the grocery store.

Katie waved, not looking at him.

He hurried next door, skipped pressing the doorbell, and knocked. The rap sounded sharp to his ears, but he didn't care. He needed an explanation.

Now.

Juliet answered in her pajamas. "Hey, I was hoping I'd get to see you."

So she could tell him about Ezra?

Roman flexed his fingers before entering her house. "You could have texted."

She closed the front door. "You worked earlier, so I didn't want to disturb you and Katie."

A likely excuse. "You had your party."

She nodded. "So I wanted to tell you—"

"What was Ezra doing here?"

"It doesn't matter."

"It does to me." Roman's voice was sharp, harsh to his own ears.

Her eyes narrowed. "I don't understand."

"Are you and your husband together again?"

Juliet did a double take. "What?"

"You're wearing pajamas, and he was here awhile."

She flinched. "Were you spying on me?"

"I didn't recognize the car in the driveway."

Juliet studied him with an unreadable expression. "It was just a car."

"That the man you're still married to is driving."

She rubbed her forehead. "I can't believe this is happening."

"Me, either. I thought we had something special. Or were on our way there."

Juliet stared at the floor. "I thought so, too."

"Katie needs you."

"Katie." Juliet's gaze jerked up. Her eyebrows furrowed. "Only her?"

Roman wouldn't put his heart on the line. Not now. He couldn't. "I can't have her get more attached to you when I was so wrong about you."

"No, I'm the one who was wrong." Juliet took a breath. She blew it out. "For your information, I was rear-ended today by Remy, who was driving Ezra's car. He came over here to tell me Remy isn't pregnant, so he wants me to come home. I told him no." Juliet held up her left hand. "I also took off my rings. We're still getting a divorce."

Oh, man. Regret slithered through Roman. He forced himself to stand straight. "I'm sorry, Juliet. I overreacted. You've made such a difference for Katie. So, when I thought—"

"No excuses." Juliet moved away from him. "Whenever I wanted to do something without him, he got jealous and accused me of horrible things. He also asked me to raise his child. You want me to do the same thing with Katie. You're acting the same as him."

Him.

She meant Ezra.

"I'm nothing like him," Roman defended himself.

"Close enough. Been there. Done that. I don't want another T-shirt."

"I don't understand."

She straightened and raised her chin. "I liked you, Roman. I enjoyed kissing you. But I'm not about to get involved with a man who jumps to conclusions about me. Who doesn't ask how I am after being in a traffic accident. Who's more concerned about my relationship to his niece over his with me."

Foul-tasting shame coated his mouth. "I dated a woman who was getting divorced. I planned to propose, had a ring, but she reunited with her husband. That's why I jumped to the wrong conclusions."

"You'll keep jumping to them until you work through your issues."

"Juli—"

"I'm sure you'll have no trouble finding someone to help you raise your niece. But that person isn't me." As Juliet gripped the handle, she opened the door. "If Katie needs me, she knows where to find me. Goodbye."

He stepped outside.

She closed the door.

The thud reverberated through him. What had he done?

As a Taylor Swift album played on Missy's cell phone, Juliet sat with her friends in the living room. An impromptu Posse gathering was what she needed. Less than an hour after she posted on the group chat, people had rallied. Four were there in person and one via video chat. Butterscotch and Lulu made the rounds for rubs and love.

Juliet wiped her swollen, puffy eyes. No doubt they were as red as when pollen released in springtime. Nell had secured an ice pack to Juliet's neck to help with swelling and pain. She didn't think she had whiplash, but Nell wasn't taking any chances and had used an online patient portal to make Juliet an appointment tomorrow. Someone had covered Juliet with a fleece. And Missy had brought a box of cupcakes. Those hadn't made things instantly better, but they helped. So had the wine that Bria opened.

Since the Posse arrived, Juliet had relayed what happened with Remy and Ezra. She'd laughed a few times and cried many tears. Okay, tears kept threatening to fall and nothing she did closed the pipeline.

Her marriage was over, but the finality of tonight hit harder than she expected. Her ring finger felt bare, and her gaze kept drifting to her left hand. It was missing something she'd grown used to wearing.

For better or for worse.

Her engagement ring and wedding band sat on the table amid the wine bottles, glasses, napkins, and a box of cupcakes. But it wasn't only Ezra causing the wellspring of emotions.

Roman's stricken expression was stuck in her mind. She feared her friendship with Katie might be another casualty of tonight. But she was afraid more tears would fall, and she needed a break, so she hadn't mentioned that part of the night yet except for a brief line on her text message. But she would when the time was right.

Tears stung her eyes.

Juliet blinked them away.

Pull yourself together, princess.

"Someone give Juliet more tissues," Selena said from Bria's laptop. "It's good to cry. Get out the emotion now rather than hold it in until later."

What if the tears don't stop?

Nell handed her a box. "Sorry for slacking on the job."

"Thanks, and you're not." Juliet took two. One for her nose and another to crumple and rip to shreds. That had been her MO tonight. "Is it time to take off the ice pack?"

Nell checked her watch. "Seven more minutes."

"Ezra and Remy deserve each other." Missy bit into a cupcake. With all the creative flavors in the box, she chose plain vanilla with white icing. "He's probably crying on her shoulder tonight."

Juliet refilled her wineglass. "I don't think he's capable of tears. Not unless they'd get him something he wanted and were fake."

"Sociopath." Nell reached for another cupcake. "I can't believe Ezra thought he could waltz in here and you'd go back to him."

Selena's face puckered as if she'd bitten a lemon. "He has some nerve, but Juliet said the right things."

"I tried. Ezra acted like this was my fault, as usual." Juliet was tired of being blamed by him or…anyone. "He was so offended I hadn't told him what Charlene said about Deena faking a pregnancy and thinking Remy did the same thing. But there's no way Ezra would have believed me before."

"Wait." Bria straightened. "Deena pretended to be pregnant?"

"I've never heard about this," Missy said.

Nell nodded. "Me, either, though it sounds like my mom knew."

"Call me clueless," Selena said.

"Guess the gossip disappeared with the fake baby." Juliet's muscles hurt, so she stretched. "Charlene told me Paul Dwyer was in love with someone else, but they broke up for a time, and he dated Deena. That mustn't have worked out because he got engaged to his original girlfriend, but Deena said she was pregnant, so he married her instead. She claimed to miscarry after the wedding, but this was in the days before HIPAA, and supposedly there was only a negative pregnancy test. Not a positive one."

"Wow." Nell stared at the blank TV. "My mom hates Deena, but she's never mentioned that to me. Did Elise tell you, Bria?"

"No, but Elise hated Deena, too. Oh, my…" Bria's lips parted. She jumped to her feet and ran into the kitchen.

A door opened, but Juliet didn't know if it was the one to the backyard or the garage.

"Was it something we said?" Nell asked.

The others shrugged, but no one appeared concerned, so Juliet remained seated. That was easiest with the ice pack.

Bria returned, out of breath. She carried a cardboard box. "This has a bunch of Elise's things. It's where I found the journal. There was also a letter, and I wasn't sure who it involved until now."

Missy rose on her knees, but she kept a hand on Butterscotch, who purred like a jet engine. "Oh, I love a good mystery."

"This one involves three people." Bria set the box on the floor and dug through it. She removed a notecard-sized envelope. "Here it is."

"Read it," Selena said on the screen.

"Come on," Missy encouraged. "I want to hear it."

Juliet nodded. "Me, too."

"And me," Nell added.

Bria pulled out a yellowed piece of paper and unfolded it. "My love. I wish with my whole heart that things could be different. I know you want to do the right thing, but I also see and hear how much you don't want to lose me. It's a tough spot to find yourself in. I know because I feel the same. And it sucks."

Missy tilted her head. "It doesn't sound like Elise."

"It's not her handwriting." Bria showed them the letter, and they all agreed. She kept reading. "I'll be honest. This whole 'be honorable' cloak you're wearing isn't helping heal my broken heart. Quite the opposite. But it proves the kind of man you are—caring and kind—and why I wanted to grow old with you at my side."

"How sad." Nell leaned forward. "Whoever wrote this is still in love."

Bria nodded before refocusing on the letter. "But I can't smile and pretend to be happy with how things turned out. I'm not like you. I'm not that big of a person. And I hate myself because I know what this means for us. Well, what's left of us because that must end, too. From this day on, we must stop all contact. I don't want you to acknowledge me, not even with a wave. I can't go back to being just friends, and your new family deserves your full attention. There is no other way."

"Oh, that's heartbreaking." Juliet wiped her eyes. This letter added to her sadness. "The person is complimenting his actions, but she's doing the same thing with hers."

"We find ourselves in an unexpected situation," Bria continued. "The future we planned is no longer possible, but the stakes are too high to ignore to put this off any longer. Doing this is the right decision. I feel that in my heart. And I also know in my heart it is one you would have made yourself eventually."

"That sucks," Selena chimed in. "But not every person you meet is supposed to be in your life forever. Some enter to teach us a lesson and leave when they've done that. Still, my heart hurts for whoever wrote this."

"So, I'm saving you the effort of having to decide this and saying goodbye now. It'll be easier for both of us. I stole my photo from your wallet. Don't be mad because it's not something you need any longer," Bria kept reading. "Forget me. Don't look back at what might have been. Start fresh. Give your heart away with no regrets. You'll always have a piece of my heart, and I'll remember enough of what we shared for both of us. I love you. I will always love you."

The only noises in the living room were the music playing and the cat purring.

"That sounds like the situation Charlene mentioned," Juliet admitted.

"Paul Dwyer would be the man. Deena, the other woman." Selena rubbed her chin. "But who was his fiancée?"

"Not Elise, based on the handwriting," Nell said.

Missy nodded. "Elise never dated Paul Dwyer. One day when we were working, she brought up old boyfriends. I'd dated only Rob, but she rattled off a dozen names. I'm pretty sure that one wasn't on there. She hated Deena, but I didn't work there until after Mr. Dwyer had died, so I never saw them interact."

"My aunt was friendly with him." Bria folded the letter and placed it into the envelope. "He came into the cupcake shop, and they spoke whenever they saw each other on the street. Maybe the letter is from a friend of hers."

"My mom was Elise's best friend, but she dated my dad throughout high school and college." Nell typed on her phone. "The handwriting isn't hers, either."

"Honorable, kind, and caring all describe the Paul Dwyer I remember," Selena said.

Juliet nodded. "He was, and this has Deena written all over it. But we need to figure out who was in love with Paul."

"I could ask Dalton," Bria offered. "He's not his mom's biggest fan, but this might hurt him if he didn't know."

"Don't mention it to him, then." Nell held up her phone. "I asked my mom if she knows more."

"Thanks," Bria said. "I hope Charlene does. I might learn something new about my aunt."

Juliet yawned.

"Tired?" Nell asked.

"A little. With the party, being rear-ended, Ezra, and Roman—"

"Wait." Bria's intense stare bore into Juliet. "You never told us more about what happened with Roman."

She blinked, hoping to cool the burning behind her eyelids. "After Ezra left, Roman came over all cave-dweller-dog-marking-his-territory-like. He assumed Ezra and I were together again and was upset. He said Katie needed me. It was like déjà vu the night I found out about Ezra's affair. When I told Roman he was wrong, he apologized and explained his reason. I understand we all have baggage. But his reaction, what he said about Katie, was too much like Ezra. I can't—won't—put myself in that position again. If I get involved in a relationship, I want one that's good for me and equal. But not right now. I need to figure out myself before I add another person to the mix."

"I'm so proud of you for putting yourself first and not settling." Selena raised her glass. "To Juliet."

Everyone cheered and drank. Juliet did, too. A little more wine and her brain might turn off so she could sleep through the night before she had to start another day with all these emotions brimming.

Something beeped.

Nell removed the ice pack. "You're doing great."

In some ways, yes. As Juliet looked at each of her friends, her love for them overflowed. With their help, she wouldn't be only great, but she would also soar.

If only Juliet could skip all the steps in between. But she knew what Selena would say to that. Elise, too. Juliet reached for another cupcake.

chapter twenty-four

B RIA WOULD RATHER be at home with Juliet, eating cupcakes and trying to crack the letter writer's identity. Unfortunately, Charlene had only heard the story through the grapevine, which surprised everyone because she and Elise had been besties their entire lives. But instead of being in Berry Lake, Bria was an hour's drive away, about to enter the county jail's building.

It was the last place she expected to be, but her father asked her to come earlier that day.

As she walked inside, her feet scuffed the floor, but a slow pace or falling on her bottom wouldn't make the visit go any faster.

The lobby wasn't crowded. Perhaps the jail staggered appointment times.

Bria signed in—thirty minutes early as required—and placed her purse, phone, and jacket into a locker. The key went into her jeans pocket. Now, all she had to do was wait until it was her turn.

She ran her sweaty palms over her thighs.

Some people sat in chairs. If Bria did that, she would only end up fidgeting. Where she stood gave her the perfect view of the door. Unfortunately, bolting and driving home wasn't an option.

That might be why they made visitors store their items in a locker. With their keys out of reach, they couldn't make a quick getaway without some effort.

Not that she would do that.

Unlike her dad, she tried not to disappoint others. Not if she could help it.

"Bria," a man called her name.

She turned to see Marc Carpenter walking toward her. The lawyer wore a suit and tie as if he'd come from his office in Berry Lake.

Her muscles bunched. "What are you doing here?"

"Brian wanted me here tonight."

Chills shot down her arms. As she breathed, her chest hurt.

"Is my dad okay?" she whispered, sounding more like a child than an adult. She wanted to be indifferent toward her father. But more times than not, she became that hero-worshipping kid who longed for her father's attention and love, even at thirty-three. Because a part of her still wanted those things.

"He's fine." Marc's dad-of-the-year voice comforted her.

Bria released the breath she'd been holding. "Thank goodness."

She hated expecting the worst. But life had taught her that. Marc's son would never have to worry about him ending up behind bars and facing years in prison like hers.

"There's no reason for you to be concerned. Brian wants to run something by you. That's all." Marc didn't sound or appear worried. "Your father wants me here because you and I will have a few things to discuss after we visit with him."

"Okay." But ever since Aunt Elise died, Bria kept waiting for the next bad thing to happen. Boulders had been sitting in her stomach for weeks. Today's unease felt more like pain between her eyebrows about to explode into a massive headache.

Marc flashed a closed-mouth smile. "Everything will be okay."

Bria half laughed. "Says the attorney standing in the county jail's lobby."

Not being alone relieved her. Dalton had wanted to come, but visiting hours ran from six to nine on Thursday nights. It made little sense for him to drive all this way when he had a meeting on Friday morning in Portland. She would see him on Saturday for breakfast.

"Now, if I were your father's defense attorney, that would be another story," Marc said.

She shivered, thinking of the tall man with a linebacker's build and intense brown eyes, who represented her father. "That guy scares me."

"He's skilled at what he does and exactly what your dad needs."

Not to mention expensive. Bria had paid the criminal defense attorney's initial retainer fee from her savings account, knowing her father would never repay her. As Selena T said, it was only money and was meant to be spent. Those words completely opposed the CPA in her and her practicality and need for security, but she wanted him to have more than a public defender with so much at stake.

"Your father isn't helping himself by remaining silent about his whereabouts that night," Marc added. "He needs an alibi. I say this not only as a lawyer but also as someone who's known your family my entire life."

Bria didn't understand why her father kept saying he was innocent, but he wouldn't back those claims with a name or location to prove it. "I'll keep trying to get him to say something."

"I'm not giving up, either. I was closer with your aunt and lost track of your dad over the years, but he and I used to run around with Paul Dwyer back in the day."

"Aunt Elise called you the three musketeers."

Marc laughed. "We were that. Good times."

That reminded Bria of the letter. "Do you know who Paul dated before he married Deena?"

"There were a few girls in high school, but he was serious with a woman he met in college."

"Someone from Berry Lake?"

"Not that I recall."

That explained why Charlene hadn't known the woman's identity. Oh well, Bria tried. She needed to focus on her father now. "If I can't convince my dad to say something, I hope you can. You've been such a big help with Aunt Elise's estate. She mentioned you would try to make things as simple as possible."

Marc nodded. "I'll keep doing that. Even after probate ends, I promised Elise to be here for you."

"I appreciate that." Her aunt had touched many lives in Berry Lake, and those people from Marc to Sheriff Dooley were doing what they could for Bria and the cupcake shop, even though Elise and the bakery were gone.

"Marc Carpenter and Bria Landon," a man called.

She and Marc followed him to a room with tables and partitions.

Her father remained seated. He wore an orange jumpsuit. Funnily enough, it complemented his tanned skin.

"Bria. Marc." Her dad welcomed them with a grin that didn't reach his eyes. "Thanks for visiting me tonight. The times aren't the most convenient."

Marc sat. He adjusted his suit jacket. "A late dinner won't hurt."

Bria took a seat next to the lawyer. "How are you?"

"I'm hanging in there, baby doll. Don't worry about me." The words came quickly, but his features remained tight. "Still dating Dalton Dwyer?"

She nodded. "It's going well."

"Have you found a new job?" Her dad's interest surprised her, unless he wanted to know when she would have money coming in again.

"I've sent out some resumes but no replies yet."

"You'll get some."

She appreciated his confidence, but she didn't need it. Bria was skilled in accounting. She would be an asset to any company. "I'm in no rush. I want to find the best fit wherever that might be."

Her dad stiffened before glancing at Marc. "You're not set on staying in San Diego?"

"No." Bria didn't hesitate to answer. "My job kept me there. Now that I don't have that, I plan to sell my condo and move to Berry Lake."

"Because of Dalton?" her father asked.

"He lives in Portland and is one reason, but my friends are there. I've been tossing around the idea of opening an accounting service."

"Reach out if you do," Marc said. "I'd love to hire someone local."

Her father's posture relaxed. "This is fantastic news."

A wide grin spread across Marc's face. "Told you this would work out."

Her dad nodded. "You did."

Bria had a feeling they'd left her out of a previous conversation. "What's going on?"

He cleared his throat. "I want to sell my share of the cupcake shop."

A good thing she was sitting, or she might have fallen flat on the floor. Most likely, face-first.

She opened her mouth to speak, but words failed her. She took a breath and another—time to try again. "You told me you wanted to sell, but I never expected, well, this. Especially right now."

Bria tried to wrap her mind around it. Her heart struggled less.

"I'd hoped for the charges to be dropped at the arraignment," he added. "When that didn't happen, I looked closer at my financial situation. You paid the attorney's retainer, and I appreciate that, but the legal fees are only going to add up from here on out. And other expenses can't wait. I need to pay them now."

Bria had no idea what those were. She assumed he lived out of a suitcase and traveled from one get-rich scheme to another. He might have an apartment or house he used as a home base. To be honest, she'd never asked him.

It wasn't as if she hadn't cared, but they'd never talked about anything other than surface level stuff. She couldn't remember the last holiday they'd spent together. Her father had missed every single life event of hers. Not that there'd been that many, but he'd even skipped Aunt Elise's funeral.

Bria dragged her upper teeth over her lower lip. "I'm not sure what to say other than thank you."

"Don't say anything." He glanced around as if to see if he were being watched. "You've been clear about your intention to keep the cupcake shop, and Marc mentioned your friends are interested in becoming co-owners."

She sat ramrod straight, her muscles tightening. The Posse discussed that in Missy's hospital room, but only the five of them had been there. Bria glanced at Marc. "How do you know that?"

A sheepish expression formed on the attorney's face. "Selena Tremblay paid me a visit when she was here last month."

Of course, she did. Probably before or after she purchased the McMurray home. Anything Selena did shouldn't surprise Bria. Her friend never waited for something to happen. She took charge, going after what she wanted, every time. Once again, it was paying off. Yet Bria had so many questions.

"So a sale like this is possible?" she asked. "I wasn't sure with probate."

"It's not, but Selena can loan Brian money. She wants the other three members of your group included, too. The Posse?"

Bria nodded. "The Berry Lake Cupcake Posse. That's what Elise called us when we worked for her one summer."

"Oh, that makes more sense," Marc said. "Brian will use his share of his inheritance for collateral. Once probate closes and you both take ownership, he can sign over his part of the cupcake shop and building to her in place of the loan repayment. I believe it's a good way to get Brian the money he needs right now."

Selena was as generous as she was successful. "It sounds like a solid solution."

"It is. I haven't spoken to Selena because your father wanted to run this by you first."

This was happening. Bria forced herself to sit still. "Thanks, Dad."

"Anything for you, baby doll," he said.

Not true. She bit her lip. But being in jail might have him rethinking things in his life, including her.

"I have information for your friends, and then they can speak to me," Marc offered.

Tingles erupted. Bria wiggled her toes. She should grab on to this opportunity and hold tight with both hands, but she had to ask her dad. "Are you sure? This isn't what you wanted."

"I'm positive. It wasn't what I originally intended, but things have changed now." He shifted in his chair before glancing around the visitation area once again. "The truth is, I convinced your aunt to leave me half the shop. I had my reasons. They seemed valid, even reasonable, at the time. But if I'd let her give you everything as she desired, someone might not have torched the place."

Someone.

Not him.

"We'll rebuild." The five of them would keep her aunt's legacy alive. "The way Aunt Elise wanted the shop to be."

Her dad smiled softly. "I know you will. And I can't wait to see what you do."

That gave Bria the opening she needed. "If you told Marc or your other attorney where you were on that Thursday night, you could help us."

"I'm innocent." Her father's firm tone matched his posture. He sounded and looked more like his old self. "I won't be convicted."

"Don't be naïve, Brian." Marc's voice was harsh. "It doesn't work that way. You had a key. You had a motive."

Her dad having a motive was a gray area in Bria's mind. "My father wanted to sell the cupcake shop. Destroying it only decreases the value. That doesn't fit if the motive was to profit."

Her dad nodded once. "Exactly. The jury will believe me."

She didn't want her father to go to jail if he was innocent. But despite what he claimed, the fact he wouldn't provide proof suggested he was guilty. That gnawed at her. "Dad, please, if you have an alibi—"

"Trust me, baby doll. Everything will be okay." His voice wavered, suggesting he wasn't as confident as he appeared. "Marc will go over the details with you, and you can discuss it with your friends."

Bria wanted to pinch herself, but something—the man sitting across from her—kept her from celebrating. "Are you really okay?"

"Elise meant for you to have the cupcake shop. It's what my sister wanted. I also have faith in my attorney and the system. I'll be fine."

Marc cleared his throat. "Brian, please don't sacrifice your freedom on the sword of justice. People assume you're the arsonist. They want you to be guilty. If you have any information, big or small, give it up to help your case. No matter your lawyer's reputation, attorneys aren't miracle workers."

"I don't need a miracle," her father replied. "I have the truth on my side."

If that were the case, would he be in jail without bail?

Still, Bria wished she had her father's faith. She nearly laughed. That was the first thing she'd wanted from him besides his love in a very long time.

On Friday, Bria sat at her kitchen table with the Posse. Afternoon tea had been Juliet's idea since Selena had to drive back to Seattle that night. It made for a long day, but she'd wanted to be here in person this time.

A pretty tablecloth covered the table. Five teapots with different flavors of tea sat next to a plate of cupcakes and triangular-cut cucumber sandwiches. There were even sugar cubes and small gold teaspoons. Not to mention flowers. Juliet had gone all out.

As usual.

Nell grabbed a cupcake. "All we're missing are scones and clotted cream."

"And tiaras." Selena raised a floral teacup. "We need to do tea right, especially when our host is a princess."

Juliet blushed. "I didn't have time to bake scones, but we can do this again. I'll see if I can get five tiaras wholesale from Charlene."

"Christmas is coming up," Missy chimed in using a sing-song voice.

Everyone looked at her. Bria was surprised to hear her sound so lighthearted.

"What?" Missy asked. "It's October. December is right around the corner."

"Duly noted." Selena sounded way too serious. "I expect your Christmas lists before Thanksgiving."

That was the perfect lead-in. "There might not be extra money this year for gifts."

Four questioning gazes stared at Bria.

"But we're all getting something much better." She drum-rolled her hands on the table. "The Berry Lake Cupcake Shop."

Selena stiffened. "You spoke with Marc and your dad agreed?"

Bria nodded. "It's a go."

Selena's eyes gleamed. "Yes!"

Nell pursed her lips. "Would someone please tell the rest of us what's going on?"

"My dad needs money, so he's borrowing it from Selena—"

"Not just me." She circled her hand around the table. "From the four of us. I'm setting up an S-corp to handle it."

"When the probate is over, he'll transfer his ownership in the building and cupcake shop and the loan will be forgiven."

"The business and building aren't worth as much post-fire, but we'll probably need the same amount we discussed before or a little more for repairs." Selena kept looking at the other three at the table. "I can provide the funds upfront, in case anyone can't afford it right now."

Juliet raised her hand. "Thanks. I'll have a better idea of my financial situation soon, but I'm willing to sell all my jewelry and designer clothes if that'll help."

"Logan supports this one hundred percent, so lack of money won't be a problem. And the terms are good. No interest." Selena beamed brighter than Sirius A, the star that lit up the night sky. "Our lawyer did some groundwork for me before I approached Marc in September."

Missy sat still. No blinking, no breathing, nothing.

"You okay?" Bria asked her.

Missy exhaled as if she had been holding her breath. "We're all going to co-own the cupcake shop. Really?"

Her disbelief and shaky tone were understandable. Bria had wanted this to happen, but that had been one more pipe dream in a long list of them. "Yes."

A smile finally appeared, making Missy look like she was back in high school. "I've saved most of the money from when Rob died. I've been saving to buy a place, but Jenny wants me to stay in the guesthouse, which works out perfectly now."

"You'll be a co-owner and the manager," Bria said. "You okay with that, Missy?"

"Yes!"

Nell wiped her eyes. "I've been saving for a house, a wedding, something I thought would make me happy in the future, but this… This is more than I imagined being able to do. I'm tingling all the way to the tips of my toes. I'm not sure I have enough, but I'll contribute what I've got to the cause."

"We have so many plans to make." Bria got up.

"Sit," Selena ordered. "We have plenty of time to figure things out. Right now, we celebrate."

Juliet refilled everyone's teacup with the right tea. How she remembered all five flavors was a mystery to Bria, but maybe that explained why her friend excelled at event planning.

"A toast." Bria raised a pink floral teacup. "To the new co-owners of the Berry Lake Cupcake Shop."

Nell raised her platinum-rimmed teacup with gray flowers. "And to Elise for hiring us to work for her that fateful summer."

Selena nodded. "Nothing is going to stop us from succeeding."

"And keeping Elise's legacy going," Juliet added. "To all of us."

Missy raised her orange teacup. "Cupcake Posse forever."

chapter twenty-five

J ULIET FILLED HER teacup with Earl Grey on Saturday morning and placed a homemade blueberry scone on a small plate. Nell had put the idea of scones in her head yesterday, and Juliet wanted to continue celebrating their cupcake shop.

Theirs.

She loved the sound of that.

Lulu sat at her feet and stared up at her with an eagerness in those brown puppy dog eyes.

"You've had your treat for this morning." If Juliet fed Lulu something each time she begged, the dog would need to go on a diet. She ate two times a day with a couple of treats as it was. "You'll have to wait until this afternoon for another one."

The dog panted as if understanding her.

Lulu probably did because she loved to eat. Sweets were her favorite food item but not good for her.

Juliet carried her breakfast to the living room and turned on the TV.

Butterscotch stretched on the top of the couch, nestled between the pillows and the wall. It didn't look comfortable, but the cat didn't seem to mind.

Today was the perfect time to get caught up on shows Juliet missed. She'd put on leggings and a T-shirt to take Lulu for a walk, or Juliet would have stayed in her pajamas all day—her new guilty pleasure when she didn't have to go into work or host a party, which wasn't often.

Not that she was complaining.

Busy meant earning money and making a name for herself.

Well, within Events by Charlene.

That was enough for Juliet.

This was her first Saturday off since mid-September—Charlene's orders, even if Juliet would put on double the number of tea parties next weekend. "Ready to binge-watch with me, Lulu?"

The dog trotted out of the kitchen, but she didn't hop on the couch as usual.

Footsteps sounded.

Bria entered the living room in a pair of jeans tucked into suede boots, a pretty burnt orange sweater, and a scarf with fall colors. "That scone looks delicious."

"There are more. Take a few scones with you, so I don't eat them all."

"We're visiting my dad after we have breakfast. I'll take him one." She headed into the kitchen. She came out with a scone rolled in a paper towel. Lulu trotted over to her. Bria patted the dog's head. "Thanks."

"Have fun with Dalton."

Heart-eyes appeared, and an adorable, lovestruck expression spread over Bria's face. "I will. Any plans for today?"

"Binging a show to catch up on episodes and chores. Though I might skip the laundry." Not doing chores on a regular schedule was an unaccustomed luxury for Juliet. With Selena's guidance, Juliet had replaced the "should do" with "wanted to do." So far, that was working well. "I have enough clean clothes to get me through a few more days."

"Then relax. There are leftovers for lunch and dinner or splurge on takeout."

"Maybe I will." Her tip money from the last event would more than cover that.

Her attorney was pleased with the divorce negotiations. Juliet wasn't counting every penny the way she had been, but she was still cautious with her spending. Ezra's lawyer had told him using an unfair prenup might cost him in the end, so Juliet would now receive money from the sale of the house and alimony for three years versus one. The only sticking point was who would pay for her totaled vehicle. However, she wasn't complaining when she'd expected so little. She'd been driving Elise's car so that Juliet didn't have to rent one.

"Though leftovers sound good, too," she added.

"If you want company, call Missy and Nell."

Bria sounded so much like her aunt. Juliet grinned, thinking about the ways Elise had left her mark. "Nell's busy with Gage and Welles."

"Oh, right." Bria bit her lip. "I hope they're doing something low-key like a movie. But as long as Nell's happy."

"Exactly. Except I worry she'll hurt herself."

"She's an adult and an RN. At some point, her self-preservation instincts will kick in."

"True, but we'll see if this continues to keep Charlene out of Nell's business."

Bria shook her head. "Maybe if Charlene didn't push her daughters so hard, things would happen as they should. And Nell wouldn't need to go out with a guy who's wrong for her."

"Not sure that's possible for Charlene." Juliet's laugh was more bittersweet than anything. "I think she intended to do the same thing with Roman and me when she introduced us."

Worry flashed on Bria's face. "I'm sorry."

"It's how Charlene is." If Juliet were honest with herself, the thought of being with him had flitted through her mind. "She can't help herself."

"Charlene probably could but won't. She and Aunt Elise were best friends but night-and-day different."

"Different is good." Juliet pictured the members of the Posse. "Look at the five of us. We're each different."

Bria nodded. "I'm the practical, boring one."

"You're the one who's smart with money and numbers. Your talent will come in handy once the cupcake shop is up and running again."

"Thank you." Bria crossed her fingers. "I hope Brew and Steep agrees with you."

"What do you mean?"

"I'm meeting with the owners in the morning to discuss my accounting services."

Juliet leaned forward. "Oh, that's wonderful. I'll plan a special dinner to celebrate your first official client."

Bria shook her head. "Let's not jinx it, but I'm hopeful. I don't want to use too much more of my savings."

That practical side of Juliet's friend was never too far from the surface. "I make dinner most nights, so it's not jinxing anything. This meeting will work out. And if they can't see what an amazing accountant you are, between Berry Lake and all the surrounding towns, you have a vast area full of potential customers. And you can even expand beyond the area, contact old clients from San Diego and meet with them virtually."

"Listen to you." Bria beamed. "You're Ms. Boss Babe Business now."

Heat rushed up Juliet's neck. "It's Selena. Oh, and Charlene. She's been teaching me more about the business side of event planning."

"It's great advice." Bria studied Juliet. "But that's pretty specific. Are you striking out on your own?"

"I thought about it for about a day. I even came up with a cute name for the business. Tiaras and Teacups."

"That's adorable."

Juliet nodded. "But I found out there's more to doing parties than food and favors. The insurance is expensive. Plus, you need other stuff."

Bria nodded. "And though Washington has no personal state income tax, businesses still pay."

"Yes, and that's another reason I decided against it. I'm making decent money without the headaches of owning a business. Working for Charlene makes the most sense, now that I'll be a co-owner of the cupcake shop." Juliet shimmied her shoulders. "I love the sound of that."

"Me, too. So much." Bria picked up her keys and a water bottle. "I need to get going, or I'll be late. Have a relaxing day."

The front door opened and shut.

Butterscotch stretched, opening his eyes but not lifting his head.

"Enjoy your nap?"

He closed his eyes as if saying he wasn't done.

"Well, sleep well on your second nap."

The cat purred. Butterscotch enjoyed playing with the red laser light and his feather toy, but naps were his favorite activity of the day. Still, he was a chill cat, rarely making a sound unless a meal was over five minutes late. "I finally found the perfect male."

Juliet giggled.

Lulu jumped on the couch, sniffing at Butterscotch before circling a few times before she lay next to Juliet.

Juliet settled back, enjoying her breakfast and the show.

Lulu's ears perked. She barked and jumped to the rug.

"It's probably a delivery or the mail."

The mail slot opened, and a padded envelope fell to the floor.

Lulu whimpered.

Butterscotch raised his head.

Juliet stood. "What's wrong?"

The little dog hunched as if in pain and groaned.

Her stomach sank.

"Oh, no." She dropped to the floor next to her. "Did you hurt yourself when you jumped off the couch?"

Juliet touched Lulu.

The dog flinched.

Her stomach fell.

Butterscotch came over to the dog and sniffed. The cat lay next to Lulu.

She grabbed her phone and hit Roman's number. He was a vet and would know what to do.

One ring…

The call clicked over to voice mail.

Ugh. She hit Sabine's number.

One ring. Two.

Juliet touched Lulu's head.

"Please answer."

The line connected. "Hello."

"Something's wrong with Lulu." The words rushed out, one after another as if strung together. She took a breath. "Lulu hurt herself when she jumped off the couch, but she's done that a hundred times since she came to live here. She's hunched and hurting. What do I do?"

"The animal clinic is open on Saturdays for both appointments and emergencies. I'll tell them you're coming in."

"Okay." Juliet's pulse raced. "I'll go right now."

"Wait," Sabine ordered. "Calm down. It's hard when an animal is hurting, but you need to drive safely."

"I know." And Juliet did. "It's just Mrs. Vernon trusts me—"

"Old habits are hard to break, honey. Whatever happened isn't your fault."

"Not my fault."

"That's right. It's not your fault. Keep saying that if you have to."

Still, responsibility bore down on Juliet's shoulders. She gripped the phone. "Okay, I will."

"Make sure you take your purse and your phone. More than once, dealing with an injured animal, I forgot one or the other or both."

Juliet grabbed her purse and car keys. "Got them. Is it okay to carry her?"

"Can she walk?"

Panting, Lulu lay on the floor.

Juliet's heart hurt. "I don't think so."

"Put her in Butterscotch's cat bed to transport her."

"Okay." Except she felt anything but okay.

"I need to take Sheridan and Michael to the airport, but Max can do it if you need—"

"See your daughter and future son-in-law off." Juliet forced the words from her dry throat. She would rather tell Sabine to please meet her at the clinic, but she couldn't. That was the old Juliet. "I can handle this."

She would keep repeating those words until she believed them.

"Update me on what they say."

"I will, thanks." Juliet disconnected from the call and dropped her phone in her purse.

Carefully, she lifted Lulu, who continued whimpering, each sound sending a this-is-your-fault dagger into Juliet's chest. She placed her on Butterscotch's bed. "I know, baby girl. But we have to go to the vet and find out what's wrong with you. They'll make you feel better."

At least Juliet hoped so.

She carried Lulu to Elise's car and placed the cat bed onto the back seat.

Her hands trembled. Juliet didn't want to get in another accident. "Breathe."

Lulu whined.

"It won't be long, sweetie."

Juliet backed out of the driveway. Her hands gripped the steering wheel in the ten and two positions she'd learned from her late grandfather. Her foot wanted to press on the accelerator to get there faster, but she drove like her grandmother on the way home from church, slow and steady and ten miles under the speed limit.

As she pulled into the clinic's parking lot, relief flooded her. "We're here."

Once again, she carefully picked up Lulu on the cat bed. "We're almost there. It's going to be okay."

Juliet said the words for both of their sakes. She used her hip to open the door and then moved to the counter where a woman with two brown braids sat. "This is Lulu. She's injured, but I'm not sure what happened."

"Sabine Culpepper called to say you'd be in. We know Lulu from when she was with Mrs. Vernon, so I pulled her chart." The woman smiled. "It won't be long. Have a seat."

"Thank you." Juliet stepped away from the counter. She didn't want to sit. It was her first health issue with anyone in her care, and Juliet was freaking out big-time. A good thing she'd never had children, or she would be an even hotter mess.

A young woman with green-striped hair stepped into the lobby. She held a file. "Lulu."

Juliet moved toward her. "Right here."

"I'm Delilah." She smiled, but the tension in Juliet's muscles sharpened. "You're a first-time pet mom."

It wasn't a question, but Juliet nodded.

"We have no appointments available today. They're all full, but we offer emergency visits."

"What's that?"

"We take your dog to triage, where they'll be examined," Delilah explained. "After that, the doctor comes out to speak with you."

"Oh, okay." Except it wasn't. Juliet didn't want to be separated when Lulu was hurting so much. What if she thought she was being abandoned again? But if those were the rules… "So I wait here?"

"Yes. Lulu will be in excellent hands. Dr. Goya is an excellent vet."

Goya, not Byrne.

Juliet blew out a breath.

Roman wasn't at work. It was a Saturday, but his schedule seemed to change. Not that she'd seen him. He must be out with Katie. Or was he dating someone?

Juliet cringed.

Stop thinking about him.

She needed to focus on Lulu.

"Can I please take her?" Delilah asked.

Juliet loosened her grip on the cat bed. "Sorry. I'm…worried."

"Not a problem." Delilah took the pillow. "It's hard to see them hurting."

With a nod, Juliet lightly touched Lulu's head. "They'll take good care of you, and I'll be out here. I won't leave you. I promise. I love you."

As Delilah opened a door and carried Lulu away, Juliet wrapped her arms around herself. The lobby was empty, so she had her choice of seats.

The only problem?

She still didn't want to sit. Except pacing wouldn't accomplish much, so she forced herself into a chair. The stack of magazines was all pet related. Not that Juliet could focus on anything.

She could let the Posse know what was happening, but that would sound the cavalry. She didn't want to ruin their plans for today.

Besides, Lulu was her responsibility. Juliet needed to handle this. If only to prove to herself she could.

chapter twenty-six

D ALTON DIDN'T MIND getting up early on a Saturday morning when his alarm blared. He and Bria had a schedule to stick to if they wanted to see Brian during visitor hours at the county jail. Now that they were together at the café, he wished he'd woken up earlier.

Bria inhaled the crisp autumn air. "This is lovely."

The water view from the Lake Café was beautiful, but she was gorgeous. Dalton had another reason for choosing this place for breakfast. The secluded deck only had a handful of tables that had to be reserved in advance. Out here, no one would wander by their table asking Bria about the cupcake shop and her father. The questions had been wearing on her since her aunt's death last month.

"I've never eaten here," she added.

"I've been here once before." With his boss, Tanner, six months ago, when they were looking over the town to assess development potential. Dalton had only wanted to get as far away from Berry

Lake and his mother. But fifteen years later, he recognized the possibilities and the money to be made from his hometown. "I thought you might enjoy this place."

"I do." As Bria stared at the water, the breeze toyed with the ends of her hair. "But I prefer being with you, whether here or at the Burger Barn."

"Same." All Dalton wanted to do was make her happy. He hoped what he said next would. "I put in an offer on the cottage on Pinewood Lane. I plan to ask Tanner if I can work from Berry Lake two days a week. I'd like Fridays and Mondays off to limit my driving between here and Portland."

"That would be great, but you mentioned you couldn't use the place until January. What will you do until then? I'm not ready for—"

"Neither am I." They didn't want to move too fast, even though they sort of were. "Tanner has a vacant lake house. No one is booked until the holidays."

"You're going all in."

"You're worth it. And you prefer to have plans."

She blushed. "Thank you for doing all this for me."

"It's not only for you. I want to do this for us." Dalton reached across the table and held her hand. "We've been given a second chance. That's not something I take for granted."

"Me, either." She glanced at her coffee cup before meeting his eyes. "What if Tanner says no?"

"Then we make the most of the weekends." Dalton squeezed her hand. "We were going to try a long-distance relationship when we were living in different states and a plane ride apart. Now we're only a short drive away from each other. This will work."

"I love how confident you sound."

"That's because I am."

She laced her fingers with his. "I am, too."

The server returned with the bill folder. Dalton signed the charge slip and placed his credit card in his wallet. "Ready to visit your dad?"

She hesitated.

"We don't have to go," he said.

"I told him I'd come."

"It's hard."

Bria nodded. "I want to support him, but everyone in town thinks he set the fire. A part of me believes it, too. Yet, he sounds sincere when he says he's innocent. I want…"

"You want to believe."

"More than anything. But what if this is one more empty pot at the end of the rainbow? What if there's enough evidence to prove he set fire to the cupcake shop and nearly killed Missy? What if he's found guilty?"

"You'll know, which will hurt, but it'll be better than the uncertainty right now."

Bria nodded. "You're right. I need to know. And I'll go from there."

"We go from there." Dalton raised her hand to his mouth and kissed it. "You said your dad is the only one you have left, but you have me. I won't include my family in that mix because you don't want them. Well, except for Ian. The rest of them aren't worth knowing. But you'll always have me."

Gratitude shone in her eyes. "Thank you."

Dalton could sit and stare at her all day, but they had a tight time window. "Let's go see your dad."

Breakfast with Dalton had been fantastic, and Bria was grateful for him. But the warm and fuzzy feeling at the café morphed into something heavier and full of dread during the hour-long drive to the county jail.

He opened the door to the lobby. "Thirty-three minutes early."

She signed in and regretfully threw the scone away. No food was allowed to be brought in. "Now, we wait."

Except it wasn't so easy to do. Her body buzzed like a bumblebee. She wanted to be anywhere but there.

Bria wrapped her hands over her stomach.

Dalton put his arm around her. "I won't ask if you're okay. It's clear you're not."

Not trusting her voice, she nodded.

"But I'm here." He pulled her closer, and she sank against him. "I meant what I said. You're stuck with me. We'll get through this."

"Thanks."

Her throat was so tight the one word was all she could manage. She appreciated her dad putting Dalton on the list of approved visitors, or she'd be seeing him on her own. Could she have handled that? Yes, but she didn't want to have to do it.

Bria was torn. It was as if half of her sided with the Berry Lake residents who demanded her father be put away for the rest of his life. The other part of her hurt, knowing her dad was behind bars and alone. Coexisting with those two halves was…difficult.

She wanted justice to be served the same as others did, but his claim of being innocent kept playing in her head on an endless loop. Yet, one question plagued her like a bad dream.

Did he set fire to the cupcake shop?

She glanced around at the other families waiting to see loved ones. It was more crowded than on Thursday night. People spoke in muted voices with eyes averted. Did they feel the same as her? Probably not, since every person's situation was different.

"I want to believe him," she whispered to Dalton.

He squeezed her tightly. "I know you do."

"But my doubts are real and keep growing. No bail means he's not only a flight risk. There must be evidence tying him to the fire, right?"

"I would assume so."

"I'm wondering if it's a ploy or some kind of delusion, and he needs help. Mental help, I mean."

"That's something to bring up with his attorney."

"I'll call on Monday. If it were that…"

"He might not have realized what he was doing."

She nodded.

"Bria Landon and Dalton Dwyer," someone called.

"Here we go." She followed the person to the visiting area where her father sat. "Dad."

He straightened, but the dark circles under his eyes and the worry etched into each line on his face broke her heart. "Bria. Dalton. Thanks for coming."

They sat across the table from him.

Her dad started to speak but stopped himself.

"What is it?" she asked.

Her dad hunched his shoulders and stared at the table. "I'm not sure where to begin."

Her heart lurched. His tone frightened her. Unable to speak, she gripped Dalton's hand.

"We have thirty minutes," Dalton reminded her father. "But we can come back on Thursday evening if you need more time."

Her dad shook his head. "It can't wait. Did you talk to your friends about the cupcake shop?"

"Yes, they're all in. Marc drew up the contract as you requested. Selena will contact your attorney on Monday."

Her dad relaxed. "Wonderful, but I need money paid elsewhere first. Today, if possible."

Huh? "I don't understand."

"I thought there was enough, but this month's payment bounced. The place understands the situation. Except I'm running out of time. This is more important than the money going to my attorney."

He made no sense. "What are you talking about?"

His face contorted. "You wanted me to give an alibi. This is it."

She sucked in a breath.

"Go to the Cliffside Manor in Wishing Bay," he instructed.

Bria had visited the small coastal town, but she hadn't been there since she was younger. "You took me on vacations there."

Her dad's expression softened. "A long time ago."

She remembered little except for building sandcastles and eating saltwater taffy.

"Introduce yourself to the receptionist. Tell her you'll be paying for room three thirteen." His chest appeared to collapse, so he sank into himself. "The place has sign-in logs and videos. Tell my attorney so he can get whatever records...evidence he needs to give me an alibi."

Every word he said floored Bria. "I will, but why did you wait so long?"

"I didn't want you to hate me."

"Dad—"

"Please don't hate me."

"I'm so confused." None of this conversation made sense.

"Go to Wishing Bay, and you'll see." He sounded adamant. "Don't wait. Go today. And pay. Please pay what I owe."

She glanced at Dalton. "I…"

"We'll go now. Unless you have something else for Bria."

"That's all." Her father's eyes appeared haunted. "I love you. I didn't always show it, but everything I did… I love you, baby doll. And I hope you can forgive me."

Bria didn't know what she would find at the Cliffside Manor, but she hoped it wasn't as bad as her dad made it sound. Because at this moment, she had no idea what to expect, and that terrified her.

chapter twenty-seven

TIME DRAGGED FOR Juliet in the clinic's waiting room. The clock's hand moved as if traveling through maple syrup and slowing with each revolution. The constant ring, ring, ringing of the phone made her want to volunteer to be the receptionist. Anything would be better than sitting here and doing nothing.

A young couple entered, checked in at the counter, and sat with a small dog in their lap. Soon, a tech called for them. They must have had an appointment.

Her knee bounced.

What was taking so long?

A man came in, paid by inserting a credit card into a reader, and left with a cat in a gray, hard-sided carrier.

Oh, no. An icky feeling trickled along Juliet's spine.

An emergency visit wouldn't be free, and depending on what needed to be done, this might be expensive. How much would the treatment cost?

She checked her banking app.

Gulped.

Her chest tightened.

Breathe. Just breathe.

Juliet tried, but what if she couldn't afford to have Lulu treated?

A lump burned in her throat. Her vision blurred.

She blinked before staring up at the ceiling, wanting to keep the tears from falling. It was one thing to cry at home. She didn't want to do that in public.

A pamphlet about payment plans through something called CareCredit sat in a plastic container on the checkout counter.

Could she qualify for that with no credit?

Probably not because everything for the past twelve years had been in Ezra's name.

There was another option. All she had to do was swallow her pride.

Stop.

This was about Lulu, not her. And it wasn't like Juliet wouldn't owe for her portion of the cupcake shop.

She blew out a breath before pulling out her phone.

> **JULIET:** *Something's wrong with Lulu. I'm at the animal clinic. Not sure I can afford her treatment. Can I borrow the money?*
> **SELENA:** *Are you at the Berry Lake Animal Clinic?*
> **JULIET:** *Yes.*
> **SELENA:** *I'll take care of it. Not a loan. You did a favor for Mrs. V. You shouldn't go into debt over this.*

Juliet wiped her eyes. Of course, Selena would say that.

> **JULIET:** *I guess going into debt over the cupcake shop is enough.*
> **SELENA:** *Exactly. I'll call them.*
> **JULIET:** *Thank you.*
> **SELENA:** *Asking for help shows how much you've changed.*
> **JULIET:** *I'm trying.*
> **SELENA:** *You're doing great. Let me know how Lulu is. Love you.*
> **JULIET:** *xoxox*

Juliet sat taller. She'd been on her own, even married and with her grandmother living in the same town. The Cupcake Posse reuniting had changed everything.

Changed her.

And at the perfect time, given her husband and grandmother were no longer part of her life.

The clinic's phone rang.

Selena.

Juliet rubbed her eyes again. Her friends were the best in the world. It was too bad they'd lost touch over the years, but none of them could change the past. All they could do was move forward, which was what she was trying to do.

She was on her own, but not alone.

Big difference.

Juliet would have the life she wanted—no more settling and living in fear of losing everything.

A woman with dark hair and brown skin and a kind expression approached. She wore a white jacket over her blue scrubs. "Are you Lulu's mom?"

Juliet nodded.

"I'm Dr. Goya." She kneeled to put herself at eye level with Juliet. "After my examination, I believe Lulu has disk space narrowing. She shows all the signs, including tightness in her abdomen. It happens in older dogs and can be aggravated by jumping or a fall. The treatment options range from pain medication and rest to surgery. It depends on the severity."

Juliet tried to process all the information. "What do you recommend?"

"I would like to take X-rays to see what we're dealing with and determine if additional imaging, a CT scan or MRI, is necessary. I have an estimate here." The vet handed over a piece of paper. "I need you to sign it."

"Please do whatever you need to do to help Lulu." Saying that loosened the knot in Juliet's stomach. She glanced at what the treatment plan entailed, managed not to wince at the four-figure price, signed on the line, and returned the paper. "Here you go."

"We'll keep you posted."

"Thank you."

As the doctor walked away, she texted Selena.

> **JULIET:** *Do you want to know the estimate?*
> **SELENA:** *Nope.*
> **JULIET:** *Thanks. Must be nice not to worry about what something costs.*

SELENA: *You're not wrong, and you'll be in this place, too.*
JULIET: *I can't wait. I've been listening to your podcasts.*
SELENA: *You're on your way.*

Juliet had been taking baby steps. Only, her strides were now getting longer, moving her a greater distance from her starting point. She stood at a fork with two paths. One was familiar, but she'd traveled that road so many times and didn't want to go in that direction again. The other was new and scary, but at the same time, exciting. That unfamiliar road was full of curves she couldn't see coming. Each step took trust and faith in herself. It was slow. But one step was better than none.

Juliet was finished standing still, frozen in place out of fear. Nothing would stop her from heading to the future she wanted.

All she had to do was believe.

Believe in that future.

Believe in herself.

What seemed like hours passed.

Juliet tried reading a magazine, but the words blurred. She closed the cover, set it on the stack next to her, and pulled out her phone to see what tea party ideas were on Pinterest.

"Juliet…"

She stiffened before turning toward the sound of Roman's voice. He stood six feet away from her and wore scrubs. His hair was a mess, and he hadn't shaved.

Her pulse kicked up. He was still handsome as ever.

She swallowed. "Working today?"

He nodded. "I saw Lulu with Dr. Goya."

It was her turn to nod. "I called you, but it went to voice mail. I didn't leave a message."

Roman rocked back on his heels, looking everywhere but at her. "I let the call go. I'm sorry. I'm embarrassed by how I reacted the other night. I wasn't sure what to say to you."

She kept her face neutral and her shoulders back. At least she tried. But anger flared at his reason for not answering because Lulu needed help—a vet's help.

Still, Juliet tried not to take it personally. This had nothing to do with her, and everything to do with him. A part of her wished things had turned out…differently. She missed him. Not in a pity party kind of way, but he'd added something to her life. Or maybe she just enjoyed the eye candy.

Whatever it was, she'd made the right choice.

She needed to put her marriage behind her and rely on herself. Not jump into another relationship before she was ready.

And she wasn't.

Not really.

Even if she could have fallen for Roman.

But if anything, he'd shown her that Ezra was wrong about her being old and unattractive. When Juliet was ready—and she wanted to be ready someday—love would happen.

In its own time.

She waited for Roman to say something.

He didn't.

Juliet raised her chin and stared directly into his eyes.

"Today is the first time I've contacted you. That's only because of Lulu. There are no hard feelings. Honest." She truly meant that. "Rumor has it, you'll have no trouble finding what you're looking for."

His face reddened. "It's—"

"None of my business." Juliet didn't want him to feel bad for living his life. If he wanted to date every single woman in town, he could, even if being in the house next door would give her a front-row seat to his love life, whether or not she wanted it.

No regrets. She'd made the best decision for herself. "I only want what's best for you and Katie."

"She misses you, Lulu, and Butterscotch."

"We miss her." Juliet swallowed. "She's welcome to come over whenever she wants."

Even though she had a long way to go in her journey, her heart of hearts told her she would help Katie and already had in small ways. And those added up.

A phone rang. It startled Juliet but amplified the sudden silence between them.

She shifted in her chair. Roman appeared no more comfortable than she was.

Funny… No, sad, given how comfortable they'd been before.

Words perched on the tip of her tongue—about Bria staying in Berry Lake and how the Posse would be co-owners of the cupcake shop. Juliet kept quiet.

There was, however, one question she wanted to ask. "Where's Katie today?"

"She slept over at Chloe's house. Alexis stayed over, too. The three have been inseparable since the birthday party. It's made a tremendous difference. They're visiting a pumpkin patch today. It looks like fun. She sent a photo of them eating apple cider donuts."

Juliet clasped her hands together. "Good for her."

He nodded. "Dr. Goya will be out shortly."

"Thanks."

Roman cleared his throat. "If you need help to pay—"

"I have it covered." He was probably going to suggest the credit program they offered.

He stared at her left hand. "I need to get to work, but I wanted to see how you were doing."

"I'm worried, but Lulu is in excellent hands."

"She is."

"See you around."

For someone who needed to work, he didn't appear to be in a hurry.

Finally, he turned and took a step toward the door before he stopped and faced her.

Weird, but the entire exchange had been as well. "Is there something else?"

"This is awkward."

Roman wasn't wrong. "It is."

He rubbed his neck.

"What?" she asked.

"I…" He wiped his palms on his scrubs. "Do you think we could start over?"

She hadn't expected to hear that. "Start over how?"

"As friends."

Juliet forced herself not to flinch. But the hits kept coming, and she had no idea what to say.

"What?" he asked.

She swallowed a sigh. "I thought we were friends."

"Oh. I…" He shifted his weight between his feet. "I saw you as something else. That was a mistake. My mistake. I'm sorry."

"It's okay." The words came automatically. But Roman wasn't Ezra. She didn't have to say anything if she didn't want to. This time, she had.

"I should have pursued a friendship first." The words rushed out. Roman took a breath. "We live next door to each other. Friends are the neighborly thing to be. Plus, there's Katie. That will make things easier with all of us."

"I suppose so." Juliet wasn't sure things would be less awkward between them based on how he was acting. "Though it sounds as if you're trying to convince yourself of that."

"I'm not, but for some reason around you, I act like a twelve-year-old talking to the prettiest girl in school, the kid who ends up making a fool out of himself each time."

That made her smile. "We've all done that."

"So, friends?" Roman's hopeful expression matched how she felt.

She hadn't had a male friend in years, not since before meeting Ezra because he got angry when she spoke to other men, including his coworkers when they came for dinner. But it wasn't only her and Roman. They had someone else to consider. And he was right—being friends with him would make her relationship with his niece easier. "Sure, it's worth a try for Katie's sake."

Roman's gaze locked on hers. "And ours."

"And ours," she repeated.

He extended his arm. "Shake on it?"

As their hands touched, a spark flashed that reminded her of their kiss. She ignored it.

Juliet had four best friends, but there was always room for another. And she would rather have Roman and Katie be a part of her life than on the outside of it. "Friends."

chapter twenty-eight

FROM THE PASSENGER seat of Dalton's car, Bria stared at the Cliffside Manor, a nursing home that looked more like a brand-new hotel than an assisted-living center in the charming small beach town of Wishing Bay on the Washington coast. "I have so many questions."

Dalton removed the keys from the ignition. "That's why we're here."

The man had shown so much patience when her nerves were getting the best of her on the drive there. But those feelings had quadrupled since he'd parked the car.

"Yes, but what was my dad doing here on that Thursday night? I thought he might have been involved in something sketchy, but now that I see this place, I'm not sure what to think. Not saying anything to the police or his lawyer makes no sense unless he was trying to swindle retirees."

"People do strange things sometimes." Dalton's voice remained steady, the way it had been since they'd left the jail. "Let's find out why your dad was here."

Bria slid from the car. Her insides trembled with uncertainty.

Why was prison a better option than her father mentioning an assisted-living home?

Bright flowers grew in neatly manicured beds. Someone had mowed the strips of green lawn recently. Not one weed was in sight. "The landscaping is nice."

"The facility is high-end."

"Well, if the residents are rich, that explains why my dad was here. He might be looking for investors."

Dalton reached for the front door before lowering his hand. "No matter what we find inside, I support you, and I love you."

Warmth flowed through her. Bria brushed her lips against his. "I love you, too. But—"

He placed his fingertip against her lips. "No buts, okay?"

She loved this man, but the practical side of her had to get this out. As soon as he lowered his arm, she had her chance. "I don't have a 'but.' It's more of a what-if."

"Go ahead."

"If my dad is being made a scapegoat by the Berry Lake Sheriff's Office and Fire Department, it means the real arsonist is still out there. They might blame Missy or me."

"If—and I'm emphasizing that word, if—that's the case, we'll deal with it. Together." Dalton laced his fingers with hers. "I lost you once because of my family. Nothing—and no one—will drive us apart. I promise."

As she nodded, contentment flowed through her. "Good, because I don't want that to happen again."

He squeezed her hand and opened the door. "It won't."

His confident voice spurred her forward. She approached the receptionist. "Hi. I'm Bria Landon. My father, Brian, asked me to pay for room three thirteen."

"Oh, hello. I'm Lauren." The woman appeared to be around the same age as her. She dressed in business casual clothes that would have been right in style at Bria's old firm. "We've been expecting you."

This was bizarre. "My dad said he was here a few weeks ago on a Thursday night."

Lauren nodded. "I'm sure Brian was here. Thursday night is date night."

Date night? Bria met Dalton's gaze, and he shrugged slightly.

"Could we…" Words failed her. She didn't know what to ask.

"Of course, go up, and then I'll have you meet with our business manager to pay." Lauren didn't miss a beat. "It's so wonderful to meet you finally. I see the strong family resemblance."

Bria didn't think she looked like her dad, but maybe Lauren saw something Bria didn't see.

Lauren motioned to a clipboard with a pen attached. "Please sign in. Put room three thirteen for the resident."

So he'd visited someone. That was more than they knew before. Except…

This was almost too easy, which gave Bria a sense of foreboding. Weird, when this place was light and cheery, clean and welcoming. She signed the form before moving out of the way for Dalton to do the same. She handed him the pen.

He filled out the line below hers. "Do you keep the sign-in logs?"

"Yes." Lauren took the clipboard from him. "Management keeps everything for a minimum of seven years."

That meant they would have proof—evidence. But that only begged a question.

What was her father hiding?

Brian Landon looked out for one person—himself. If Bria thought her dad had changed, the way he'd convinced her aunt to leave him half the cupcake shop showed her he was the same as always.

Lauren handed over two badges, and they each clipped them to their shirts. "I'll buzz you through the double doors. Take the elevator to the third floor. Follow the signs to room three thirteen. Enjoy your visit."

"Thanks." Bria only hoped they walked out of there with more answers than questions.

A few minutes later, they stood in the elevator. The doors closed.

"You okay?" Dalton asked.

She inhaled deeply. "I'm not sure."

He placed his arm around her and pulled her against him. "The good news is there's the video of your dad's visit and a log with his name and the time he signed in and left."

Bria nodded. "But this place… It makes so little sense. Aunt Elise never mentioned my dad coming to Wishing Bay."

The elevator dinged. The doors opened.

"Third floor." Dalton motioned for Bria to exit first. "The sign says the room is on the left."

As they walked in that direction, the numbers went down from three twenty. Several doors were decorated for fall with wreaths and autumn-inspired swags. Others had golden leaf garland wrapped around the doorframe. A few were decked out in skulls, bats, and skeletons. One even had lights.

They reached three thirteen. The door was undecorated with no nameplate. It was ajar.

She glanced at Dalton.

"You can do this," he whispered. His eyes held only strength and love.

With a nod, Bria tapped lightly on the door. "Hello?"

No one answered.

She knocked again. That pushed the door open more.

"Go in," Dalton encouraged her.

Bria took a tentative step inside as if she were entering an alternative universe or a black hole.

The room was bland except for a pretty bouquet of mixed flowers in a glass vase on the nightstand. A chair sat near the wall on the far side of a hospital bed.

Someone was asleep and covered with a quilt.

Wait. Bria recognized that quilt.

A shiver ran along her spine, coiling at her tailbone, ready to hiss and bite.

She peered closer, trying to remember where she'd seen the pattern and fabrics before.

Bria took a step and then another.

A woman with brown and gray hair faced away from her.

Bria couldn't see anything from this distance, so she moved to the side of the bed. It was impossible to tell whether or not the woman was asleep. Waking her wouldn't be polite, but curiosity got the best of Bria. "Hello?"

The woman turned toward her.

Bria gasped. The face. It was like staring in a mirror. Well, if she added twenty-five years to her age.

The woman smiled. "Hi."

She trembled. "I'm Bria."

"Pretty name." The woman sounded almost childlike. "Mol."

A lump scorched her throat. Bria struggled to breathe, afraid she might throw up. "Molly?"

The woman nodded.

No. This wasn't happening.

Molly.

Bria hadn't heard the name in years, but she knew it, even if she didn't know this woman.

"Your name is Molly?" Bria asked again, unsure what she wanted the answer to be.

Another nod.

Her blood turned to ice. She dug her fingernails into her palms.

Why, Dad? Why?

But suddenly, everything made sense.

From not wanting to give his alibi to asking her not to hate him. But questions rammed into her, one after another.

Who else knew? Did Aunt Elise?

Tears stung Bria's eyes. Hot tears. Bitter tears. Sad tears.

Regretful tears.

This wasn't her fault.

Selena, Juliet, Nell, and Missy would tell Bria that.

Dalton came up behind her and placed his hands on her shoulders.

A million thoughts ran through Bria's brain, but she didn't think she could string words together.

The woman's gaze sharpened on Dalton. Her lips parted. "Paul?"

"Dalton," he said.

Molly shook her head. "My love. Paul."

Air rushed from Bria's lungs.

"Do you know who this is?" Dalton whispered.

"Yes." Bria wiped her eyes. Needing his strength, she leaned back against him. "Molly is my mother."

If you want to know what happens next to Bria, Juliet, Missy, Nell, Selena, and the Berry Lake Cupcake Shop, read *Kittens & Kisses*, the third book in the series. For more info, visit:

https://melissamcclone.com/blcp3

Want to learn more about Jenny and Dare or Sheridan and Michael? Check out my Beach Brides/Indigo Bay miniseries which contains prequels to the Berry Lake Cupcake Posse series, visit:

https://melissamcclone.com/blcp_prequels

Join Melissa's newsletter to receive a **FREE** sampler collection, and hear about new releases, sales, freebies, and giveaways. Visit:

https://melissamcclone.com/join

about the author

USA Today bestselling author Melissa McClone has written over forty-five sweet contemporary romance novels. She lives in the Pacific Northwest with her husband, three children, a spoiled Norwegian Elkhound, and cats who think they rule the house. They do!

If you'd like to find Melissa online:
melissamcclone.com
facebook.com/melissamcclonebooks
facebook.com/groups/McCloneTroopers

other books by melissa mcclone

The Berry Lake Cupcake Posse Series
Can five friends save their small town's beloved bakery?
Cupcakes & Crumbs
Tiaras & Teacups
Kittens & Kisses

The Beach Brides/Indigo Bay Miniseries
Prequels to the Berry Lake Cupcake Posse series…
Jenny (Jenny and Dare)
Sweet Holiday Wishes (Lizzy and Mitch)
Sweet Beginnings (Hope and Josh)
Sweet Do-Over (Marley and Von)
Sweet Yuletide (Sheridan and Michael)

One Night to Forever Series
Can one night change your life…and your relationship status?
Fiancé for the Night
The Wedding Lullaby
A Little Bit Engaged
Love on the Slopes
The One Night To Forever Box Set: Books 1-4

The Billionaires of Silicon Forest
Who will be the last single man standing?
The Wife Finder
The Wish Maker
The Deal Breaker

Mountain Rescue Series

Finding love in Hood Hamlet with a little help from Christmas magic...

His Christmas Wish
Her Christmas Secret
Her Christmas Kiss
His Second Chance
His Christmas Family

Her Royal Duty

Royal romances with charming princes and dreamy castles...

The Reluctant Princess
The Not-So-Proper Princess
The Proper Princess

Quinn Valley Ranch

Two books featuring siblings in a multi-author series...

Carter's Cowgirl
Summer Serenade
Quinn Valley Ranch Two Book Set

A Keeper Series

These men know what they want, and love isn't on their list.
But what happens when each meets a keeper?

The Groom
The Soccer Star
The Boss
The Husband
The Date
The Tycoon

For the complete list of books, go to:
melissamcclone.com/books.com